Nowhere
to Hide

By the same author

Cold, Cold Heart

JAMES ELLIOTT

Nowhere to Hide

PIATKUS

Copyright © 1997 by James Elliott

First published in Great Britain in 1998 by
Judy Piatkus (Publishers) Ltd of
5 Windmill Street, London, W1

This edition published 1998

***The moral right of the author
has been asserted***

*A catalogue record for this book is available
from the British Library*

ISBN 0 7499 0413 5

Book design by Deidre C. Amthor

Printed in Great Britain by
Mackays of Chatham plc

This book is dedicated to the memory of William J. Caunitz.
A fine writer and a dear friend. I'll miss him, always.

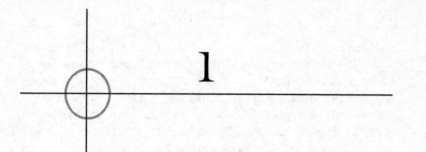

1

ALL HE ASKED of her was to be held. That was all. Fully clothed. Just to sit beside him on the silk brocaded sofa, hold him, run her fingers through his thinning silver hair, and listen to him coo and moan in an infantile voice as he snuggled his head to her breasts. It was strange behavior, to say the least, but far from the strangest behavior Nicole "Niki" Bass had encountered during the past eighteen months.

Classical music played softly in the background, always Chopin nocturnes, as she cradled him to her shoulder and stroked his head. Every so often, in her best motherly tone, she would repeat, as instructed: "There, there, Billy. That's a good little boy. Such a good little boy. Mommy loves you."

Sometimes she varied the words with comforting innovations of her own, which always seemed to please him. For this she would be paid one thousand dollars an hour, with a two-hour minimum, 50 percent of which she got to keep. And he was a good tipper, always another thousand, of which she kept the entire amount.

His name was William Ryland Bradford III, of the South Carolina Bradfords, and he was a steady client. At least once a month. Bass guessed he was well over seventy years old, and obviously very wealthy. The two-bedroom luxury suite he leased on a yearly basis on the seventeenth floor of New York City's exclusive Carlyle Hotel cost him twenty thousand dollars a month.

Carolyn Chambers, the woman who founded and ran the escort service for whom Bass worked, had nicknamed Bradford "the Hugger." He had been Bass's first "client," as Chambers insisted they refer to the men who called for their services. Never "trick," or "john," as in the street-hooker vernacular. The Hugger had been Chambers's way of breaking Bass into the business gently. He was a soft-spoken, kindly, true south-ern gentleman who treated Bass as an old friend whenever they got to-gether for dinner in his suite followed by three hours of hugging. It was always the same, precisely four hours and a thousand-dollar tip.

She liked the old man, and felt almost guilty as she glanced at her watch. But business was business. It was ten o'clock and time to gently remind him that his four hours were up. The Hugger thanked her gra-ciously for her time, and paid in cash, as all of their clients did. Bass put the money into one of the zipped compartments of the oversized shoul-der bag she carried when working. The bag was constructed to conceal a hidden compartment with Velcro fasteners in the center between the two main sections, readily accessible without opening the bag; this was where she kept the .380-caliber semiautomatic pistol she took with her whenever she went out at night.

Bass gave the Hugger a kiss on both cheeks. She lingered a moment to feign a regretful parting, told him, truthfully, that she looked forward to seeing him again, and left. She exited the elevator into the hotel lobby to hear her pager chirp softly from inside her shoulder bag. She glanced at the display to see that Chambers was calling her from the service, and then walked to the far end of the lobby to the pay phones off the Gallery, a cozy sitting area just inside the Madison Avenue entrance to the hotel.

Normally, the call from Chambers would be to make certain that all had gone well—no rough stuff and the client had paid promptly. She al-ways checked when she knew the client's scheduled time was up. But she never called when the Hugger was the client.

Carolyn Chambers was the closest thing Bass had to a friend in the city, and she did not regret for one minute accepting her offer to work for her eighteen months ago. The elite escort service had no name, did not advertise, had an unlisted telephone number, and handled only ten "girls," as Carolyn referred to them. Ten exceptionally attractive, edu-cated women, of which Niki Bass was the reigning queen and the most in demand. All were former international fashion models, having worked the Milan, Paris, London, Tokyo, and New York runways just a few short years ago; Bass had even had a short run as a cover girl for the fashion magazines. They were all between the ages of twenty-five and thirty-five, and all had the sophistication, elegance, and social graces to handle any situation.

Their high-powered clients expected no less for the premium prices they paid. Chambers personally selected and screened all of her girls, setting down strict dress codes, and hard and fast rules of behavior for them and the clients. No wham-bam-thank-you-ma'am service, the typical evening often included a cocktail party, or a diplomatic reception, the theater, or dinner at an expensive restaurant, usually followed by two or three hours with the client at his apartment or home. Nothing kinky or perverse—just straight sex if the client initiated it, which most did. Hotel calls were limited to men like the Hugger who were vouched for by trusted, long-term clients.

Other escort services sent their girls—the more acceptable-looking street hookers funneled into mob-controlled services—out on as many calls as they could jam into a single night, often into questionable, even dangerous, situations. They kept 60 percent of the two-or-three hundred dollars the girls earned from each client, and cheated them at every opportunity. Chambers considered her girls friends, and treated them with respect and consideration, and had never attempted to cheat them in any way. A three-thousand-dollar night, which was what Bass netted that evening, was not the exception but the rule. Occasionally clients arranged for entire evenings, from six until midnight or two in the morning, and sometimes overnight. Bass had even had two trips with clients that year: a weekend in Paris, and another in London. Both first-class, with a weekend rate of fifteen thousand dollars for special clients. The girls saw only one client a night, one of Carolyn's rules, and worked five days a week, with Monday and Tuesday off.

All of their clients were referrals from the original base Chambers had established three years ago from among her many wealthy and socially prominent contacts, consisting of diplomats, politicians, bankers, and corporate CEOs. She had built a reputation for exclusivity and discretion, and women who, more often than not, stunned the client with their beauty and elegance upon their first meeting.

Bass always looked at the bottom line, and her present bottom line was that she had had an interesting year and a half, netted a little over nine hundred thousand dollars, lived and dressed well, and still managed to squirrel away six hundred thousand dollars. Two months shy of her thirtieth birthday, and looking even younger, she knew she had at least another five years in the business, but she did not plan to stay that long. Perhaps two more years, just until she saved enough to fulfill her dreams.

Bass crossed the Gallery to the pay phones in the hallway beyond, ignoring the hopeful smile from a handsome, well-dressed young man who did a double take as he came out of Bemelmans Bar adjacent to the Gallery. She smiled to herself, enjoying the compliment, and dialed the number for the service to hear Chambers answer on the first ring.

"Was the Hugger his usual sweet, endearing self?"

"Couldn't have been sweeter."

"I thought you might like to know that Michael Onorati called a few minutes ago. He wants to see you. Tonight. I told him you were unavailable, but he said it was very important. 'Urgent' is the word he used."

"Did he say why?"

"No. And I didn't ask. I said I'd see what I could do. Since the Hugger is a no-sex client, if you want to see Onorati, I don't mind bending the rules. It's your call."

"Where is he?"

"At his apartment at One Beekman. Shall I call him back and tell him you're available?"

Bass hesitated for a moment. She was tired, but not that tired. She liked Onorati. He was a steady client—twice a month, sometimes more, for the past year. He was a highly successful lawyer, and a CPA, and, from what Bass judged from his pillow talk, operated in the upper echelon of financial circles. Middle-aged, divorced, and relatively attractive despite his pattern baldness and spreading paunch, he was a gentle lover who made few demands, and often gave her expensive gifts as well as good tips.

"Okay," she told Chambers. "Give me about forty-five minutes."

Bass enjoyed walking in the city, and she had on the right shoes, no heels—the Hugger was only five six. The twenty-five-block walk to Onorati's apartment would be good exercise and loosen up muscles stiff from four hours of sitting.

Bass stepped out into the cool, crisp October night and breathed deeply of the scent of autumn coming from the park a block away. She strolled south along Madison Avenue, window shopping in the smart designer shops that lined both sides of the street: Givenchy, Ferre,

Valentino, Dior, Saint Laurent, Armani. She paused in front of the Armani display window and noted that the same stylish pants suit she was wearing was on the mannequin in the window—a far cry from her cousin's hand-me-downs of her teenage years. No one laughed at how she dressed now.

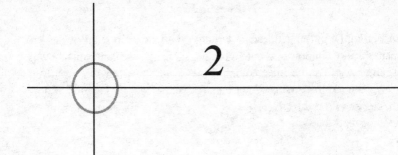

2

AS HEAD OF the Gambino crime Family, and the "boss of bosses" of all five New York Mafia Families, Vincent Genero was the most powerful and most feared mobster in New York City. Every inch the new-generation Mafia don, he was visible to the public and press, swaggering, arrogant, and reveled in his status and position. Standing before him, one knew that one was in the presence of a powerful man, a man who knew how to wield that power to destroy those who got in his way. One look into his onyx eyes told anyone with half a brain that it was best not to upset him.

His foul mouth, explosive temper, and frequent violent outbursts were legend, and tonight he was in a full-blown rage, his face turning purple, the veins in his neck and at his temples throbbing as he climbed into the back of the black Mercedes parked at the curb in front of his favorite Italian restaurant, just off Arthur Avenue in the Bronx.

Big Paulie and Johnnie "Socks," Genero's driver and bodyguard, two bull-necked hulks whose shoulders touched as they sat stiffly in the front bucket seats, remained silent, afraid to speak without being spoken to as they listened to Genero ranting and raving to Carmine Molino, his underboss and chief enforcer, who sat beside him in the back of the Mercedes.

"What are you waiting for?" he snapped at Big Paulie.

"Where to, Mr. Genero?"

"Just drive, what I pay you to do," Genero said.

Big Paulie pulled out immediately, unaccustomed to not having specific instructions from his boss.

Genero turned to Molino. "How much did the fuck steal?"

"Looks like fifteen or eighteen million."

"Fifteen or eighteen? That's a three-million-dollar difference. What kind of moron accountant you got, can't narrow it down?"

"He's still trying to figure it out. Goes back about five years," Molino said. "Onorati laundered maybe eighty, ninety million through the Caymans like he was supposed to. But he skimmed off a chunk for himself every time he did it."

"How'd he get away with it this long?"

"He ain't dumb, Vinnie, you know that. He doctored up the set of books he kept for us, makin' it look like he was investing the money in real estate and construction projects. Most of it he did. Condos, town houses, resorts, piece of this, piece of that. Good investments we was makin' money off of. But fifteen or eighteen million of it was just smoke and mirrors. The real estate is nothin' but empty lots in shit neighborhoods, and the construction projects don't even fuckin' exist. We'd a probably never gotten wise to him if the accountant I hired to go over the books for the company I started runnin' some of the drug money through didn't accidentally spot somethin' out of whack."

"That motherfucker! I want to know to the fuckin' penny what he stole!" Genero shouted, the anger taking hold again as he pounded the center armrest with his fist. "I trusted that fuck. Like a brother. I know him all my life. All my fuckin' life. Helped the fuck out by bringin' him into the family. Made him a rich man without stealin'. Wasn't for me that cocksucker would be nothin' but another scumbag ambulance chaser."

Genero fell silent, staring straight ahead, the look in his eyes one of pure menace. He and Michael Onorati had grown up in the same Bronx neighborhood. Had gone to Catholic school together. Genero had dropped out in the tenth grade to work for his mob-connected uncle, while Onorati, with financial assistance from Genero, had gone on to college and law school.

Genero, with an IQ of 150 and an intuitive intelligence bordering on brilliance, got his education in the streets. Through guile and intimidation, and an uncommon ruthlessness and murderous brutality, he rose quickly through the ranks of the wise guys. At the age of twenty-six he became the youngest capo in the history of the Gambino crime Family. Fourteen years later a series of federal convictions resulted in long-term prison sentences for the top members of all five Mafia Families in New York, leaving a power vacuum throughout their organization.

Within weeks a bloody, internecine struggle erupted, and Vincent Genero emerged as the new don of the Gambino Family. Due to his ability to make money, and the fear he instilled in the new heads of the other Families, he was soon chosen, in an effort to keep the peace, as the "boss of bosses." It was then that Genero hired his trusted friend as his chief financial officer, placing Onorati in charge of laundering and investing all of the Family's money, and eventually, through Genero's glowing recommendation, a considerable amount of the ill-gotten gains of the other four Families.

"I'm gonna take care of that piece-of-shit traitor myself," Genero finally said. "You know where he is right now?"

"At his apartment in Manhattan," Molino said. "But you'd better let me arrange to have it taken care of. This is a piece of business you might not wanna be too close to."

Genero fixed a hard gaze on his underboss. "Hey, Carmine! This is personal. And I'll take care of it personally. You got that? I'll take Paulie and Johnnie with me," he added. "You go back to the restaurant. I'll call you when I'm finished."

"Okay," Molino said, knowing better than to argue with Genero when he was in one of his moods. Genero's one weakness was his volatile temper, which occasionally overwhelmed his better judgment. Molino always tried to curb his boss's more impulsive actions, but knew enough not to cross the line when it came to telling Vincent Genero what he should or should not do.

"The accountant says that Onorati has got to have a record of where he's been hiding the money he stole," Molino said, carefully wording what he felt Genero should know about the situation. "You know, how to get access to it and shit? So you might wanna make sure you got all that out of him . . . in case things get out of hand."

Genero nodded absently. "Take Carmine back to LaRosa's," he told his driver.

Big Paulie, still unnerved by his boss's mood, immediately and expertly swung the car into a tight U-turn on the narrow street, sending his passengers in the back sliding into each other.

"Hey, Paulie, the feds got a tail on us?"

"No tail, boss."

"Then slow the fuck down!" Genero growled, smoothing out his hair and his impeccably tailored custom-made suit.

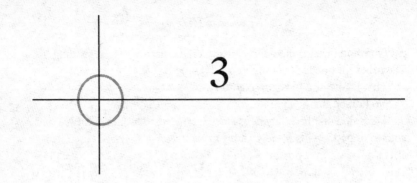

3

BEEKMAN PLACE, AN enclave of elegant town houses and condominiums, ranks high among the most fashionable addresses in Manhattan. A quiet, narrow, tree-lined street only two blocks long, off First Avenue, between Forty-ninth and Fifty-first Streets, it stretches along the East River, offering spectacular views for those fortunate enough to live on the east side of the street. Michael Onorati was one of the fortunate; his fifteenth-floor penthouse apartment at One Beekman Place took up the entire southeast corner of the building and had a wraparound terrace with panoramic views of the river and the city.

As Nicole Bass entered the lobby of the graceful brick building, she smiled at the familiar faces of the doormen, who smiled back and nodded a good evening from behind the reception desk.

"Go right on up, Miss Bass," one of the doormen said as the other rang Michael Onorati to announce her arrival.

Bass stepped from the elevator into the private foyer serving Onorati's apartment to find him standing outside his door waiting for her, stylishly dressed in a double-breasted Brioni suit. She embraced him and kissed him on the cheek, only to have him hug her emotionally, then hold her at arm's length and stare strangely into her eyes before leading her into the apartment.

"I'm sorry I called so late," Onorati said as Bass followed him to the built-in bar in the tastefully decorated living room. "But it's been a hectic day, to say the least."

"It's alright, Michael. I'm happy to see you anytime."

"Go out on the terrace and enjoy the view while I make us a drink. The usual for you?"

"That'll be fine."

The French doors were open to the cool night air, and Bass crossed the room and stepped outside. The broad, expansive terrace was filled with trees and shrubs in huge decorative urns and planters, creating the effect of being in a private garden. The sound of traffic from the FDR Drive directly below was only a faint hum at that hour, and the lights from the Fifty-ninth Street bridge sparkled off the dark waters of the East River. A dramatic scene, peaceful and quiet, with only an occasionally whoop-whoop of a distant siren to remind her that she was in the heart of the city.

Onorati brought the drinks and stood beside her. He was in an odd mood, more subdued, not his usual amorous self.

"Carolyn told me you said it was urgent? Is something wrong?"

"Nothing you can't fix with the right answer."

Bass gave him a puzzled look. "I don't understand."

"How long have we been seeing each other?"

"A little over a year."

"And we've had fun? We've enjoyed each other's company?"

"Of course." Bass had no idea where the conversation was leading. The look on Onorati's face was one she had not seen before.

"And we're compatible; we enjoy the same things?"

"Yes." And then it dawned on her. He was looking for a permanent arrangement. Something she considered anathema.

Onorati leaned against the waist-high wall enclosing the terrace and watched in thoughtful silence as a brightly lit yacht moved slowly upriver. Then, at length, he put his arm around Bass's waist and held her close.

"I'm selling this place. As a matter of fact, I have it sold already. I'm leaving New York permanently, and I want you to come with me."

Bass turned to face him, intent on handling the situation as diplomatically as possible. But as she began to speak, he interrupted.

"Before you turn me down, let me state my case."

"Michael—"

"Please, Niki. Come inside with me, I want to show you something."

Onorati led her back inside the apartment, through the living room to the walnut-paneled study off the master bedroom. The doorway leading from the study to the bedroom was open and Bass noticed three half-filled suitcases on the king-size bed. She followed Onorati to his desk, where he opened an ostrich-skin briefcase. Over his shoulder, Bass caught a glimpse of the neatly banded packets of one-hundred-dollar bills that filled the inside of the case. She estimated there was at least fifty thousand dollars.

Onorati snapped open the accordion-file compartments built into the top of the case and removed a passport and two airline tickets. He gave Bass a quick look at the outside of the passport.

"A Spanish passport?" she said as he put it back in the file compartment, closed the briefcase, and slipped it under his desk.

"I'm starting a whole new life, Niki. A new name, a new nationality. A new me. And I want you to be a part of it. I want you to be my wife."

"Michael, I can't just—"

He held up a hand to silence her. "I'll make you happier than you can ever imagine. Whatever you want is yours. I've put a great deal of money aside over the years, and I promise you, I can give you as luxurious a life as anyone could possibly want."

He reached into the pocket of his suit coat, removed a small blue-felt box, opened it and held it out. Bass stared at the exquisite five-carat diamond ring inside.

"I can't accept that." She took a step back, sorely tempted by the beautiful ring but unwilling to make the commitment that went with it.

"Please. It's a token of my sincerity and to show just how much I appreciate your being in my life."

"Michael, I've enjoyed the time I spent with you. And you've been good to me. But, I don't love you, and I have plans for my life as soon as I save enough to get out of this business."

"Let me take you out of the business. Besides, love is highly overrated," Onorati said with a hopeful smile. "We're already friends. I admit I've fallen in love with you—I think you've known that for a while. I know you don't feel the same way, but I do know that you like me and we're compatible, and that's a solid beginning for any relationship."

"Michael, I can't do this. It would never work."

"I can make it work. We'll have a home on Majorca in the summer, a winter place in the Caribbean. St. Barts, I think. Do you like St. Barts? And we can travel, anywhere you want, as often as you want."

"It sounds wonderful," Bass said, her tone more firm, "and I hope you have a good life, but I can't be a part of it."

"I know this is unexpected. I hadn't planned to just spring it on you, but I didn't have the time to do it right. Some things happened sooner than I expected. I've got to leave tomorrow morning. But if you'll come with me, and give it a chance, I promise that if in one month you still feel the way you do now, I'll give you one hundred thousand dollars and kiss you goodbye with no hard feelings. What do you say?"

Bass shook her head and was about to respond when Onorati placed a finger on her lips to stop her.

"No. Don't say anything yet. Please, go out on the terrace and think about it. All you have to say is yes, and the details will take care of themselves." He held up the airline tickets he had taken from the brief-case. "Two tickets on the Concorde from JFK to London, leaving at eight forty-five in the morning. We'll have dinner in London tomorrow night."

"I don't have to think about it. It's a wonderful offer, Michael, but it's not for me."

"Niki, please. As a personal favor. Just think about it, that's all I ask. I have some last-minute calls to make."

She decided to give him that, and opened the double doors leading from the study to the terrace, a night breeze billowing the delicate curtains around her.

"And you won't have to worry about packing anything," he called to her as she stepped outside. "I'll buy you a whole new wardrobe in Paris or Milan, or anywhere you like."

Bass didn't reply. She had no intention of accepting his offer. She knew a few of the other girls in the escort service would have jumped at the opportunity. Playing him along for the month just for the money and all the gifts and clothes they could stockpile before they left, maybe even marry him, but Bass had her own set of rules.

Yes, she was a prostitute, but on her own terms and for her own reasons. But that wasn't all she was, and she didn't aspire to celebrity or enormous wealth or a life of luxury. Her goals were specific and finite; enough money, invested properly, to make her financially independent, able to live comfortably, free to make her own choices in life and to put her out of the reach of those who would use her.

The path she had chosen was high-risk, but she took every precaution: safe sex, monthly gynecological exams and AIDS tests, the medical reports turned in to Carolyn Chambers on the first of every month—another of her rules. She never used drugs, and if a client even suggested it, it was the last time she saw him. She had accepted that if what she was doing now was the price she had to pay to reach her goals, then so be it. She had tried it the right way, the "straight and narrow," as her father would have said, and it had gotten her nowhere. The naive, trusting, sixteen-year-old kid who had arrived in New York City from the hills of eastern Tennessee chasing a dream, a believer who took people at their word, no longer existed. She had learned the hard way—lessons not easily forgotten. She would never again allow herself to get into a situation where others could control her life.

And there was something else bothering her. Onorati's new identity and his rush to leave made her suspect his departure in all probability wasn't voluntary. She knew something about phony passports and new identities. Maybe the government was after him, the IRS, the FBI; he was running from something, she felt certain of that. She knew the signs, had seen them before. Not that it mattered, she would not have gone with him regardless of the circumstances.

Bass sipped her drink slowly, enjoying the view and the night air. She thought of other men in her life, men who had made offers that sounded great in the beginning but had later proved to be the worst mistakes she had ever made. She had trusted them, too. They had given their word, then used her, and in the end betrayed her.

She looked back into the study to see Onorati in the soft glow of the desk lamp, gesturing as he spoke on the telephone. She didn't need, or want, Michael Onorati or anyone else to take care of her. She turned away and walked around the corner of the terrace to look out over the river, determined to end the discussion once and for all as soon as he got off the phone.

4

AT TWENTY MINUTES after eleven the black Mercedes sedan moved slowly down the narrow tree-lined street to slip quietly into the curb in front of One Beekman Place. Big Paulie immediately cut the engine and the lights. From outside the car, the dark, reflective tint on the windows made it impossible to see Vincent Genero sitting silent and motionless in the back seat, staring out the window at the entrance to the apartment building. His earlier outward display of anger had diminished to the calm, icy determination he always exhibited once he decided on a definite course of action.

"Gimme your piece," he finally said to Johnnie Socks, his bodyguard.

The huge man in the front passenger seat immediately took the 9-millimeter semiautomatic pistol from his shoulder holster and threaded the silencer to the barrel before handing it to Genero.

"There's a round in the chamber, boss, and the safety's on. And you got a full magazine; twelve rounds."

"Both of you come with me," Genero said, taking one last look through the double glass doors at the entrance to One Beekman. Satisfied that the lobby was empty except for the two doormen on duty, he climbed out of the car before his driver could run around to open the door for him.

Genero tucked the gun inside the waistband of his trousers, his wary eyes scanning the street as he stood in the deep shadows beneath a towering maple tree in front of the building. Both sides of the street were deserted, with the exception of a doorman from a building in the next block who stood just outside the entrance, his back to them, taking a smoking break. Genero pulled on a pair of thin leather gloves; Big Paulie and Johnnie Socks did the same.

"We don't want no witnesses," Genero told his men, who were close on his heels as he moved swiftly off the sidewalk and opened the door to One Beekman. The three men strode purposefully into the lobby to be immediately confronted by one of the doorman, who eyed them with suspicion.

"May I help you gentlemen."

"I'm here to see Michael Onorati. Fifteen-A, right?" Genero continued toward the elevators only to have the doormen step in front of him.

"Is he expecting you?"

"I wanna surprise him."

"I'm sorry, sir, but I have to call him to get permission to send you up."

"Yeah?"

"Yes, sir."

Genero gave only the briefest look to Johnnie Socks. The powerful bodyguard grabbed the doorman from behind, used both arms to grip his head and neck, and twisted with all his strength. A short, helpless yelp was followed by a sickening snap and crunch.

Big Paulie walked over to the reception desk where the other doorman had picked up the telephone to call the police. "You don't wanna do that."

The frightened doorman's eyes were wide with horror as he watched his friend's lifeless body slide from the arms of the man who had snapped his neck. His gaze shifted to the gun Big Paulie was pointing at him, and he lowered the telephone.

Johnnie Socks watched the entrance as Genero crossed the lobby to the reception desk. "Why don't you just give me the pass keys to the apartment, save us all a lot of trouble?"

The doorman was too terrified to move. A dark wet spot spread down the right leg of his uniform as he involuntarily relieved himself. A small puddle formed around his shoe. Genero smiled and nodded to Big Paulie.

"Open your mouth," Big Paulie said, then immediately grabbed the doorman's face in his huge hand and squeezed until he forced his jaw to drop. He shoved the tip of the silencer to the back of the man's mouth and cocked the hammer.

"Get the fuckin' keys now. Or get dead now."

The doorman pointed a shaking finger toward the package room behind the reception desk.

Big Paulie kept the gun in the man's mouth while Genero opened the door to a room the size of a walk-in closet. A peg board on the wall on the right contained pass keys for all of the apartments in the building. Genero saw Onorati's name over 15-A, and removed the keys. He nodded to Big Paulie as he came out of the room.

Without hesitation, and with as much forethought as he gave to scratching his crotch, Big Paulie pulled the trigger twice. The gun made no more noise than a loud finger snap followed by a metallic clank as the receiver came back to pick up the next bullet and inject it into the chamber. The doorman fell back against the wall, sliding down to a sitting position, his chin on his chest, his dead eyes open, staring unseeing at the floor.

"Put 'em in there," Genero said, indicating the package room.

Johnnie Socks and Big Paulie dragged the bodies inside the room and shut the door, then hurried across the highly polished marble floor to catch up to Genero as he stepped into the elevator.

Nicole Bass sat on one of the decorative wrought-iron chairs on the terrace, staring out at the spectacular Manhattan skyline. She looked over her shoulder to see Onorati still talking on the telephone. She assumed they would not be making love that night, and was eager to leave, but felt she at least owed him the courtesy of a proper goodbye.

Onorati looked up and saw her watching him. He shrugged apologetically, then pointed to his watch and held up five fingers. Bass nodded and got up to walk around to the front of the terrace overlooking the river. She finished her drink and decided to go back inside to make another.

It was then that she saw the three men enter the living room. Two of them had guns. The man leading the way, shorter than the other two, but still powerfully built, looked vaguely familiar to her, but she couldn't place him. Probably someone Onorati had introduced to her when they were out to dinner one night, she thought; he enjoyed showing her off to his friends. Except these men were obviously not friends.

They were not looking in her direction, and being careful not to draw their attention by any sudden movement, Bass inched her way around the corner of the terrace and hid behind a large planter that concealed her from view, but allowed her to see most of the study. Onorati, still seated at his desk, had just hung up the telephone. He was unaware that the shorter man now stood directly behind him in the doorway.

Bass looked across the terrace to the chair she had been sitting in; her shoulder bag, with her gun inside, was hanging by its strap from one of the arms, in plain view of anyone looking outside from the study. She continued to move along the wall of the building to get closer to the bag, but soon realized there was no way she could reach it without being seen.

Genero stood motionless in the doorway as Onorati turned in his chair to reach for some papers on the corner of his desk. It was then that Onorati saw the dark shape in his peripheral vision and was startled by the presence of the man he least wanted to see.

"How ya doin', Mike," Genero said, still leaning against the doorframe. "I'm not interrupting anything, am I?"

"Vinnie. No. No," Onorati said, recovering his composure. "I was just making some calls. Come in. Sit down."

He assumed that, while talking on the telephone, he had not heard Genero ring the doorbell, and that Bass had let him in. That was until Big Paulie and Johnnie Socks appeared from the living room, looming behind their boss and glowering. Onorati's expression of surprise changed to one of total defeat, telling Genero that he knew precisely why he was there.

Genero motioned with a quick jerk of his head for his driver and bodyguard to go back into the living room. The two men disappeared without a word.

"Why'd you do it, Mike?" Genero's voice was low and dispassionate.

Onorati's first thought was to deny everything, but he knew it would be futile. "I was going to pay it back, Vinnie. I swear."

"And when were you plannin' on doin' that?"

"Soon. I was just using it to make some extra money for myself. I was going to transfer it all back into your accounts within a few months."

"Yeah?"

"Absolutely. I was just borrowing it for a while."

"Why? I don't pay you enough? Five hundred thousand a year, plus bonuses. You can't live on that?" His voice was growing tighter now, the anger beginning to rise again as he stared into the face of the old friend who had betrayed him.

"I got carried away. You know, things got out of hand, I spent more than I should have. I was going to come to you for help, but I was too embarrassed."

Genero's demeanor changed. His eyes bored into Onorati as he moved from the doorway to stand next to the desk. "Stop insulting my intelligence, Mike. You've been skimming money for five fuckin' years. The accountant says fifteen to eighteen million."

"I'm sorry, Vinnie. I know I let you down, but—"

Genero's voice turned to a snarl. "Let me down? You fuck! You made me look like a goddamn fool."

"I still have it all," Onorati said, and opened one of the desk drawers.

Genero immediately grabbed his wrist. "You don't have a gun in there, do you, Mike? No, you don't. I forgot who I'm talkin' to. If you did, you wouldn't have the balls to use it." He released his grip but still watched him closely.

Onorati removed a computer disk from the drawer. "It's all here. The account numbers, the access codes."

He turned on the computer, waited until it booted up, then inserted the disk. After a few keystrokes the screen was filled with a table of five rows with three columns, representing various offshore banks, the telephone numbers to access their computers, the codes to effect electronic transfers, and the secret numbered accounts. Genero squinted at the screen to verify what Onorati had told him.

"See? It's all there. I can put it back into your accounts first thing in the morning. I can do it by computer, send authorization and instructions for the transfers."

"Just like that, huh?"

"Just like that. If you have the account numbers and the access codes, that's all the identification you need." Onorati turned off the computer and removed the disk, placing it in Genero's outstretched hand.

Genero put the disk in his coat pocket and backed away from the desk. He turned to look into the living room, where Big Paulie and Johnnie Socks had made themselves a drink and were standing at the bar. Something caught Genero's attention as he turned back to face Onorati. He moved closer to the doorway to the master bedroom and saw the half-filled suitcases on the bed.

"You goin' somewhere, Mike?"

"A little vacation. Just for a few days."

"Yeah?"

"Yes. Honest, Vinnie." His eyes went to the two airline tickets on top of the desk, and he added, "Just a quick trip to London."

"You're a lying fuck, Mike." Genero pulled the gun from inside his waistband and held it at his side.

"Vinnie, no."

"I trusted you. Got you set up. Gave you business people'd kill their mothers for. Treated you like a brother. And you fucked me."

"Ah, Vinnie. I was just trying to make some extra money; get out of the hole I got myself into."

"You got that right, Mike. A hole six feet deep is what you got yourself into."

"Vinnie. Come on. Hey. I'll make it up to you. I promise. Give me a break. We go back a long way."

Genero was icy calm again. "I don't whack you, I look weak to the other families. They think I'm weak, I got problems."

"Vinnie, please. What can I do? Tell me. I'll do anything."

"You can die like a man, Mike. I'll make it quick—'cause we go back a long way. If we didn't, you'd die real slow." Genero's eyes went flat and emotionless as he raised the gun and held it to Onorati's forehead.

"Please, Vinnie! Please! I'll do anything. God! No!" Onorati lowered himself from the chair to kneel before Genero, pleading, crying.

Genero scowled in disgust and pulled the trigger twice in rapid succession. Onorati rocked back on his knees, then slumped over onto his side. A significant portion of the back of his head was blown away, and six feet behind him, blood and brains smeared the bottom of the curtains on the doors to the terrace. Genero stared down at him for a long moment, then walked back into the living room.

Nicole Bass had witnessed it all. In an attempt to get close enough to the chair to grab her shoulder bag, she had moved even closer to the open doors of the study, behind one of the large urns containing an evergreen tree. She had checked on the location of the other two men, peering through a casement window to see them standing at the bar making drinks. Just as she was about to take the few steps that would have put her within arm's reach of her bag, the man with Onorati had moved closer to the desk and in the direct line of sight of the chair outside. She heard only snatches of the conversation, not enough to understand what it was about. But she had seen the computer screen glow and then go dark, and she saw Onorati drop to his knees and heard him begging for his life. And she had watched in horror and revulsion as the silencer-equipped gun was pressed to his forehead, and had seen the calm, merciless look on the man's face as he fired.

She fought off the fear-induced paralysis that gripped her when she saw Onorati topple over dead on the floor, and she struggled to remain calm enough to think clearly and rationally despite the adrenaline rush that jolted her system. Her only concern now was to stay hidden until they left, and then sneak out of the apartment and get as far away as she could before the body was discovered.

Then the sound of the shorter man's voice made her realize that she would have to come up with an alternate plan. She needed to get out immediately.

"Check the rest of the apartment, and the terrace," Genero told Big Paulie and Johnnie Socks. "Make sure nobody else is here. I'll check the bedrooms on this end, you get the kitchen, and I think there's a maid's room or somethin' back there, too."

Genero walked back into the study and on into the master bedroom. Bass again looked through the casement windows to see the two men leaving the living room. The one with the gun headed to the opposite end of the apartment, while the other started toward the open French doors leading from the living room to the terrace, just around the corner of the building from where Bass was hiding. Bass seized what she saw as her only chance of getting out alive. She moved quickly from the shadows behind the urn, grabbed her shoulder bag, and ducked into the study.

She paused to step over Onorati's body, and out of the corner of her eye, saw the ostrich-skin briefcase braced against the side of the knee-hole under the desk. Remembering the money inside, she grabbed the case and crossed to the doorway into the living room. She paused again, to make certain neither man had returned, then took the gun from her shoulder bag, entered the room, and moved quietly toward the entryway. As she reached for the door handle, a shout from the terrace almost caused her to freeze in panic.

"Hey, you!" Johnnie Socks shouted at her, and ran into the living room. "Boss! Paulie!" he called out. "There's a broad headed for the door!"

Johnnie Socks was halfway to Bass when she turned to face him, pointing the gun at him.

"She's got a piece!" he shouted, stopping in his tracks twenty feet away.

"Back off!" Bass said, thumbing the hammer back and leveling the gun at his head.

Johnnie Socks took a few steps back as Bass pulled open the door and immediately slammed it shut behind her.

Out in the foyer Bass instinctively dismissed the elevator as a means of escape, but she was thinking clearly enough to hope to use it as a ruse, giving her a few more seconds of lead time. The elevator door was still open, and she slapped at the button for the lobby on the inside panel to close it, then ran to the end of the foyer and pulled open the door to the emergency stairwell.

Big Paulie ran out into the foyer, crouched low, and quickly scanned the area, the barrel of his gun following the movement of his eyes. The elevator door was almost closed, and he lunged at the narrowing gap and stuck his arm in, sending the door shuddering back in the opposite direction. A quick glance told him the elevator was empty. At that moment Genero and Johnnie Socks appeared in the foyer.

"Where is she?" Genero shouted.

"Must of went down the stairs," Big Paulie said.

"Why the fuck didn't you shoot her when you saw her?" Genero snapped at Johnnie Socks.

"You got my gun, boss."

"Fuck!"

Genero led the way to the stairwell. He paused at the landing and heard the sound of footsteps skipping down the stairs below, and then they suddenly stopped.

Bass stood silently on the twelfth-floor landing. Within seconds she heard heavy footsteps above her, rapidly approaching. She started running again, and, after descending two more floors, realized they were gaining on her. She made a spur-of-the-moment decision and went down one more flight, then quietly opened and closed the door leading into a foyer that served four apartments. She frantically looked for a place of concealment. A chest-high credenza with a flower arrangement on top, against the wall to her right, was the only place to hide in the large open foyer.

Bass got behind the credenza, placed the briefcase on the floor beside her, and holding her weapon expertly in both hands, braced her forearms on top of the credenza. She took steady aim at the door to the stairs, sights aligned and ready to fire the moment anyone came through it. She took slow, deep, even breaths to calm herself as her heart thumped against her chest. Things were coming back to her, flashing through her mind. Things she thought she had forgotten, hoped she had put behind her. She cursed softly under her breath and stared at the door to the stairs, watching for the slightest movement.

Genero and his men paused just outside the foyer on the ninth-floor landing. Again listening for footsteps. The stairwell was silent.

"She could'a ducked into any one of these floors," Genero said. "Maybe she lives here. We gotta get the fuck out before she calls the cops or somebody else does, finds the doormen."

"But she saw us, boss," Johnnie Socks said.

"I know she saw us. You get a good look at her?"

"Yeah. Real good. Nice body. Great ass."

"You fuckin' moron. You ever see her before?"

"No. But ya know, I think she was carryin' that briefcase you gave Onorati for Christmas last year, or one just like it."

"What?"

"The brown one with the pimples; cost like four grand or somethin'."

Genero stared at him for a moment. "The ostrich-skin one?"

"Yeah, that one. You had me pick it up at Gucci's. Get it wrapped nice. Remember?"

"I remember," Genero said. "Come on, we'll take the stairs the rest of the way down, in case anyone comes up in the elevator."

"We just forget about her?" Big Paulie said.

"No, we don't just forget about her. I'll take care of it. I got other ways of findin' out who she is."

Genero led the way as the three men descended the stairs. He checked the lobby to see that it was empty before entering, then sent Big Paulie out to check the street before he left the building. Big Paulie waved them outside, and all three men climbed into the black Mercedes to disappear around the corner moments later.

. . .

Bass looked at her watch again. Ten minutes had passed since she ducked into the ninth-floor foyer. She suspected they had given up, assumed she had gotten away, or perhaps thought she lived in the building and had returned to her apartment and called the police. Logic told her they would not waste any more time looking for her, and that she should get out of the building as soon as possible.

She picked up the briefcase and moved cautiously toward the door, keeping the gun trained on it as she approached the small inset window. She did a quick look through the glass and saw that the landing was empty. Staying inside the foyer, she cracked the door a few inches, held it open with her foot, and listened. The stairwell was silent. She stepped out onto the landing and slowly descended the stairs. Finding the lobby empty, she held her gun inside her jacket and forced herself to walk calmly to the door.

Once outside, she saw that the street was deserted, and she ran the short distance to the corner of Forty-ninth Street, then over to First Avenue. She crossed the avenue and slowed to a casual walk, and was about to hail an approaching taxi when another old lesson learned came back to her: she did not want there to be anyone who could remember picking up a fare in the vicinity of the crime.

She continued walking along the sidewalk to Fifty-third Street, then turned west until she reached Third Avenue. She grabbed a taxi there, headed uptown, and had the driver drop her three blocks away from her apartment building.

5

JOE EARLY AND his partner, Tommy O'Brien, along with two other detectives from the 17th squad, were working turnaround, a tour that required them to sleep at the station house in the bunk beds in the small room off the main squad room. They were about to turn in for the night when, at 12:42 A.M., they heard the call come over the radio reporting a double homicide at One Beekman Place.

The response time for the 17th Precinct was quicker than the average throughout the city, due to the high-rent area it encompassed. But this call, more than others, sent the detective squad into action in record time. The location of the double homicide, in an exclusive building where apartments cost well over two million dollars, and were owned by more than a few tenants with the political clout and connections to call the mayor or the police commissioner directly, assured that this would be a "press case" with an extremely high profile.

Joe Early caught the case and immediately called DBM, Detective Borough Manhattan, asking the supervisor to give him all the help he could spare from the night watch and any detectives from the Homicide Task Force, who were about to go off-duty at 1 A.M. He was informed that eight detectives would be sent over immediately to help with the canvass of the area. Early then called the Crime Scene Unit and Emergency Services Unit, to make certain the uniformed officer first on the scene had informed them of the situation. Having done that, he and

O'Brien, along with the two other on-duty detectives from the 17th squad, left for Beekman Place.

Early angled the unmarked car into the curb in front of One Beekman among the phalanx of blue-and-whites that had responded to the scene. His predictions of it being a press case proved accurate; the media were already there in force, with more arriving every minute.

The yellow crime scene tape was being strung as Early and O'Brien got out of their car. The uniforms had already used their blue-and-whites to block both ends of the two blocks running north and south, and the intersection with Fiftieth Street, effectively sealing off access to all of Beekman Place and keeping the press out of the immediate area.

Early and O'Brien found the first officer on the scene, patrolman John Hernandez, in the lobby, talking to a well-dressed older man who sat on an upholstered bench just inside the entrance. Hernandez left the man's side to join the two detectives, leading them over to the reception desk, where the bodies of the doormen were visible through the open door of the package room.

"The guy over there—Mr. Lewis," Hernandez said, pointing to the man on the bench, "got back from a weekend at his country place in Connecticut about twelve-forty. Didn't see the doormen around. He says his lawyer was supposed to send a package over for him earlier today. He decided to check if it was there himself. He opened the door to the package room, found the two bodies, then after he finished puking over there"—Hernandez pointed to a small, viscous, yellowish puddle near the reception desk—"he called 911. He didn't see anything or anyone. Got no idea what happened or why."

"Keep everyone away from the bodies until the medical examiner and the Crime Scene Unit get here," Early told Hernandez, then turned to O'Brien. "You thinking what I'm thinking?"

O'Brien nodded. "Nobody came in here just to kill two doormen."

Early, being careful where he stepped, looked inside the package room and saw the peg board containing the pass keys to the apartments. He immediately noticed that the keys for apartment 15-A were missing. The others were all there.

"Come on," he said to O'Brien, and led the way to the elevator.

"What's up?"

"If I'm right, we just caught one hell of a big case," Early said as the elevator doors closed. "The pass keys to apartment 15-A were missing."

"Who's in 15-A?"

"The name on the board says 'M. Onorati.'"

"Michael Onorati? Mobbed-up lawyer? Connected to the Gambino Family?"

"The very same, unless there's two M. Onoratis in the building."

Both men recalled the fiasco a year ago, when they were in the immediate area and responded as backup to a radio call reporting a suspicious van with blacked-out windows parked on Beekman Place just up from Onorati's building. With two foreign consulates occupying town houses in the same block, such reports were taken seriously and responded to in force. Early and O'Brien, and four uniforms, had dragged three embarrassed FBI agents out of their surveillance van. After they had calmed down, they explained that they were conducting a surveillance operation on Michael Onorati. Early suggested that in the future they let them know when they were operating in their precinct, a suggestion that fell on deaf ears.

Early stepped out of the elevator and immediately saw the open door to apartment 15-A. "Oh, yeah," he said. "I can see it all now, Tommy. We'd better be perfect on this one. There's going to be so much brass looking over our shoulders we'll think we're in the middle of the St. Patty's Day parade."

Early and O'Brien entered the apartment, keeping close to the wall, walking along the edge of the carpet, well away from the normal traffic patterns through the rooms, in order to preserve the crime scene. They quickly scanned the living room, taking note that no one had tossed the place as would be expected if a robbery had occurred. Nothing was disturbed. As they reached the doorway to the study, they both stopped in their tracks.

"That's our boy," Early said. "A little worse for the wear, but it's definitely Michael Onorati." He stayed in the doorway, looking around the room. Again, nothing was disturbed. "Ten to one it was a hit."

"No gun near the body," O'Brien said, leaning in to get a good look at the side-by-side entry wounds in Onorati's forehead. "Double tap to the head. Kind of rules out a suicide, huh?"

"Oh, yeah. We got ourselves a triple homicide."

"Yeah, and if it's a mob hit, it's going to be a lot of fun finding witnesses, not to mention getting them to testify."

"A real challenge, Tommy me lad, but it sure breaks the monotony. And if we do real good, detective second grade here we come."

"And if we screw it up, we kiss our gold shields goodbye and spend the rest of our careers in the bag in some shit precinct in the Bronx or Harlem."

"High risk, high gain," Early said. "Let's get moving."

Both men retraced their footsteps through the apartment until they were outside in the private foyer.

"You secure the apartment until the Crime Scene Unit gets here," Early said. "I'll go back down to the lobby and fill the task force sergeant in on the situation."

Early reached the lobby just as the task force sergeant and the Crime Scene Unit arrived. A quick look around reinforced the high-profile nature the case was rapidly assuming. He saw the chief of detectives, one of the department's five superchiefs, and the deputy commissioner for public information, obviously interrupted during a night on the town judging from the tuxedo he was wearing; they were huddled in a corner with the Homicide Task Force commander, the platoon commander, and the patrol supervisor.

Early gave the task force sergeant the details of what he had discovered in apartment 15-A and informed the Crime Scene Unit supervisor of the third body. He then went behind the reception desk, where he pulled on his latex gloves, picked up the telephone, and, holding the receiver between his thumb and forefinger, dialed a number that rang in the Intelligence Division's operations center.

The telephone call Early placed had more to do with career opportunity than anything connected with his investigation at this point. Four months ago he had put in for a transfer to the Intelligence Division's Organized Crime Monitoring Unit. He had been through two interviews already; one with the commander, a deputy chief, and another with Tony Rizzo, the lieutenant in charge of OCMU, who had assured him that he was in as soon as a slot opened.

The phone call, patched through to Rizzo at his home on Staten Island, waking him from a sound sleep, was Early's way of demonstrating that he was already a team player, informing Rizzo about something that fell well within his purview and would be of immediate interest to him.

Nicole Bass sat on the small balcony of her twentieth-floor apartment on East Sixty-ninth Street between Lexington and Third Avenues. Her legs were tucked under her and she was bundled in a thick terry cloth bathrobe against the chill early morning air. She finished her second glass of wine and poured another from the Chianti bottle on the small table next to the chair.

She cried for Michael Onorati. Not because she loved him, but because he was a dear, sweet, gentle man who had been kind to her. The image of the bullets shattering his skull as he toppled over on the floor kept coming back no matter how hard she fought to keep it at bay. She thought the wine might calm her nerves and stop her hands from shaking. But she recognized the condition for what it was, the ebbing of the adrenaline that had flowed through her body as she ran for her life from the apartment. It would run its course, wine or not.

When she felt calm and collected enough to organize her thoughts, she picked up the cordless phone in her lap and called Carolyn Chambers at home, telling her what she had witnessed and how she had escaped, leaving out any mention of the briefcase she had taken.

"Oh, my God, Niki! Are you okay?"

"I'm fine now, a little rattled, but I've got it under control."

"Do you want me to come over?" Chambers was only a few blocks away, at her town house on East Seventy-fourth Street just off Madison.

"Thanks, but I'll be alright. I am going to take a few days off, though, maybe take a trip, I don't know."

"Take as much time as you need. It must have been horrible, seeing Michael killed right in front of you. And then having them come after you. Do you know who they were?"

"The one who shot Michael looked familiar. I may have seen him before. I'm not sure."

"Do you think he recognized you?"

"He didn't see me. One of the men with him did, but I've never seen him before."

"Did you call the police?"

"Are you out of your mind?"

"No. No. I wasn't suggesting that you should. I was just worried that if you did, then the people who were chasing you would eventually find out who you are."

"This never happened, Carolyn. Do you understand? I was not at Michael's apartment tonight."

"Of course. It's not in either of our best interests to tell anyone, Niki, but I'm more worried about you."

Bass knew Chambers was sincere in her concern. "Well, don't worry about me. I'll be okay. I've been through worse."

"I can't imagine what could be worse."

"Just don't worry about me. I'll call you next week."

"You take care. If you need anything, call me . . . anytime."

Bass hung up and began going over the night moment by moment in her mind's eye, recalling every detail she could from the time she left Onorati's apartment until she got in the cab on Third Avenue. There had been no one in the lobby, she had passed no one on the street until she was two blocks away on First Avenue—an old man walking his dog, and he had not even looked at her. The only person who knew she was there was Carolyn, and that base was covered. Except the doormen—the damn doormen. They saw her come in. Knew Michael was expecting her.

Oh, Christ! They'd tell the cops she was there. What time she arrived. Should she call the cops now and get it over with? No. Wait until morning. Until she was thinking clearly and could concoct a story that might convince them she had left before anything happened. She could tell the cops she didn't call right away because she was too frightened to think rationally. No. That wasn't right. If she wasn't there when it happened, what the hell would she be calling the cops for. She'd have to wait until they contacted her.

And where were the doormen when she left at . . . what time? Twelve or twelve-fifteen. If they occasionally left their stations, that could work to her benefit. She could claim they were not there when she left. Would they remember precisely when they were and were not at their stations? And in a building like that, why had they left the entrance unguarded in the first place? They probably wouldn't admit they had left. It would be her word against theirs. The cops would believe them—she didn't kid herself about that.

And even if she did manage to convince them that she left before anything happened, what could she say she was doing there? Delivering something to Michael, or had come just to say goodbye before he flew to London. Left ten minutes later. He was fine then. She'd have to think of something. And who knew when they would discover the body. Time of death could be established only within a few hours, she recalled, which gave her some leeway. And the briefcase. She would have to get rid of the briefcase.

Bass got up and stood at the balcony railing, looking out over the city, forcing the maddening circular barrage of hypothetical questions and answers from her mind. She was losing it now. Her thought processes were cluttered. She would wait until morning, make her decision then. She went back inside, sat on the sofa in the living room, turned on the television, and tuned to New York 1, the twenty-four-hour all-news channel, to see if the police had found Onorati's body.

At first the live feed from Beekman Place didn't register, then it dawned on her what she was staring at. The camera shot over the reporter's shoulder showed the entrance to One Beekman, the sidewalk in front of the building filled with cops. Bass turned up the volume to listen to the reporter.

"The police are not commenting on the details of the triple homicide here at One Beekman Place. But this reporter has learned that the victims were the two doormen on duty at the time and one of the tenants . . ."

Bass didn't hear the rest of what the reporter said. The doormen had been killed! She was home free. She felt a brief sense of shame about being so elated over the deaths of the two men, but then she had done nothing to cause them. The fact was that now there was no one to place her at the scene of Michael's murder; other than the men who were responsible, and they certainly weren't going to the cops.

My God! They killed the doormen. Who the hell were they, and what had Michael done to them to get himself killed? It had something to do with money, she recalled from the bits and pieces of the conversation she had heard. She remembered hearing the man who killed him saying something about an accountant and "fifteen to eighteen million." People had been killed for a whole lot less.

Bass changed the channel and lay down on the sofa, staring at an old black-and-white movie, not caring what she watched, just needing something to stop the images of the night's near-fatal encounter that flashed through her mind like a looped tape. Over and over again. She lay there for more than an hour, until the wine and sheer exhaustion put her to sleep.

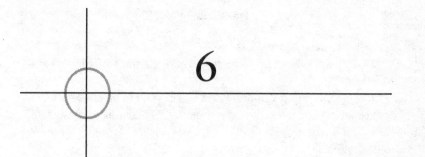

6

AT ONE THIRTY-FIVE in the morning, Detective Jack Kirby was the only customer left in Eddie Boyle's Tavern on Manhattan's Upper West Side. He was sitting in a booth in a darkened corner nursing a drink when his pager interrupted his painful reverie.

He pulled the pager from the waistband of his jeans and pressed the button that illuminated the display. "Ah, shit!" he muttered upon recognizing the number as the home telephone of his boss, Tony Rizzo, the head of the Intelligence Division's Organized Crime Monitoring Unit.

Kirby got to his feet too fast, feeling the effects of the three double Jack Daniels he had polished off. He steadied himself and walked over to the bar, where Boyle, a retired cop with thirty years in the Job, having heard the pager from across the room, handed him the telephone and went to the other end of the bar to give him privacy.

"Lou, it's Kirby," he said, calling Rizzo by the diminutive for "lieutenant" used as a term of respect throughout the Department.

"There's a triple homicide over at One Beekman Place," Rizzo told him. "You know where it is?"

"Yeah."

"Well, you might want to get over there."

"What's that got to do with us?"

"One of the victims is Michael Onorati."

Kirby shook some of the fuzziness from his head. "Somebody whacked him?"

"Looks like it."

"Who are the other two victims?"

"Doormen," Rizzo said, detecting the slight slur to Kirby's words. "You okay?"

"If you're asking if I'm drunk, I was supposed to be off-duty for the next two days, Lou. So with all due respect, I'll get shit-faced if I want to."

"I wasn't passing judgment, Jack. Just concerned about your ability to do the Job."

"I'll manage," Kirby said. "I'm on my way."

"Get some breath mints. The place will probably be crawling with bosses."

"Yeah."

Rizzo hung up and propped a pillow under his head, staring at the darkened bedroom ceiling. He knew what was tormenting Kirby—it was the reason he had arranged for him to be off-duty at a time that was going to be difficult for him, to say the least. There were few in the detective bureau, or for that matter in the Department, who didn't know the story, a tragic incident that struck home to every cop who heard it.

Fourteen months ago Kirby had been on duty for thirty-six straight hours—a surveillance operation. He came home at seven in the morning, physically and mentally exhausted, and went directly upstairs to the master bedroom of his small Cape Cod–style house in Queens. He kissed his wife as she got out of the shower to start her day, forgetfully put his gun on the nightstand instead of in the lockbox on the top shelf of the closet where he always kept it, then flopped on the bed fully clothed and fell immediately to sleep.

Kathleen Ann Kirby, age six, before leaving for school, ran upstairs to give her daddy a hug and a kiss goodnight. Her eyes immediately went to the gun on the nightstand. Daddy's gun. She had always been fascinated with it, watching him put on his shoulder holster, slip the gun inside, then hide it under his coat.

Jack Kirby was startled from a deep sleep by the roar of the gunshot. The image of his little girl, their only child, his precious Kathleen, whom he loved more than life itself, lying dead on the bedroom floor from a gunshot wound to the chest, was burned forever into his memory.

His wife and his family and friends had forgiven him, but he could not forgive himself. The marriage had been on less than solid ground for the previous year, and the divorce came three months later. The home in

Queens went up for sale, they split the proceeds, and both went their separate ways, taking with them a void that would never be filled; a part of their souls irretrievably torn from them in one terrible moment. For the past fourteen months Kirby had lived with a cold loneliness, his heart as hard as stone. The run-down one-bedroom apartment he rented on the Upper West Side reflected the shambles his personal life had become.

Kirby was a good cop, highly decorated, and one of the youngest ever to earn the coveted gold shield, becoming a detective at age twenty-three, after only two years in the Job. That was seventeen years ago. Career advancement meant nothing to him. He had never taken the sergeant's exam, wanting to continue to work the streets and avoid ending up in a desk job or as a supervisor.

He was ten months away from having his twenty years in and the option of retiring with half pay, but he had no thoughts of leaving the Department. The Job was his life now, he had nothing without it, and he intended to stay in it until they forced him out. And then, he occasionally thought in his darker moments, it would be time to eat his gun.

After the death of Kirby's daughter, Rizzo covered for him through the worst of it, which lasted about two months. Since then it was only necessary on the occasions when it came back to haunt him, occasions when Kirby couldn't stand to be with himself, and neither could anyone else. This was one of those occasions. Kathleen Ann Kirby would have been eight years old today.

Kirby stood bent over the sink in Boyle's men's room, tossing cold water on his face. He ran his hands through his thick unruly hair and stared into the mirror. His rugged good looks were muddied by a two-day growth of stubble, and his intense, piercing blue-gray eyes, which normally intimidated the hell out of anyone they locked on, were streaked with red and rimmed with deep circles. The white mock turtleneck he wore under his leather jacket had a small dark stain on the chest—a remnant of the greasy cheese-steak sandwich he had eaten for dinner. He shrugged—nothing he could do about it now. No time. He splashed more cold water on his face, smoothed back his hair with his hands, then left the men's room to find Eddie Boyle waiting with a cup full of steaming coffee for him.

"One for the road," Boyle said.

"Thanks, Eddie."

"You're not plannin' on driving, are you?" Boyle called out as Kirby reached the door.

"I'll grab a cab. See ya."

The immediate area outside the perimeter of the crime scene had reached critical mass by the time Kirby got out of the taxi on First Avenue and walked up Fiftieth Street to the police line at the intersection with Beekman Place. Television news trucks, satellite dishes and antennas bristling from their roofs, crowded the end of the narrow side street that provided a clear angle of view to the entrance of One Beekman Place thirty yards away.

Kirby estimated at least sixty reporters and ten TV news crews were massed at the yellow crime scene tape. They shouted questions to anyone who came out of the building, and turned on their klieg lights to film anything that looked like it might possibly be of interest, casting harsh, glaring light across the deeply shadowed street.

Kirby wore his detective shield on a beaded chain around his neck as he angled and shoved his way through the crush of reporters. An attractive young woman with a microphone in her hand spotted his shield and stepped in front of him, signaling to her cameraman to roll tape. The lights from the camera momentarily blinded Kirby as the television reporter shoved the microphone in his face.

"Marni Thompson, Channel Four News," the reporter said. "Detective, can you tell us who the victim on the fifteenth floor is? And do you have any idea who killed him?"

"Aliens," Kirby said. "Landed on the roof about twelve-fifteen. They've killed all the tenants and seeded the building with pods. Some of them are about to hatch. Film at eleven."

"Very funny," the reporter said, and signaled to her cameraman to cut the lights and stop taping. "Thanks for nothing."

Kirby ducked under the crime scene tape and crossed the street to enter the lobby of One Beekman. The first person he saw was the last person he needed to see that night, given his mood and condition: Pete Davidson, a uniform whom Kirby had briefly had as a partner when he was working undercover narcotics. Davidson was a coward and a liar who had nearly cost the lives of Kirby and two other men.

Kirby had punched Davidson silly one night when he could no longer tolerate his incompetence and cowardice, telling him that if he did not put in for a transfer immediately he was going to kill him himself, before he got someone else killed. Davidson had transferred out, and was one of the few cops who did not get a gold shield after eighteen months of undercover narcotics work. He blamed Kirby for that, but everyone in the task force knew about Davidson, and it was the commander who laid the bad report on him.

Kirby tried to get by him in the lobby without incident, but Davidson saw him and was not about to let the opportunity pass.

"If it isn't the great Jack Kirby. A legend in his own mind."

"Don't press your luck, Pete."

"I heard they put you in the rubber gun squad," Davidson said. "Down in the motor pool with the rest of the losers and psychos, after your kid killed herself with your gun. You stupid bastard."

Davidson never saw the left hook that hit him hard enough to cross his eyes and send him to his knees, stunned and semiconscious, where Kirby began kicking him in the ribs.

Davidson's uniformed partner, a huge black man, grabbed Kirby in a bear hug and pulled him across the lobby, away from Davidson, who was struggling to his feet.

"Hey, Kirby. I don't like the son of a bitch either, but look around, will ya? How bad you want to hurt yourself here."

Kirby pulled himself free and looked about the lobby. It was full of brass and a few heavyweights from headquarters; all eyes were on him. Including those of John Kane, the chief of detectives, who was storming toward him. They had met on two previous occasions, when Kane had decorated him for bravery. Reaching Kirby's side, he took him by the elbow and led him off into a corner.

"What the hell is wrong with you, Kirby."

"He asked for it."

Kane got a whiff of Kirby's breath and shook his head in disgust. "Look, I'm aware of your loss, and you have my deepest sympathy. I know you've had a rough time. But if you ever show up drunk on the Job again, I'll have your shield."

Kirby's temper calmed as quickly as it had flared. "Sorry, chief. It won't happen again."

Kane grunted. "What are you doing here?"

"My boss called and said to get over here, that Michael Onorati got whacked."

"Then do what you came to do . . . and don't go talking to the press. You look like hell and you smell like a goddamn brewery."

"Yes, sir," Kirby said. "Who caught the case?"

"Joe Early. He's up on the fifteenth floor with the Crime Scene Unit in Onorati's apartment."

Kirby headed for the elevator, catching Davidson's eye as he stood leaning against the wall holding his ribs. Kirby blew him a kiss as the elevator door closed.

The Crime Scene Unit was in full swing in Onorati's apartment, collecting and bagging any and all samples, particles, and whatever detritus they found on or around the body. The CSU photographer finished taking the official pictures of the scene, while a technician did the formal sketch, taking measurements and relating them to the compass points. Four technicians were on the terrace, going over every inch of the outside area.

"Who's Early?" Kirby asked one of the CSU technicians working the living room.

The technician pointed to a stocky, muscular man with reddish-brown hair and the countenance of a pit bull. He was standing near the entrance to the study and scribbling in his notebook. Kirby went over to him.

"Early? Jack Kirby. OCMU."

"Yeah. How ya doin'?" The two men shook hands. "I called your boss. Thought you might want to get in on this from the beginning. Also, I'd like to be able to reach out to you guys for help when and if I need it."

"No problem," Kirby said. "What do you have so far?"

"M.E. says the time of death was around eleven, eleven-thirty. Doesn't look like anything's missing. My guess is it's a hit. The shooter, or shooters, must have used silencers; nobody in the other apartments heard any shots. And I'd say the victim knew whoever did it."

"What makes you say that?"

"He didn't put up a fight. Two glasses on the bar over there with some scotch left in them. Maybe he made whoever was here a drink."

"Any prints?"

"None on the glasses on the bar, which makes me think whoever used them was wearing gloves or wiped them off; which means there might have been at least two of them; victim's not going to wipe down his own glass before he gets killed."

"Or the killer didn't remember which one he drank from and wiped them both down before he left."

"That, too," Early said. "Also, we found another empty glass outside on the terrace, got some partials off that one. Technician says they may not be good enough to do anything with, though."

Kirby watched as Onorati's corpse was zipped into a body bag by two attendants from the Mortuary Division, then he and Early stepped aside as it was carried from the study.

"I don't know too much about how the wise guys operate," Early said. "But I thought the usual procedure was to take their victims for a ride, whack them, then bury them at some construction site under a couple tons of dirt. Not to kill two innocent civilians when it wasn't necessary."

"That was the old days. When they were well organized and efficient and had people working for them with IQs over fifty. The new generation are a bunch of psychos who saw the *Godfather* movies too many times. Most of them are stupid, love playing the role. Think they're Al Pacino."

"So what's your take on this?" Early asked.

"Onorati wasn't a soldier or a made man; he was a lawyer and a CPA who laundered money for the Gambino Family. Whatever he did to get himself killed, he did it to them."

"Any ideas who specifically might have done it?"

"Sure. Vincent Genero."

"He's the 'boss of bosses,' right?"

"Right."

"And you think he did this himself?"

"He and Onorati were close friends since they were kids. Nobody killed him without Genero putting out the contract. If he didn't do it himself, he ordered it done. But this kind of senseless shit, whacking him in his apartment, killing the doormen, has Genero's arrogance all over it."

"Yeah? I remember reading some stuff about him; busted ten or twelve times for killing his own kind. D.A. didn't have enough to get the grand jury to indict on any of them."

"Eleven times, to be exact. Unlike most of them, he's smart and he's slippery," Kirby said. "The guys doing the canvass come up with any-thing?"

"A doorman up the street saw a black Mercedes or BMW parked in front of the building around eleven-thirty. Couldn't see anybody inside; says it had tinted windows. Didn't notice the license plates. Didn't see it leave; it's not there now."

Early looked at his notes. "And some guy in the lobby of Beekman Towers, that apartment hotel around the corner? Says he saw a good-looking woman go by in a hurry around twelve. He was coming down from that rooftop bar. Had half a load on. The description he gave isn't much better than a stick figure."

"That's it?"

"So far," Early said. "Oh, yeah, you're gonna love this. They got kind of a neighborhood watch committee around here. They hire a private se-curity firm, rent-a-cops, no guns. Just to show a presence; gingerbread uniforms and a car with their logo on it. Two of their finest were parked around the corner on Fifty-first. Asleep in the goddamn car. One of the first uniforms to respond to the scene woke the morons up. Bottom line? They didn't see shit."

Kirby looked out through the open doors to the terrace, to a building beyond with a direct line of sight into the study. "Anybody canvassing the apartments in that building off the terrace?"

"They're next on the list. DBM only sent me eight detectives. They're still working this building and the others on Beekman Place."

"The doorman who saw a BMW or Mercedes? Genero rides around in a black Mercedes," Kirby said. "There would have been two others with him: his driver, Big Paulie Arturo, and his bodyguard, Johnnie 'Socks' Giordano. I'll get some pictures out of our files and send them over to you first thing in the morning. See if anyone can ID them. If Genero was here, they were here; he doesn't go anywhere without them."

"Thanks, I appreciate it."

"I want Genero worse than you do. I've been trying to nail that piece of garbage for the past six years," Kirby said. "I'll work close with you on this, give you whatever I come up with. I'll get back to you tomorrow."

Kirby returned to the lobby and went outside. He walked to the north end of Beekman Place, where East Fifty-first Street ended, and took the stone steps down to the overhead footbridge that spanned the FDR Drive. He crossed over the drive and walked down to the small promenade along the banks of the East River. Three of the benches along the railing were occupied by homeless men, bundled in rags and asleep, or passed out drunk under sheets of cardboard. He found an empty bench at the far end and sat staring out across the water toward Roosevelt Island.

He closed his eyes to see his daughter come running across the lawn and leap into his outstretched arms, giggling and squealing with delight as he hugged her and spun her in a circle.

"Happy birthday, honey, wherever you are," he whispered. "Daddy loves you, and he always will." And then the tears began.

Kirby spent the rest of the night on the bench overlooking the river, tormented by bittersweet memories. He left when the first trace of dawn appeared on the horizon.

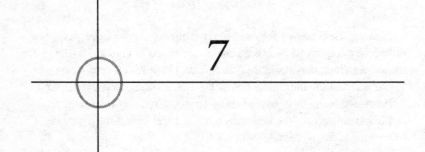

7

NICOLE BASS WOKE shortly after dawn with a headache from too much wine and a stiff neck from sleeping on the sofa. She dressed in her running clothes, did her stretching exercises, then left the apartment to run her daily five-mile route through the city streets. It was just what she needed to relieve the tension and stress that had allowed her little more than a few fitful hours of sleep. Her headache and stiff neck gone, feeling refreshed and thinking clearly, she was back in the apartment in time for the beginning of the *Today* show. She did a light workout with free weights, followed by six sets of stomach crunches, as she anxiously awaited the local news break at seven twenty-five.

A live camera shot of One Beekman Place filled the screen, and Bass turned up the volume to listen to the reporter's voice-over. The police had released Michael Onorati's name and the names of the doormen to the press. Onorati was described as a wealthy lawyer and investment counselor who lived in a penthouse apartment on the fifteenth floor. They showed an interview taped early that morning, when the chief of detectives, with the deputy commissioner for public information at his side, squinted against the bright lights from the cameras and stated that there was no apparent motive for the triple homicide and he was not going to speculate. The press would be kept advised of any and all developments. The report was followed by a commentary on the city's rising crime rate, specifically the increase of violent crimes such as the one at One Beekman, how no neighborhood could be considered safe or immune, and how the police department seemed incapable of doing anything about it.

Bass switched to *Good Morning America* and ate her usual breakfast of orange juice and a bowl of cereal as she waited for the local ABC affiliate to give its version of the story at the seven fifty-five news break. The report was much the same. No mention of suspects, witnesses, or any speculation on who might have done it, or why.

Bass had now fully regained her emotional equilibrium after her harrowing experience. For the second time she sat calmly going over the details, trying to remember if she did anything, or left anything behind, that could lead the police to her. She thought of the glass she had left on the terrace, but dismissed it as inconsequential; she had never been fingerprinted. She could think of nothing that would implicate her.

She turned off the television, took a long shower, then pulled on her robe and went back into the living room, where she reached under the sofa to retrieve the briefcase she had taken from Onorati's apartment. She flicked open the gold-plated locks and opened the case, resting it on her lap. She began counting the stacks of one-hundred-dollar bills, banded into one-thousand-dollar packets, laying them out on the coffee table before her. She counted them twice and came up with the same amount: sixty-five thousand dollars. She took a deep breath and smiled to herself. What the hell, it wasn't as though poor Michael had any use for it anymore. And he had no family.

Bass sat staring at the money, then, having decided what she would do with it, she separated fifteen thousand dollars from the neat rows she had formed and put the remaining fifty thousand back in the case to be deposited in one of her investment accounts.

Twenty minutes later she came out of the bedroom dressed in a navy blue Givenchy suit, looking like the international fashion model she had once been. She placed the fifteen thousand dollars in one of the zipper compartments of her shoulder bag, slid the briefcase back under the sofa, and left the apartment for a morning of shopping and a leisurely lunch at her favorite restaurant.

Bass limited her extravagant shopping for designer clothes to those she deemed necessary for her work, saving and investing every penny she could. But this was found money, she reasoned, and after last night's near-death experience, what could be more life-affirming than a shopping spree.

Charlie, her favorite doorman, gave her an exaggerated once-over and a thumbs-up approval of her outfit as she got off the elevator. Bass gave him a broad smile and a wink, doing a slow, graceful runway turn for him as she left the lobby.

She headed west on East Sixty-ninth Street, toward Madison Avenue and a shopper's nirvana. First stop, Valentino's, and a blouse she had coveted but couldn't bring herself to spend the eight hundred dollars they were asking.

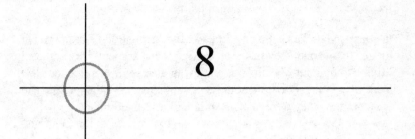

8

VINCENT GENERO HAD purchased his estate on Centre Island, Long Island, for very specific purposes: privacy and seclusion. A long, winding driveway, secured by electronic gates, led to the Tudor-style mansion situated on a point of land at the very end of the main road through the island. The property was heavily wooded, with an occasional broad expanse of lawn and sweeping views of Oyster Bay. Conducting a surveillance operation anywhere near the property without being spotted would have been impossible, plus Genero had a contact within the local police department who informed him whenever an outside law enforcement agency was operating on the island.

Every week Genero had his car and house swept for electronic bugs by experts in the field, and he never used his home telephone, or the cellular phone in his car, to discuss Family business. He also never went to the social clubs in Little Italy, or Bensonhurst, or Ozone Park, or any of the other places frequented by members of his Family. He knew all too well that the city, state, or federal organized-crime task forces—sometimes all three without telling each other what they were doing—had audio and video surveillance on all the known Family hangouts. Genero discussed business only in places he knew were secure: on long walks in areas chosen on the spur of the moment as they drove about, or in a series of randomly chosen restaurants scattered around the five boroughs, or on the grounds of his Centre Island estate.

Late last night, after leaving Onorati's apartment, he had returned to LaRosa's restaurant in the Bronx to talk with his underboss and second-in-command of the Gambino crime Family, Carmine Molino, informing him of the woman they had seen leaving the apartment. He instructed Molino to find out who she was and to tap their sources inside the New York City Police Department to see if they knew about a witness, and what progress they were making with their investigation.

Aware that Genero was a late riser, Molino arrived at the Centre Island estate at ten-thirty the following morning. He was escorted to the garden terrace off the kitchen by Johnnie Socks, to join Genero for a breakfast of coffee and sweet rolls. The boss of bosses was resplendent in a cream-colored Sulka silk shirt worn beneath a black custom-tailored wool crepe blazer and gray slacks, his tasseled Gucci loafers polished to a glossy shine.

In stark contrast to his boss, Molino was a slovenly man who cared nothing about what he wore or how he looked. His clothes were usually rumpled and unpressed, giving one the impression he had been tossed out of a washing machine in the middle of the spin cycle. Anything but vain, the only time Molino looked in a mirror was when he shaved, while Genero could not pass any reflective surface without checking his appearance.

Molino stood before Genero wearing a cheap, poorly cut olive-drab suit with a drooping crotch and two rings of sweat stains at the armpits. His ample stomach hung over his belt, but despite his excess weight, and the fact that he had not exercised in fifteen years, a sense of strength and ability emanated from his stocky, thick-set body that gave any potential challenger pause.

Genero gestured for Molino to sit at the table, and having no patience for the old-fashioned, exaggerated pleasantries of his predecessors, he got right to business.

"So, you come up with anything?"

"Yeah. Some good news." Molino tore off a chunk of sweet roll, stuffing it in his mouth, and washing it down with a gulp of coffee. "The cops aren't looking for no witness; they don't even suspect there was one."

"Who'd you talk to?"

"The captain we got on the hook in the chief of detectives' office. It's solid information. They got nothin'."

"Why'd you tell him you were asking?"

"Don't worry, I covered it. I said we were really pissed off that someone whacked our good friend Michael Onorati and that we would appreciate knowing any details he could give us."

"What about those scumbags in the organized-crime unit?"

"Our source over there says a detective by the name of Kirby was called in, but he don't got no more than the cops in the Seventeenth Precinct who are handling the case."

"And what about the broad? Any idea who she is?"

"We got a possible lead. Somebody who might know."

"Yeah? Who?"

"One of our guys, Jimmie Vicarro. I used him to deliver the suitcases full of cash once a month to Onorati. Then he'd drive him out to La Guardia to the private jet we hired to take him to the Cayman Islands. You know, make sure him and the money got off safe. He'd also pick Onorati up the next day when he got back from laundering the cash down there; take him home or back to his office."

Genero shifted impatiently in his chair, giving his underboss a stop-telling-me-what-I-already-know look. "So Jimmie knows who the broad was?"

"Not exactly. When I asked him if he knew anybody Onorati was seeing kind of regular, he remembered four, five times when he picked him up at the airport, on the way home he used his portable phone to call some broad."

"He hear a name?"

"He thinks maybe Vicki, but he ain't sure what it was. But Jimmie's sure he was calling some kind of call girl—an escort service. He heard him tell somebody on the phone that he wanted to see a certain person at a certain time. And then tell them for how long he wanted to see her; six or eight hours, or whatever."

"So does Jimmie know who she is, or doesn't he?"

"No, not himself. But he says that once or twice, when Onorati got back later than expected, he tried calling a number, couldn't get no answer. Then he'd call his office and tell his secretary to keep calling this number and tell some broad that he was going to be late. He done that just last week. So what Jimmie's saying is that Onorati's secretary's got to know who the broad is."

"You send somebody over to talk to her?"

"I wanted to check with you first."

"So send somebody."

"I was thinkin' Nino Totani and a few of the guys from his crew."

Genero thought for a moment. Nino Totani was a capo who ran the most productive crew in the Family. Deadly and resourceful, he handled things discreetly without making a ripple, and could be relied on in extremely sensitive matters.

"I don't want no army running around asking questions; attracts too much attention. Just Nino, and Johnnie Socks, he saw her. Make sure if the secretary knows anything, and if the cops come around for any reason, she don't tell them what she tells us."

"I'll take care of it."

Molino got up to leave, sitting back down when Genero put out a hand to stop him; his eyes hard and unyielding, boring into his underboss as he spoke.

"You tell Nino I don't want nobody else knowing our business. He don't tell no one about who we're lookin' for or why. Make sure he understands that; I don't want the other Families finding out I got a potential problem, and I definitely don't want the cops getting wind of what we're doin'."

"Nino's real closed-mouth. But I'll make sure he understands."

"Makes sense the broad was a hooker," Genero said after a long pause. "She hasn't gone to the cops to report what she saw, and Johnnie Socks says she stole a briefcase out of the apartment. They're all fuckin' sneak thieves. How many escort services we into right now?"

Molino thought for a moment. "Four or five, in the city."

"You tell Nino if the secretary doesn't have nothin' for us, start checking with the people we got runnin' the whores."

"From what Jimmie says, it don't sound like Onorati was dealing with none of our services. Sounds like it might be a little higher-class operation."

"So how many of them can there be?"

"I don't know. Doesn't matter. We'll check 'em all."

"What about the money that fuck stole?"

"I'm gonna give that computer disk you gave me to the accountant who discovered the money was missing. I set up a meet with him for one o'clock. I'll tell him like you told me; empty out the accounts Onorati set up for himself, transfer it back into our accounts. You want me to keep usin' him to handle the cash until you find somebody to replace Onorati?"

"No, I want you to whack him. One less person to worry about."

"You sure?"

"Yeah, I'm sure. Think about it. He knows we found out that fuck was stealing from us. Last night we kill him. Today you give him the disk to transfer the money back into our accounts. Unless the guy's a moron, he knows we did the hit. So, after he makes the transfers, take him somewhere he won't be found."

"I'll do like you say, Vinnie, but the guy's too scared of us to talk; he's got a wife and four kids we could get to."

"And the feds find out about him, threaten to put his sorry ass in prison for the rest of his life if he don't talk? Promise him if he testifies for them they'll protect him? I don't need to be worryin' about that shit. You could hang yourself with loose ends. I want him out of the picture."

"Okay. Who do you want me to get to handle the cash?"

"I'll find somebody. You concentrate on finding the broad. And get back to me as soon as Nino talks to that secretary."

Genero got up from the table and walked with Molino to his car. "Ya know, we're gonna be okay on this, long as the cops don't find out about the broad before we get to her."

"I cleaned my plate of all other business, Vinnie. I'll find her."

"You do that. Soon."

"When I do, you want to talk to her first?"

"What would I want to talk to her for? Just get rid of her."

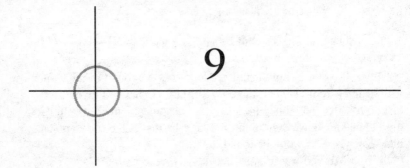

9

THE THIRTY-THOUSAND-MEMBER New York City Police Department is run from its headquarters at One Police Plaza, a modern, arsenal-like building in lower Manhattan. But the Department's most closely guarded and sensitive secrets, gathered by detectives who are considered by their peers to be some of the best in the world, are kept at the Intelligence Division's headquarters in a three-story brick building at 72 Poplar Street in Brooklyn Heights, almost underneath the eastbound exit ramp of the famed Brooklyn Bridge.

Tasked with gathering intelligence information on organized crime, criminal conspiracies, and terrorist groups, the Intelligence Division runs intricate webs of undercover and deep-cover officers and confidential informants, and is capable of conducting the most sophisticated of electronic surveillance operations. They have liaisons with the FBI, the DEA, the ATF, the CIA, the U.S. Marshals Service, and the Secret Service, occasionally working directly with these agencies when they are operating a joint task force within the city. But the exchange of information with the federal agencies, as the NYPD has learned to their disappointment over the years, is usually a one-way street, with the feds giving little in return unless it suits their purposes.

The Intelligence Division's Organized Crime Monitoring Unit, located in a squad room on the second floor of the Poplar Street building, is separated into modules of specialization. Each team of detectives within the OCMU has its own area of expertise: the Italian desk deals with the Italian Mafia, the Russian desk the Russian mafia, and so on, carrying out intelligence-gathering operations against the full range of organized criminals throughout the city: the Colombian cartels and Jamaican posses, the Chinese triads and other Asian gangs, along with various smaller, but equally deadly loose-knit groups and organizations dealing in everything from drugs and guns to stolen merchandise.

Jack Kirby's area of expertise for the past six years was the Italian Mafia. Specifically the Gambino crime Family and their ever-expanding heroin- and cocaine-trafficking. With Genero at the helm they were brutal and ruthless in their conquests, taking over the Jamaican and Colombian territories at the first signs of weakness and killing anyone who got in their way.

As a permanent reminder of who the enemy was, Kirby had a pyramid of booking photos of the upper echelon of the Gambino Family tacked to a corkboard on the wall above his desk. Genero's arrogant face, fixed with a defiant grin, was at the top of the pyramid, daring Kirby or anyone else to bring him down, a challenge that Kirby took personally and considered his primary goal in life. Beneath the boss-of-bosses photo were the side-by-side mug shots of his underboss, Carmine Molino, and his consigliere, the Family counselor, and beneath them, three rows of seven photographs each of the twenty-one capos who ran fifteen- and twenty-man crews for Genero, crews with their own areas of specialization that included loan-sharking, extortion, bookmaking, hijacking, auto theft, and drug-dealing.

Kirby had gone home only long enough to shave, shower, and change clothes. He was at his desk in the OCMU squad room at seven thirty-five, eating a breakfast of onion bagels and coffee at a time of day when he was usually grabbing a few hours of sleep. Working organized crime meant working nights; that was when the wise guys were most active. He liked the surveillance side of the work, outsmarting the bad guys, and the other benefits: no caseloads or clearance rates to worry about, and no dealing with self-important assistant district attorneys or tedious court appearances. The downtime, however, the writing of seemingly endless reports, bored him to distraction, but it was a small price to pay for the freedom and independence working for the Intelligence Division allowed. Results were what counted at OCMU, and creative approaches that brought results were encouraged and rewarded.

Kirby had never quite adjusted to sleeping during the daylight hours, but the lack of sleep didn't bother him anymore; his body rhythms had somehow adjusted to getting by on a few hours each day. The times when it caught up with him, he would crash for ten or twelve hours on his days off. At eleven o'clock he had just finished compiling a folder of unclassified information and photographs for Joe Early at the 17th Precinct when he looked up to see Lieutenant Tony Rizzo, head of the OCMU, enter the squad room. Rizzo, having just returned from attending a briefing by the chief of detectives at One Police Plaza, motioned with his head for Kirby to join him in his office.

"The Chief putting the pressure on about the Onorati hit?" Kirby asked as he closed the door behind him.

"Among other things."

Rizzo, a wiry, darkly handsome man in his mid-forties, fixed his large liquid brown eyes on Kirby, studying him for a brief moment, looking to see if the demons were gone from the man he both liked and respected. "By the way, I heard about your little altercation at One Beekman last night. Did you have to kick the guy's ass in front of the chief of detectives?"

"Actually it was his ribs I kicked, not his ass," Kirby said, deadpan. "He just shot off his mouth at the wrong time."

"You didn't have to come in today, you know."

"It's okay. I told the Seventeenth squad I'd work close with them on this one."

"How do you plan to handle it?"

"I thought I'd start with some of our lower-level snitches on the fringes of the Gambino organization, see what they're saying on the street about Onorati getting whacked."

"What about the feds? The FBI's had Genero and some of his people under audio and video surveillance for the past six months."

"I've got a call in to our liaison. But I don't hold out much hope of getting anything from her. You know how damn turf-conscious they are. And if I had to guess, I'd say they didn't have anyone on Genero last night, or if they did, he shook them and they aren't about to admit it."

"What about the task force and the D.A.'s squad?"

"They won't have anything current. The task force has been working the Jamaican posses since the bloodbath up in Washington Heights last month, and the D.A.'s squad is concentrating on the Russian mafia's latest gasoline tax swindle."

"Crime Scene Unit come up with anything?"

"Nothing. They found a lot of latent prints, but they'll probably turn out to be the cleaning woman or the maintenance people, whatever. If Genero was careful enough to make sure they picked up the spent shells after they shot the doormen and Onorati, he sure as hell made certain they didn't leave any fingerprints around."

"I just can't see Genero doing this himself. Molino usually takes care of the wet work. It doesn't make sense Genero would put himself at risk."

"Trust me on this one, Lou. He did it. Him and Big Paulie. And Johnnie Socks, who probably snapped the doorman's neck; that's his style. But Genero pulled the trigger on Onorati. I'd bet my shield on it."

"I don't know. Maybe Onorati got caught up in a turf war. According to the latest take from the Bonanno Family surveillance, some of their crews have been attempting to move in on Genero's territory."

"No way. Onorati only did two things for Genero, and both involved money—laundering it and investing it. Even if there's a turf war going on we don't know about yet, that's no reason to whack Onorati. He's not a made man and he's not a soldier. The only thing that could get him killed is stealing money, and if he stole from Genero, that psycho would go ballistic."

"Did you check the take from the bugs we've got in place on Genero's crews?"

"Yeah. Two of the low-grade morons in DiAngelo's crew in Brooklyn were talking about the hit early this morning at their social club, but it was just speculation. They don't know who did it."

As Rizzo was about to speak, Kirby's beeper went off. He looked down to check the call-back number on the display, then removed it from his belt to look again, making certain there was no mistake.

Only three digits appeared on the display: 432. The number 4 meant that the caller, a deep-cover police officer assigned to OCMU, was requesting an immediate emergency meeting. The number 3 told Kirby that the caller wanted to meet at the third of five predesignated clandestine meeting sites they had established. And the number 2 told Kirby the time—within two hours of the call. The deep-cover officer had never used the emergency code number in all of the six years that Kirby had been his handler.

"Something up?" Rizzo asked, reacting to the concerned look on Kirby's face.

"Tommy Falconetti."

It took Rizzo a few seconds to place the name. He had never seen the man in person or talked directly with him, and Kirby usually referred to him in conversations and in his written reports by his code name, Fonzi. Only four people in the Department knew that Falconetti was a police officer working under deep cover: Kirby, Rizzo, the Intelligence Division's deputy chief, and the chief of detectives.

Falconetti's name was rarely mentioned out loud, and so compartmentalized were the details of his operations that only Kirby, as his handler, knew precisely where Falconetti was and what he was doing at any given time. The deep-cover officer reported in every two weeks, calling a telephone-answering unit with an hour-long message tape. Connected to a separate line set up by the division's technical unit in Kirby's apartment, the number for the answering unit was officially listed in the telephone company records for a Cathy O'Neal at an apartment in Queens—an Intelligence Division safe house.

In other than emergency situations, Kirby and Falconetti met face-to-face once every three months, allowing time for complete, in-depth debriefings on what the deep-cover officer had learned. The second, and equally important, reason for the face-to-face meetings was to allow Kirby an eyes-on assessment of the physical and mental condition of Falconetti and to allow him, if only for a brief time, to relax and have an unguarded conversation with another human being without being afraid of blowing his cover.

"Is he still inside one of Genero's crews?" Rizzo asked.

"Yeah. Nino Totani's. One of the few capos working for Genero who's got a brain that functions above the level of a reptile. What bothers me is Falconetti's not due for a face-to-face meet for another six weeks."

"Maybe he's got something for us on Onorati."

"That, or he's coming apart at the seams. He's been under for six years now, Lou, and the last time I saw him, there were signs that the stress was beginning to take its toll."

Kirby looked at his watch. It was eleven-fifteen. "The meet's on the

Upper East Side. A small park on Sutton Place. If I leave now, I've got time to check in with Early at the Seventeenth, and then get set up to observe the site before Falconetti gets there."

"Make sure he's alright. If it looks like he's starting to lose it, bring him in right then and there, before anything happens to him."

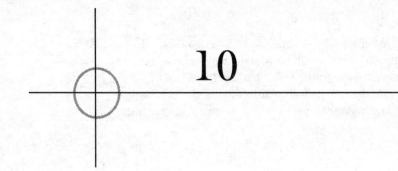

10

THE MAÎTRE D' at Nello's restaurant, a suave, handsome Greek by the name of Yorgi, greeted Nicole Bass with a broad smile and out-stretched arms, taking both her hands in his and kissing her lightly on each cheek. It was the reception Bass always got, and one of the reasons she ate lunch there at least three times a week.

Yorgi, and the owner, Nello, were aware that she had once been a top fashion model and treated her like a celebrity; they knew nothing of her present occupation. On the restaurant's wall of fame, just inside the en-trance, a photograph of Bass, with Nello and Yorgi beaming on either side of her, was prominently displayed among a large collection of sim-ilar snapshots of the rich and famous and beautiful who frequented the restaurant.

The food and service at Nello's were as good as any restaurant's in the city, and better than most; the atmosphere was inviting and relaxing. But they were not the only reasons for its popularity. Location was re-sponsible for some of its success, for it was situated between Sixty-second and Sixty-third Streets on Madison Avenue, in the heart of the Upper East Side, the city's most fashionable shopping area, and home to many of the most wealthy and successful people in the city. But that, again, was only part of the reason.

The dominant reason for Nello's popularity was to be found in its clientele. The lunch and dinner crowds, more often than not, included a disproportionate number of dazzling fashion models, and the new gen-eration of teenage hopefuls who emulated them and hung on their every word, hoping that some of their success might rub off. On the heels of the models came the actors, rock stars, writers, producers, and moguls, who in turn brought the paparazzi and the gossip columnists. Barely a week went by without some columnist mentioning that so and so were seen together at Nello's. Men, young and old, role-played and postured to impress, in the hopes of becoming acquainted with, or walking off with, one of the sleek, gorgeous creatures they came to ogle.

Nicole Bass could more than hold her own with any of the current crop, receiving her share of approaches and entreaties from eager admirers on a regular basis, all of whom she politely turned away. For very specific and personal reasons, she had not dated anyone since going to work for Carolyn Chambers eighteen months ago.

After unburdening Bass of her collection of shopping bags and placing them in the cloakroom, Yorgi escorted her to her favorite table, in a corner just inside the folding glass doors that ran the full length of the front of the dining room, looking out on Madison Avenue. It was a brilliant, crisp October day, the kind that makes even jaded New Yorkers smile with appreciation, and the glass doors were open to the fresh air and the fully charged atmosphere of the city of cities. A solicitous waiter immediately brought Bass a glass of dry white wine, knowing well the likes and dislikes of the familiar customer who, unlike most of the other models—who believed that the pleasure of serving them should be gratuity enough—tipped extremely well.

Bass took a welcome sip of the wine and settled back to people-watch, a constantly changing minidrama of which she seldom tired. The avenue was more crowded than usual; the Spanish Columbus Day parade, held the week prior to the Italian celebration of the same occasion, had begun an hour ago in lower Manhattan and would go on for the better part of the afternoon. Its main route was up Fifth Avenue, and though it would not reach this far north for another few hours, the crowd of spectators was already spilling over onto Madison.

Bass was beginning to feel like her old self again. The stress and emotional upheaval of the previous night were mostly gone now. Only a dim, frightening memory remained, kept at bay by the knowledge that there was no one who knew she had been at Onorati's apartment who would, or could, report her being there to the police. Her morning shopping foray had been successful and had bolstered her spirit. To the uninitiated it would be hard to conceive that the small collection of bags she had handed to Yorgi contained nine thousand dollars' worth of clothes, but they did: the coveted silk blouse from Valentino's, plus a second one from their fall collection she simply could not resist, an evening dress from Gianfranco Ferre, a pants suit and a dress from Armani, and a cashmere sweater and a cocktail dress from Ferragamo.

The last purchases had brought back poignant memories and a strong, unwelcome reminder of all that she had lost: she had once been Ferragamo's favorite model, showing their clothes at their best on runways around the world. And less than five years ago, though it now seemed a lifetime to Bass, she had been the feature model in their fall fashion catalogue, which led to her getting the cover of *Glamour* magazine.

Bass forced the bitterness the wistful recollections brought with them from her thoughts and relaxed with her wine. The waiter returned to recite the day's specials, then brought her a complimentary appetizer of bruschetta when he returned to take her order for a salad and the angel hair pasta. It was just past noon, and the lunch crowd was beginning to trickle in. Yorgi, always attentive to Bass's needs, topped off her wineglass and offered her his copy of the *New York Post* so she could read her favorite columnists, telling her that the restaurant had again been mentioned—a current Broadway star had been seen there with someone other than his wife.

As Yorgi retreated to the door to welcome another customer, Bass unfolded the paper and was about to open it to the gossip column section when she gasped audibly. She quickly composed herself as her eyes locked on the huge, bold headline across the front page:

MOB MONEY MAN MURDERED!

The *Post* had scooped everyone—its rival papers and the electronic media. A well-sourced crime reporter had discovered the connection between Michael Onorati and the New York Mafia's boss of bosses, and the paper had rushed to get the story into the late city final edition shortly after the murder. Below the headline was a file photograph of Vincent Genero with two of his lawyers on the steps of a courthouse, surrounded by cameramen and reporters, dozens of microphones and tape recorders stuck in his face. Bass's hands began to shake. She carefully folded the paper so she could lay it on the table to read the article.

She then held her wineglass in both hands to hide the tremors and took a slow, deep breath to calm herself.

Now she knew why the man had looked so familiar. It was not that Onorati had ever introduced her to him. She had seen his picture in the papers and film of him on the television news as he emerged victorious from his occasional courtroom battles.

Michael in the Mafia? She could not believe it. He hardly seemed the type. She began reading the article, the details of how it was alleged that Onorati had laundered and invested money for the mob. But she couldn't concentrate. Her mind began to race as the magnitude of what she was involved in overwhelmed her. She had witnessed a Mafia godfather commit a murder. A powerful man, a man at home with violence. A man whose tentacles of power reached everywhere, with no laws or rules to give him pause.

He knew she had seen him. He knew she could put him in prison for the rest of his life. And there was no doubt in her mind that that knowledge must, at this very moment, be an overriding constant in his every thought. No matter how hard she tried to convince herself that she was safe, that it was highly improbable he would find out who she was, she had a sinking feeling in the pit of her stomach that her ordeal was far from over.

Bass put the paper aside and stared unseeing out at the avenue, her thoughts flashing by in quick vignettes of all that had happened the previous night. Again, she went over every moment in her mind's eye, trying to think of anything she might have forgotten that could lead them to her. There was nothing. She was positive. Nothing to place her at the murder scene, nothing that could lead to her identity being discovered by Vincent Genero or the police.

Then she remembered the briefcase. The police would have to connect her to the murder before they ever searched her apartment, a highly unlikely scenario, but the briefcase was the one thing that could place her at the scene of Onorati's murder. She would get rid of it as soon as she got back to the apartment.

She ate little of her lunch, drinking another glass of wine as she forced herself to think logically about what, if anything, she should do. Go somewhere and just disappear for at least a month, until Michael's murder was old news and put on the back burner by the police? If the investigation wasn't being actively pursued, and without solid leads, and with the constant stream of new murders in the city demanding their attention, that would eventually be the case; Vincent Genero would begin to feel more secure, and less concerned with finding her. But she knew she couldn't count on that happening. She had to think things through, calmly and deliberately. Not make any impulsive decisions.

Bass paid her bill, collected her shopping bags, and said goodbye to Yorgi, then stepped out onto the sidewalk and, within seconds, disappeared in the crowd. She would drop her bags off with the doorman at her apartment building, then go for a long walk. She always thought best when she walked.

11

THE SMALL MINIPARK was just off a tree-shaded cul-de-sac where Fifty-seventh Street ends at the East River. Set between the stylish Georgian town house that serves as the New York residence for the secretary-general of the United Nations and the elegant brick apartment building at One Sutton Place, the park is no more than fifty feet square, with a small sandbox playground at its center. Benches line the sides and front of the cloistered area, taking full advantage of the river view.

Access to the park is down a broad ramp that serves, among others, the elderly, wheelchair-bound wealthy who live in the exclusive neighborhood. Accompanied by their private nurses, weather permitting, they are wheeled there to enjoy the fresh air and the view. Sunny, lazy afternoons find nannies supervising their young charges at play in the sandbox.

During weekday lunch hours the park is a popular place to bring a sandwich and while away a quiet hour. It is not uncommon for complete strangers to share a bench in the picturesque setting overlooking the river. Given the few benches available, and the desirability of the location, even surly New Yorkers usually accept the intrusions without malice, unofficially declaring the park a demilitarized zone free of the rudeness and inhospitable attitudes for which they are known the world over.

Jack Kirby was familiar with the location, and had carefully scouted the area, watching for signs that the park was under surveillance by anyone other than himself. Satisfied that the meeting had not been compromised, he claimed one of the benches along the railing at the front of the park, looking out over the river toward Roosevelt Island—virtually the same view, only from a lower elevation and a different angle, as seen from Michael Onorati's penthouse apartment, six blocks south of the park.

Kirby positioned himself in the center of the bench, declaratively alone. He had on khakis and running shoes and a black mock turtleneck under his dark brown aviator-style leather jacket. With his hair worn long, over the collar and ears, he looked like anything but a cop. He sat watching a tugboat move slowly up the river as he nibbled on a pastrami sandwich he had picked up at a deli on Lexington Avenue. He glared at one, then a second, person who approached and eyed the bench with a look that suggested Kirby should move to one end or the other. In a city that leads the world in the number of people around whom you shouldn't make a sudden move, or start a conversation with under any circumstances, Kirby's body language and his steady, menacing glare, which he had perfected for just such occasions, were all that were required to keep those who considered sitting next to him at bay.

Tommy Falconetti had spent the hour since calling Kirby's beeper making certain no one was following him to the meeting site. After leaving his car at an Upper East Side parking garage, he first walked a circuitous route, doubling back on himself and making quick changes of direction in mid-block, before stopping at Bloomingdale's, where he went to the men's department on the basement level. He strolled casually among the clothing displays, pausing ostensibly to examine a jacket or a shirt, his senses sharply attuned to any signs of surveillance.

The huge department store had an individual rhythm, a normal flow of movement, that even the most experienced person following him could inadvertently violate. Visual incongruities that stood out against a composite of normal patterns—people entering and leaving, some walking briskly with purpose and determination, others browsing, passing time, an ethnic mix of age and style and attitude, and an ordinary randomness as they paused or stopped in response to something that caught their eye, or to get their bearing—any violation of this normal mix and flow of activity would, under careful observation by a knowledgeable subject, eventually betray a surveillance.

Detecting nothing out of the ordinary, Falconetti left the store by the Third Avenue exit and continued the process of filtering out anyone who might be following him. He varied his pace with erratic stops and starts, then doubled back to enter a delicatessen, where he bought a takeout sandwich and a Pepsi. At the next corner he stopped to light a cigarette, looking back to see if he recognized anyone he had seen in the deli. He continued on, pausing in front of shopwindows along the fast-paced avenue, using the reflections in the glass to look for any coinciding disruptions in the normal pattern of foot traffic. Satisfied that he was not being followed, he headed directly for the park at Sutton Place.

Kirby sat sideways on the park bench, at an angle that allowed him to observe the entrance to the park. He checked the time. Falconetti was twenty minutes late. He would give him another fifteen minutes, then follow the prescribed procedures for their meetings: in the event either of them could not keep the appointed time, they would try again at the fallback time, two hours later. If either of them failed to show then, the meeting was aborted until it could be established what had happened, and a new time and place could be set up.

Just as Kirby was about to leave, Falconetti appeared. Kirby moved to one end of the bench as he saw him pause at the top of the ramp. Twenty-eight years old, dressed in a black leather blazer over an orange silk shirt worn open at the neck to reveal two gold chains, he was the quintessential young wise guy in his walk, his attitude, his slicked-back hair, and in his choice of clothes. Even his manner of speech was part of his cover, using only the crude street patois of the mob.

Kirby well remembered the inherent dangers and pitfalls of living a double life. Working under deep cover meant never stepping out of character for a single moment, even when meeting with your handler, for fear that in doing so you might later, at the wrong time and in the wrong place, have a lax moment and say something that would blow your cover. You had to walk the walk and talk the talk every waking moment. Your life depended on it.

Falconetti's eyes moved slowly over the park, studying the faces of the people seated on the benches, showing no sign of recognition as they passed over Kirby. After a few moments he walked casually in his direction and sat on the opposite end of the bench. Without acknowledging his handler's presence, Falconetti took his sandwich and soda out of the bag and placed them between him and Kirby, then unwrapped the sandwich and began to eat as he stared out across the river; just another New Yorker on his lunch hour taking a break from the frenetic pace of the city.

The two men ignored each other as they observed their surroundings, watching for anyone entering the park who seemed to be looking for someone. Kirby had immediately noticed the deterioration in Falconetti's condition. In the six weeks since he had last seen him, he appeared to have lost a considerable amount of weight and was as twitchy as a tundra caribou in the middle of deerfly season. A nervous tic in his left eye fluttered intermittently, and his head moved as though it were on a swivel. After five minutes Kirby finally broke the long silence.

"What have you got for me?"

Falconetti popped the top on his Pepsi can, took a long drink, then spoke without turning to face Kirby. "I think Genero whacked Onorati."

"Jesus Christ, Tommy! You called a high-risk meeting to tell me something I already figured out."

"You also got it figured out there was a witness?"

Kirby almost turned to face Falconetti, then caught himself and immediately looked away and talked into his sandwich. "Someone saw Genero make the hit? A civilian?"

"That's the word."

"Who?"

"Don't know."

"You don't know? How do you know there was a witness?"

"I was at the club this morning with Nino Totani and a couple of the crew when Carmine Molino and Johnnie Socks came in. Molino took Nino outside for a private conversation, but Johnnie Socks stayed with us, runnin' his mouth, like usual. Full of himself. Tryin' to impress us with how tight he is with Genero. He said that he and Nino had a special job to do for the don. They were supposed to find some broad—a hooker who saw them take care of a piece of business last night."

"You sure the piece of business he was talking about was Onorati?"

"Yeah. While he was braggin' about how smooth and cool Genero was, the stupid bastard said, 'He made sure that fancy lawyer fuck ain't gonna steal from him no more.' "

Kirby fell silent, considering what Falconetti had just told him. He restrained himself from getting too enthused about the possibilities, but he knew if it was true, then it had finally happened. Genero had screwed up big-time. The only thing that did not sound right was Onorati having a street hooker at his penthouse at One Beekman Place. It didn't fit.

"It was a hooker, huh? You sure?"

"That's what he said." Falconetti paused, thinking, then added, "Actually what he said was they were lookin' for 'some high-priced call girl cunt.' And that 'we chased the bitch but lost her.' "

Kirby smiled. A high-class call girl. That made more sense. "And what else?"

"That's it. But Nino and Johnnie Socks left in a hurry. We were supposed to set up this hijacking for tonight, but before Nino left, he told me to let it go until after he took care of something for Molino."

"A witness! Son of a bitch! Good work, Tommy."

"Yeah. I thought you'd wanna hear about it right away. I know how bad you want Genero. If you can get to the witness before Nino does, you might be able to put that piece of shit away for good."

"Did Johnnie Socks say anything else about the hit? Or if they had any idea who the witness was? Where they were going to start looking?"

"Nothin'. I'm pretty sure they don't know who she is—they're lookin' to find out."

Kirby studied his deep-cover officer out of the corner of his eye. He was clearly rattled. "How are things going for you?"

"I'm hangin' in there."

"Tommy, you look like shit. Talk to me."

Falconetti hesitated, then: "Nino's acting a little different towards me since six of his crew runnin' the auto-theft operation were busted on the information I gave you. He's no dummy, Jack, he knows it had to come from inside."

"You think he's onto you?"

"Not yet. But when the task force came down on the operation, they shouldn't have busted the car dealer in Queens who was fronting for them. I warned you about that. Outside of Nino, only me and two other guys in the crew, Jimmy DiAmato and Sammy Casella, knew about that dealer being in on the operation."

"I'm sorry that happened, but it was out of my hands. The FBI had to be brought in because the dealer was shipping the cars overseas. Those assholes busted him without telling us they were going to do it."

"Yeah, well, shit happens."

Kirby watched Falconetti's eyes. They were jumping all over the place. It was time to bring him in. Kirby knew the signs; just as his handler had seen the signs in him seventeen years ago and pulled him out despite his protests.

Kirby's career as a police officer had started exactly the same as Falconetti's. The chief of detectives and the deputy chief who headed the Intelligence Division had combed the list of applicants for the police academy, several thousand young men mostly in their twenties, looking for potential candidates for assignment as deep-cover officers. Kirby was one of only three selected and received a telephone call asking if he was interested in a secret undercover assignment.

Upon accepting the offer, all records of his ever having applied to the police department were sealed, and no one, family or friends, was to be told of his assignment; he was simply to state that he had lost interest in becoming a cop. When his class entered the academy, he did not. He received no training as a police officer, nor was he exposed to any police information or jargon or ways of thinking that could betray him under stress. He was given no instructions on how to proceed with his deep-cover assignment, no set of rules to follow, the theory being that any behavior or procedure he memorized would be unnatural and a dead giveaway.

In an unceremonious rite, witnessed only by the head of the Intelligence Division and the OCMU detective assigned as his handler, Kirby, at age twenty-one, became a cop without the support system all other cops could depend on. His shield was placed in his right hand as he took the oath, then the shield was taken back, sealed in an envelope, and placed in a safe. It would be the last time he ever saw his white shield. Promoted to detective grade, and given his gold shield upon completion of his deep-cover assignment, he then went through the academy, a situation that proved awkward, to say the least, given what he had been through the previous two years, and that all of his classmates were raw recruits.

Both Falconetti and Kirby had been selected for the same reasons. High test scores, and low profiles—they had both come to New York City from somewhere else. Kirby from Philadelphia, where he was born and had lived all of his life before going to college at Pennsylvania State University for two years, and Falconetti from New Haven, Connecticut, where he had joined the Marine Corps out of high school.

Kirby had made some tough friends in the predominantly Irish-

American neighborhood where he grew up, which gave him an acceptable background and credentials for his assignment. He was to infiltrate the infamous Irish gang on the west side of Manhattan known as the Westies, who at that time were at the height of their criminal activities, terrorizing and murdering at will. Kirby spent two years inside the vicious and deadly gang, his work resulting in arrests, convictions, and long prison sentences for the leaders. The gang had been effectively neutralized and was never again a threat.

Falconetti had numerous friends and acquaintances in the Italian-American community in New Haven, two of whom were mob-connected and had vouched for him as a stand-up kid when he worked his way into Nino Totani's crew in New York City. Falconetti had now been under longer than any deep-cover currently operating. Much too long, in Kirby's opinion.

"I think it's time for you to come in, Tommy."

"Not yet."

"Look at yourself. You're a fucking mess."

"I know . . . I know. I'm startin' to hear footsteps. But I want to stay with it just a little while longer. At least until you nail Genero for whacking Onorati."

"It's not worth the risk."

"Fuck if it isn't. I thought bringing Genero down was what this was all about?"

"It is, but getting that psycho isn't worth your life."

"It isn't that bad yet. Look, with Nino in charge of finding the hooker, I'm in the perfect position. You're gonna need someone inside to let you know how close they're gettin' to her, who she is, and like that; get the information to you so you can snatch her before she ends up in some landfill in Jersey."

"I don't know, Tommy." But he did know. Falconetti was right. Having him inside Totani's crew would be invaluable in learning the identity of the witness.

"What are we talkin' about? A few days at the most? Fuck, Jack. I've been under six years. Couple days ain't gonna make no difference. Besides, Nino's not thinkin' about who ratted out the auto-theft operation right now; he's workin' on finding the hooker."

Kirby yielded. "Okay. But as soon as I know who she is, I'm pulling you out. Understood?"

"Absolutely. I ain't no hero."

"The hell you're not," Kirby said, and got up from the bench and left the park, leaving Falconetti there to finish his lunch.

Two blocks from the Sutton Place park Kirby stopped at a public telephone on Second Avenue and called Tony Rizzo at his OCMU office. The enthusiasm in Rizzo's voice echoed Kirby's.

"A high-class call girl?"

"That's what he said. I'm on my way in right now. I just called to suggest you might want to put a surveillance team on Molino. If I'm right, Totani's going to be reporting in to him. As soon as he does, we can put a couple teams on him and Johnnie Socks. One we make sure they spot and lose, and another one they don't. If we can't find the witness on our own, they might just lead us to her."

"What are the chances the FBI's picked up the same information?"

"No chance at all. Falconetti told me that after the task force busted six of Totani's crew for the auto-theft operation, he got real serious about having the club swept for bugs every week. So nobody's listening in on their conversations."

"Good. Let's keep this to ourselves. I don't want us tripping over the feds while we're looking for the witness; and if they get to her first, we're out of the picture."

"I'm not about to tell them."

"This is your baby, Jack. Find her, and fast. I'll get the surveillance going right away."

Kirby hung up and jogged over to the Third Avenue parking garage where he had left his car. In the six frustrating years of trying to nail Genero, he had never come this close. With a little luck and timing, it now seemed to be within his grasp. Ignoring most of the traffic laws of the City of New York, he made the trip downtown and across the bridge to Brooklyn in record time.

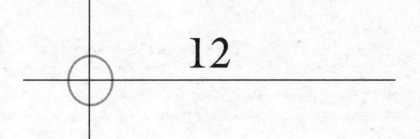

12

NINO TOTANI, BORN in Palermo, Sicily, forty-one years ago to a four-generation Mafia Family, was taught to live with and by violence. Six years ago Vincent Genero brought him to the United States, at a time when others like him were imported by all of the New York Mafia bosses, immediately following the spate of arrests and convictions that had decimated the hierarchies of the five Families. The Zips, as the Sicilians were called for some unknown reason, were brought in to restore order and discipline and carry out "hits" on those who were challenging the authority of the new dons.

With their work completed, the bloody internecine Mafia war over, most of the Sicilians returned to their native country, but Totani, who had come to like New York City, remained. Shrewd and resourceful, his skills and the effectiveness of his methods were recognized and admired by Vincent Genero. At the new don's request, he eagerly agreed to stay and became a "made man" in the Gambino crime Family in appreciation of the work he had done. Quickly earning the respect and trust of Genero, within two years he rose to the position of capo with his own crew and soon proved his worth; his hijacking and loan-sharking operations alone brought in more money than any three of the other crews combined.

Tall and lanky, Totani had none of the bulky, tough-guy look about him, yet he emanated a sense of power and authority out of all proportion to his physical size. It was clear who was the leader as he and Johnnie Socks strode purposefully down Madison Avenue, Johnnie Socks

almost abreast of the capo, but staying a half pace behind, showing him
the respect he had earned. People in their path had a tendency to give
them a wide berth, and the two men paid no attention to the rhythm of
the street; the pedestrian shuffle of pauses, half steps, and sidesteps that
New Yorkers followed to avoid bumping into each other. Such subtleties
and considerations were lost on Totani and Johnnie Socks, who walked
down the center of the sidewalk expecting others to get out of their way.

A natty dresser, Totani emulated his don with his expensive Italian
designer suits and tastefully coordinated socks and shirts and ties. On
the surface he did not look like what he was: a cold-blooded enforcer
and professional killer. Pleasantly handsome, with a smooth olive com-
plexion, black hair that glistened in the sunlight, and dark brown eyes,
he had an engaging charm and ease of manner. He was not given to
Genero's volatile outbursts, but was all the more menacing for the detached, unemotional way with which he handled any and all situations.

In comparison, Johnnie Socks, a slack-jawed hulk, wearing a three-
quarter-length leather coat, his massive shoulders threatening to tear
apart its seams, looked and acted precisely as one would expect. He was
muscle, a brutal, bullying borderline moron who believed that if you did
not understand something it was best to punch it first, then ask questions. The perfect sycophant, an original idea would have sent him into
convulsions.

After checking the directory in the lobby of the office tower on the
corner of Thirty-eighth and Madison, the two men got off the elevator
on the twenty-sixth floor and followed the hallway to Michael Onorati's
office at the northwest corner of the building. The plush, two-room suite
had an expansive reception area and an inner office paneled in a rich
walnut and furnished with expensive antiques and Persian carpets.

Totani and Johnnie Socks entered to find Maria Padron, Onorati's
secretary, removing files and personal items from her desk and cabinets,
sorting them into separate boxes lined up on the floor behind her desk.
She was at the far end of the reception area, rummaging through a file
cabinet, and had not heard the door to the suite open. She startled when
she turned to see the two men watching her from the entryway.

"You're Maria, right?" Totani said, giving the attractive, raven-haired
woman a smile and an appraising look.

Maria nodded, her eyes wide with surprise, then narrowing to caution as she focused on Johnnie Socks and walked toward them. "I don't believe I know you."

"Carmine Molino said to give you his regards."

Maria's change of expression told them that she now understood who they were. "Is there something I can do for you?"

"We'll do it for ourselves," Totani said. "I'm just going to look through Onorati's office, then maybe I'll have a few questions for you later."

Totani hoped to find an address book that would tell him who the call girl was without having to let the secretary know his area of interest.

"I'm afraid I can't let you into the office. The police called and said the detectives would be over this afternoon. They instructed me to leave Mr. Onorati's office just the way it was before he died."

"I have some different instructions for you." Totani looked to Johnnie Socks. "Keep Maria company while I check out the office."

Totani brushed past the secretary and opened the door to the spacious inner office. The room was dominated by an oversized, ornately carved mahogany desk with two leather wing chairs set before it. All but a twelve-inch border of the highly polished wood floor was covered with an exquisite silk Persian carpet. Sunlight streamed through the large windows behind the desk, making the rich paneling glow with an inner warmth.

Totani noticed the open wall safe, with the painting that normally concealed its presence propped against the wall on the floor below. He crossed the room and looked inside the safe to find it empty. He next went through the desk drawers, finding them just as empty, with the exception of a few pens and legal pads. A glance at the overflowing bin of the paper shredder in a corner next to a custom-built computer workstation told him of the precautions Onorati had taken before leaving his office for the last time.

Totani returned to the reception area to see Johnnie Socks looking up Maria Padron's skirt. She stood on a library ladder with her back to him, removing the last of the leather-bound volumes from the top shelf of a wall unit once filled with books now packed in boxes. Totani walked over to where Maria was climbing down from the ladder.

"Did you empty out the safe?"

"No. Mr. Onorati did."

"What was in it?"

Maria hesitated.

"I asked you a question." Totani's tone of voice had not changed, but his body language and the look in his eyes had.

"Money, a passport, some computer disks and personal papers . . . I'm not sure what else. That's all I ever saw him put in there."

"And he took it all with him?"

"Yes. He put it in his briefcase and left."

"The one with the pimples?" Johnnie Socks asked, getting a curious look from Totani.

"Excuse me?"

"The briefcase with the pimples . . . that Austrian one."

"Oh, you mean the ostrich-skin briefcase."

"Yeah, that one."

"Yes. He took it with him when he left."

"What else did he do before he left?" Totani asked.

"I believe he made a few international calls, but I don't know to whom."

Totani took Maria gently by the arm, led her across the room, and sat her down in the chair behind her desk. "I need you to tell me something."

"If I can."

"Onorati had a girlfriend. A professional girlfriend. A call girl. I need to know her name and where she lives."

"I was not involved in any of Mr. Onorati's personal affairs. I wouldn't know anything about that."

Totani propped a hip on the edge of the desk and leaned over to take Maria's hand. She tried to pull it back, but he held it firmly.

"I think you do know about that. Now, why don't you think about it for a moment and carefully consider your answer this time."

Maria shrunk back into the chair from the terrible look in Totani's eyes. "Her name was Nicole. That's all I know."

Totani squeezed Maria's hand in a tight grip, painfully pinching her fingers together, but said nothing. He continued to stare directly into her eyes, silently conveying to her that he knew she was lying.

Maria, unnerved by his steady gaze, and the pain in her hand, looked away. Then, "I remember calling a number once or twice for Mr. Onorati to leave a message for her . . . Nicole . . . with another woman, Carolyn, when Mr. Onorati was going to be late for their date. I still might have the telephone number where she can be reached."

Maria leaned forward in the chair, and with her free hand, reached into a packing box at the side of the desk and removed an address book. She placed it on the desktop and turned to a page of entries near the center of the book.

"Yes, here it is, Nicole. But there's no last name and no address, just the telephone number." She handed Totani the address book and pulled her hand free.

Totani tore out the page and gave the book back to her. He then looked across the desk to a photograph he had noticed earlier. A snapshot of a smiling Maria with a beautiful little girl sitting on her lap on a swing in a park. He picked it up and smiled at the image of the beguiling child.

"Your daughter?"

"Yes." Maria's eyes grew wide. She began to reach for the photograph, but the look Totani gave her made her stop.

"How old is she?"

"She'll be three next month."

Totani pointedly looked at the photograph as he spoke. "When the police come and talk with you, we weren't here, and if they ask, you know nothing about the woman named Nicole. You lie to them just the way you lied to me when I first asked you about her. You tell them nothing."

Totani again smiled at the image of the little girl in the photograph. "She's very beautiful. You must love her very much."

"Yes, I do."

"It would be a shame if anything should happen to her." He held the photograph up for Johnnie Socks to see. "Wouldn't you agree, Johnnie?"

The top button of Maria's blouse was open, revealing an ample cleavage, and Johnnie Socks had positioned himself to look down on her. "Yeah. A real shame," he said without looking away.

"I won't tell anyone anything," Maria said. "I promise. You have my word."

Totani stood and reached an open hand toward Maria's face. She pulled back, drawing a sharp breath. He smiled and gently patted her cheek. "I'd appreciate that."

As Totani and Johnnie Socks came out of the building and headed north on Madison Avenue, Totani noticed a dark blue Chevrolet sedan with two men in it double-parking at the curb.

The driver of the car placed a laminated police parking permit on the dashboard, announcing to the traffic cops who the car belonged to and not to tow or ticket it, then he and his partner got out and walked toward the entrance to Onorati's office building.

Johnnie Socks had noticed them, too. "Cops."

"Doesn't matter," Totani said, smiling confidently. "Like the lady said, she won't tell them anything."

13

JACK KIRBY HAD spent the past hour in the records section with Janet Morris, a police administrative aide. Morris was one of a dozen or so civilian PAAs in the Intelligence Division, who, after extensive background checks, were hired to do clerical work and to transfer the division's vast accumulation of files and records to computer databases.

Kirby questioned the wisdom of allowing civilians access to highly classified files, but Morris did not bother him as much as some of the others. With ten years' experience working in the chief of detectives' office at One Police Plaza, she had volunteered for a transfer to the Intelligence Division to help with their changeover to computers. A hard worker, she proved to be a welcome addition; the ten years in the C-of-D's office had taught her the jargon and the myriad acronyms that were an everyday part of the cop vernacular, which meant, unlike the new civilian employees, she did not need everything explained to her. Her sunny disposition and perky cheerleader face made her a favorite throughout the division, and she was never too busy to stop and help the detectives learn the new filing system, often doing some of their dreaded paperwork for them.

A genius with a computer, Morris was, apart from her abilities as a programmer, an exceptionally skilled hacker who could get in and out of virtually anyone's database, no matter how secure. Upon discovering that Michael Onorati had a portable cellular phone, Kirby decided to put Morris's covert skills to immediate use. Rather than going through time-consuming proper channels, and in part not to tip his hand, he had Morris access the telephone company's records for Onorati's cellular phone for the past six months.

Reasoning that any escort service operating in Manhattan would have a local telephone number, Kirby did not bother checking the bills for Onorati's home and office phone, which would list only long-distance calls. But if Onorati had requested a detailed billing for his cellular phone, which many business subscribers did, all of the local calls, along with the time and date placed and the duration of the call, would be listed on his bill. But Onorati had not, and they were not.

Kirby then asked Morris to search the Organized Crime Monitoring Unit's files, going back five years. As Kirby had feared they would, the OCMU files revealed only the lower-class prostitution operations run by the wise guys that had cropped up during OCMU investigations. Morris was now in the process of doing a global search of all the division's files, looking for any reports on upscale escort services and individual high-class call girls.

Kirby returned to the OCMU squad room and placed a call to the Department's Public Morals Division, asking for that same information. Twenty minutes later he got an interdepartmental fax listing some eighteen escort services believed to be currently operating in the city, six of them considered upscale. He then reached out to friends, placing calls to detectives in the 19th, 20th, 23rd, and 24th Precincts, encompassing the Upper East and Upper West Sides of Manhattan. He requested any information they had on low-profile, elite escort services operating in their precincts and specializing in well-heeled clientele—the type of service, Kirby believed, someone of Onorati's means would use.

Kirby had purposely not called Detectives Early and O'Brien at the 17th. He did not want to tell them about the existence of the witness until he had something solid. Any information about an eyewitness who had seen Genero kill Onorati, information that Early and O'Brien had not turned up in their own thorough investigation in the immediate area of One Beekman Place, would strongly point to only one source, someone wired into the wise guys. Kirby was not about to take any chances, no matter how remote, of compromising his deep-cover officer. When he found the witness, and had brought Falconetti in, he would then bring Early and O'Brien up to speed, and, if he was lucky, provide them with a witness who would make their case for them.

Having done what he could for the moment, and hoping to come up with something that would narrow down the list of escort services the witness might be affiliated with, Kirby returned to the records section to check on the PAA's progress.

"I'm about three-quarters through the files," Morris said, scribbling some notes from the information on the computer monitor. "And so far I've gotten one hit. A surveillance operation the Counterterrorist Squad ran about seven months ago."

"That's not going to give us anything. It's highly unlikely the person I'm looking for is involved with terrorists."

"Oh, ye of little faith," Morris said with a smile and a wink. "You detectives are such linear thinkers. If you got into computers, you'd learn how to think in more lateral and oblique ways."

Kirby smiled back at her. "Okay, so educate me."

"Last March your Counterterrorist people were conducting a surveillance on a United Nations diplomat believed to be involved with some suspected Iranian terrorist. They ran background checks on all of his companions during that period. One of them was a high-class call girl."

"Got a name?"

"That's where I came up short. A confidential informant told your guys that she was a call girl, but he didn't know her name or who she worked for. The surveillance team only saw her on one occasion, and the detective who followed her that night, after she left the diplomat's apartment"—Morris glanced at her notes—"Detective Sullivan, lost her somewhere in midtown Manhattan. About two weeks later the surveillance was terminated when it was established that the diplomat in question didn't have any connection to the terrorists."

"Then we're back to square one."

"Maybe. Maybe not. There's a follow-up report attached to the file. Before the diplomat came up clean, Sullivan kept digging on the escort-service angle, thinking that it might be a cover for some of the terrorists' operations. What he didn't find is interesting in and of itself."

"What he *didn't* find?"

"He picked up bits and pieces of information about an elite escort service with a number of diplomats and other heavy hitters as clientele. Again, no one seemed to know the name of the service, or any of the people involved. And according to Sullivan's report, he kept running into stone walls whenever he asked the wrong people questions about a mysterious escort service specializing in diplomats and politicians."

"The wrong people being the feds?" Kirby asked, suspecting, as often happened, they had inadvertently trampled on an FBI operation.

"No. According to the report, it was from within the NYPD. It might be worth your while to talk to Detective Sullivan. What do you think?"

"I think you should keep looking. I've got to find this woman fast, before the bad guys do. So I don't have time to go back over old territory that didn't turn up anything in the first place."

"Should take me about another half hour to check the rest of the database."

"Thanks, Janet. I'll be in the squad room."

Nicole Bass had been walking for the past hour, with occasional stops to browse in some of the shops along Fifth Avenue, and to stand at the curb behind the police barricades to watch part of the early stages of the lively and colorful Spanish Columbus Day parade. The first wave of bands and sound trucks and marchers and costumed dancers had reached Forty-fifth Street and were rocking, swaying and gyrating their noisy, rhythmic way up the broad avenue.

Bass had called Carolyn Chambers from a public phone inside the Trump Tower, to let her know that she now knew who the man was she saw kill Onorati. Chambers had seen the same front-page story in the *Post* and had suspected as much. Bass reinforced that it was now more important than ever not to mention to another living soul that she had been at the apartment that night. Chambers again swore her oath of silence and fidelity.

Bass had been thinking things through as she walked. Going over and over the same scenarios she had been examining in her mind since the previous night. But the revelation that the most powerful Mafia boss in the city was the man she had seen commit a cold-blooded murder now cast an even deadlier pale over her situation. She had heard stories of how the mob could find you anywhere, and they never gave up. But no matter how much she played devil's advocate against her earlier conclusions, she still could not see how they would ever find out that she was the one who had witnessed the killing of Michael Onorati.

The unrelenting stress of the past fourteen hours was taking its toll, weakening her inner strength, the steely resolve that for the last two years had allowed her to keep the past in the past, and to not let it ruin her life any more than it already had. She thought of all she had lost, all she had hoped for in life, how her childhood dream of becoming a model had been achieved and then turned into a nightmare. And then she thought of her father. She was all he had left, and he had died alone, in a hospital bed in Johnson City, Tennessee, and she had been unable to be there to comfort him in his final hours, or even to attend his funeral.

She tried to shake the disturbing thoughts as she picked up her pace along the crowded avenue. But she no longer heard the street noise, or the sound of a passing band, as once again her father's voice, clear as a church bell ringing in a distant hollow, called to her across the years. His gentle, loving words spoken in the east Tennessee twang of her youth: "You can be anything you want to be, little darlin', and don't you ever let nobody tell you no different."

Overcome with a sudden wave of emotion, Bass stopped before a store window to hide her face from the passing crowd while she composed herself and blinked away the tears that welled in her eyes.

"No, Daddy," she whispered, staring at her reflection in the window. "I'm sorry, but I can't be what I want to be. And you wouldn't be very proud of your darlin' little girl right now."

14

NINO TOTANI USED the car phone to call Carmine Molino, who in turn called a Family source with the telephone company. Using the reverse directory, the phone company contact gave Molino the name and address for the number listed in Onorati's secretary's address book under Nicole's name. It took no more than twenty minutes after leaving Onorati's office for Totani and Johnnie Socks to get the information from Molino and arrive at the high-rise on East Sixty-first Street. The directory in the lobby showed the office of Carolyn Chambers, Public Relations Consultant, to be on the thirty-first floor.

The space Chambers leased was simply one large room with half-glass walls separating a small office cubicle from a living-room–like reception area tastefully decorated with comfortable furniture: a cozy grouping of two armchairs and a sofa, all in glove-soft tan leather, with a marble-and-brass coffee table in the center. A friendly, intimate environment where prospective clients could be screened in personal interviews conducted only after they had been recommended to Chambers by established clients.

A photo album on top of the coffee table contained eight-by-ten glossies, full face shots, of the ten women who worked for her service. A large-screen television and VCR in one corner of the room provided the prospective clients, once Chambers decided they were suitable, the opportunity to make their selection after viewing videotapes of the women, dressed for an evening on the town, introducing themselves as they sat in a chair talking to the camera.

Chambers was in the glassed-in office space, working at her computer, when the front-door chime sounded and drew her attention to the reception area. She frowned at the sight of the two men who entered and tried to imagine who might have recommended the huge, crude-looking muscular man, then thought perhaps he was merely accompanying the darkly handsome one, carrying the attaché case, who at least appeared to have first-sight qualifications. But she had not received an introductory call from any of her clients advising her that they were sending someone over.

"May I help you gentlemen," Chambers said, turning off the computer as she got up from her desk and stepped out into the reception area.

"I'm sure you can," Totani said, offering a charming but brief smile as his eyes moved slowly over her, appreciating her understated beauty.

Although Chambers no longer went out with clients herself, and had not for the past ten years, at forty-five she was still in excellent physical shape, a highly desirable, attractive woman with a trim, compact figure and stunning bright blue eyes.

"I'm looking for someone who works for you. Nicole."

Johnnie Socks flopped down on the sofa and began paging through the photo album as Totani crossed the room. Chambers's antennae went up. She instinctively knew the two men were not cops. Then it struck her, and the fear showed in her eyes.

"Nicole? I'm afraid I don't know anyone by that name," Chambers said, by force of will remaining calm. "Are you sure you have the right office?"

"Oh, yeah. I'm sure," Totani said.

"Well, again, I run a one-person office here, and I don't know anyone by that name."

"I know what you run, lady. So let's stop playing games."

"Yeah," Johnnie Socks said, holding up the album, overly proud of his discovery. The photo on the page he held up for Totani to see had the name "Nicole" typed on a tag across the bottom. "If you don't know nobody named Nicole, then what the fuck is her picture doin' in here?"

Chambers's first thought was to run for the door and out of the office. As if reading her mind, Johnnie Socks got up and turned the dead bolt, grinning at her as he returned to the sofa.

"That's an old photograph," Chambers said, her mouth gone dry, her voice an octave higher. "She no longer works for me. I just haven't gotten around to updating the album."

Chambers did her best to compose herself, but the effort had little effect. "I'm sorry I lied to you at first, but if you know the business I'm in, you can understand why I'm not forthcoming about any of my girls . . . or former girls."

"Sure, I can understand that," Totani said, smiling again. "Maybe you can tell me where I can find her."

"I believe she moved to Los Angeles. Yes. I'm sure of it. I got a letter from her a few months ago and she raved about how much better she liked it than New York."

"Is that right?" Totani continued to smile. "Then maybe you could explain to me why Michael Onorati's secretary called you to leave messages for her a couple of weeks ago, and why Nicole was with him at his apartment last night?"

"She wasn't. I don't know who told you that, but someone has made a mistake. She used to date Mr. Onorati, but—"

Totani held up his hand to silence her, his charming smile gone, his eyes narrowed, menacing. "I want you to listen to me. Very carefully. I know how to play games you never heard of; you understand? So stop lying to me, or this conversation is going to turn ugly, real fast."

Chambers was nearly paralyzed with fear. But Nicole was her friend, and she had promised to protect her. She held out hope that she could still convince them that she was not lying.

"Please believe me, I'm telling you the truth. Nicole left three or four months ago and the letter is the only contact I've had with her since."

"You're not going to let me do this the easy way, are you?"

"I can't tell you what I don't know."

Totani nodded to Johnnie Socks, who got up from the sofa, moving with a quickness that belied his size and bulk. Chambers let out a short, pitiful yelp as he wrapped one of his massive arms around her, pinning her arms to her sides. He used his free hand to cup her mouth while Totani opened the attaché case and removed a roll of duct tape. He tore off one strip and placed it across her mouth, then a second, longer strip, using that to tie her hands behind her back.

Chambers struggled to no avail; her muffled screams barely carried across the room. Johnnie Socks lifted her bodily, taking advantage of the situation to fondle her breasts before he sat her down in one of the leather chairs flanking the sofa.

Chambers's eyes widened as she watched Totani take a small cylindrical object from the attaché case. It had a short metal tube that protruded from one end, and was no larger than a bottle of vitamins.

Totani flicked a lever, and a bright blue-and-white flame shot out of the miniature, butane-fueled blowtorch.

"You let me know when you're ready to cooperate."

Totani shoved Chambers's skirt up to her hips, exposing the soft white flesh of her inner thighs. With one hand, he pushed her legs apart; with the other he brought the blowtorch closer to the surface of her skin.

"We'll start here. Then move up to your breasts. Then to your face. You can stop me at any time by telling me what I want to know."

Chambers's eyes went wide with pain and terror. A tortured, muffled scream escaped the tape across her mouth as Totani brought the blowtorch into play.

15

JANET MORRIS, THE PAA in the records section, found nothing more in the Intelligence Division's files that was of any help in narrowing down Kirby's search for an elite escort service. In the interim Kirby called fourteen of the eighteen services on the list he received from the Public Morals Division. He asked each of them if they had anyone he could take to a charity ball who would not look out of place at a black-tie affair. The soft-spoken sexy voices that answered the calls assured him they could provide someone who would meet all of his requirements. When he tried to pin them down about any of the women who worked for them who might date lawyers, politicians, or wealthy businessmen exclusively, they became suspicious and immediately hung up. It was a lame approach and he knew it from the start, but with nothing else to go on, it was the best he could do.

He also knew that he was losing precious ground to the wise guys hunting for the witness, and they could operate with none of the restrictions with which he had to contend. With no alternatives he was about to call another of the services on the list when the phone on his desk rang just as he reached to pick it up to dial.

It was Mike Jacobs, a detective with the 19th squad. Kirby had called him earlier to ask about escort services in his precinct.

"Hey, Jack. Not for nothin', but I might have something that ties in with what you asked me about."

Kirby sat up straight in his chair. "What have you got?"

"My partner and I just finished interviewing a woman by the name of

Carolyn Chambers. A robbery victim, so she says. According to her, two guys came into her office, tied her up, tortured her, then robbed her of a few hundred dollars in cash."

"So what? Is she a call girl?"

"Claims to be a public relations consultant. What the sign on the door says. But I ran across her name once before."

"And?"

"Hold your water and let me finish with the background first."

"What makes you think it wasn't a robbery?"

"She says they stole a couple hundred dollars, right? Yet she has this Piaget watch on her wrist must be worth about fifteen grand, plus a gold necklace worth another two or three. The perps didn't bother to boost them."

"So what's your take on it?"

"Considering a phone call she made, which I'll get to in a minute, I'd bet my pension what they wanted was information, not money. They burned the shit out of her thighs and tits with what she says was some kind of miniature blowtorch."

Kirby recalled a report he had read a few years ago on a woman worked over in the same manner by one of Genero's soldiers, but he couldn't remember which one. He said nothing and let Jacobs continue.

"She'd be dead if one of her friends from an office down the hall hadn't come in when he did. Whoever worked her over meant to kill her; they left her tied up with a clear plastic bag taped over her head. She was turnin' blue when the guy ripped the bag off. So he calls it in, and by the time the uniforms got there, this Chambers was recovered enough to be on the phone in her office. Callin' some guy named Nicky. The uniforms couldn't hear everything she said, but they heard enough to know that she was warning this guy that someone was coming after him; crying and apologizing all over the place for giving him up. They said it sounded like maybe she was talkin' to an answering unit.

"Anyway, I caught the case, and by the time me and my partner got there, the victim was pretty well composed. Said she never saw the perps' faces, they were wearing ski masks. When we asked about the phone call, she said the uniforms had misunderstood what she was saying, and she stuck to the robbery story. Make any sense to you?"

"If she runs an escort service, yeah, it does."

"You didn't hear this next part from me, okay?"

"Understood."

"Chambers supposedly has a string of high-class hookers who specialize in real heavyweights: politicians—rumor is one of them is a U.S. senator—lots of prominent citizens, influential, well-connected, big-money guys who can pick up the phone and get the mayor or the commissioner on the line no sweat. You hear me, Jack?"

"Loud and clear."

"Year, year and a half ago, Public Morals was about to bust her operation wide open, until the word came down from on high to lay the fuck off. So tread lightly, my friend."

"I'll do that."

"You at liberty to tell me what you're working on?"

"Not now. But if I pull it off, you'll read about it."

"Just don't mention my name in the report. I like where I am, you know. And I got seven years until retirement. I don't want to spend it in Brooklyn North dodgin' bullets and walkin' around up to my ankles in blood and crack vials. Know what I mean?"

"No problem. Got an address on this Chambers?"

"Yeah. Me and my partner drove her home after she refused to let us take her to the hospital to get the burns treated; said she'd have her own doctor take care of her. Like I said, name's Carolyn Chambers. Lives in a brownstone worth at least a million and a half at 48 East 74th between Madison and Park."

"How long ago did you drop her off?"

"About fifteen minutes."

"I owe you a big one, Mike."

"And you know me, I'll collect."

"Anytime."

Nino Totani hung up the car phone after reporting what he had learned to Carmine Molino. He turned to Johnnie Socks, who sat slumped in the front passenger seat, his hooded eyes fixed on the semicircular driveway in front of the upscale high-rise apartment building at 150 East 69th Street between Lexington and Third Avenues. The car was parked at the curb across the street, at an angle that provided an unobstructed view of the entrance to the building.

"Let's just go in, whack the bitch, and get it over with," Johnnie Socks said. He was hungry, sulking because Totani had refused to stop and wait for him to get a pizza at a place they had passed a few blocks back.

"It's a security building. You don't get past the doormen unless they call upstairs and get the person's okay."

"Fuck 'em. We could do what me and Big Paulie did last night. Take them out, too."

"We don't need those kinds of complications," Totani said patiently. "We find out if she's home first. Then we sit on her until she comes out; we hit her on the street and drive away. Nice and clean."

Totani dialed the number Carolyn Chambers had given him as he was about to use the blowtorch on her face. He put the call on the external speaker that played through the car radio and heard the phone ring three times before it was picked up by an answering machine.

"Hi. This is Niki. I'm sorry I can't take your call at the moment, but if you leave your name and number and a brief message, I'll get back to you as soon as I can."

Totani hung up at the sound of the beep.

"Fucker ain't home," Johnnie Socks growled. "So whatta we do now?"

"We wait until she gets home."

"We whack her on the way in?"

"If we see her in time. Before she gets too close to the entrance. Otherwise, we wait until she comes out again and we follow her. Gives us more time to set it up at just the right spot."

"I thought her name was Nicole? That broad says her name's Niki."

Totani rolled his eyes. "Same thing. A nickname."

Totani took the eight-by-ten photograph of Bass from above the sun visor and studied her face.

"Great-lookin' broad, huh?" Johnnie Socks said. "I'd pay to fuck her."

Totani smiled. "You always pay to get laid, Johnnie."

"So what? It's better that way. They do whatever you tell them to do, shit a normal broad wouldn't do, and you don't have to talk to them when you're finished."

Totani laughed softly to himself, his eyes fixed on the sidewalk, watching the approaches to the building.

Johnnie Socks suddenly sat bolt upright, leaning forward until his face almost touched the windshield. The focus of his attention was a woman who had just turned the corner off Lexington Avenue.

Totani saw her, too. He studied her carefully, then looked at the photograph, then back as she approached the semicircular driveway.

"That's her," Johnnie Socks said. "Least I think it's her."

"What do you mean, you think? You saw her last night, didn't you?"

"Yeah. But mostly I was starin' at the barrel of the fuckin' gun she pointed at me."

Totani looked at the photo again. The woman in the picture had her hair up; the woman he was watching had shoulder-length hair and looked more like a college student than a call girl. The woman's hair in the photo looked dark, almost black. The woman across the street had chestnut-brown hair, highlighted by the sun on it. The photo was taken in a studio, Totani reasoned; lighting could make it look darker than it really was. And her face would look different framed in shoulder-length hair.

Johnnie Socks squinted as he watched her walk up the driveway, away from them and toward the entrance to the apartment building.

"Oh, yeah. Fuckin' A. That's her alright. That's the same great ass I seen runnin' out of the apartment last night. Want me to whack her right now?"

"Not now. Too many people around. She'd be right at the entrance by the time you got close enough to put a couple in the back of her head."

"Fuck's the difference? In this city everybody knows better than to say they seen anything when they did."

Totani settled back in the driver's seat. "Relax, Johnnie. Now we know where she is. We'll take her when she comes out."

16

SHORTLY AFTER ONE-THIRTY Jack Kirby pulled into the curb a few doors down from Carolyn Chambers's four-story brownstone on East Seventy-fourth Street. He stepped out of the car to hear the pulsating beat of a Latin band as the lively Spanish Columbus Day parade, now in full swing, proceeded up Fifth Avenue one block west of where he stood.

He walked up the steps of the brownstone and was about to ring the bell when the door suddenly opened. He heard a woman's voice say, "Thank you for coming, Dr. Lewis," and a well-dressed middle-aged man carrying a small black bag came out.

"I'll be back in the morning," the doctor said, then nodded to Kirby and continued down the steps to the sidewalk.

Carolyn Chambers stood in the doorway, her eyes suddenly growing wide with fear as they locked on Kirby. She was about to slam the door when he reached inside his leather jacket and pulled out his shield and ID case, flipping it open for her to see.

"I've already told the police all that I know," Chambers said, closing the door partway and peering out from behind it.

"You didn't tell them about the person you were trying to protect."

"I was robbed. That's all I know. Now please go."

"Well, whoever *robbed* you left you for dead. When they find out you're not, they may damn well come back to finish the job. I've got an undercover female police officer from the Intelligence Division on her way here to stay with you until we get this sorted out."

"I don't want your help. Two men robbed me. I can't identify them. I have nothing more to say. If you have any more questions, you can talk to my lawyer."

Kirby put his foot against the bottom of the door as she went to close it. "If you don't tell me which one of the women who work for you was at Michael Onorati's apartment last night, she's going to end up dead before the day's over."

Chambers hesitated, tears forming in her eyes. "I don't know what you're talking about. Please leave me alone."

"Look, Ms. Chambers, whoever she is, I'm her only chance right now. I'm not interested in causing you any trouble, but your friend's going to die if you don't cooperate with me. Now, may I come in?"

Kirby entered the foyer without invitation. Chambers took a step back and let him pass. She was wearing a loose-fitting velour jogging suit, the zipper on the mock turtleneck top left open enough for Kirby to notice two ugly burn marks covered with a white salve on the side of her left breast.

Chambers walked stiffly, her face etched in pain as she led Kirby, without further protest, into an expensively furnished and elegantly decorated sitting room off the entrance foyer. She indicated a chair across from the sofa where she carefully lowered herself into a sitting position, obviously in great pain from what had been done to her. She wasn't at all what Kirby had expected; she talked, looked, and carried herself as though she were well bred and well educated.

"If you already told the two men who tortured you where they could find your friend, I don't have much time, and the clock's ticking, if I'm not too late already. So please, no games. I don't care what you do for a living, and I'm not going to read you your rights, so nothing you say can be used against you in a court of law. This isn't about you, it's about saving your friend. I just need to know who she is and where I can find her."

Chambers took a slow, deep breath of resignation, then: "I didn't want to tell them about Niki. I tried not to, but they hurt me so much."

"Nicky who? We talking about a man?"

"N-I-K-I. It's short for Nicole. Nicole Bass. She works for my public relations firm."

"Whatever. Was she conducting public relations in Michael Onorati's apartment last night when he was killed?"

Chambers nodded slowly. "She saw him kill Onorati."

"Saw who kill him?"

"The Mafia boss. Vincent Genero."

Kirby took a deep breath himself. He definitely had the arrogant son of a bitch now, if he could just get to the woman first. "You called her from your office and warned her they knew who she was, right? What did she say? Is she going into hiding someplace?"

"She wasn't home. I left a message on her answering machine."

"That was what? An hour ago?"

"I called again, just before you arrived. She still isn't home."

"Good. That means she hasn't been back to the only place they know to look for her. And the odds are they won't hit her right away. Genero likes things neat and clean. Which means we have some time."

The expression on Chambers's face said that the finality of Bass's situation had set in.

"Can you describe the men who assaulted you?"

"The one who burned me was tall, thin, dark-complected, well dressed, and handsome. The man with him was huge and crude and had mean, narrow eyes set close together."

Kirby recalled what Falconetti told him he had heard and seen at the social club that morning. "Probably Nino Totani and Johnnie Socks."

"The tall one called the other one Johnnie."

Kirby leaned forward in his chair, making direct eye contact with Chambers. "Carolyn, I'm going to level with you. And I want you to level with me. May I call you Carolyn?"

Chambers nodded again. "I won't press charges against them, and I won't admit that I saw their faces. So if you're thinking of arresting them for what they did to me, don't waste your time. I can't afford the publicity. I have friends . . . contacts . . . who can let them know that I'm no threat to them."

"Fair enough. I know you operate an exclusive escort service. That's not at issue here, and I give you my word that whatever you tell me will not leave this room."

"What do you want to know?"

"Everything you can tell me about Nicole Bass."

"She began working for me about eighteen months ago. She used to be a top fashion model until something happened that destroyed her career."

"What happened?"

Chambers hesitated, then: "I'm not certain. I have very thorough background checks done on my girls before they ever begin working for me. None of them have a criminal record and they have never been involved with drugs. Nicole had no criminal record, but she confided in me that she had been in the government's Witness Protection Program for a short time before I met her."

"Why was she in the Witness Protection Program?"

"I don't know. She would never talk about it. She's a very private person; doesn't let anyone inside. She did assure me that she was no longer in any danger, that whatever it was that required her to go into that program was no longer a problem for her or anyone else."

"And how long ago was she in the program?"

"Again, I don't know. Some of my girls remembered her from her modeling days. They told me that four years ago she was making over two hundred thousand dollars a year and was on the verge of becoming a supermodel. Then she just disappeared from the scene for two years. None of her old friends seem to know where she went, or why. I would imagine that was when it all started."

"She was making two hundred thousand a year and she became a hooker?"

Chambers gave Kirby a harsh look, but didn't respond to the use of the term she abhorred. "By the time she came back to modeling, her chance had passed her by. The top models were younger then, a different look. She couldn't get a job anywhere. That's when I met her."

"Do you have a photograph of her?"

Chambers started to get up from the sofa, grimacing in pain.

"Tell me where it is and I'll get it for you," Kirby offered.

"In the top section of the secretary desk against the wall. The cabinet on the left."

Kirby crossed the room to the secretary, removed a fat photo album, then returned to his chair and handed the album to Chambers.

"They took a photograph of Niki from the album in my office," she said as she flipped through the plastic-covered pages. "But Niki rarely made herself up like that unless she was working. The pictures in here were taken at some of the parties I gave for the girls, when we were just relaxing and being ourselves."

Kirby was leaning forward, craning his neck to look at the photographs as Chambers turned the pages. "They sure don't look like hookers."

Chambers's voice took on an edge. "That's the second time you've used that word. They aren't hookers as you think of them, Detective Kirby. They're all intelligent, educated former models who earn an average of seven hundred thousand dollars a year. They leave the business after five or six years. Some marry wealthy clients, others use the money they've invested to start a business. I doubt that any of them will ever cross the line again."

"Sorry. No offense meant."

"None taken."

Chambers stopped paging through the album and removed a five-by-seven snapshot of a remarkably beautiful woman, taken on the beach at Chambers's summer home on Fire Island. The occasion was a party she had given for her girls. Bass was sitting on the beach, smiling broadly, long, shapely legs crossed, a glass of champagne raised in a toast to whoever was holding the camera.

"This is how Niki looks most of the time, and how she dresses—very casual."

Chambers handed the snapshot to Kirby. He stared at it, stunned by the woman's quiet, haunting beauty. Her features, framed in shoulder-length chestnut-brown hair, were strong, yet feminine and sensuous. "Captivating" was the word that came immediately to mind. She appeared to be wearing no makeup and was dressed in jeans and a sweatshirt. Something he again had not expected, given the stereotypical image of the glamorous, high-class call girl: heavily made up, laden with jewelry, slinky, sultry, with a hard edge to them that told you they were manipulative, streetwise opportunists.

But Bass's beauty was natural, open, friendly, and inviting. Beneath softly arched eyebrows, dark brown wide-set eyes reached out with a touch of sadness, hinting at the intelligence behind them; they were not so much seductive as they were challenging and direct, capturing whoever they held in their steady, self-confident gaze.

"You mind?" Kirby said, putting the snapshot in the inside pocket of his leather jacket.

"No. I have others if you think they'll help."

"This is fine. She looks like a college kid. How old is she?"

"Almost thirty. But you're right, she looks twenty-five, or less."

"How tall?"

"Five ten."

"I'll need her address and telephone number."

Chambers again started to get up, but Kirby handed her his notepad and pen and she wrote them down.

"It's apartment 20-B."

"Nicole Bass is her real name? Most hookers . . . call girls use an alias."

"My girls don't use an alias. With our clients it isn't necessary."

"If she got the message you left, where do you think she would run? Friends?"

"She doesn't have any close friends; she keeps to herself, and doesn't socialize with the other girls unless I ask her to come to one of the parties I occasionally give for them."

"Any boyfriends, guys she dates nonprofessionally?"

"No. She once told me that she would only date clients until she left the business. She said she didn't need the inevitable complications that would arise."

"Can you tell me anything she said about what she witnessed last night?"

Chambers told her what Bass had said about seeing Genero murder Onorati. "She called shortly after it happened . . . and she said something strange, but then, as I told you, she's always been somewhat of a mystery to me."

"What was it she said?"

"I told her it must have been terrible to see someone killed right before her eyes, and she said that she had been through worse."

"Any idea what she was talking about?"

"None whatsoever. But of all my girls, Niki is the one I worry about least. Underneath that soft, feminine surface, she's tough, and I suspect quite able to take care of herself."

Kirby looked at his watch. He had arrived less than twenty minutes ago. Bass's apartment house was only five minutes away.

"Anything else you can tell me that might help convince her to trust me?"

"Not really, except that she's highly intelligent; always taking courses at NYU to improve herself. And she's a good person; most of her clients fall in love with her. For what it's worth, I can give you an opinion that may allow you some insight into her personality."

"Like I said, anything you think might help."

"Somewhere along the way, someone she trusted and believed in hurt her badly. She's not a very trusting person anymore, so that may prove to be a problem for you."

Kirby got up from his chair, thanked Chambers for her help, and, after scribbling three numbers on the back of his card, handed it to her.

"My work number's on the front, my home, pager, and cellular numbers are on the back. I'll call Bass on my way over to her apartment, but if you hear from her before I talk to her, tell her to call me immediately."

Chambers made an effort to get up as Kirby started to leave the room.

"Please, stay where you are. I'll see myself out."

The doorbell rang as he reached the foyer. He looked through the peephole to see the female undercover he had asked Lieutenant Rizzo to send standing on the landing outside. She had a small overnight bag with her and was holding up her shield. He opened the door and let her in.

"In there," he told the young woman, indicating the sitting room, where Chambers could be seen still sitting on the sofa. "Don't let her out of your sight. You get into any kind of a situation, you call for backup right away."

Kirby skipped down the steps and jogged over to his car. As he pulled out from the curb, he opened his flip phone and dialed Nicole Bass's number.

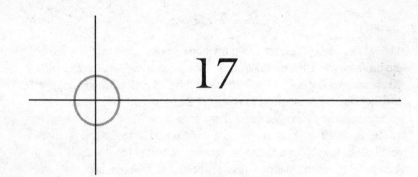

17

NICOLE BASS HAD gone directly into her bedroom upon entering her apartment. She unpacked the clothes she bought, modeled them in the full-length mirror, and tried different accessories and shoes with them before putting them away in her closet. It wasn't until she went into the living room to turn on the all-news channel, to see if there were any updates on Onorati's murder, that she saw the blinking light on her telephone answering unit.

She pressed the playback button as she crossed the room to get the remote control for the television, stopping midway there at the sound of Carolyn Chambers's voice. Her frantic words rushed out between sobs:

> *"Oh, God, Niki! I'm sorry, I'm so sorry. I had to tell them. You can't imagine how much they hurt me. Please forgive me. I gave them your name and address. One of them is big, mean-looking, wearing a black-leather car coat. The other one is good-looking, tall; he has on an olive-colored double-breasted suit. Oh, God. Please, please forgive me. Run, Niki. Before they get you. Forgive me. Please forgive me."*

Bass stood in the center of the room, unable to move. Her mind was reeling. She turned one way, then another, then finally made it to the sofa, where she sat with her elbows on her knees, her head in her hands, her entire body trembling.

"Oh, no. Not again," she whispered, her breathing shallow, a tightness in her chest. She forced herself to think clearly, not to let the fear paralyze her. Use the adrenaline rush to your advantage, they had taught her, and she forced herself to take slow, deep breaths. She had to get out. Now. The audible time stamp on the message said the call from Carolyn had come in over an hour ago. Where were they? Outside waiting for her? They wouldn't come up to the apartment. No. Too risky. They would be waiting outside. That might not be a problem. *Get out now!* The voice inside her head screamed, forcing her out of her inactivity.

She ran into the bedroom and slipped out of her dress, pulling on jeans, a silk T-shirt, a black wool blazer, and running shoes. She next took the wig from the box on the shelf in her closet, standing before the mirror to get it on just right. Short and sandy blond, it changed her appearance considerably. She took the Vuarnet sunglasses with the large round frames from the top of her dresser and put them on, completing the disguise.

Dragging a tan leather carry-on bag out of the closet, she began tossing in underwear and a few changes of clothes, all casual and easily packed. She put her toilet articles and a travel kit containing her makeup and dryer in last, zipping the bag closed before running back out to the living room. The briefcase, she thought. Onorati's briefcase and the rest of the money. She pulled it out from beneath the sofa, shook out the remaining fifty thousand dollars, and stuffed it into the carry-on with her clothes.

Something else fell out of the briefcase, lightly striking Bass's foot. A computer disk. She stared at it for a moment, recalling the disk Onorati had given to Genero. She put it in her jacket pocket, then got her small notebook computer from the desk at the other end of the living room and slipped that into one of the outside pockets of the carry-on bag.

Get rid of the briefcase, she thought. Where? The trash chute was out in the hall.

Bass first took her pistol from her shoulder bag, checking the magazine to make certain it was full. Seven rounds. One in the chamber gave her eight. She slid the compact semiautomatic pistol into her waistband at the front of her jeans. The black blazer concealed it from view.

She went out into the hall and ran the short distance to the small utility room near the elevators, where she tossed the briefcase down the trash chute. She kept her hand inside her jacket on the pistol grip, her eyes scanning the hallway until she was safely back in her apartment. As she closed and locked the door behind her, the telephone rang. She let out a sharp, startled cry. Calm down! she told herself. Calm the hell down! Use the fear and the adrenaline.

She let the phone ring until the unit clicked on, then listened to the deep, unfamiliar voice leaving the message.

"Nicole Bass, my name is Jack Kirby. I'm a detective with the New York City Police Department Intelligence Division. If you're there, pick up the telephone. [A long pause.] I need to talk to you immediately. Your life is in danger, and right now I'm the best chance you have of staying alive. Ms. Bass? Are you there? [Another pause.] I just left Carolyn Chambers. I'm aware of your situation and I want to help you. When you get this message, call me immediately at 981-6630, my cellular number. There isn't any time to waste, Ms. Bass. I'm on my way over; if you're there, wait."

Bass now stood directly over the phone, her hand reaching to pick up the receiver. No, she told herself. You don't know who he is. It could be anyone. She heard the disconnect, then after the tape rewound, she played back Kirby's message, jotted down his cellular number, and considered calling him. She decided against it, putting the number in her pocket as she erased both messages. No complications right now. She had to go somewhere and think things through.

First she had to get out of the building, past the men waiting for her, if they *were* outside waiting for her. But where would she go? Time to think about that later. First she had to get away from where they knew they could find her. The phone rang again, just as she was about to leave. She let the answering unit get it, and at the first sound of Carolyn Chambers's voice, she picked it up.

"It's alright, Carolyn. I understand and I forgive you. I've been there. I've got to go now. I'll call you when I'm safe."

Without giving her a chance to respond, Bass hung up, put on a lightweight raincoat from the entryway closet, grabbed her carry-on and her shoulder bag, and left the apartment.

18

NINO TOTANI HAD called Carmine Molino again, to tell him where Bass was and that they were still sitting on her, waiting until she came out. Molino's only words were, "The boss ain't happy. Get her out of the picture. Now."

"Yeah, so I can fuckin' eat," Johnnie Socks said as Totani hung up, growing more irritable with each passing moment from the lack of food. He was slumped in his seat, staring at the entrance to the apartment building, when he saw the tall good-looking woman with short blond hair come out and walk down the driveway to the sidewalk. He studied her as she stood at the curb, the large carry-on bag in her hand, signaling to a taxi that passed her by. She appeared nervous, her eyes moving constantly up and down the street. Then she turned, and her back was to him as she looked toward Lexington Avenue. He leaned forward in his seat.

"Hey, Nino. The broad lookin' for a taxi."

Totani had seen her and dismissed her. "Yeah?"

"Legs all the way up to her ass? That's her. Yeah, she's got a wig on and sunglasses, but I'm tellin' ya, that's her. She's got a bag with her. She's skippin'. I'd bet a yard on it."

With that Johnnie Socks jumped out of the car and started across the street, his eyes fixed on Bass, who had begun to walk toward Lexington Avenue to try for a taxi on the much busier street.

Bass looked back over her shoulder and saw the man across the street get out of the car. Huge. A black-leather coat. Then the other man, tall, olive-green double-breasted suit, got out and started after him. Bass turned and ran back up the driveway to her apartment building.

Puzzled to see his favorite tenant come back into the lobby after just leaving, Charlie the doorman came up to her as she stood staring back down the driveway, breathing heavily.

"Can I help you, Ms. Bass?"

Bass turned, startled by his voice. She hadn't seen him approach. "Yes, Charlie. Will you please go down to the corner and get a taxi for me and have it come up to the door."

"Sure, Ms. Bass. Going on a trip?"

"A short one. To visit some friends," she said absently, her attention still focused on the end of the driveway. The two men were no longer in sight.

"I like the wig. Different look." Earlier, when Bass had come out of the elevator and crossed the lobby, it had taken him a few moments to recognize her; then he recalled that he had seen her wear the blond wig once before.

Bass forced a smile. "Sometimes I get bored with what I see in the mirror."

"No one else does."

"Thank you, Charlie. You're a sweetheart."

Troubled by the wide-eyed, anxious look about her, he said, "Are you okay?"

"I'm fine, Charlie. Just a little nervous about the trip. I hate flying."

"Know what you mean," Charlie said, and left to jog down the driveway, heading to the corner of Third Avenue to hail a taxi.

Bass sat on one of the bench seats in the lobby that allowed her an unobstructed view of the driveway. Twenty yards away, on the sidewalk, she saw the big man in the black-leather coat walk past, then return, his eyes on the entrance to the building. She watched as the second man walked up to him and jerked his thumb toward their car. Then both men walked back to the car and got in.

The taxi arrived five minutes later. Bass had her raincoat open and the blazer unbuttoned. Her right hand was inside her blazer resting on the pistol grip as she moved quickly outside, tossed her carry-on into the taxi, thanked Charlie profusely as she handed him a twenty-dollar bill, and climbed into the back seat.

The driver turned in his seat to flash a toothy grin. He wore an orange tam-o'-shanter cocked at a rakish angle on his head and a garland of colorful beads around his neck. What Bass thought was zither music played on the car radio.

"To where, please?"

"Just get out of here fast. I'll tell you where as we drive."

"To where is that?"

"Drive. Just drive."

"F and DR Drive?"

Great! Bass thought. Another New York cabbie who speaks no known language. "Just drive. Away from here."

The cabbie shrugged, mumbled something, and drove slowly down the driveway. He pulled onto East Sixty-ninth Street only to be stopped by two cars in front of him waiting for the traffic light to turn green at the corner of Lexington Avenue.

Bass turned in the seat to look out the rear window of the cab. "Oh, shit!"

Johnnie Socks was getting out of the car across the street, his eyes hard on Bass. Another car turned the corner off Third Avenue and came to a stop behind the taxi, blocking Johnnie Socks's view of the back seat of the cab. Bass watched him come out from behind the car and move slowly toward the cab. Then she saw his hand go inside his coat and bring out a large, semiautomatic pistol with a silencer attached to the barrel.

"Move! Goddamnit!" Bass screamed at the driver and ducked down in the seat.

"No move." He gestured toward the traffic light.

Bass looked up, saw there were no cars parked at the curb on their left for the fifty or sixty feet to the intersection.

"Go around them! Use the sidewalk!" she shouted, then lay back down on the seat.

"Oh, no. No sidewalk." He looked back and saw Bass scrunched down in the seat. "Why are you like that? You are sick? No get sick in cab, please."

At that moment, a loud *crack* filled the interior of the taxi as a bullet came through the rear window; the glass spiderwebbing as the round thudded into the side pillar just behind the driver.

"Oh, look goddamn," the cabbie said, staring at the ruined window. "What did that?"

"They're shooting at me!" Bass shouted. "Get us out of here!"

"Shoot my window. I punch their stupid face."

"They have guns, you moron! Drive up on the sidewalk!"

As Bass raised her head, another shot slammed through the rear window, blowing out a chunk of the spiderwebbed glass as it zinged past her ear and impacted in the dashboard to the driver's right.

Bass glanced at the traffic light ahead. It was still red. The driver behind them scrambled out of his car and ran wildly down the street, yelling at the top of his lungs for the police. Johnnie Socks was now standing openly in the middle of the street, directly behind the taxi, his gun in plain view, pointed at the rear window. People on the sidewalk scattered, some taking cover behind parked cars and garbage cans, others running out of sight around the corner.

Bass threw open the rear door of the cab, and in one continuous fluid motion, jumped out, drew her gun, and crouched into a stable firing stance. She fired two shots in rapid succession at Johnnie Socks, who for a split second stood staring at her in stunned disbelief. One of the bullets tore through the sleeve of his coat, just missing flesh and bone. The other penetrated the windshield of the car behind him as he rolled over the hood of another car parked at the curb and landed on the sidewalk beside Totani. He immediately jumped back up and returned fire, the poorly aimed shots well wide of their mark.

Bass's unsilenced shots had echoed loudly off the surrounding buildings, causing even more pandemonium in the street.

Totani, who was crouched low behind the car parked at the curb, moved behind the next car, working his way around to the side of the taxi to get a clear shot at Bass. He was furious that Johnnie Socks had precipitated the action before he was ready, and seriously considering shooting him in the head right then and there.

Bass caught sight of Totani in her peripheral vision as he popped up behind a car parked directly opposite the taxi. She quickly turned to face him, firing over the roof of the cab, again squeezing off two rapid-fire shots that ricocheted off the wall of the building behind him, missing his head by mere inches as he dropped to the ground.

"Fucker can shoot for a broad, huh?" Johnnie Socks said, his finger probing the hole in his coat as he crouched behind the car.

"Shut up, you idiot!" Totani spat out the words as he raised his head to peer over the roof of the car at the curb. He slowly rose to his full height and swept the area in front of him with the silenced pistol, but he didn't have a shot. Then he saw Bass appear from behind the rear fender of the taxi, her gun instantly trained on him. She fired once, the round tearing into the roof of the parked car just as he ducked down.

Bass felt the cab move backward. The driver had been lying flat on the front seat, terrified. Now jolted out of his inaction by the gun battle in the street, he was backing up to get around the car in front of him. Bass dove back inside just as the cab lurched forward, swung hard to the left, jumped the curb, crumpling the taxi's right front fender and the rear left fender of the car in front of them, and scraping the side of the car first in line at the traffic light. The whoops and wails of sirens could now be heard behind them on Third Avenue, approaching fast and increasing in volume and number.

Bass looked back to see Totani and Johnnie Socks retreat toward their car, stuffing their guns back inside their coats. The police cars had not yet reached the corner, and the bottled-up traffic at the Third Avenue intersection would prevent them from gaining immediate access to the hopelessly gridlocked street.

The now hysterical taxi driver, his hands clenching the steering wheel in a death grip, ran the light and fishtailed, tires howling, out onto Lexington Avenue. A large restaurant supply truck, heading south on the broad one-way avenue, swerved to avoid him and careened out of control into a building on the far corner, demolishing a plate-glass display window. Four of the cars behind the truck rear-ended each other as the first car slammed on its brakes to avoid hitting the taxi. Pedestrians bolted for safety in every direction.

The frantic cabbie drove at breakneck speed down Lexington Avenue, veering in and out of the traffic in front of him. He ran the next red light and narrowly missed broadsiding a limousine. His voice now a strident screech, he was screaming at the top of his lungs to no one in particular in a language Bass did not recognize as he swung into the curb and skidded to a stop, turning to shout at his passenger in his best English.

"Out of cab! Out! Out!"

Bass was watching the street behind them, looking through the hole blown out of the rear window, and forcing herself to take slow deep breaths to overcome the sheer terror that gripped her. She turned and pointed the gun at the cabbie. "Drive, goddamnit! And keep driving or I'll blow your head off!"

"Don't shoot. Don't shoot. I drive. Only joking. See, I drive now." With that he roared back out into traffic and continued his erratic high-speed run south on Lexington.

Bass looked back to see the green Pontiac coupé the two men were in pull out from the corner, but that was as far as they got. The traffic tie-up caused by the collisions at the intersection made it impossible for them to make the left turn and continue the pursuit. She watched as they wove their way through the cars stopped at odd angles, then saw them speed west on Sixty-ninth Street.

The cabbie made four green lights in a row, and at Sixty-fourth Street, Bass told him to turn left. They continued east for three blocks, when Bass instructed him to turn left again onto First Avenue, heading uptown.

"You can slow down now," she told the still-rattled driver. "We've lost them."

When they reached Eighty-second Street, Bass told him to pull over. She opened her shoulder bag and removed five banded packets of money, each containing one thousand dollars in one-hundred-dollar bills, most of what was left from her shopping spree. She handed them to the driver, who stared at the money in disbelief.

"For your trouble, and your window and fender. And some English lessons."

Bass was out of the taxi and moving quickly along Eighty-second Street toward Second Avenue before the driver stopped shouting his thanks to her and pulled out, still waving as he disappeared, heading north.

Now where? No one to turn to. Not that there had been since her father's death. Need to collect yourself. Think this through. Can't run blindly, you'll make mistakes. Never let the panic take hold. It'll destroy you if you do. Fight it. Use the things they taught you; the only positive things that came out of it all.

Bass was walking at a fast pace and forced herself to slow down as she crossed Lexington and continued on toward Madison. And then she knew what to do, at least for the moment. The Carlyle Hotel. Only six blocks south. She could hide there, relax, organize her thoughts. Check in under another name. Pay in cash. Yes. Small. Exclusive. Excellent security. Great room service. The lap of luxury. Jacuzzis in the bathrooms. Just what she needed to calm down and think things through. A long soak in a hot tub.

19

JACK KIRBY USED the siren on his unmarked car three times to get through bottlenecks on the Upper East Side caused by the rerouting of traffic to compensate for Fifth Avenue being closed for the Spanish Columbus Day parade. It had taken him twenty-five minutes to travel the five blocks from Carolyn Chambers's brownstone to East Sixty-ninth Street. He had forgotten about what the parade would do to the traffic situation, and with the circuitous route he was forced to take, he realized now he could have left the car on Seventy-fourth Street and jogged the distance in under ten minutes.

It was almost two-thirty when he sped up Third Avenue and shot across the intersection at Sixty-eighth Street. His portable radio was tuned to the Intelligence Division frequency, and he had not heard the central dispatcher report the "shots fired" call in the 19th Precinct. His chest tightened when he saw the flashing-light bars on the roofs of two patrol cars up ahead, barring access to Bass's block.

Fearing the worst, he slammed his fist into the steering wheel. "They got to her! The bastards got to her." He expected to find Bass lying dead in the street, or zipped up in a body bag on her way to the morgue.

He pulled in parallel to the patrol cars blocking the street and jumped out, flashing his gold shield at a uniformed cop who was about to tell him to move. The street was cordoned off at both ends of the block, and Kirby estimated there were thirty or forty cops in the area between the barricades.

The 19th Precinct, covering the Upper East Side, was the most high-profile precinct in the city, and the turnout in force was to be expected. A blue-and-white Emergency Services Unit truck was parked just past the patrol cars; the heavily armed men who had climbed out of it were searching the immediate area to make certain the shooters were no longer there. Detectives from the 19th squad and the Borough Task Force were interviewing eyewitnesses and canvassing the nearby buildings for anyone who might have been looking out their window at the time of the incident.

Halfway up the block, Kirby saw a group of detectives and uniforms gathered around the duty captain and the operations lieutenant. One of the detectives moved away from the group. Kirby tucked the back flap of his ID case into his waistband so his shield hung over his belt in plain view and approached him.

"Kirby, Intel," he said. "Whatcha got?"

"Gunfight at the O.K. Corral," the detective said. "Best guess is some druggies at war with each other. Strange neighborhood for it, though. What's Intelligence got to do with this anyway? You know something I don't?"

"Just passing by. Heard the call. Anyone killed?" Kirby held his breath.

"Nope. No stiffs, no blood around, so nobody wounded either."

"How many involved?"

"Three shooters. One woman, blond. Two men. One big, husky, other one tall and slim. Caucasian or Hispanic, depending on who you talk to. Guy shoots into the back of a cab. Woman gets out, returns fire. He shoots. She shoots. Other guy shoots. And like that. Witnesses say she got the best of the two guys, pinned them down. She jumps back in the cab, driver uses the sidewalk, runs the light and turns Lexington into a demolition derby, then takes off heading south. The two guys tear out after them in a green, blue, black, or gray Pontiac, Buick, Ford, or Oldsmobile. End of story."

"The female shooter was blond?"

The detective looked at his notes. "Tall. Blond. One witness says great legs. Good-lookin'."

"You find the cabbie involved?"

"Yeah. His cab was shot up, so he reported it to his dispatcher. She called it in. Couple uniforms interviewed him. He dropped the blonde off around Eighty-second, says he wouldn't recognize her if he saw her again."

"Where did he pick her up?"

"Uniforms didn't get that. We'll have to get a full statement from him later."

"Did he drop her off at an address?"

"No. Corner of Eighty-second and First. Says she headed west on Eighty-second."

"How was she dressed?"

The detective consulted his notes again. "Silver-gray raincoat. Black blazer under it. Jeans. Olive or beige T-shirt. Running shoes." The detective's eyes narrowed and he gave Kirby a look. "You're just passin' by, huh?"

"Yeah. You know how it goes."

"What unit you with at Intel?"

"Organized Crime."

"This was a wise-guy shoot-out, wasn't it?"

"I don't know."

"Witnesses say the guys doing the shooting had silencers. Now that you mention it, sounds like it might be wise guys to me."

"I didn't mention it, and lots of bad guys got silencers these days."

"I could use a little help here, Kirby. The blond shooter didn't happen to be one of your undercovers, did she?"

"Absolutely not."

"So you got nothin' for me?"

"All I know is what you told me. Thanks." Kirby then turned and walked toward the driveway leading to Bass's apartment building.

"Right," the detective called after him. "And thank you, for nothin'."

As Kirby entered the lobby of the apartment building, the congregation of cops outside on the street began to break up. With no one killed or injured, the remainder of what would amount to a cursory investigation would be left to the precinct detective squad.

Charlie the doorman stood inside the lobby at the floor-to-ceiling plate-glass window, watching the activity out on the street. He saw Kirby enter and immediately noticed the gold shield looped over his belt.

"Can I help you, detective?"

"Anyone been in here to talk to you and the other doorman?"

"Not yet."

"You see what happened?"

"Some of it."

"You know who was involved?"

Charlie hesitated, looked around, then: "You with the One-Nine?"

Kirby smiled. He had himself a cop buff; he could work him, no problem. The doorman liked to use the lingo, even though he had it wrong. Precincts like the 24th were spoken as the Two-Four, and the 70th the Seven-Oh, but the precincts in the teens were always referred to as the 19th, the 17th, never splitting them into two words. No one had ever written the curious anomaly down, to Kirby's knowledge, but every cop knew the jargon.

"No. I'm with Intelligence."

Charlie's eyes widened. "No kiddin'?"

"No kidding. Detective Kirby." He extended his hand and the doorman shook it.

"Charlie Adamson," Charlie said.

Flatter him first. "Sounds like you used to be on the Job."

"No. No. Not that I didn't try. I took the test for the academy about twenty years ago, but I didn't make the cut, I guess. I used to do private security up until last year. Liked the work, but this pays better, good tips."

A rent-a-cop. Perfect. "Miss the action, though. Don't you?"

"Yeah. Sure do. So what can I do for you, detective?"

Kirby put an arm around Charlie's shoulder and steered him to a private corner of the lobby. "Call me Jack."

Charlie beamed. "Okay, Jack."

"Listen, Charlie, I got a situation here, and I could really use your help. But it's got to be strictly between us. You know what I mean?"

"Sure. I can keep my mouth shut. I know the drill. Intelligence, huh?"

"Yeah. Organized Crime."

"Whoa! Into some heavy stuff."

"It gets that way sometimes." Kirby leaned in close. "So, the blond woman involved in the shoot-out. You know who she is?"

"She's not in any kind of trouble with the police, is she, Jack?"

"Absolutely not. I'm trying to help her."

Charlie looked around the lobby again, then in his best conspiratorial voice: "Yeah. I know her. But she isn't a blonde."

"Eyewitnesses say she was."

Charlie smiled. "She had on a wig."

"How about that? What's her name?"

"Nicole Bass. Nice lady. Real looker. Used to be a model."

"Yeah? About what time did she leave the building?"

"Couple minutes after two . . . five at the most. She was going some-where on a trip. Had an overnight bag with her. Tan leather," Charlie said, and winked. "I got an eye for details. She goes out to the curb to grab a cab, next thing I know she comes running back inside looking really up-set. Asked me to run down to the corner at Third and get her cab for her. So I did. She leaves, and a minute or two later the shooting starts."

"You see her shooting at the two guys?"

"I didn't actually see her. The cab was further up the street. But I did see the two guys who were shooting at her; they were right near the end of the driveway. At least I assume it was Ms. Bass they were shooting at, you know, 'cause I didn't actually see her involved."

"That's okay. Witnesses say the shooter who got out of the cab was a tall, good-looking blond female. Wearing a gray raincoat, black blazer, jeans."

"Yeah. That's what Ms. Bass had on; must have been her then."

"Any idea where she might have gone?"

"No. She's a real private person. You sure you're not looking to arrest her for something?"

"No. Like I said. She's not a suspect. She's a victim. I'm looking to save her life, if I can find her, Charlie."

"I'd sure hate to see anything happen to her. She's the kind that brightens up your days, you know?"

"I heard that about her. She entertain anybody in her apartment? Men, women, like girlfriends, boyfriends?"

"You know, in the year and a half she's lived here, I don't think I ever saw her with anybody. Male or female. Strange, huh?"

"Like you said, she's private. Listen. I really got to get some kind of handle on her if I'm going to figure out where she might run and find her before the bad guys do."

"Who do you think's trying to kill her?"

"I don't know yet. But if I could get a look around her apartment, maybe I might see something that could give me a clue where she would have gone. What do you think?"

"I don't know. I could lose my job. You don't have a warrant, do you?"

"No. Nothing official. And like I said, she's not a suspect. We could keep this just between us, our own little covert operation. It'd be a big help to me, Charlie, and to Ms. Bass." Kirby knew he was on thin ice, but he needed something, anything, to go on.

Charlie scrunched up his face, staring at the floor, wanting to help, but not wanting to get caught at it. "She's really good people. I like her a lot."

"Sometimes you just have to do the right thing, Charlie. Even if it means sticking your neck out a little. So what do you think? Can we do it? It's not like I'm going to toss the place or anything. Just a quick look around."

Charlie chewed on his lower lip for a moment, then looked past Kirby to his counterpart, Pete, the doorman at the desk. "Could you sort of distract Pete, the other doorman, while I get the spare keys for her apartment?"

"Absolutely. Good thinking."

"Then you could go up to the twentieth floor and I could meet you there in a couple minutes. It's 20-B. I'll make some excuse, like I'm going up to check on you."

"Sounds like a plan to me."

Kirby crossed the lobby and motioned to Pete to come out from behind the desk. He took him over to the same corner where he and Charlie had talked, asking him for his version of events while keeping one eye on Charlie as he got the spare keys to Bass's apartment. It took most of his self-control to keep from laughing out loud when Charlie gave him a big thumbs-up and held up the keys in triumph. Kirby thanked Pete for information that he already had, then told him he was going to check to see if any of the tenants with apartments facing the street had seen anything more.

Kirby had barely gotten off the elevator on the twentieth floor when the doors opened on the adjacent elevator and out stepped Charlie, keys jangling in his hand.

"Got 'em, Jack."

"Good work. Why don't you just let me have them. I'll go in and look around myself, keep you out of it just in case anyone complains later on."

Charlie was crestfallen. "Okay. But maybe I should wait out here in the hall as a lookout for you."

"No. That would just advertise that something was going on."

"Right. Right. I'll wait down in the lobby for you then, okay?"

"Good idea."

Kirby gave him a fraternal slap on the shoulder and waited until he stepped into the elevator before entering Bass's apartment.

The living room was clean and uncluttered, a place for everything and everything in its place. News magazines—*Time, Newsweek, U.S. News*—a current copy of *New York,* and the morning's newspapers—the *New York Times* and the *Wall Street Journal*—were arranged on a coffee table set before an overstuffed sofa and two comfortable-looking armchairs, their down pillows neatly fluffed. A StairMaster exerciser filled one corner of the room, while a rack of dumbbells filled another; a barbell, holding what Kirby determined was seventy-five pounds, lay on the floor beside the weight rack.

Kirby's attention was drawn to the wall opposite the intimate grouping of furniture. He counted seven framed covers from past issues of various fashion magazines, all between the years 1989 and 1991, and all showing Nicole Bass in glamorous poses. A section of bookshelves on the wall behind the sofa contained a sizable collection of knickknacks: vases, small bronze statues, ceramic animals. An eclectic selection of books filled the lower shelves. Mostly nonfiction: history, philosophy, finance and investing, a few self-help pop psychology, and others with titles Kirby thought to be in Spanish. One of the titles he roughly translated as a history of Bolivia and its people.

In the center of the middle shelf, at eye level and flanked by two ceramic horses, was a framed black-and-white photograph of what Kirby estimated was a fourteen- or fifteen-year-old Nicole Bass. Smiling and happy, in a T-shirt and faded jeans, a thumb hooked into a front belt loop, one hip cocked, Bass stood in the center of a clearing surrounded by dense, hilly woods. She had an arm around the waist of a tall, slender, older man whose knotty forearms gave the impression that he was made of twisted steel cable. He had a craggy, hardscrabble face that told of long hours of strenuous work with little to show for it. The strong family resemblance was evident in the eyes; the same direct, never-quit gaze of his daughter—there was no doubt where she got it. Bass's head rested against the proud father's chest as he hugged her to his side, his sharp features softened by a half smile of such gentleness and kindness that one would have thought that depth of emotion impossible from the tough, gnarled look of him.

In the background of the photograph a horse with spotted hindquarters that Kirby recognized as an Appaloosa craned its neck over a split-rail fence enclosing a small paddock and a weathered barn with gaps in the siding and a precarious lean to it. Directly behind where father and daughter stood was a one-story log cabin with a sagging front porch, and to the right of the cabin, at the very edge of the photograph, an outhouse could be seen behind the cabin. Kirby stared at the image of the young Bass. Even at that age, without makeup or a sophisticated hairstyle or expensive clothes, though still a bit gangly, she was just as beautiful as she appeared in the framed photographs from the fashion magazine covers.

Kirby scanned the other shelves, but saw no photographs of the mother. He then walked through the kitchen/dining room, toward the guest bedroom, pausing to hit the playback button on the telephone-answering unit, checking for any messages left on the tape. There were none. She had gotten Chambers's message and his and erased them. According to the doorman's time frame, she would have been in the apartment when he called. Probably listened to him leaving the message. But she hadn't called. Not a good sign.

Maybe after the shoot-out with the wise guys, she was running scared and after thinking it over would realize he was her best chance of staying alive. But somehow Kirby doubted that. The task force detective had said she got the best of Nino Totani and Johnnie Socks, both of whom Kirby knew were good with guns, practicing their skills at an indoor shooting range in New Jersey a few times each month. The fact that Bass had shot it out with them and not simply panicked and run meant that somewhere along the way she had had considerable training, and some real-life experience in tight situations.

He pulled open the drawer of the table that held the telephone and the answering unit, but found no address book or lists of telephone numbers, only a menu from a delicatessen on Third Avenue that delivered.

After a cursory examination of the guest bedroom, he was surprised that so far he had found nothing, other than the photographs, books, and exercise equipment, of a personal nature. No matchbook covers of favorite restaurants, no pictures from vacations or getaway weekends with friends or lovers, or wall posters that told of places she had been or longed to go, or might run to in time of crisis. Not a single photograph of a man other than her father. It was as though she had no personal life outside of her profession.

The master bedroom revealed little more. The one exception was a large painting on the wall at the foot of the queen-size bed. It again told something of her background: an oil painting of morning mist drifting through a mountain forest brilliant with fall color. In the background, through the trees, gently rolling hills rippled into the distance, and the steeple of a backcountry church could be seen rising from a hollow where the ground sloped steeply at the edge of the painting. Hillbilly country is the way Kirby would have described the scene.

One of Bass's closets in the master bedroom was filled with what Kirby knew by the labels was expensive designer clothing. All neatly arranged by season and occasion. A rack built into one end of the huge closet held a dozen or more pairs of shoes with heels of varying heights. The second closet, smaller and less organized, was stuffed full of casual clothes, the floor littered with at least six pairs of running and cross-training shoes. Separating the professional from the nonprofessional, Kirby thought, wondering if she was successful at doing that beyond her wardrobe.

He looked through the drawers of the nightstands on either side of the bed, finding nothing but a hardcover book that promised to teach readers how to invest their money wisely. A bookmark stuck out three-quarters of the way through the thick volume. A quick look through the drawers of a high chest and a dresser on opposite walls yielded nothing of interest. A large four-tier jewelry box on top of the dresser contained a broad selection of relatively expensive necklaces and bracelets, gold and semiprecious stones, but no diamonds or rubies or emeralds.

Kirby returned to the living room and stood looking around to see if he had missed anything. He realized that, with the exception of a brief glimpse into Bass's background, and the fact that she was neat, with perhaps a compartmentalized mind, kept abreast of current affairs, and probably invested her money wisely, he knew no more than he had when he entered the apartment. Certainly nothing that would help him get a fix on where she might run when in trouble.

He thought of one possibility, and picked up the phone and dialed Carolyn Chambers's number. He asked her where Bass was raised and if she had that address. Chambers told him she believed Bass came from somewhere near Johnson City, Tennessee, but that she had no immediate family left, her father having died a few years ago.

With that, Kirby dug out the card Detective Joe Early of the 17th

Precinct had given him the previous night. It was time to bring Early up to speed on the shooting incident and what he had learned so far, and to enlist his help in finding Bass. He detected a note of anger in Early's voice when he asked how long Kirby had known about the existence of a witness, but Kirby smoothed it over with the promise to be more forthcoming with information as he got it. He also assured Early that on his way back to Intelligence Division headquarters, he would drop off a photograph of Bass for him to get copies made to aid in the city-wide hunt that was about to begin.

Kirby was staring at the photograph of the teenage Bass and her father when it struck him. In his haste to find her and get her into protective custody, he had completely forgotten to call in and have someone check the files of the Witness Security Program, its proper name as opposed to Witness Protection Program, which most people called it. Why had she been put in the program? He needed answers, and fast.

The Intelligence Division's liaison with the U.S. Marshals Service, which ran the Witness Security Program, was Tom Quinn, a man Kirby knew on a first-name basis and occasionally had a beer with when their paths crossed. He used his flip phone to place the call from his car as he drove back downtown. He reached Quinn at his office at St. Marks Plaza and asked him to run Bass's name.

Kirby was pulling into the curb in front of the 17th Precinct station house when Quinn called him back.

"She was in the program for six months," Quinn said. "Left it voluntarily eighteen months ago. Came back to New York and started using her own name again."

"What name was she using in the program?" Kirby asked, thinking that she might use it again while running from Genero's men.

"Martha Johnson."

"Who put her in the program?"

"DEA."

"Let me guess, she was busted for drugs and made a deal with them to testify against someone?"

"None of the case history came up with her file," Quinn said. "DEA's got it classified—you'll have to get the details from them."

Kirby thanked Quinn and hung up, then immediately dialed the number for the Drug Enforcement Administration's liaison with the Intelligence Division: Charlie Castanza. He and Kirby were casual friends after working on a number of joint investigations into the Mafia's narcotics-trafficking operations. Castanza was at his office on lower Manhattan's west side, and Kirby told him what he needed.

"I'll see what I can do. You know Dirty Ed's?"

"Grungy cop bar in the West Village, a couple blocks from DEA headquarters?"

"That's it. Give me about an hour and meet me there."

20

VINCENT GENERO'S FIST pounded the glass-topped wrought-iron table on the patio outside the study of his Centre Island mansion. The vibrations sent a Venetian glass vase full of freshly cut chrysanthemums from his wife's flower garden tumbling off to shatter on the flagstones below.

"What the fuck you mean there's nothin' in them?"

Carmine Molino slowly shook his head; this was not the kind of news he relished bringing to Genero. "Two accounts in the Caymans, one in the Bahamas, one in the Netherlands Antilles, and one in Liechtenstein. Zero balances. He cleaned them out."

"Cleaned out fifteen, eighteen million? Where the fuck did he put it?"

"The accountant says he could have transferred it into other accounts."

"So—what other accounts? Where's the fuckin' money right now?"

"We got no way of knowin'."

"You tellin' me we're out fifteen, eighteen million . . . and which the fuck is it anyway? Fifteen or eighteen?"

"We still ain't sure. Onorati done some real creative bookkeeping."

"That fuck! That fuck!" Genero's chest heaved, his face crimson; he was working himself into another of his purple rages.

Molino was not about to mention that Genero had screwed up bigtime. Killing the only guy who could get to the money, before he knew for sure he had it back. And then there was the problem of explaining the loss to the heads of the other four Families; almost half of the money belonged to them, entrusted to Genero, to safeguard and invest.

Molino simply shrugged and said, "Probably moved it into the same kind of secret, numbered accounts in some other banks, maybe the same banks. Without the codes, there's no way we can trace it. The accounts on the computer disk he gave you was where it was before he did it."

"That sneaky fuck. Thought I wouldn't kill him. Let it slide for old times' sake. Make me think he gave it all back. Then figured he'd fuckin' make a run for it after we left. That rotten fuck!" Genero's fist thundered onto the glass tabletop again, this time sending a starburst of cracks shooting in all directions.

Molino discreetly inched his chair back from the table. "He must have had another disk with the new accounts on it somewhere."

"Yeah? Well where the fuck is it?"

"Nino went through his office this morning and found nothin' except the telephone number that led him to the broad. The secretary said Onorati cleaned out the safe: cash, personal papers, some computer disks. Stuffed it all in his briefcase and took off. Maybe it's somewhere in his apartment."

"We can't go near that apartment right now. Fuckin' cops probably got it sealed."

"Maybe we can get to one of the doormen on the day shift. Convince him to check it out for us when the cops ain't lookin'."

Genero wasn't listening; he was staring off somewhere in the middle distance, his eyes narrowed. "What was that you said before?"

"About gettin' to one of the doormen?"

"Before that. About the briefcase."

"Onorati's secretary said he emptied out his office safe, stuffed it all in his briefcase, then took off."

"The broad's got the briefcase."

"What broad?"

"The fuckin' broad that saw me whack that fuck; *that* fuckin' broad."

"How do you know that?"

"Johnnie Socks says he saw her with it when she ran outta the apartment."

"You think she knows what she got?"

"Fuck would I know? Fuckin' whore probably took it just to hock it. Or knew there was money in it. And what are those morons doin' about finding her? Fuckin' Nino. I thought at least he had some brains. Fuckin' broad outshoots him. You believe that shit?"

"They're tryin' to find her . . . but we got another problem."

"Yeah? What's that?"

"The cops know about her." Molino braced himself for a renewed outburst of temper; it came without pause.

This time Genero simultaneously slammed both fists down on the glass top, shattering it to pieces and sending chunks of the safety glass down through the table's open framework. Molino jumped to his feet and backed away as Genero kicked a piece of the glass off his Gucci crocodile loafers, then slowly rose and walked off across the lawn. Molino followed at his side, remaining silent until Genero spoke.

"You sure they know?" He was surprisingly composed now. The cold, calculating calm had descended.

"Yeah. A detective by the name of Kirby from Organized Crime got onto her. But we got somebody inside lettin' us know what they got."

"Those fucks! How'd they find out? Nobody knew but us."

"Probably the broad who runs the escort service. They left her for dead and she wasn't."

"Fuckin' idiots." Genero fell silent, then stopped walking and turned to face Molino. "Or maybe the cops got somebody inside, too."

"Only person I told was Nino. Outside of you, me, Big Paulie, John-nie Socks, that's it. Nobody else knew nothin' about her."

"Make sure. Just in case. Maybe somebody inside Nino's crew. Tell him, look into it."

"Yeah, okay." Molino knew better than to argue when Genero was in the grip of the paranoia that ruled many of his actions.

"The cops know any more than we do?"

"Not yet. Maybe even less. They were one step behind Nino and John-nie Socks."

"Find her, Carmine. And tell Nino don't fuckin' kill her. I want her alive until we find out what she knows about the money. Bring her to that warehouse over in Brooklyn. I'll talk to her personally there."

"I'll take care of it."

"And see if you can put someone on that Organized Crime detec-tive—Kirby. Maybe the cop fuck'll lead us to her." Genero again looked off in the distance. "That name sounded familiar to me first time you mentioned him. How come?"

"Couple years back when you skated on that murder rap? He's the one got in your face on the courthouse steps. Said no matter how long it took him he was gonna put you in prison for the rest of your life."

"Yeah. Yeah. Called me a piece of shit. And don't I remember somethin' else in the papers about him? Shot his own kid, right?"

"Same guy."

"Stupid fuck."

Molino approached the next subject gingerly. "You think maybe we should tell the heads of the other Families what happened about the money? You know, be up front with them? Tell them we'll make things right?"

"Fuck 'em. Those assholes. They'll start whinin' like a bunch of pussies. I got enough problems with that broad still runnin' around. We'll straighten the money out later. Turns out she's got it, we don't have to say nothin'. Never happened."

Molino turned to leave and Genero grasped him firmly by the upper arm. His voice was a low growl. "You don't tell nobody nothin' about that computer disk and the money. Fuckin' nobody! Not Nino, not nobody. We're lookin' for the broad 'cause she was a witness and that's it."

"Right. I won't say nothin' to nobody."

Genero released his underboss's arm. "And make sure those morons understand I want her alive and able to talk. Don't bust her up till I'm finished with her."

Molino was across the lawn at the gate leading from the grounds to the driveway when Genero called after him.

"And Carmine, I don't want no more bad news."

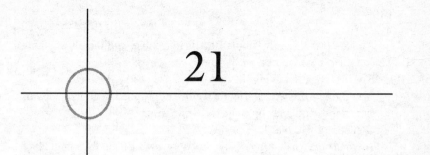

21

KIRBY WAS GREETED by the overpowering odor of stale beer and cigarette smoke as he entered the dimly lit bar in the West Village. After the few moments it took for his eyes to adjust, he saw that the place was empty except for the bartender and Charlie Castanza, who sat in a booth in a dark corner nursing a long-neck bottle of beer.

The bartender had big hair and wore a short leather skirt and fishnet stockings; she looked through Kirby like he wasn't even there when he ordered a club soda. He crossed the room and slipped into the booth, reaching across to shake Castanza's hand, a beefy paw that went with the rest of his squat, 230-pound, power-packed body.

"You sure struck a raw nerve with this one, Jack."

"What did you find?"

"I ran Nicole Bass's name on the computer. Comes up her file's sealed—no one gets in except on a real high level. But I noticed that one of the names connected with the case was Cliff Mahanes."

"Do I know him?"

"He's a group supervisor here at the New York Field Division. One of the good guys. When I asked him why the file on Bass was sealed, he asked me why I wanted to know, and I had to tell him you were looking for her."

"So what did he have to say?"

"First things first. You didn't get this from me, or anyone else at DEA. We didn't even have this conversation, right?"

"Right."

"And another thing. If Nicole Bass is in trouble, and there's anything we can do to help her out, we'll do it."

"The way you're talking, it sounds as if she used to be an agent."

"You figured she was a druggie we busted, flipped, and then she rats out her friends and ends up in the program, right?"

"Something like that."

"Anyone else was asking, that's probably what I'd tell them and leave it at that. But we got history, Jack, so I know you well enough to know you'll do the right thing. I'll give it to you straight, just like Cliff Mahanes gave it to me."

Castanza took a long pull on his beer and began. "About four years ago, when Bass was a fashion model, she was in Rome working for some designer. Just a kid from the hills of Tennessee getting her first taste of the big time. Twenty-four, twenty-five years old, new to the game, but making about two hundred twenty-five thousand a year, on the fast track to being a supermodel, but still pretty much wide-eyed, naive, and trusting. Then a real scum wad by the name of Ernesto Calderon enters her life."

"Never heard of him."

"Bolivian drug trafficker. At the time, the whole upper echelon of the Bolivian government was nothing but a drug cartel that made the Colombians look like pikers. Calderon was the brains behind their operation."

"I remember reading something about that. The CIA was looking the other way to keep the right-wingers in power."

"Yeah. For a while. Then their cozy little arrangement started to generate too much heat. The press got hold of it and raked them over the coals, so the CIA's Counter Narcotics Center ran a joint operation with us to bring the cartel down."

"How does Bass fit into all of this?"

"I'm getting to that. The DEA's country attaché in Italy at the time was Bill Crawford. Real hard charger, go-get-'em, can-do guy, do anything to make a case. Occasionally got people killed with some of his harebrained stunts."

"In other words, a real prick nobody wanted to work with."

"You got it. But the suits in Washington considered him God's gift to the war on drugs. Made a lot of big cases that made them look good in the press. Anyway, Ernesto Calderon was in Rome for a high-level meeting with the Sicilian Mafia, putting together a distribution deal for the heroin they were bringing in from the Middle East. He had a real eye for the ladies. Especially models. He started sniffing around Bass, showing up backstage at the shows with flowers. But she wanted nothing to do with the greasy fat bastard. But Crawford had Calderon under surveillance, hotel room bugged, the whole nine yards. He'd been trying to get someone inside the Bolivian's operation for three years, and when he saw Calderon chasing after Bass, he saw her as his chance to nail him.

"So he makes his approach, asks her to play along with Calderon, see what she can learn. Appeals to her patriotism and all that. She says thanks but no thanks. Turns him down flat. Well, glory boy Crawford doesn't like that one goddamn bit. So he decides to use an alternative method of persuasion."

"He set her up?"

"Big-time. She's getting off a flight from Rome to Milan going to work another fashion show, and what do you know? The DEA resident agent in Milan is waiting with a couple of Crawford's buddies from an Italian narcotics task force, supposedly acting on a tip from a confidential informant. And what do they find but a fuckin' kilo of pure, uncut heroin in Bass's luggage."

"The Italians were in on the setup?"

"All the way. So naturally, Bass claims to know nothing about it. It's all a big mistake. They lock her up, charge her with narcotics-trafficking, tell her since she was caught carrying weight she's going to spend the next thirty years in an Italian prison. They let her sit in a fuckin' cell for about a week, then our hero Crawford comes along, tells her he can help her if she helps him."

"Bass didn't ask for help from the embassy?"

"Sure she did, and at first her friends didn't buy into it and went to the State Department on her behalf. But the striped-pants pussies at the embassy simply went to Crawford and asked him for his read on it. He lies and tells them he's had Bass under surveillance for a couple weeks and she's guilty as sin. They buy it and bow out. Her friends figure if the State Department says she's guilty, then it must be true. Plus Crawford tells them to shut the fuck up about the bust or they'll regret the day they were born; Bass was clean, but a fair share of her model friends were putting powder up their noses to stay skinny, so they backed off fast. Then the modeling agency Bass works for drops her like a used condom.

"So there she is, busted in Italy on a narcotics rap, facing thirty years, her friends and her agency desert her, she knows she's innocent, but no-body wants to hear about it. Then some scumbag wop lawyer fleeces her for a hundred grand, most of the money she had saved, before he tells her there's nothing he can do; Crawford even set that up. Wanted her broke and desperate. So Bass takes what she thought was the only way out."

"And Crawford gets her to work as a confidential informant for him."

"Oh, he went a lot further than that. There was no official record of the phony bust, and Crawford made sure it didn't hit the papers, so Calderon wouldn't hear about it and get suspicious, figure out we were dangling Bass in front of him as bait. Then Crawford arranges for Bass to be somewhere where he knows Calderon will run into her. He does, thinks it's fate, makes his move, Bass agrees to go out with him as in-structed, and the game's afoot.

"Then Crawford goes down the hall to his CIA counterpart at the Rome station, tells him what he's got in the works. The CIA wants in, sees a chance to get someone deep inside the Bolivian drug cartel, offers to train Bass, designs a whole new operation around her. Know what the cold-blooded bastards called it? Operation Armani. After the fashion de-signer."

"Nice touch."

"Next phase. Crawford instructs Bass to tell Calderon she has to go back to the States for about a month, and then she'll accept his offer to visit him at his ranch in Bolivia that takes up about half the fuckin' country. The piece of shit is beside himself. Sends her flowers every day, offers to fly her all over the place in his private jet. Fucker's in love. From what Mahanes told me Bass is a real looker."

"And then some."

"So anyway, the CIA hustles her off to Camp Peary, their secret train-ing base in Virginia, and puts her through a month of intensive training in some basic tradecraft: combat pistol course, escape and evasion, clan-destine meetings, surveillance detection, self-defense, and a bunch of other stuff, including a crash course in Spanish. Mahanes said she was a natural, tough and smart, excelled at it."

Kirby nodded, now understanding her expertise and composure in the shoot-out with Totani and Johnnie Socks.

"To make a long story short, she spent eighteen, twenty months living and traveling with Calderon, built a case for us you wouldn't believe. Took a lot of risks, pulled off shit most experienced agents couldn't have done. We're ready to bust the cartel, so the CIA sets up a scam to get the top guys from Bolivia to Miami so we can grab them in this country. Works like a charm. Bass is supposed to be kept clear of all this, so she can walk away after the busts go down.

"Fuckin' chickenshit assistant U.S. attorney in Miami? Wants to make sure he wins his case, so after promising Bass she won't have to come out in the open, he names her as an undercover for us, forces her to testify at the trial. Damn near got her killed. Twice. First time she blew away two of the cartel's gunslingers in a parking lot. Second time they try to take out her and the two agents driving her to the courthouse. Car with four half-ass hit men in it pulls alongside and starts blasting away. Can't shoot worth a shit, and the stupid bastards weren't watching the oncoming lane and run smack into a semi, head-on, doing about eighty. A thing of beauty, I was told."

"And that's why she ended up in the Witness Security Program."

"Right. But about six months after she's in the program, Calderon gets hit in jail, and the Cali cartel wipes out the rest of his Bolivian buddies for moving in on their territory. Payback's a bitch. So there's nobody left who gives a shit about Bass testifying. She wants her life back, tells us she wants out of the program, and leaves. That was about eighteen months ago, and that's the last Mahanes or anyone else heard of her until you called today."

"And your glory boy Crawford went on to bigger and better things, huh?"

Castanza smiled. "Oh, no. That's the only good part of the story. Proof positive that there is indeed a God. About two months later the greedy prick was caught stealing three million in cash he seized in a bust. He's doin' twenty-five-to-life in Leavenworth for that and some other shit he pulled. Word is he's established a real close involuntary relationship with a guy named Leroy with a ten-inch dick. When Leroy gets bored with him, he loans him out to his buddies for a couple of packs of cigarettes. The way I hear it, Crawford's dance card's always full."

Kirby laughed and reached across the table to again shake Castanza's hand. "Thanks, Charlie. I owe you a big one."

"I just want you to know, none of us are proud of what that sleazeball did. Bass was a nice kid, from what Mahanes says, and Crawford fucked her over royally. Destroyed her life, her career, and forced her into being a whore for that fat, disgusting pig Calderon."

"I can see why her file's sealed."

"Yeah. Wasn't exactly one of our finer moments. But you got your share of scumbags on the Job and we got ours. Crawford was one of the worst." Castanza finished his beer and leaned across the table. "Mahanes asked me to ask you what Bass is doing now, and why you're looking for her."

Kirby told him. Castanza shook his head slowly as he listened.

"That's too bad, Jack. She can't seem to catch a break, can she?"

"Not lately."

On the drive back to Brooklyn, Kirby kept thinking of what had happened to Bass, how she had been betrayed and raped by her own government, by people she was supposed to be able to trust and turn to for help. If and when he found her, it would not be an easy task convincing her to testify against Genero. He would first have to convince her that although there would always be Crawfords in this world, there were also people still worthy of her trust, who did not see everyone who crossed their paths as pawns to be used in pursuit of their personal goals, or every relationship as an opportunity.

He desperately wanted to find Bass and bring her in—it was his job—and if he never accomplished anything else as a cop, he wanted to put Genero away for the rest of his life. But he now promised himself that in pursuit of that goal he would not use Bass as others had. He would do everything he could to make certain no further harm came to her as a result of anything he did.

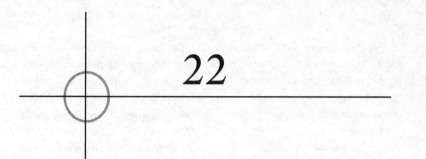

22

NICOLE BASS WAS too tense and anxious to sit and soak in a tub. She instead opted for a hot shower, letting the forceful stream of water massage her shoulders and the back of her neck, soothing her jangled nerves as the last of the adrenaline slowly worked its way out of her system. Her hair swathed in a towel, her body wrapped in the thick terry cloth robe provided by the hotel, she sat at the small desk across from the foot of the bed, a bottle of Perrier from the minibar in her hand as she turned on her notebook computer.

She inserted the disk found in Onorati's briefcase and brought up the directory. It listed only one file: ACCOUNTS.MO. She instructed the computer to copy the file to her word-processing software, then activated the program and accessed the file, filling the screen with its contents.

Bass sat staring at the five rows of three columns. The first column in each row contained a string of numbers separated by hyphens, which she soon realized were foreign telephone numbers preceded by their country codes. It was the country codes for the Netherlands Antilles (599) and Liechtenstein (41) that led her to the discovery. Among the numerous courses Bass had taken at New York University over the past eighteen months were an advanced course in computers and others in money management and international finance. With the further help and advice of Peter Bechtal, a wealthy investment banker she had met through the escort service, she deposited all of her money in two foreign banks. One in Liechtenstein and the other in the Netherlands Antilles, effectively putting the difficult-to-explain large amounts of cash she earned out of reach of the Internal Revenue Service and into low-risk investments with moderate growth.

She had a program on her computer, an address book/desktop dialer, that contained a listing of all of the world's country codes. She opened the program and found that one of the other country codes on the screen, used for two of the entries, was for the Cayman Islands, and the last one was for the Bahamas. She immediately suspected that the numbers following the country codes were telephone numbers for offshore banks, but the numbers for Liechtenstein and the Netherlands Antilles did not match the numbers for her banks in those countries.

Under the premise that the system used by her banks held true for others that specialized in no-questions-asked numbered accounts, she assumed that the telephone numbers would not respond to a voice call, only to electronic calls from computer modems, and were used specifically to access their main computers. And if she was correct, the second set of numbers in the columns were the codes to effect transfers that were to be entered once the connection was made. The third set of numbers she reasoned to be the access codes to the secret numbered accounts.

Bass closed her eyes and tried to recall the parts of the conversation between Onorati and Genero she had overheard, particularly after Michael had turned on his computer. She had heard only bits and pieces of the exchange: "I was going to give it back." "You've been skimming money for five years." "Fifteen to eighteen million." "It's all here." "I can put it back in the morning."

But hadn't she seen Onorati give the disk he took from his computer to Genero? She was certain she had. But if he hadn't? And this was the only record of the accounts and their access codes? Perhaps she had found a way out of this nightmare. Something with which to bargain. But wouldn't Genero have her killed anyway? She was still the only witness to the murder and would remain a threat to him as long as she was alive. But if he knew she was playing straight with him, returning the key to millions of dollars . . . ? That might convince him that she was sincere if she told him she would never testify against him.

Even better, she could tell him that she really hadn't seen anything. Only Michael lying dead on the floor as she ran out. That she had no idea who shot him or why. It was worth a try; not that she had a host of other choices unless she wanted to spend the rest of her life running and looking over her shoulder.

She looked at the numbers on the screen again and considered using her computer's internal modem to access the accounts and check the individual balances, to make certain she had something of value to Genero, something with which to bargain. But she reconsidered, wanting to talk to Peter Bechtal first, to be absolutely certain that the same procedures for her accounts applied to the accounts in these banks. Any mistake, any variation in the procedure, could trigger automatic alarms that would then lock her out of the computer and possibly alert the bank that the account security had been compromised, blocking further access until the bank could determine that the person trying to gain access was indeed the one authorized to do so. They were the security procedures her banks had assured her they followed.

She again called up the address book program on her computer and got Bechtal's telephone number. She reached him at his office.

"This is a pleasant surprise. And rather clairvoyant. I was just thinking about you."

"I need to see you, Peter. I need some advice."

"Anytime, Niki. You know that."

And she did. Bechtal, divorced from his second wife, had asked Bass to marry him at least four times in the fourteen months since they had met.

"Could you possibly meet with me this afternoon? I apologize for asking on such short notice, but I won't keep you long."

Bechtal didn't even bother checking his schedule for the remainder of the day. He would have his secretary cancel or postpone anything to be with Bass, no matter how short the encounter.

"Where and when?"

"In Bemelmans Bar at the Carlyle. As soon as you can get there."

Bechtal detected the note of urgency in her voice. "Are you alright?"

"I'm fine, Peter. I just need a little advice and counsel."

Bechtal looked at his watch. It was three-ten. "I can be there in twenty minutes."

"You're a dear. See you in twenty minutes."

Bass hung up and thought long and hard before following through on

the next stage of her rudimentary plan, finally deciding to jump in with
both feet. She recalled the *Post*'s article about Michael Onorati's murder
she had read that morning; it stated that Genero lived on Centre Island,
Long Island, near Oyster Bay. She called information and asked for his
telephone number, feeling fairly certain that it would be unlisted. Much
to her surprise it was not, and she dialed it. A gruff, no-nonsense voice
answered. Bass almost lost her nerve.

"Yeah?" was all the man said.

"I'd like to speak to Mr. Genero, please."

"Who's callin'?"

"Nicole Bass."

A brief silence was followed by "Yeah? Okay, you don't go nowhere.
I'll get him for ya. Right away."

Big Paulie ran from the kitchen wall phone to the study at the opposite end of the house. He stopped abruptly at the open door to the large
chestnut-paneled room and knocked on the doorframe. Genero, sitting at
his massive, ornately carved and inlaid desk, half-glasses perched on the
end of his nose, looked up from the financial report on his loan-sharking
operations he was reading and motioned for his driver to come in.

"You're not gonna believe this, boss. But unless somebody's playin'
some kinda stupid game, that broad's on the phone askin' for you."

"What broad?"

"That Bass broad. You know . . ."

Genero stared in disbelief. "You're shittin' me."

"No, boss. That's who she says she is."

Genero motioned for Big Paulie to leave, then glanced at the red light
glowing on the publicly listed line of the two-line telephone. He picked
up the handset and pressed the button for the active line.

"This is Vincent Genero. What can I do for you?"

Despite the fact that he was certain his telephone lines were not bugged,
he was taking no chances; whoever was on the other end of the line could
be setting him up.

"Do you know who I am, Mr. Genero?"

"Yeah. You said your name was Nicole Bass."

"Yes. But do you know who I am?"

"I heard your name before. What do you want?"

"I'd like to meet with you. I believe I have something of importance
to you."

"Yeah? What's that?"

"I don't think you want me to be specific on the telephone, but I will if you insist."

"No. That's okay. That won't be necessary. This got somethin' to do with business, right?"

"Yes. Something that belonged to a former associate of yours. I thought we might be able to make an arrangement. I'll give you what I have, and then I'll go away. You'll never have any reason to worry about me again, nor will I have to worry about you. Is that possible, Mr. Genero?"

"Anything's possible. But you're right. We should meet. I'll send somebody over to pick you up, bring you out to my house where we can talk private. Where are you?"

"Please, Mr. Genero. I'm not stupid, and if you continue to insult my intelligence, this conversation is over."

"No problem. What did you have in mind?"

Bass hesitated, staring out of the tenth-floor window of the corner hotel room. One block west she could see the intersection of Seventy-sixth Street and Fifth Avenue and Central Park beyond. The heart of the Spanish Columbus Day parade had now reached the Upper East Side, and she could hear the muffled sound of the music and caught glimpses of the colorfully costumed marchers passing by. There was a reviewing stand directly across from where Seventy-sixth Street intersected Fifth Avenue, on the park side, and the sidewalks were lined with onlookers and police standing behind barricades barring entrance to all vehicular traffic. Bass wanted to meet someplace out in the open, in clear public view, and the park would be perfect with the spillover crowd from the parade and the cops within shouting distance.

"I'll meet you in Central Park. At the Conservatory Water."

"Where's that?"

"Between East Seventy-third and Seventy-fifth Streets. It's a pond where they sail model boats."

"Oh, yeah. I took my kid there once. What time you wanna meet?"

Bass thought for a moment. Her meeting with Peter Bechtal would take no more than thirty minutes. "In an hour."

"I could be there then."

"I'll look forward to our conversation, Mr. Genero."

Genero hung up and thought for a moment. He allowed himself a small smile. *So the broad does have the disk. I'll give her a conversa-*

tion. Smart-mouth bitch. And I ain't goin' nowhere near her. Could be a
setup. Cops could have gotten to her. And meetin' with her could add
weight to whatever story she told them. I got people to handle these
kinds of situations. What I pay them for. He picked up the phone and
called Carmine Molino.

Bass sat staring unseeing out the hotel window, wondering if what she
was doing had any chance of working. She knew now that the disk was
of value to Genero; he knew precisely what she was talking about. But
how valuable? She would access the accounts after talking to Peter. She
looked at her watch. It was three-fifteen. She called the concierge's desk
in the lobby of the hotel and asked what time the parade would end. The
concierge told her it was scheduled to be over no later than five o'clock
but it would probably be closer to five-thirty before the last marchers
finished and the crowd dispersed. Which told Bass that the police and
the crowd would still be around when she met with Genero. Safety in
numbers, she thought.

She took a blank disk from a compartment of her computer case, removed Onorati's disk from the computer, and inserted the blank one.
She used a sheet of hotel stationery to write down all of the numbers in
the order in which they appeared on the screen, then closed the file,
copied its contents onto the blank disk, and deleted the file from the
computer's hard drive. She next slipped the original disk into her shoulder bag, along with the sheet of stationery containing the handwritten
numbers, then zipped the copy she made of the disk into an inside
pocket of her carry-on bag.

Deciding that the wig she had worn was no longer necessary, she
tossed it into her carry-on and blow-dried and brushed out her hair. She
wore the same clothes she had worn earlier and, before leaving the room,
remembered to take the spare magazine for her pistol from her shoulder
bag and replace the near-empty one, giving her another seven rounds of
ammunition.

She stopped on her way out the door and stared at herself in the mirror over the dresser. Despite the inner turmoil, she looked calm and in
control. "I hope the hell you know what you're doing," she said to the
image before her, then tucked the pistol into her waistband at the front
of her jeans, buttoned her blazer to hide it, and left the room.

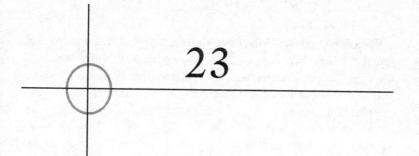

23

NINO TOTANI HAD returned to the Gambino Family social club in the Bensonhurst section of Brooklyn to organize and oversee the search for Nicole Bass. He first put a Family contact with the airlines to work, to find out if Bass had made reservations on a flight out of the city. After getting Molino's approval to use more men, he sent two of his crew to watch the Port Authority Bus Terminal, and two each to watch the ticket counters for the trains at Grand Central and Penn Stations. It was all he could think of doing, and had told Molino so, adding, "Chances of spotting her aren't good, and if she's got a car stashed somewhere, or rents one, and drives out of the city, we're fucked."

Totani held out some hope that the cops might lead them to Bass, but so far the two men he had assigned to tail Jack Kirby were sitting in a car watching the entrance to Intelligence Division headquarters; their source had reported that he was in the OCMU squad room.

At three-twenty Carmine Molino called the Bensonhurst social club from a public phone and instructed Totani to call him back from a pay phone outside the club. Totani's relief at the news of Bass contacting Genero was clearly evident in his voice when he told Molino not to worry, he'd finish her off this time.

"No. Vinnie wants her alive. So you don't do nothin' to her except snatch her up and throw her in your trunk. Then you bring her to the ware-house."

"It could be a problem dragging her out of the park to wherever we leave the car."

"You don't grab her in the park. You don't go near her there. You just watch her. Make sure she don't have no cops backin' her up. Wait until she thinks nobody's gonna show, then when she leaves the park, you follow her and snatch her off the street."

"There's a parade going on. We might have to park on the West Side, and she might leave the park on the East Side."

"Hey, Nino! Fuckin' work it out! Put a car on the East Side and the West Side. I gotta fuckin' tell you everything. Those are Vinnie's instructions, he told me to tell you. So you do it like he says. And this time don't fuck it up."

Molino gave him the time and place for the meeting, and Totani returned to the club. He gathered five of his crew in the back room, Johnnie Socks and Tommy Falconetti among them.

"We're going into the city. The woman we're looking for called the boss to arrange a meeting in about an hour."

"Fuck she do that?" Johnnie Socks said. "She got a death wish?"

"How would I know?" Totani said. "Maybe she's going to beg for her life. Anyway, the boss isn't going to show, so we're supposed to grab her and bring her to the warehouse."

"Where's the meet?" It was Tommy Falconetti.

Totani gave him a hard look. "You don't need to know that right now, Tommy. All you do is take Jimmy and Sammy in your car. I'll take Johnnie and Tony with me. You follow me into the city. I'll have a plan worked out by the time we get there."

"My car's parked four blocks away at my apartment," Falconetti said. "I'll go get it, bring it around."

"Take Jimmy and Sammy with you. I'll be parked out front waiting."

Falconetti left, with Jimmy DiAmato and Sammy Casella in tow. Two blocks from the club Falconetti stopped in front of an Italian grocery he knew had a pay phone in the back. He told the two men where the car was parked and that he would meet them there.

"I wanna grab a couple packs of smokes."

Falconetti went to the front counter of the store and bought two packs of Winstons, then looked out the window to see DiAmato and Casella turn the corner. He walked quickly to the pay phone at the back of the store and dialed Jack Kirby's pager, punching in the number of the pay phone he was calling from and a two-letter code as soon as the pager beeped its ready signal.

. . .

Detective Joe Early of the 17th Precinct detective squad swung into immediate action after Kirby dropped off the snapshot of Nicole Bass. He rushed the picture to the photo unit at One Police Plaza and, with the importance of the search for Bass verified by the chief of detectives, had two hundred copies within thirty minutes. He then had uniforms from the 17th Precinct distribute the copies to the Port Authority police, who patrolled the bus station, and to the Metro North and Long Island Railroad police, whose domains were Grand Central Terminal and Penn Station, respectively.

When a check of the state motor vehicle records showed no vehicle registered to a Nicole Bass of New York City, additional photos were distributed to the outlets for all of the rental-car companies operating in Manhattan.

Early and his partner, Tommy O'Brien, reinforced by six detectives from the Borough Task Force, were now checking the larger hotels in Manhattan on the chance that Bass had decided to hole up somewhere rather than leave the city and would choose a place where she could get lost in the crowds of tourists. Certain she would not register under her own name, on advice from Kirby, the detectives checked under Martha Johnson, to no avail, and were now visiting each hotel, showing Bass's picture to the people working the reception desks and to hotel security. They explained that she might be wearing a blond wig, asked if anyone who looked like her had recently checked in, and if not to keep an eye out for her.

Kirby had returned to the OCMU squad room, where he enlisted the help of Janet Morris, the police administrative aide, to check the airlines, again to no avail. Rather than sit on his hands waiting for others to bring him information, Kirby decided to check out some of the smaller hotels on the Upper East Side himself, particularly those in the vicinity where the cab driver had dropped Bass off at Eighty-second and First and where she was last seen walking west. If she went as far as Park or Madison Avenues, being someone accustomed to the finer things in life, Kirby reasoned she might have checked into one of the small, exclusive hotels in that area, one with excellent security that would quickly challenge anyone who was not a guest. There were four hotels he could think of that fit the description. Two were on Madison Avenue only five or six blocks south of Eighty-second Street. The Mark and the Carlyle. And two on Park he would check out first.

He was driving across the Brooklyn Bridge, on his way to Manhattan, when his beeper sounded. The two-letter code after the telephone number on the display told him that the caller was Tommy Falconetti. He used his cellular phone to call him back, turning onto the FDR Drive as the call was answered on the first ring.

"Jack?" Falconetti's voice was tight.

"Yeah. What's up?"

"I got to make it fast. The witness called Genero to arrange a meet."

"What?" Kirby couldn't believe what he had just heard.

"You heard me right."

"Where's the meeting? When?"

"In about an hour. Somewhere in Manhattan. I don't know where. Nino got closemouthed all of a sudden. Me and two guys are supposed to follow him and two other guys from the crew into the city. He's gonna tell us the plan when we get there."

"This is crazy. Why the hell would she meet with Genero? He's not dumb enough to show. He'll just have her whacked on sight."

"No. Nino's orders are to snatch her and bring her to the warehouse in Brooklyn."

"Why?"

"Don't know that either."

"Which warehouse?"

"You know the one Genero runs his olive oil business out of?"

"Yeah."

"That one. Look, I gotta go. Nino's gonna wonder what's keepin' me. I get a chance I'll call you when I know when it's gonna happen."

"Listen, Tommy. If you can't get back to me, I want you to grab her yourself if you can. Bring her in."

"If I try that, there'll be gunplay, guaranteed. I'm probably gonna have to kill a couple of them, and the witness could get popped in the middle of it."

"Use your best judgment. If the opportunity presents itself, grab her. Don't worry if you have to blow any of that scum away. It'll be judged a righteous shoot, hands down."

"Okay. But I'll try and do it clean."

"And if you don't get the chance to get her away from them, just let it go down. I'll have the warehouse staked out long before they get her there. We'll take them when they show. Either way, Tommy, you're comin' in. Your undercover days are over."

"Like I said before, we get the witness in safe, I'm outta here, no argument. I think Nino's pretty much decided I'm a snitch anyway."

"Play it safe, Tommy. No Rambo bullshit. I want the witness, but not at any cost. So remember, if you can't pull her out from under their noses, let it slide. I'll have ESU sew that warehouse up tighter than a gnat's ass."

"No problem. By the way, what's her name and what does she look like? Nino's got a picture of her, but I didn't get a look at it yet."

"Tall, dark brown hair, could be wearing a blond wig. Long legs. And she's drop-dead gorgeous. Looks like a model; that's what she used to be. Her name's Nicole Bass, friends call her Niki."

"Okay. See you when I see you," and he hung up.

Kirby thought of returning to headquarters to organize the stakeout of the warehouse, but if Falconetti managed to call him with the meeting site, he wanted to be in Manhattan where he could respond quickly. As he continued north on FDR Drive, he called Tony Rizzo at OCMU and filled him in, requesting that he get an Emergency Services Unit team in position at the Brooklyn warehouse as soon as possible.

Kirby turned off the FDR Drive and headed west, then north on Park Avenue, toward one of the hotels he thought might be a possibility. Why the hell would she want to meet with Genero? It made no sense. They already tried to kill her, and now she thinks she can talk them out of it? Something wasn't right. He turned his portable radio to the frequency for the 19th Precinct, reasoning that since that was where Bass was last seen, she might have set the meeting for somewhere in the same precinct. If Falconetti had to take out any of the wise guys, the "shots fired" call would come on that frequency.

Kirby calculated he had four things working for him now, which made him feel a lot more positive than he had after the shoot-out on East Sixty-ninth Street. First, there was always an outside chance he might find Bass at one of the hotels before she went to the meeting with Genero. Failing that, Tommy Falconetti might get back to him with the meeting site and he could call in backup and surround the place. Or Falconetti could get her out of there himself and bring her in. And if none of that worked out, they would definitely be in a position to grab her at the warehouse in Brooklyn. At least her harebrained decision to meet with Genero had its positive aspects.

But then Murphy's Law could come into play, he thought as he ran a light and pulled a U-turn on Park Avenue after spotting the first hotel he planned to check out.

Tommy Falconetti slipped behind the wheel of his black Chevrolet Camaro and started the engine. Sammy Casella, sitting in the back, leaned forward.

"Gimme one of them smokes you got. I'm out."

Falconetti stiffened. In a hurry to get back to the car, he had left the cigarettes on the shelf below the pay phone. He patted the pockets of his leather jacket, then, feigning disbelief, threw up his hands.

"You believe this shit? I left them on the fuckin' counter."

"Yeah?" Casella said.

"Yeah. Must be losin' it."

"Comin' down with that old-timer's disease, I guess, huh?"

"Somethin' like that."

Casella sat back in his seat. "Better get that checked out right away. I heard you could die from that."

Falconetti forced a laugh and glanced at the rearview mirror. Casella sat with his massive arms folded across his chest, staring back. He wasn't smiling.

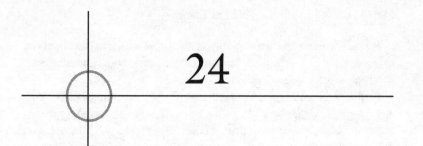

24

PETER BECHTAL, TALL, elegantly dressed in a charcoal-gray, chalk-striped Turnbull & Asher suit and carrying an English hand-tooled leather attaché case, was the picture of the patrician banker as he entered the quiet, softly lit bar off the Hotel Carlyle lobby. He spotted Nicole Bass sitting at a corner table to his right and flashed a warm, friendly smile as he crossed the room, bent down to kiss her on the cheek, and sat opposite her.

"It's good to see you, Niki."

"You, too, Peter. I apologize again for calling on such short notice."

"No apology necessary." He reached over and squeezed her hand. "You sounded a little distressed on the telephone. You're not in trouble, are you?"

"Nothing I can't handle."

"Whatever it is, you know I'm here for you."

A waiter approached and Bechtal ordered the same thing Bass was having, a glass of dry white wine. When the waiter retreated, Bass took the sheet of hotel stationery from her shoulder bag, unfolded it, handed it to Bechtal, and told him what she believed the numbers represented.

"Is there any way you can find out if the numbers following the country codes are for computers at banks in those countries?"

"Certainly." Bechtal opened his briefcase and removed a flip phone and dialed his office. He read the series of country codes and telephone numbers to his executive assistant and asked her to call him back as soon as she had the information.

He studied the list for a few moments, then gave it back to Bass. "If I had to hazard a guess, I'd say the other numbers are access codes and accounts."

"That was my guess, too."

Fourteen months ago, when Bass first learned about offshore banking and confidential numbered accounts, she had been fascinated by the intricacies and machinations of the process. She had heard of movie stars and supermodels who protected much of their wealth from the IRS, but until Peter Bechtal taught her the ins and outs of the arcane world of international finance, she would never have imagined she could do the things she now took for granted.

With his help and guidance, she had set up a corporation and a confidential numbered account in Liechtenstein, and then a separate identical account with a trust company in the Netherlands Antilles. Once a month she flew to Toronto and deposited her cash in one of the Liechtenstein bank's Canadian branches. She then controlled her newly created corporation through the trust company in the Netherlands Antilles, her identity protected by their impenetrable secrecy laws. The Caribbean branch of the Liechtenstein bank then "lent" her her own money, and if ever questioned about the source of her income, she could point to her loan from a respected international bank. With her banks having no branches in the United States, and unaccountable to U.S. tax laws, she had effectively sealed her finances from the prying eyes of the IRS.

The banks cared little or nothing about the source of her funds, or of any other clients' funds, drawing the line at accepting money from illegal sources that were patently obvious and tainted to the point of causing the bank embarrassment or legal problems if they were discovered and made public. The billions in drug money that moved through the financial world were more than welcome, providing the money was well laundered before it got to the bank. It had all been a fascinating education for Bass, and she had Peter Bechtal to thank for it.

The waiter returned with Bechtal's drink. He took a sip, then held Bass's gaze, his brow knit with concern.

"Whose accounts are they, Niki?"

"I'm not sure," she hedged. "But what I'd like to know is if I can access them to find out the balances."

Bechtal hesitated. "If the accounts aren't yours, you're talking about doing something illegal. I'm not being judgmental, but I can't advise you properly unless I know what I'm dealing with."

Bass gave him a reassuring smile. "I haven't done anything illegal."

Bechtal's portable telephone chirped and he answered it. He took a notepad and pen from his attaché case and wrote down the information given him.

"You were right," he said when he hung up. "The numbers are for computers at two banks in the Cayman Islands, and one each in Liechtenstein, the Bahamas, and the Netherlands Antilles." He read off the names for her. "They all specialize in the same type of accounts I recommended to you last year."

"Do you know if they operate under the same principles as my banks?"

"In what way?"

"If I use my computer modem to access the bank's computers and the accounts, can I issue instructions to transfer the balances to other accounts? In other banks?"

"Yes. Almost all offshore numbered accounts are set up in much the same manner. As far as the banks are concerned, whoever has the code numbers is the rightful owner of the accounts and they can be accessed in the same way as the ones I recommended for you."

"So by using the codes I have here, I can access the accounts and do whatever I want with whatever is in them."

"With only one caveat. If the accounts are set up with an additional identifier, perhaps a code word, that word would have to be entered after the numbered code before access to the accounts is granted."

"If that's the case, and I try to access them without the identifier or code word, what will happen?"

"You are automatically locked out of the computer at that point. With most security systems you would have a total of three attempts to enter the correct series of numbers and any additional identifier. If on the third try you do not get the codes or identifiers right, you would again be locked out and the computer would immediately notify the bank security that someone other than the authorized person may be trying to access the accounts. And something you will want to bear in mind: all of the banks on this list have security systems sophisticated enough to automatically trace the call."

"But assuming that all of the codes and identifiers are entered properly, and I instruct the bank's computer to transfer the balances to other accounts, will those transactions leave a trace that anyone can follow, other than the bank?"

"Niki, I don't like the direction in which this conversation is going."

"Please, Peter. I need to know."

"You've got to understand, if the accounts are not yours, and you happen to have gotten hold of someone else's codes, what you are talking about doing is highly illegal and violates at least six international banking laws that come immediately to mind, not to mention criminal statutes in the countries where the banks are located."

"Without going into things you really don't want to know about, I can assure you that no one is going to notify the authorities about my accessing these accounts. And I give you my word that you will in no way be involved. We never even talked about it."

"Don't mistake my concern for condemnation, Niki. I'm only worried that something will happen to you."

"I know that, Peter. And I appreciate your concern. But tell me, can the transactions be traced by anyone outside of the bank?"

"No. The same secrecy the bank applies to the ownership of the accounts is applied to any transactions carried on within those accounts. Any and all information about account activity is given only to the client. If for any reason that client has lost or otherwise cannot produce his or her code numbers, they must present themselves in person, with proper identification, to one of the bank's officials."

"And you're certain that as far as these particular banks are concerned, whoever has the proper codes is the rightful owner of the accounts."

"Yes. I'm more than familiar with these specific banks; I have current dealings with them on a weekly basis. And as with the banks I recommended to you, they issue stern warnings to their clients to keep their account codes in a safe place because possession of the codes is tantamount to ownership as far as they are concerned. It's the one risk you take when you opt for secrecy and the ability to bank electronically with them."

"Thank you, Peter. You've been a great help."

"Promise me you'll be careful about what you're doing."

"I promise."

Bechtal settled back in his chair and sipped some more of his wine. He looked at Bass with open adoration. He was a handsome man, aristocratic good looks, with salt-and-pepper hair and dark blue eyes with friendly crinkles at the corners. Twenty years older than she, keeping trim and physically fit made him look half the age difference. A kind and considerate person with the solid self-confidence and optimistic outlook on life that come with enormous wealth, Bass found him to be enjoyable company and comfortable to be with. He was hands down her favorite client.

"It was rather coincidental that you called when you did. I was just about to call Carolyn and arrange to see you. I have a wonderful idea. Seven days on my sailboat in the Caribbean. We can take the corporate jet down to St. Martin on Friday. My captain will meet us there, and we can sail over to St. Barts and then down to Antigua, or anywhere else you like."

Bass had been on Bechtal's eighty-foot luxury sailing yacht the previous winter and had enjoyed it immensely. But she had no intention of dragging him or anyone else into the middle of her current troubles.

"It sounds wonderful, Peter, but I can't just now. May I have a rain check for sometime next month?"

"Of course."

"And this trip won't be through the service. I'll accept the invitation as your friend."

"That's very thoughtful of you, Niki, but it isn't necessary."

"Yes it is. You've been good to me, and I appreciate it."

"I'll look forward to it. As a matter of fact, I'll count the minutes."

Bechtal stood when Bass got up from the table. She embraced him and kissed him on the cheek. "Thank you so much, Peter. I'll be in touch."

"If there's anything more I can do—"

"I know," Bass said. "All I need to do is call."

Bechtal lowered his voice and said, "If someone were to attempt to access those accounts illegally, they should not do it from a telephone that could lead Interpol or the FBI to their doorstep."

Bass smiled and squeezed his hand, releasing it as she walked away. Bechtal's adoring gaze followed her until she was through the door and into the hotel lobby.

Bass returned to her room, immediately turned on her notebook computer, and inserted the original disk from Michael Onorati's briefcase. She connected the telephone cord from the internal modem to the jack

on the wall behind the desk and brought up the communications program. Registered under a false name at the hotel, she was not worried
about the call being traced back to the room if things went wrong.

She entered the number for an outside line, and the first country code
and telephone number in the dial directory, and clicked on the DIAL button. Fifteen seconds later the computer at the Bahamian bank answered,
asking for the access code needed to proceed. Bass typed in the code
number and waited as the dark blue screen went blank with the exception of a red circle pulsating in the center.

Five seconds later she was past the first security stage, and the computer asked for further instructions. Bass typed in the code for the account number and held her breath. If a code word or further identifier
was needed, this is where she would run into the problem. Another five
seconds and Bass breathed a sigh of relief. She was in. The screen was
filled with a menu offering her a selection of options, two of which were
"Show Current Balance" and "Transfer Funds."

Bass chose the "Show Current Balance" option, and it quickly appeared in a small box at the bottom of the screen. She wrote it down, exited the accounts section, and disconnected from the bank's computer.
She repeated the procedure for the remaining three banks and four accounts, writing down the balances. When she finished, she sat staring at
the total amount in all five accounts scribbled on the paper before her:
$18,586,000.

There was now no doubt in her mind why Vincent Genero was so eager to get his hands on the codes. She definitely had something with
which to bargain.

She returned the disk to her shoulder bag and looked at her watch. It
was four-ten. She still had twenty minutes to get to the Conservatory
Water in Central Park, only a casual ten-minute stroll from the hotel.

Bass left the Carlyle by the Madison Avenue exit and walked the short
distance to the corner of Seventy-sixth Street, where she waited for the
crosswalk light at the busy intersection. Looking one block west, to
Fifth Avenue, along the eastern border of Central Park, she could see the
crowds lining the sidewalks and the parade proceeding noisily northward. The knot in her stomach tightened as she thought of the imminent
meeting with Genero. Ahead of her the lively beat of a Latin band fol-

lowed by a colorfully costumed line of marchers dancing up the avenue did nothing to ease the tension and soothe her jangled nerves.

The light changed, and as she crossed the intersection, she did not notice the unmarked police car that turned the corner off Madison onto Seventy-sixth and swung into the open parking space in front of the main entrance to the Carlyle. Nor did Jack Kirby see Bass step from the curb and start across the avenue not fifty feet from where he flashed his shield at the doorman, who was about to tell him to move the car as he gave the revolving door a shove and disappeared into the hotel lobby.

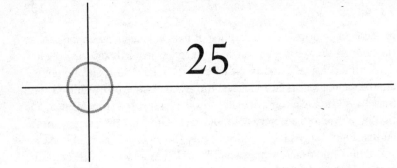

25

SHOULDERED TOGETHER ALONG Fifth Avenue and Central Park West as far as the eye can see, Manhattan's towering skyline rises dramatically above the trees just outside Central Park, a stunning backdrop to the fragile, peaceful setting. Surrounded by the frenetically paced city, contained within its muscular embrace, the 843-acre park is a pastoral retreat that soothes the harried urban soul with its miles of wooded footpaths, broad green meadows, mirrored lakes, and leafy dells. From inside looking out, it is the most flattering vantage point from which to view New York City; yet once deep inside the park, the city seems to vanish altogether, its sounds reduced to the soft whoosh of distant traffic and the footfalls of nearby joggers.

Most of the park's charms were lost on Nino Totani, who, when he thought about it at all, considered it nothing more than a huge public toilet for homeless wackos and winos, and a target-rich environment for rapists and muggers and every other sick, twisted motherfucker in a city with a never-ending supply of them.

He left his car on the East Side, just off Madison on Seventy-third, and ordered Tommy Falconetti to park on the West Side, one block off Central Park West. The six men then met near the Conservatory Water, where Totani assigned them observation posts with a commanding view of the model boat pond and the paths leading to it.

The area around the pond was crowded with people on benches and lounging on the grass, enjoying the golden warmth of the Indian summer day. Totani estimated their numbers at two hundred or more. Men

and women with their children, tired of the parade, some wearing colorful sweatshirts proudly proclaiming their nationality, or carrying tiny
flags representing the entire gamut of Hispanic countries, strolled
around the pond and in front of the model boat house and the small café.
Some stopped to buy ice cream and sit on the terrace to watch the
flotilla of remote-controlled model boats being maneuvered across
the sparkling water by their owners along the banks.

Tommy Falconetti sat on a grassy slope at the southeast corner of the
pond. His eyes moved constantly over the people seated or walking
about, and those approaching on the half-dozen footpaths leading into
the area. Having had no opportunity to call Jack Kirby with the location
of the meeting, his mind sorted through possible scenarios for getting
Nicole Bass safely out of the park by himself. He studied the faces of
the women walking alone, comparing them to the photo that Totani had
finally shown to those in the crew who had not yet seen it.

Bass waited at the corner of Seventy-sixth Street and Fifth Avenue for a
break in the parade's near-constant stream of bands and dancers and
marchers. She angled her way through the crush of onlookers at the
curb, who were swaying and rocking to the loud, lively rhythms of a
passing Brazilian band, until she spotted an opening and skipped across
the avenue to enter the park.

The meandering network of footpaths and trails tended to subvert
one's sense of direction, but this section of the park was familiar territory
for Bass—the mile-and-a-half track around the reservoir and then another three and a half miles through the paths below it were her alternate
routes for her morning run. One day the city streets, the next the park.

She walked south, along a wooded trail ablaze with autumn color and
dancing with dappled patches of late afternoon sun and shade. Skirting
the rocky, wooded thickets of the Ramble, she reached the Conservatory
Water and sat on a bench near the statue of Hans Christian Andersen, on
the opposite side of the pond from the model boat house and the Ice
Cream Café. She had ten minutes until the appointed time, and sat alternately scanning the approaching footpaths for any sign of Vincent Genero and watching a man sail a remote-controlled sailboat that reminded
her of Peter Bechtal's invitation.

She struggled to maintain her composure and sat patiently at first, going over and over in her mind what she would say, refining it until she felt it would not sound as though she was threatening him, something she felt certain the Mafia don would take a dim view of. She would make it a straight business proposition. His money for her life, and the promise that she would never testify against him. Insisting that she had not seen who shot Michael Onorati.

She decided to tell another lie: she would tell Genero that if she did not show up alive and well within one hour after the time set for their meeting, she had left instructions with a friend to transfer all of the money from Onorati's accounts into other banks where Genero would never find it. It was a safeguard she would have taken had she known anyone she trusted enough to carry it out. But she believed the bluff would have the desired effect. No one in their right mind would take the chance of losing eighteen million dollars; yet the inner voice of past experience countered that Genero damn well might if it came down to the money or spending the rest of his life in prison. He could always get more money. This was a man who killed people, or had people killed, as a way of resolving problems. And he had good reason to have her killed.

Her willpower and self-confidence were diminishing with each passing moment, and the longer she sat on the bench, her eyes constantly moving about the park, the more apprehensive she became. And as the time for the meeting drew near, every instinct told her to get up and get as far away from the area as she possibly could. To get out of the city immediately. To run and keep running and never look back. But she had had enough running and hiding and pretending to be someone other than who she was. And she had vowed never to put herself through that again. No matter the cost.

The first thoughts that went through Tommy Falconetti's mind when he saw Nicole Bass enter the area and walk around the model boat pond was that the photo he had seen did not do her justice. And that Jack Kirby had grossly understated how attractive she was; in his eyes, "drop-dead gorgeous" only began to describe her.

She had entered the Conservatory Water from the east side of the park, and Falconetti reasoned that with Fifth Avenue only a short distance away, rather than walk across almost the entire breadth of the park, she would leave the same way she had entered. He immediately checked the positions of the men with whom he would have to contend if he was somehow going to get Bass out of the park and into protective custody. Twenty-five yards to his left, leaning against a tree on a rise above the pond, almost directly behind where Bass was sitting, was Jimmy DiAmato. His assignment was to follow Bass if she headed west when she left the park. On his right, approximately thirty yards away, Johnnie Socks stood beside a bench where two paths intersected, looking like a demented, overgrown mugger waiting for his next victim. To Johnnie Socks's right, Tony Damiano sat on a bench overlooking the model boat house. Falconetti watched as he mouthed something to a bag lady who pulled her cart up and sat down beside him. The woman left in a hurry.

Nino Totani was at the opposite end of the pond, near the statue of Alice in Wonderland, far enough away that if Falconetti managed to get to Bass as soon as she got up to leave, he would not have to contend with him. If it came down to a shoot-out, of all the crew members surrounding the area, Totani was the man he wanted most to avoid. With the exception of Johnnie Socks, the others were merely muscle, who couldn't hit the broad side of a barn if they were inside it with the doors closed, let alone a moving target. He could handle Johnnie Socks, who was slow to react to any situation, but Totani was another story altogether.

How he had missed killing Bass outside of her apartment, Falconetti did not know, but he suspected it had something to do with Johnnie Socks screwing things up. One thing he did know: Totani would not hesitate to kill him if he thought he was helping Bass to escape, which did nothing to lessen the tightness in his chest and calm his jittery nerves as he focused his attention on Bass.

Falconetti decided that making his move as soon as Bass got up to leave would be the best tactic. But first, with only a matter of seconds to pull it off, he would somehow have to convince her that he was not a threat, and get her to come with him voluntarily, a major obstacle he had not yet worked out.

He watched as Bass kept checking the time and nervously glancing about the area, then got up and moved closer to where she was sitting.

Jack Kirby hoped against hope that Bass was still in her room at the Carlyle. After identifying himself to the assistant manager at the front desk and showing Bass's picture to him, he learned that she had registered under the name Catherine Adams and was in room 1009. The assistant manager rang the room, but no one answered, and Kirby was now on his way up in the elevator with one of the hotel's security guards—an ex-cop who retired five years ago after thirty years on the Job.

The security guard unlocked the door to the room with his pass key and let Kirby inside, going in with him as the assistant manager had instructed. A quick look through the open door to the bathroom to the right of the entryway, and a glance about the empty bedroom, told Kirby that he was too late. Whatever happened now was in the hands of Falconetti or the ESU team at the warehouse in Brooklyn. There was nothing more he could do at the moment, other than conduct a thorough search of her belongings, which, without a warrant or any probable cause, he did not want to do with the hotel security guard watching over him.

"You mind waiting outside the room?"

The ex-cop smiled, understanding what Kirby was going to do. "Sure. You got to use the bathroom, right?"

"Right. I won't be long."

"Take your time. Can't rush Mother Nature."

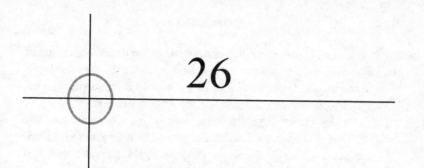

26

NICOLE BASS HAD been sitting on the bench at the model boat pond for thirty minutes. Twenty minutes past the time she had arranged to meet Vincent Genero. Her apprehension was gradually becoming a gnawing fear as she strongly suspected she had been set up. But she had considered that a possibility from the outset and had seen no signs of it. She stopped concentrating on only the people approaching her and began to look beyond the immediate area around the model boat pond and the paths leading to it where she had been watching for Genero to appear. She carefully studied the people sitting on the grass ahead of her and to her right, this time taking in the far perimeter, on top of the grassy slope where the woods closed in.

And then she saw him. Off in the distance, standing at the top of the slope beneath a large maple where two paths intersected, one foot propped on a park bench. The same no-neck monster who had fired into the back of the cab. He was staring at a young girl in a halter and shorts sitting on the grass not far from where he stood. Bass quickly looked away, before he realized she had seen and recognized him.

Bass felt her skin grow cold and clammy. Her heart raced and her breathing quickened. She cursed herself for not following her gut instincts to forget the meeting and run for her life. Genero never had any intention of showing up; he had sent his men instead. Probably to kidnap her and bring her to him. How could she have been so naive and stupid to believe he would strike a deal with her? But then she knew how; it was what she needed to believe would be the outcome, so she had allowed herself to believe it.

She carried on an inner dialogue as she tried to calm down and think clearly. Clear, decisive thinking. It was the only way out. Think your way through it. Don't panic. Panic and it's all over for you. They want you alive until they get the computer disk. That's your edge. If they simply wanted you dead, they would have killed you by now. Right out in the open. Just as they had tried on the street outside your apartment building.

Bass regained some of her composure and began looking carefully over the surrounding area, this time scrutinizing everyone she saw in a different light. The surveillance detection lessons she had learned, in what now seemed like another lifetime, came back to her. She watched for the small mistakes that gave away a careless or untrained surveillant.

Then she spotted another one. Sitting on a bench beneath a tree on the path leading down to the model boat house. He quickly looked away as her eyes passed over him. A dead giveaway. And then she saw another, on the grass to her right; the one with the black leather sport coat and orange silk shirt. Earlier she had seen him move closer to her, but had thought nothing of it, just one of the crowd enjoying a sunny October afternoon in the park. He was staring directly at her now.

Bass gave no indication she had seen any of them when she rose from the bench and looked at her watch, shaking her head as though angry that Genero was late. She began to walk slowly around the pond toward the model boat house and the café. She kept a casual pace and, reaching the other side, bought an ice-cream cone, a ploy she hoped would allay any of their suspicions about her moving to the other side of the pond, placing her close to the paths leading out of the park on the east side. Fifth Avenue, the parade, the attendant police, and the chance to get lost in the crowd were now only a short distance away. No more than one hundred yards through the woods.

She stood on the terrace in front of the café pretending to be looking for Genero, all the while checking the locations of the men she had spotted and trying to determine how many more of them were watching her, and where they were. She looked casually about, but could not spot anyone else. She felt certain that if there were three of them at her end of the pond, there were probably an equal number at the opposite end, and running in that direction, away from the ones closest to her, would only give the others more time to respond.

Her best course, she decided, was between the no-neck hulk and the man sitting on the bench. One of the paths to her left cut through the woods at almost an equal distance between them. She had used it often near the end of her runs through the park and knew it led directly to Fifth Avenue at Seventy-second Street.

She noticed that No-Neck was still preoccupied with the young girl and had not moved from where she first saw him. The man on the bench was still there, feigning disinterest. But the younger one in the orange shirt, the one who sat on the grassy slope and had moved closer to her, had moved again. This time in the direction of where she now stood. Still making eye contact. He was either very stupid and very bad at his job, or smarter than the others and suspected what was on her mind and didn't care if she knew it.

Running to the first cop she saw was an option, but one she immediately dismissed as visions of all that it would eventually mean flashed through her mind. Protective custody. Court appearances. And when they were through with her, they would go on with their lives and she would spend the rest of hers looking over her shoulder and wondering when the mob would exact its retribution for her testifying against one of their own. No. That was one road she would not travel again.

If she disappeared on her own, the end result would still be the same, but at least without the boring inconvenience of being locked up in a hotel room for months on end, waiting for trial appearances, with a bunch of cops guarding her, who might or might not succeed in keeping her alive. First she had to get out of her present situation, then make the hard decisions she had been avoiding until now.

She left the terrace at the Ice Cream Café and strolled slowly along the edge of the water until she was directly opposite the path she had chosen. She made one last check on the men she had identified—they were still holding their positions, with the exception of the one in the orange shirt, who was now pacing her as she moved.

She turned and walked closer to the entrance to the path, then paused and took a deep breath, briefly closing her eyes to mentally prepare herself for what was to come. Hugging her shoulder bag to her side, she dropped her ice-cream cone and broke into an all-out run.

She sprinted up the path, dodging and weaving through the people ahead of her, veering off onto the grass to avoid a man in a wheelchair, then glancing over her shoulder as she ran back onto the hard surface.

The man in the orange shirt was cutting through the woods. He was fast, matching her stride for stride, gaining on her due to the angle of his approach. But at the speed she was running, he would not overtake her before she was out of the park.

She looked behind her and saw No-Neck huffing and puffing as he lumbered up the path, shoving people out of his way. At least forty yards back, he was too slow to be an immediate threat.

Bass's legs were strong, her breathing deep and even, not labored. Each morning she ended her five-mile run with a hundred-yard flat-out sprint, and she was nowhere near the limits of her endurance as the path rose toward the opening in the sandstone wall enclosing the park and the sounds of the parade and the crowd grew louder.

Tommy Falconetti briefly lost sight of Bass as she gained the top of the path and ran out of the park to the sidewalk along Fifth Avenue. He saw her again as he crashed through some shrubs and vaulted the wall without breaking stride. She was darting across the avenue through a group of brightly costumed samba dancers, who followed a flatbed truck carrying a Latin band complete with amplifiers and massive speakers that sent the music out over the crowd at a volume that drowned out all other sounds. A mariachi band marching ahead of the truck added to the blaring cacophony, competing for attention with the musicians on the flatbed.

There were no cops at the intersection at Seventy-third Street. A few stood in front of the barricades one block north, and another group stood talking to a mounted patrolman midway down the block in the other direction. None of them were aware of the chase.

Falconetti saw Bass look frantically over her shoulder as she ran. Their eyes met for an instant, just as she reached the opposite sidewalk where, amid angry faces and shouted protests unheard above the music, she shoved her way through the onlookers lined up six deep at the curb and continued running down Seventy-third Street.

It was then that Falconetti saw Tony Damiano run out of the park twenty yards to his left and bolt across the avenue straight through the middle of the mariachi band ahead of the flatbed truck. He had seen Bass and, upon reaching the other side of the avenue, began to gain on her.

Falconetti ran across the street, heedless of the samba dancers, who were now swaying and dancing in place as the flatbed stopped to accommodate a slowdown up ahead. He shoved them roughly aside, knocking one couple down in an attempt to get to Bass before Damiano did.

Totani, Casella, and DiAmato, positioned farther away from where Bass made her break at the pond, were nowhere in sight. And Johnnie Socks, just reaching the exit from the park, was so out of breath he was barely able to walk.

Bass had now been running flat out for over three hundred yards. She felt her legs tiring. Her thighs burning. Her breath growing short and raspy. She couldn't run at this pace much longer. She had to find someplace to hide. The block had no shops or restaurants, and screaming for help would have been useless with the blaring music and the inclination of most New Yorkers to run away from someone in trouble rather than toward them. The crowd thinned out on the narrow cross street, consisting of a few vendors closing up their carts for the day and a steady stream of widely spaced parade watchers heading home.

If she could reach Madison Avenue before they caught up to her, there were any number of shops and restaurants she could duck into. But what would prevent them from coming in and dragging her out, or simply killing her when they realized that was their only option?

Bass again looked over her shoulder and caught a brief glimpse of the man she had seen sitting on the bench, followed by the man in the orange shirt. They were just rounding the corner onto Seventy-third Street and hadn't seen her yet.

She was at mid-block when she looked to her left and saw a wrought-iron gate open to an alleyway between two apartment buildings. In a moment of careless impulse she quickly ducked into it, immediately realizing her mistake. The alleyway dead-ended at the back of another building not sixty feet away. She stopped halfway into the narrow, deeply shadowed passageway. She was walled in with only one way out, and had given up too much ground to run back out to the street. Her heart sank, her spirit accepting defeat.

And then her thoughts were filled with an incongruous split-second flashback to an evening long ago, in the failing light, when her horse had spooked and galloped wildly out of control into a steep-walled, dead-end hollow in the east Tennessee mountains. The horse had thrown her as he reared and ran back out of the hollow, leaving her with a sprained ankle, stranded miles from home in the rough, mountainous country. But she had toughed it out. Frightened and in pain, she had limped home through the pitch-black night.

She shook off the errant memory as she saw the door at the rear of the building on her left. A collection of trash cans were lined up against one wall and she ran past them to the door. She pulled the handle with all her strength. It was locked and wouldn't budge.

Damiano had slowed to a jog when he lost sight of Bass. He was watching both sides of the street when he came abreast of the alleyway and saw her at the far end, struggling with the door. He paused and smiled, then walked through the open gate, stopping fifteen feet from where Bass stood, still tugging at the door, unaware of him. He pulled his pistol from the shoulder holster beneath his coat.

Bass sensed Damiano's presence and looked to her left. Her eyes locked on the pistol in his hand. She took a deep breath of resignation. She was still facing the door, and Damiano could not see her right hand as she slipped it inside the waistband at the front of her jeans and placed it around the grip of her pistol.

"Fun's over," Damiano said. "Time to give it up and come along like a good little girl." Winded from the chase, he was breathing heavily, barely getting the words out. "Boss just wants to talk to you on his own turf. No big thing. So let's go."

Bass, still standing at an angle to him, the front of her blazer hanging open and hiding what she was doing, withdrew the pistol and held it out of sight, along the side of her leg. She said nothing, her eyes now looking past Damiano to Falconetti as he entered the alleyway.

"You wanna do this the hard way?" Damiano said. "I could knock you out. Then carry you like you was sick or somethin'. Nobody'd say shit about it."

Falconetti came up behind him, causing him to spin around in surprise. In the brief moment it took for Damiano to return his attention to Bass, she had turned to face him and brought her gun up in a two-handed grip, aimed at his head. Her hands were rock steady, her eyes hard and unyielding, revealing none of the raw fear coursing through her body and causing her heart to race.

"Back off!" she shouted. "Both of you. Stand against the wall with your hands behind your heads."

Damiano grinned. "Ain't gonna happen, lady." His gun was at his side. Pointing at the ground.

Falconetti stepped forward, positioning himself between Bass and Damiano. Bass quickly trained the gun on him.

"Go get Nino," Falconetti said to Damiano. "I'll keep her here until you bring the car around."

"You get Nino. I'll watch the broad."

Bass kept the gun on Falconetti. "Get out of my way!" she shouted, her voice strong and forceful. "Back against the wall until I get past you."

Neither man moved.

"Don't press your luck. I'll shoot both of you if I have to."

Falconetti was blocking Bass's view of Damiano, who took advantage of the moment to step to the side and bring his gun up to point it at Bass. He never got the chance.

Bass fired without hesitation the moment she saw Damiano's gun hand move. The bullet struck an inch above his left eye. His body shuddered for a brief moment, his eyes went wide and blank, then he toppled forward on his face, dead before he hit the ground. Bass instantly trained the gun on Falconetti, who threw up his hands just as quickly.

The gunshot had echoed loudly off the walls of the surrounding buildings, but contained and channeled upward by the twenty-story concrete walls on three sides of the narrow alleyway, it attracted no attention from the street, where the music from the parade was still the dominant sound.

Falconetti took a step forward. "I want you to listen to me. We don't have much time. I'm a cop. And I've got to get you out of here before the others find us."

"And I'm Mother Teresa." She motioned with the barrel of the gun for him to step aside. "I'm not going to tell you again. Get out of my way."

"Look, I really am a cop. I can help you. Take you into protective custody. But we've got to get out of here right now."

Bass, rattled, unnerved after shooting Damiano at point-blank range, and near the end of her ability to continue, thought she saw something in Falconetti's eyes. "Show me some identification."

"I'm an undercover. I don't carry any ID with me."

"Right. Get out of my goddamn way! Now!"

Bass started to move around him, keeping the gun aimed at his head.

Falconetti made no attempt to stop her, having no doubt she would shoot him without pause as she had Damiano.

"Hey, Nicole. Niki. I swear, I am a cop. You've got to let me get you somewhere safe. They're gonna keep coming after you until they get you. We can protect you."

He took a step toward her and saw her increase pressure on the trigger. The hammer was already cocked, and it wouldn't take much more for the gun to fire. He backed off immediately.

"Give me your gun," Bass said. "Take it out with just your thumb and index finger on the grip." Her eyes kept flicking to her right, to the sidewalk at the end of the alley, watching for anyone else who had been with them in the park.

"Niki, I swear—"

"Do it! Now!"

Falconetti complied, slipping the 9-millimeter semiautomatic pistol from the shoulder holster under his left arm and laying it on the ground at Bass's feet before he stepped back.

Bass dropped to one knee and, keeping her gun trained on Falconetti, expertly one-handed his pistol, released the magazine, put it in her pocket, then tossed the gun behind the garbage cans. She next picked up Damiano's gun, pocketed the magazine, then kicked it, sending it skittering across the concrete into a corner at the end of the alleyway.

"Now get out of my way or you're going to end up like your friend."

"Okay. Okay. You don't have to believe me. But when you're tired of running, you call Jack Kirby at the Intelligence Division. He'll help you."

Bass recalled the name from her answering unit but said nothing.

Falconetti looked down the alley toward the street. "You better get out of here fast. There's four more on the way."

Bass sidestepped past him and ran from the alley, tossing the magazines from the pistols behind her as she disappeared around the corner. Falconetti retrieved his gun and magazine and took off after her, trying to keep her in sight. As he reached the sidewalk, he all but ran into Johnnie Socks and Nino Totani, with Casella and DiAmato coming up fast behind them.

The three men had regrouped with Johnnie Socks at the exit from the park. They were held up by a mounted patrolman, who blocked them from crossing the street as a dozen Argentinean gauchos, their horses prancing proudly, passed in review, followed by a slow-moving clean-up crew and a seemingly endless group of schoolchildren carrying tiny Puerto Rican flags.

"Where is she?" Totani demanded.

He looked around Falconetti, into the alley, and saw Damiano on the ground, his damaged head in a pool of blood.

"What the fuck happened?"

"Tony D. caught up to her first. She shot him just as I got here."

"And you let her get away?"

"Hey, Nino! She had a fuckin' gun pointed at my head."

"Which way'd she go?"

Falconetti pointed east toward Madison Avenue. Bass was nowhere in sight.

"You goddamn pussy," Totani said. They had lost her and he knew it. "You let a broad bluff you out."

Falconetti held his ground. He gestured toward Damiano's body. "That look like a fuckin' bluff to you? Huh? Try wakin' him up. And like you did a whole hell of a lot better against her this afternoon?"

Totani's eyes went cold. His face a stone mask.

"Shit happens," Falconetti said.

"Yeah, Tommy. Especially when you're around."

"Don't try to lay this off on me, Nino. Not my plan. Not my fault. You wanna blame somebody, blame this stupid fuck." He jerked his thumb at Johnnie Socks.

"Hey, fuck you, Tommy. I didn't do nothin'."

"You spooked her. You fuckin' imbecile. Standin' out in the open to get a crotch shot of some broad layin' on the grass. She saw your fat ass and remembered who you were."

"Shut the fuck up!"

"Both of you shut up," Totani said. "We gotta get out of here. The cops find us anywhere near Tony, they'll think we whacked him. Get the cars and we'll meet back at the club. I can't wait to hear what Carmine says about this cluster fuck."

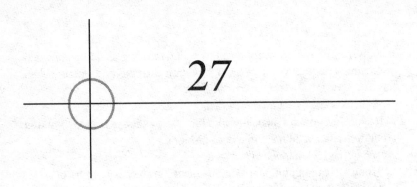

27

THE ASSISTANT MANAGER at the Hotel Carlyle handed Jack Kirby the information he had requested: a printout of the telephone calls made from Bass's room. Kirby recognized the number for Genero's Centre Island home, and was puzzling over the five international calls when his pager beeped. He looked at the display and did not recognize the call-back number. Thinking that it might be Tommy Falconetti, he immediately left the lobby to return the call from his car.

Nicole Bass stood territorially in front of one of the pay phones outside the ladies' room on the lower level of Barneys clothing store on Madison Avenue. She was badly shaken, the aftereffects of shooting Damiano and of running for her life and barely escaping twice within the past four hours. The tremors started in her hands, then spread until her teeth chattered and her entire upper body shook uncontrollably. Her skin felt cold to the touch, yet her forehead was damp with perspiration.

She knew the stress was getting to her. She could not keep running without a plan, waiting until the next crisis to take whatever action occurred to her on the spur of the moment. She doubted she could survive another confrontation. She needed time. A respite from constantly looking over her shoulder. Time to think things through, to put things in the proper perspective and to distance herself from the near-constant state of anxiety.

In her haste to get out of her apartment that afternoon, she had left things behind; things from her past that she would need if she was going to get away without leaving a computer and paper trail that even a rank amateur could follow. Unwilling to take the risk of returning to get them now, feeling certain someone would have the building under surveillance, she reluctantly accepted the cops as her only way out alive, at least until she had a well-thought-out plan in place. Cooperating with the police for the moment had definite benefits. She would use them as others like them had used her. Turnabout was fair play, and right now they could provide the security and breathing space she desperately needed.

Bass snatched the phone off the hook the second it rang. She tried to calm herself and speak in the steady voice of someone who was still in control, but she did not quite pull it off.

"Jack Kirby?"

"Yeah. Who's this?"

"Nicole Bass. You're the detective who called my apartment and left the message for me earlier this afternoon?"

"That's me."

"I need your help. Some people are trying to kill me."

"Yeah, well I told you that was going to happen. You okay?"

"I've been better."

Kirby was about to ask if Tommy Falconetti was there, then realized that if Falconetti hadn't identified himself to her, mentioning his name would be a serious mistake in the event Genero's people got to her before he did.

"Where are you? I'll come and get you right now."

Bass hesitated. His voice sounded friendly and full of self-confidence. Reassuring. But she was taking no chances.

"No. So far you're just a name and a voice on the telephone to me. You could be anyone; one of them. I'll meet you somewhere."

"Okay. Your rules. Just tell me where and when."

Bass thought for a moment. "Do you know where the Promenade is in Brooklyn Heights?"

"Yeah. I'm familiar with it."

The location was three blocks from Intelligence Division headquarters. Kirby sometimes walked there to eat his lunch and enjoy the spectacular view of lower Manhattan across the river. But he didn't tell Bass that for fear she would change her mind and spoil a perfect opportunity to secure the area before either of them got there.

"You want to meet there?"

"Yes. Near the park at Pierrepont Place."

"When?"

"I can be there in about forty-five minutes."

"So can I. And if you're worried about my not being who I say I am, call the Intelligence Division, OCMU. Ask for Lieutenant Tony Rizzo. He's my boss and he knows all about this. Okay?"

"I might do that." Bass had intended to do precisely that as soon as she hung up, but with Kirby encouraging her to do so, she now thought it unnecessary. She considered changing her mind about the location for the meeting, and to simply have him pick her up in front of Barneys. But she did not know what he looked like, and still preferred a meeting where she could observe him before she made her approach.

"I don't have to tell you how serious these people are who've been chasing you, so don't jerk me around on this. Be there."

"I will."

Kirby sped across the Upper East Side toward the FDR Drive, sounding the siren liberally as he ran lights and cut in and out of the rush-hour traffic. He used his cellular phone to call Rizzo as he drove.

"Where are you?"

"On my way to Brooklyn. Bass is coming in. She set up a meet on the Promenade."

"When?"

Kirby looked at the dashboard clock. "Thirty-five minutes. She's probably on her way there now. My guess is by cab."

"I'll get some people in place to secure the area."

"I thought you might wanna do that. Tell them to stay well out of sight. She's not too sure about me, so anything's liable to spook her."

"No problem."

"Did she call you to check me out?"

"No. Isn't Falconetti with her?"

"I didn't ask, but I don't think so. He would have made the call."

"As soon as we have the witness in protective custody, I'm sending some people to snatch him up."

"I told him we were bringing him in when this was over; he's expecting it."

"Good work, Jack. Now let's get Ms. Bass in from the cold and put that son of a bitch Genero away until his teeth fall out."

"From your mouth to God's ear," Kirby said as he came down the access ramp onto the FDR Drive. In the background he heard Rizzo talking to someone else who stepped into his office.

"Jack?"

"Yeah. Still here, Lou."

"We just got a call from a detective from the Nineteenth squad. Somebody whacked Tony Damiano. They found him lying in an alley off Fifth Avenue on Seventy-third Street. Back of his head blown out."

Kirby thought for a moment, then: "Could have been Tommy, helping Bass get away. We'll find out when we bring her in."

"Yeah. But didn't that task force detective tell you Bass held her own in the shoot-out with Johnnie Socks and Totani? Maybe *she* took Damiano out."

"Maybe."

"Approach her with caution, Jack. I mean, other than she's a high-class hooker and that the DEA screwed her over, what do we know about her? Not enough to know what we're dealing with yet. And she's proven she's not hesitant about using a gun."

"Okay. I'll keep it in mind."

At that moment Kirby saw a black Cadillac looming large in his rearview mirror. It had swerved across two lanes of traffic to get behind him.

The driver, not realizing Kirby had pulled into a slower lane while talking on the phone, thought he was getting ready to get off the Drive. He tried to cover for his mistake and backed off, but not before Kirby recognized him and the man beside him in the front passenger seat as two of Nino Totani's soldiers.

"Hey, Lou. I'm going to take a little detour."

"What's up?"

"Totani's got a tail on me. I don't want them following me to Brooklyn. I'm getting off the FDR at Fifty-third. I'll pull over to the curb at Second Avenue. Give Central a call and have the dispatcher send a radio car from the Seventeenth to intercept these guys and get them off my ass."

"Gimme a description."

"Black ninety-six Cadillac Seville. Driver's Tootie Tomisello; passenger's Joey Arena."

"I'll take care of it. Stay on the line."

Tomisello pulled into the curb on East Fifty-third Street, halfway down the block from where Kirby stopped just short of Second Avenue. He put down the window and craned his neck to see if Kirby was getting out of the car, saw him with the phone to his ear, and sat back to wait until he began to move again.

Three minutes later a blue-and-white swung in at an angle in front of the Cadillac, blocking it from pulling out. Tomisello swore an oath, realizing he had been made. Kirby drove away, heading south on Second Avenue, as the two uniforms climbed out of their radio car and motioned for Tomisello and Arena to get out of the Cadillac.

Tommy Falconetti sat at a table in the front room of the Bensonhurst social club, drinking an espresso and flipping through an old issue of *GQ* magazine that belonged to Nino Totani. He had twice tried to make an excuse to leave the club, to call Kirby and fill him in on what had happened with Bass, but Johnnie Socks had told him to stick around, Nino wanted to talk to him. He looked up when the door to the back room opened and saw Johnnie Socks motion to him.

"Hey, Tommy. Nino wants to see ya now."

Falconetti got up from the table and entered the room Totani used as an office. Johnnie Socks closed the door as Falconetti walked over to where Totani sat behind a beat-up oak desk, his elbows perched on the arms of a swivel chair, his fingers steepled beneath his chin.

"Yeah, what is it?"

"I just wanted to clear a couple things up."

"Like what?"

"Like Sammy tells me you stopped to get some cigarettes in old man Augelli's store, but you didn't have any when you got to the car."

"So what? I forgot them."

"Yeah? You forgot them, but that's the only thing you went in there for. Right?"

"Right. I was in a hurry to get to the car; you were waitin' on us."

"That's funny, because I checked with old man Augelli. He has glasses like the bottom of Coke bottles, but he doesn't miss much, ya know?"

Falconetti shifted his weight and looked over his shoulder to see Johnnie Socks positioned between him and the door to the front room, glowering at him.

"So what's the big deal?"

"The big deal is the old man says you went in the back and made a phone call, then hung up right away. Then like maybe a minute later somebody calls you back. What was that about?"

Falconetti thought fast, making it up as he went along, hoping he was showing none of the fear that was tying his stomach in knots.

"Hey, Nino, if ya gotta know, I was callin' my girl. We were gonna get it on this afternoon, then you say we gotta go into the city. So I called to tell her I couldn't make it. She's got call waiting and was talkin' to somebody. Said she'd call me right back."

"Yeah? That was who you called? Angela?"

"Yeah, Angie. I gotta tell you everything I do?"

"You called her where? At home?"

"Yeah, at home."

The look on Totani's face told Falconetti he had made a serious mistake. Totani knew he was lying. He had set him up perfectly.

Totani smiled and nodded. "You're a lying fuck, Tommy. Angela was working this afternoon at the beauty parlor. She didn't get any call from you. I figured you might say that, or maybe say you called Pete the Bank to place a bet on the ponies, so I checked with both of them."

"Hey, Nino. What's goin' on here?" But Falconetti knew what was coming next, and the look in Totani's eyes told him he was not going to be able to bluff his way out of it.

"What's goin' on is you're a rat, Tommy. You ratted out that sweet deal we had going with the stolen cars. And today you tried to rat out the meeting with the broad. But this time you fucked up."

Falconetti did not hear Johnnie Socks move up behind him. He did hear the hammer of the gun being cocked close to his ear, and then felt the press of cold steel at the base of his skull.

Totani got up from behind the desk, pulled Falconetti's leather sport coat aside, and took his pistol out of the shoulder holster. With Nino's mind closed to all other avenues of appeal, Falconetti saw no point in continuing to deny the accusations.

"You got one other problem, Nino."

"No, Tommy, you're the only one here with a problem."

"I'm a cop. Or ain't you figured that out yet?"

"Yeah, I figured it. So what?"

"So what? So you gonna kill a cop?"

"Hey, Tommy. You know me. I'll kill anybody. Especially a rat-fuck cop."

Falconetti saw Totani nod briefly to Johnnie Socks, who still stood behind him, holding the tip of the silencer to the back of his head. Falconetti closed his eyes, waiting for the gunshot he knew he would never hear before it killed him.

"Open your eyes, Tommy. It isn't over yet. You think I'm gonna have Johnnie double-tap you in the back of the head, don't you?"

Falconetti opened his eyes, half-believing he was getting a last-second reprieve.

"You're wrong. That would be too easy. And I don't like you that much."

Falconetti saw a brief flash of the wire loop that passed in front of his face. He felt a sudden tightness around his neck, his breath cut off in an instant as Johnnie Socks gripped the ends of the braided-wire garrote in both hands, pulling with all of his considerable strength in opposing directions.

Falconetti scratched and clawed at his neck, desperately trying to grab the wire as it cut deep into his skin. Johnnie Socks kicked him in the back of the knee, knocking him off balance, then supported his weight on his massive chest as he choked the life out of him.

Falconetti's eyes bulged. His face turned red. His legs kicked and flailed as he fought to gain his balance and free himself. But Johnnie Socks was too strong and expert at his task. It ended with a terrible guttural gasping sound as Falconetti's body went limp. Johnnie Socks loosened his grip and let the lifeless body drop to the floor.

"Throw that piece of cop shit in the river," Totani said, stepping over Falconetti's body as he left the room.

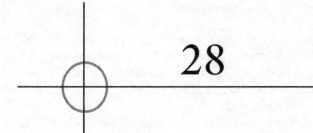

28

REMOVED FROM THE crowds and the hectic pace of Manhattan, yet only minutes from Wall Street by subway, the historic Brooklyn Heights neighborhood of elegant old brownstones with their wrought-iron flourishes and stained-glass windows looked much the same as it did at the turn of the century. Nicole Bass was familiar with the area, having visited Peter Bechtal's town house hideaway only three blocks from where she got out of the taxi and walked along a quiet tree-lined street.

She had regained some of her composure by the time she turned right at Pierrepont Street and continued past the tiny park and playground at the entrance to the Promenade. She paid no attention to the couple sitting holding hands on one of the benches where the sidewalk opened to the broad walkway along the banks of the East River. And she took no special note of the man who whizzed by on Rollerblades who heard, through the headset he was wearing, the voice of the woman holding hands on the bench alerting him that the subject of their surveillance had just arrived.

The last traces of the late afternoon sun disappeared below the horizon as Bass stopped for a moment to look out across the river at the magnificent panoramic view before her. To her right the Brooklyn Bridge soared majestically overhead, and directly across the river, backlit by a darkening burnt-orange sky, the lights in the skyscrapers of lower Manhattan twinkled on. Within the hour, as night settled over the city, the world's most spectacular skyline would sparkle in its full glory.

The dramatic beauty of the setting was lost on Bass as she began walking along the railing, watching the dozen or so people seated on the benches and strolling along the Promenade. She returned the smile of a man walking a well-behaved Doberman, unaware of the molded ear-piece the man was wearing or the thin wire hidden by his long hair as it fed into the collar of his jacket.

The sight of another couple, locked in a lovers' embrace as they stood at the railing looking out across the river, reminded Bass of the things missing in her life and brought a brief, wistful smile. She did not see the woman cast a sideways glance in her direction as she stood on her toes to gently kiss her companion's forehead, nor did she see her whisper into the microphone hidden in the sleeve of her coat as she watched Bass turn and walk back in the direction of the park.

Bass looked at her watch for the fifth time in as many minutes. Less than fifteen minutes had passed since she arrived at the Promenade, but she was growing increasingly nervous as she paced back and forth along the railing. Her emotions were stretched thin, her inner strength and re-solve depleted, and her nerves frayed to the point where she was afraid she might collapse. She looked up to once again study the people around her, and it was at that moment that she saw him.

He came out of the park and walked toward the railing, his cool blue-gray eyes constantly moving, checking his surroundings, missing noth-ing. She would not have pegged him for a cop, casually dressed in khakis, running shoes, and a black mock turtleneck worn beneath a brown aviator-style leather jacket; at first glance, he looked more like an out-of-work actor. His thick, unruly hair was roguishly long, worn over the ears and curled up at the base of his neck.

Bass estimated he was just under six feet tall, with broad, sloping shoulders and a trim athletic build. Perhaps forty, maybe younger. His walk brought to mind a leopard on the prowl, cunning and fearless. He stopped and stood at the railing overlooking the river. He had a stillness about him, a coiled sense of readiness; the only movement was in his in-tense, watchful eyes. Everything about him told of a man accustomed to and comfortable with danger and violence. Bass had seen men like him before. Men she categorized as dangerously handsome. Trouble for any-one foolish enough to get involved with them. If he had been on the op-posing side, he would have been bad news.

Kirby spotted Bass the moment he stepped onto the Promenade, as well as noting the detectives from the Intelligence Division staking out the immediate area. He decided to observe Bass first, in deference to Rizzo's advice. He stood at the railing watching her out of the corner of his eye. She walked past him toward the playground, then turned around and approached from the opposite direction.

Kirby gave her a nod and a small smile as she walked by, thinking that she was even more beautiful in person. And again he was drawn to her eyes; dark brown, almost black, challenging, but not the hard, cynical, kiss-my-ass eyes of the street hooker. The direct self-confident gaze he had seen in the snapshot Chambers had given him was there, but there was more, something irresistible, almost disturbingly alluring.

Not entirely convinced that this was the man she was waiting for, Bass slipped her right hand inside the center compartment of her shoulder bag, where she had placed her pistol after removing it from her waistband when the tip of the barrel dug into the top of her thigh as she sat in the back of the taxi. The specially designed center compartment allowed her to fire through the other end of the bag without drawing the weapon.

Kirby saw her hand disappear inside the bag. He tensed, and unzipped his jacket to let it hang open, allowing unrestricted access to the pistol secured in his shoulder holster.

Bass walked up to the railing and stood a short distance away on Kirby's right, then turned to look directly at him.

It was then that he saw there was a frailty about her, a vulnerability he had not expected. She was trying to be calm and collected, but it wasn't working. Under the surface, just behind the steady eyes, she was anxious and wary, like a rabbit in the shadow of a hawk, ready to bolt from impending doom.

He moved along the railing to stand beside her. "So are we going to pretend we don't know each other for a while, or shall we introduce ourselves?"

Bass visibly relaxed at the sound of his voice. "Nicole Bass."

"Detective Kirby."

Bass's right hand came out of the shoulder bag and she extended it to him. "That's a strange first name—Detective."

Kirby smiled and shook her hand. "It's Jack. And how about you? You prefer Nicole or Niki?"

"My friends call me Niki."

"Then let's try Niki, see if we end up friends."

"As I told you on the telephone, I need your help."

"And I need your help. Think we could build on that?"

"I don't understand. How can I help you?"

"What, are you kidding? You saw Vincent Genero kill Michael Onorati last night, didn't you?"

Bass hesitated. "I'm not sure what I saw."

Kirby held her gaze. "You told your friend Chambers you witnessed the murder. Now you're saying you didn't?"

Bass avoided his hard, penetrating stare. She looked out over the river and said nothing.

"Then maybe you can tell me why you think it is Genero put a contract out on you?"

"He thinks I saw something."

"And why would he think that?"

"I don't know. You're the cop, you figure it out. All I know is I need your protection."

"Hey. This is a two-way street here. You help me. I help you."

"Do I have to remind you what your job is, *Detective?* To protect and serve; isn't that what you do?"

"Not me. My job is to put the bad guys away, and you're my ticket to nailing one of the worst animals in this city."

"That's not why I'm here. You left a message on my answering unit that you could help me. I'm here to take you up on your offer."

"Alright. You want to knock off the bullshit, tell me what's goin' on?"

"You already know. Twice today people have tried to kill me. I want you to stop them from doing that."

"I can stop them by putting the son of a bitch responsible for it behind bars for the rest of his natural life. But in order to do that I need your help."

"Locking Genero up isn't going to stop them; it'll just make them try harder."

"Whatever. I'm still the only hope you have of staying alive. Genero believes you're a threat to him, so his soldiers are going to keep looking for you. And when they find you, and they *will* find you, you'll be lucky if all they do is kill you."

"Are you trying to frighten me more than I already am, Kirby?"

"I'm trying to make you realize who and what you're dealing with. Do you know what those animals did to your friend Chambers?"

"No."

"They worked her over with a blowtorch."

Bass flinched and looked away.

"Cooperate with me and I can prevent that from happening to you, and maybe even give you your life back."

Bass let out a short, derisive laugh. "Get something straight, Kirby, you're not dealing with a virgin."

Kirby cocked an eyebrow. "No shit."

Bass smiled, despite herself, realizing what she had said. "Poor choice of words."

Kirby couldn't help but return the disarming smile, breaking the mounting tension between them. "You mind elaborating on that?"

"What I meant was, I know how the system works, and it doesn't work to my advantage. You're going to tell me that all I need to do is identify Genero in a lineup and you'll arrest him and charge him with murder and he won't get out on bail, which we both know doesn't mean anything because that won't stop his people from coming after me.

"Then you, or the district attorney, will promise me that I'll never really have to testify at the trial. That you may not even need me for the grand jury appearance because you'll get one of the two men who were with Genero to roll over and testify against him, which gets me off the hook with you, and them. And it's all bullshit; the testimony of a coconspirator, who probably has a long criminal record and has made a deal to save his ass, is virtually worthless to you, so then you're back to having me as your only hope of convicting Genero.

"Or maybe, if the assistant district attorney who prosecutes the case is really sneaky, he'll tell me that even if he doesn't get one of the men with Genero to roll over, he'll develop corroborating testimony before the trial and he'll simply name me as an anonymous reliable source. Which is stupid, because considering who he's dealing with, he'll never get any corroborating testimony, and even if he does, calling me an anonymous source won't make a damn bit of difference, they already know who I am. How am I doing so far, Kirby?"

"Back up a few sentences. You saw two other guys with Genero when he killed Onorati?"

Bass hesitated. "I didn't say that. I was speaking hypothetically."

Kirby's temper flared. "Let me break this down for you, Bass."

"What happened to 'Niki'?"

"We're not friends yet. Look, you want to play hardball? For starters, I can lock you up for forty-eight hours as a material witness."

"And what's that going to get you?"

"Time for you to get your mind right. And if that doesn't work, the D.A. can indict you for hindering prosecution and put you away for a couple of years."

"The only way I can hinder prosecution is if I saw something I refuse to testify to. How do you plan on proving that?"

"Look, I know you've been through all this before with the DEA. You came out of that okay. Right?" Kirby immediately realized his mistake and the insensitivity of what he had just said.

Bass bristled with a flash of anger. "You've been checking up on me?"

Kirby decided not to tell her all that he knew. "Carolyn Chambers said you had been in the Witness Security Program. I checked with the marshals—they said you testified for the DEA in some big case and they put you into the program."

"And what did DEA tell you?"

"Nothing. My contact there said your file was sealed. Care to tell me why?"

"That's none of your goddamn business. And if you want this conversation to continue, don't bring it up again."

Kirby looked away, slowly shaking his head. Angry with himself for what he was doing, exactly what he had vowed he would not do: use Bass the way the DEA had. Browbeat her and threaten her into cooperating. She was frightened and vulnerable, and he was taking advantage of her when she had little in the way of defenses left. He turned back to Bass. His tone softer, apologetic.

"This is crazy. This isn't supposed to be an adversarial relationship. You don't want to get killed, and believe me, I don't want to see you get killed. So why don't we start over?"

Bass closed her eyes and gave an acquiescent nod. She was tired. Tired of running. Tired of being scared and, she reminded herself, desperately in need of a reprieve from the constant stress. The words came out in a whisper of resignation.

"I saw Vincent Genero kill Michael Onorati last night."

"Now that's what I call a great beginning."

"For you, maybe."

"This is going to work out, Bass. I promise you."

"You do, huh?"

"Absolutely. Tell me, what the hell were you thinking when you set up a meeting with Genero?"

"I guess I wasn't . . . thinking."

"You can put him away for the rest of his life and you thought what? Maybe you could talk him out of killing you by promising you wouldn't testify?"

"I was terrified. I couldn't think of any other way out except running, and I didn't want to live my life like that. I guess I hoped I could reason with him."

"Guys like Genero don't know the meaning of the word."

"I know that now."

Kirby remained silent for a long moment; a harebrained move like meeting with Genero didn't fit with what Castanza had told him about Bass, but he let it pass.

"I've got a few questions I've got to ask you. No offense meant, but it reflects on your credibility as a witness. But even if it's all bad, the D.A. can probably work around it."

"If what's all bad?"

"When I run your name through the computer, am I going to come up with a rap sheet that makes Ted Bundy look like the pope?"

"I have no arrest record, and I've never committed a crime."

Kirby raised an eyebrow. "I don't know how to break this to you, but prostitution is still a crime in New York City."

Bass offered a small, mischievous smile. "Correct me if I'm wrong, Detective Kirby, but it's my understanding that to have a crime you must have a victim. And I can assure you, you'd be hard-pressed to find any of my male friends who would describe themselves as victims."

Their eyes met and Kirby smiled. "Yeah. I see your point."

"Besides, what makes you think I'm a prostitute?"

"You're right. I don't know that for a fact, and if you've got no record, neither does anyone else. But it's a safe bet Genero's lawyers will dig it up and try to use it to discredit you as a witness."

"You're losing ground here, Kirby. You're supposed to be talking me into this, not discouraging me."

"Just covering all the bases. And another thing, are you carrying?"

"Carrying what?"

"A gun."

"Yes. In my shoulder bag. It's licensed and I have a permit to carry a concealed weapon."

"Did you kill Tony Damiano?"

"Who?"

"A wise guy found dead in an alley off Seventy-third Street. Someone shot him around the same time you were to meet with Genero."

Bass shrugged. "I'm not saying that I did, but hypothetically, killing someone in self-defense who's pointing a gun at you isn't a crime. So why muddy the waters with something that wouldn't make any difference in the end?"

Kirby nodded. On a personal level he considered the killing of Damiano a public service. He tried a different tack to get at the information he was after. "Let me put it this way. Was anyone else around when Tony Damiano met his untimely death by whatever means?"

"Another man who was with them in the park. He said he was a cop. He knew your name."

"And what happened?"

"I didn't believe him and kept my gun on him until I got away."

"And no one else was around?"

"Only the man you called Damiano. Was the other one a cop?"

Kirby saw no harm in telling her. They planned to bring Falconetti in within a matter of hours. "Yeah, he's one of our undercovers."

Bass nodded reflectively. "Then my instincts were right. I was just too frightened to let myself believe him."

"So, what about drugs?"

"What about them?"

"Are you a user?"

"No. And I never have been."

"Okay. One more question."

"You're a man with a lot of questions, Kirby."

"I don't want any unpleasant surprises when we bring you forward as our star witness."

"What's your question?"

"Where'd the fifty thousand in cash you have in your bag at the Carlyle Hotel come from?"

Bass was caught by surprise. "How did you trace me to the hotel?"

Kirby wiggled his eyebrows and grinned. "It's what I do. The cash? How'd you get it?"

"I earned it picking up cans on the highway and cleaning windshields at stoplights during rush hour. What business is it of yours?"

"I need to know if it's going to come back to haunt us."

"There won't be any repercussions from it. Now is that all?"

"Yeah. That about covers it."

"I want to get my things from the hotel."

"We'll take care of that later."

"So where do we go from here?"

"Right now, you come back to Intelligence Division headquarters with me and look at a photo array. If you can pick out Genero and the two guys who were with him, we'll have them arrested within the hour."

"I'm not sure I can identify both of them. I only got a good look at one. The same one who did most of the shooting in front of my apartment this afternoon."

"If you can tag Genero as the shooter last night, that's all I care about."

"And then what?"

"Then the detectives from the Seventeenth squad will arrest him, bring him in, and we'll go over there and see if you can pick him out of a lineup. If you can, we lock his ass up and protect you until it's time to testify before the grand jury to get him indicted."

"And then you baby-sit me until the trial, after which you hand me over to the Marshals Service and they give me a new identity and put me back in the program."

"Like you said. But one more thing. I've got to know now, before we put the process in motion. No games. No second thoughts. Are you in or out?"

"It's not like I have a multitude of choices." Bass made direct eye contact with him. "One small favor."

"If I can."

"Don't lie to me. I can deal with the truth, whatever it is. But I can't stand being lied to by people who have asked me to trust them."

"You have my word. I won't lie to you."

Kirby turned and signaled to the six detectives securing the area. They immediately moved toward him.

Bass's surprise was genuine. "They're all cops?"

"Yep. Didn't want to take any chances."

"I'm impressed."

"You wouldn't be if you knew them." He flashed his own mischievous grin. "Only joking. They're friends of mine."

The detectives virtually surrounded Bass and Kirby as they left the Promenade and turned north toward Intelligence Division headquarters, only a few short blocks away.

The detective couple who were holding hands on the bench walked in front of them, the "lovers" at the railing behind them. The dog walker paced them from the opposite sidewalk, while the man on Rollerblades skated a slow serpentine course down one side of the street. A woman appeared from the playground and brought up the rear; she was pushing a baby carriage containing a lifelike doll and a riot gun beneath a blanket. Another man stepped from a doorway at the corner ahead, then joined the procession as they passed by.

"With all this protection, I feel like the president," Bass said.

Kirby lowered his voice and leaned toward her. "You don't like . . . know him . . . ah . . . professionally? Do you?"

Bass turned to stare at him in amusement.

"I mean, I heard your . . . business was strictly high-class, you know, with real exclusive clients, a lot of heavyweight political types."

Bass continued to stare, a small smile at the corners of her mouth.

"This isn't an official inquiry or anything. And if I'm out of line, just—"

"Oh, shut up, Kirby."

"I'm shutting up."

29

WITHOUT THE SLIGHTEST hesitation, Bass picked Vincent Genero's photograph out of the fifteen mug shots spread out before her. Sitting at Kirby's desk in the OCMU squad room, she next looked over the photo array of members of the Gambino crime Family. She positively identified Johnnie Socks as one of the men who shot at her in the street that day, and as one of the two men with Genero when he killed Michael Onorati. She was less certain about Big Paulie and Nino Totani, and could not positively identify either of them.

The door to the squad room opened and Tony Rizzo, the OCMU lieutenant, entered, followed by Kendal Taylor, the Manhattan assistant district attorney Kirby least liked and often referred to as "that yuppie puke" for his ineptness and frequent refusals to prosecute what Kirby deemed to be perfectly good cases OCMU had painstakingly developed through surveillance and confidential informants.

Taylor, dressed in a navy blue pin-striped three-piece suit and rep tie, looked as though he had just stepped out of a Brooks Brothers display window as he postured in the center of the squad room. Having been briefed by Rizzo and the deputy chief of the Intelligence Division on all that had happened and all they had learned, his eyes settled on Bass. He straightened his tie and smoothed his lapels, then walked over to where she sat at Kirby's desk with Kirby standing beside her.

"This is your witness?"

Kirby nodded. "Nicole Bass, this is Assistant District Attorney Kendal Taylor."

Taylor extended his hand and Bass shook it without getting up from behind the desk.

"Ms. Bass, I appreciate your coming forward. You're doing this city a great service."

His voice was nasal and haughty, and Bass took an immediate dislike to him.

"Now. First things first. Let me tell you how it's going to be. After you identify Vincent Genero in a lineup, we will immediately take you to a hotel somewhere here in the city where we will provide round-the-clock security for you until we take you before the grand jury, which will take no longer than six days. You will then testify before the grand jury, telling them what you witnessed, and we will get an indictment against Vincent Genero. He will then be denied bail and will go to jail, and you will be moved to more comfortable and permanent quarters until the trial, where the same round-the-clock security will be provided and all efforts will be made to make you as comfortable as possible."

The ADA's innate arrogance and condescending tone set off something deep inside Bass. Her expression changed as though a mask had dropped from her face. Taylor reminded her of Crawford, the DEA agent, who had the same derisive tone and who had forced her to do things she did not want to do.

Italy. Four years ago. Getting off the Rome-to-Milan flight on her way to a fashion show. Walking across the terminal to be arrested and put in an isolation cell where she was confronted by a man she soon learned to hate. It all came back to her, setting off a visceral reaction and placing her on an emotional course over which she had little control. The images of that fateful evening in the Milan airport stayed with her as she got up and came around from behind the desk to stand directly in front of Taylor in an unmistakable confrontational manner.

"Are you finished?"

"Yes. With the exception of assuring you that I fully understand how frightened and confused you must be at this point in time. I was told there was initially some reluctance on your part to come forward. So I want you to know that there is always the possibility that, in the end, you may not have to testify at all. After you've had a chance to settle in and recover from what must have been a harrowing day for you, I'll explain precisely how that would work. For now, rest assured that you made the right choice."

Bass looked at Kirby, standing a short distance away. She made a see-what-did-I-tell-you face, then turned back to Taylor.

"Now are you finished?"

"Yes."

"Well, Mr. Kendal Taylor, my yuppie prince, let me tell *you* how it's going to be."

Kirby had seen it coming and did his best to stifle a grin, failing miserably as Bass continued to tear into Taylor.

"I will stay in my own apartment, and this man," she indicated Kirby, "will be my personal bodyguard twenty-four hours a day."

Kirby's grin quickly faded. "Hey! Wait a minute."

"You promised to protect me, detective."

"I didn't mean me personally."

"I did. Do you have a wife and family?"

"No. But I have a life, and a lot of work I'm behind on."

"I'm holding you to your word."

Bass turned back to Taylor. "I will not be cloistered in some hotel room, living like a mole, protected by people I don't know. People who Genero may damn well get to. And don't tell me it hasn't happened before. Every one of you in this room knows it has. Cops aren't immune to bribes and coercion."

Taylor was stunned to find himself dealing with someone far removed from the frightened, docile, and compliant witness he had expected. He was about to try to gain the upper hand when Bass went on, her eyes boring into him, causing him to blink more than once.

"Detective Kirby will stay in my apartment with me. In my guest bedroom, in case you're worried about me corrupting one of New York's finest. And he alone will be responsible for my personal safety. I don't want anyone else around. I prefer dealing with people on a one-to-one basis."

"So I've heard."

Bass was going to ignore the snide remark, but her rising anger and the animus Taylor triggered would not allow it.

"I don't apologize for my life to *anyone*, Taylor. So why don't you pucker up and kiss my royal Irish ass."

"Reverting to type, are we, Ms. Bass?" He regretted the ego-driven remark as soon as he made it. Realizing he was on the verge of losing his witness, he raised his hands in mock surrender. "I apologize. That was uncalled for."

But Bass was not about to let it go unanswered. "Detective Kirby's interest is in putting a killer in prison; I understand and respect that. But you're just like the rest of your kind; a self-serving prick whose only interest is in advancing your political career, and you'll use and screw over anyone to further that end. And since you've accused me of reverting to *type,* let me put it this way for you: at least when I fuck someone, they go away with a smile on their face."

An OCMU detective at a desk on the other side of the squad room snorted a laugh into his hand. Another laughed out loud until Rizzo silenced him with a glance.

Kirby was taken aback by the bitterness and rancor in Bass's tone. He could see his chances of getting Genero going up in smoke before him.

Taylor tried to recover some semblance of authority. "We can make some adjustments in the arrangements," he offered. "But we still have to follow well-established procedures."

"I don't care about your well-established procedures. I am not under arrest. I'm here voluntarily, and I will decide *what* I do, where and when I do it, and with whom I do it."

"Regulations require that a policewoman be assigned for the arrangements you're suggesting."

"These are not suggestions, Taylor. They're my terms. Take them or leave them. But I will give you one suggestion: take them unless you want my memory to fail me at a crucial moment."

Taylor bristled. "I had hoped this arrangement would be amicable and voluntary. However, if you think you can dictate to the district attorney's office by threatening to refuse to testify, we will not shy away from forcing you to get on the stand if that turns out to be our only option. And believe me, Ms. Bass, you don't want to get into a contest of wills with us."

"Quit while you're ahead, Taylor. I've been lied to, threatened, and bullied by people far better at it than you. So don't insult my intelligence any more than you already have."

Taylor's face turned crimson with anger and embarrassment, but he checked his impulse to retaliate in kind. If Bass's demands were met, he still had his witness, and, he reminded himself, that was all that mattered. He did not relish the prospect of telling the district attorney that his ego and temper had caused him to lose the cooperation of their only witness in the case.

"I'll have to take this up with the district attorney. In the meantime—"

"In the meantime, stay away from me, you sanctimonious son of a bitch."

"I was going to say that, in the meantime, we will proceed with the arrangements you've requested."

Bass turned to face Kirby. "Detective Kirby?" Her voice now lost some of its acerbic edge as her anger diminished. "Are you going to hold up your end of the bargain, or do I walk out of here alone and take my chances?"

"Let me talk to my lieutenant."

Kirby pulled Tony Rizzo aside. They went into his office. Bass sat at Kirby's desk, spun the swivel chair around, and stared out the window into the courtyard below, her back purposely to Taylor.

Kirby closed the door to Rizzo's office. "Hey, Lou. You've got to get me out of this. With all the legal maneuvering Genero's lawyer will do, it could take a year before the case comes to trial. Christ, I can't baby-sit her for a goddamn year."

"How long have you been trying to put Genero away?"

"I know. I know. Six years. You don't have to remind me."

"If we lose Bass, it could take maybe another six years to get him again. And maybe we never will. As long as she's alive and willing to testify, we've got him nailed for murder two. That's twenty-five to life, Jack. You want to take the chance of blowing a shot like that at Genero?"

"You come up with anything when you ran her name?"

"Nothing. NYSPIN, BCI, NCIC, FBI, no record anywhere. Like she told you. She's clean as a whistle."

"There's something she's not telling us."

"Like what?"

"I don't know. It's just a gut feeling." Kirby gestured toward the squad room, where through the glass partition Bass could be seen sitting at his desk. "That lady out there is too damn smart to have thought she could meet with Genero and talk him out of killing her by swearing she wouldn't testify against him, but yet that's exactly what she says she did."

"Most people don't think too clearly when they're desperate, Jack."

"Desperate, maybe, but terrified to the point of doing something that scatterbrained? Not her. And she as much as admitted to me she whacked Tony Damiano. Probably up close and personal."

"Not our concern. And if she did, it was self-defense. So it doesn't matter anyway."

"Lou, come on. A little help here. Find some way to get me out of this deal."

"It's not going to happen. Taylor isn't going to take the chance of losing Genero. He's probably already choosing his wardrobe for all the press conferences on the courthouse steps. He'll get the D.A. to pull the strings to get Bass anything she wants; and right now you're what she wants. So I'm afraid it's a done deal."

"I can't protect her by myself, Lou. You know that."

"I'll talk to the chief. He'll talk to the chief of detectives, and we'll make an arrangement with the Seventeenth squad. We can draw some people from them, some from our own division, and some from the task force if necessary. We'll secure the apartment building and the street outside round-the-clock. Bass doesn't have to know they're there."

"Ah, Jesus."

"We give her what she wants for now. See how it shakes out. She might get sick of having you around after a few days. I know I would."

Kirby smiled, reluctantly accepting the inevitable. Rizzo was right: if he refused, the district attorney had the clout to have him assigned as Bass's bodyguard regardless of any excuses or objections he could come up with.

"Besides," Rizzo added, "look at the bright side. She's real easy on the eyes."

"You got that right."

"Which brings up another issue. No personal involvement."

Kirby dismissed the warning with a shake of his head.

"Bottom line, she's a hooker, Lou. And it doesn't matter whether they work the streets or the penthouses, they're all bent in one way or another. You can't trust them any further than you can spit them."

"Can you blame her after what the DEA did to her?"

"No, I can't. And I'm sorry about what she's been through, and I can understand why she's screwed up, but there's no way in hell I can trust her. And I guarantee you she isn't leveling with us."

"So don't trust her. Just keep her alive until we get Genero. Then she's somebody else's problem."

• • •

Kirby had not said a word since he and Bass drove away from Intelligence Division headquarters. Bass finally broke the silence when they came off the bridge into Manhattan and headed uptown on the FDR Drive.

"I'd like to get my things from the hotel."

"First we go over to the Seventeenth to do the lineup, then I've got to stop at my place to pick up some stuff. We'll hit the hotel on the way over to your apartment."

"Where's your place?" She was making small talk, anything to ease the tension.

"On the West Side, off Columbus Avenue on Eighty-second."

"Pretty upscale neighborhood for a cop."

"It's a rent-controlled hole-in-the-wall I've been subletting from a friend."

Kirby looked in the rearview mirror and spotted the unmarked police car with two detectives in it three cars behind them. He knew that well before they reached Bass's apartment two more cars would be in position on East Sixty-ninth Street at opposite ends of the block in front of her building, and two more detectives would be posted inside in the lobby.

Kirby stared straight ahead, weaving his way through the last of the rush-hour traffic, silently grumbling and cursing his luck at being stuck with what amounted to an open-ended protection detail and the crushing boredom that went with it. And the display of willful determination and temper Bass had put on in the squad room left no doubt in his mind that the assignment was going to be anything but a day at the beach.

Bass tried again to lighten the mood. "Cheer up, Kirby. I know you may find this difficult to believe, but there are people who actually enjoy my company."

"I don't have that kind of money."

Bass was stung less by the remark than by the harshness with which it was delivered. "You don't have to be mean. I didn't want any of this to happen, but since it has, I've got no choice but to make the best of it. You can do the same, or you can pull over and we'll part company right here. Your choice, but I'm not going to sit here and let you take your frustrations out on me."

Kirby shrugged. "Yeah, you're right. Truce. Huh?"

"Truce."

30

VINCENT GENERO STOOD before the ornate gold-framed mirror in the foyer of his Centre Island mansion tying a perfect knot in a colorful silk tie that complemented the dark gray double-breasted Brioni suit he had chosen to wear for his arrest. His lawyer for the past eight years, David Kasanoff, dressed just as smartly, stood off to the side with Carmine Molino, who, in his wrinkled, sweat-stained, baggy suit, looked like he was about to ask them for a handout.

Within ten minutes of Bass's arrival at Intelligence Division headquarters, Molino had learned through his sources that she was in protective custody. Knowing that the don's arrest was imminent, he had called Genero first, then Kasanoff, who he had picked up and driven to Centre Island to be there before the police arrived. Kasanoff made a call of his own and learned that a warrant had also been sworn out for Johnnie Socks.

Both men waited patiently until Genero was satisfied with his appearance, not willing to risk setting him off again. Genero had flown into a rage when Molino, speaking cryptically about "that thing this afternoon," told him how badly it had gone in Central Park, and that the cops now had Bass. Molino was thankful he had delivered the bad news on his car phone. Genero had screamed a string of obscenities into the phone so loud that Molino had to hold the receiver away from his ear; had he been standing in front of him, he believed Genero might have shot him dead on the spot. By the time he arrived at Centre Island with Kasanoff, Genero had calmed down and was now more concerned with his wardrobe.

Genero stepped back from the mirror to make certain his tie was the precise length he wanted, the point just touching his belt buckle. He then turned to Kasanoff.

"I'm gonna have a private talk with Carmine before the cops get here. Stuff you don't wanna hear."

Kasanoff went into the living room and made himself a drink at the bar while Genero huddled with Molino in a corner of the foyer.

"I want you to take care of a few things for me."

"Sure. Anything."

"You called Johnnie Socks, told him to go hide someplace where the cops can't arrest him?"

"Yeah. It's taken care of."

"Good. Good. You know I don't like no loose ends. So you tell Nino, make sure Johnnie Socks don't ever come out from where he's hiding. Then he takes care of Big Paulie, same thing. Understand?"

Molino nodded that he did. He had expected it. But he did not expect what came next.

"And when that's done, you personally take care of Nino."

"Nino? You sure? He wasn't around when you whacked Onorati."

"He's the only guy you spoke to directly about findin' the hooker, right?"

"Right. But—"

"And him and Johnnie Socks did the shootin' in the street, and worked over that broad runnin' the escort service. He can tie me to that, too. Fuckin' D.A. can use that as collaborating testimony or somethin'."

"Yeah. But Nino's a solid guy, Vinnie. You know that. I wouldn't worry none about him flippin'."

"Yeah? That's what Gotti thought about Sammy the Bull. Now Johnnie Boy's spendin' twenty-three hours a day sittin' in an underground cell in Colorado. No fuckin' sunlight, watchin' his hair fall out, and Sammy's still squealin' his fuckin' brains out for the feds, tellin' everything he knows, shit he doesn't know and makes up. You do like I said."

"Yeah. I was just sayin'—"

Genero's temper flared. He leaned forward, his face inches from Molino's, his index finger jabbing his underboss's temple. "And I'm sayin' the minute the cops snap the cuffs on me, you start takin' care of things."

"Sure, Vinnie. Sure. Absolutely. No problem."

Genero stepped back, his temper subsiding as quickly as it had flared. "Nino took care of that problem in his crew?"

"It's done."

"And Falconetti really was a cop, huh?"

"He admitted it right before Johnnie Socks choked the fuck to death."

"What? Five, six years in Nino's crew. You never know, do ya?"

Molino nodded in agreement. "I'm lookin' into who it was recommended him."

"Okay, you do that. Now listen close. After those other things are taken care of, here's what I want you to do. Put a call in to Joey Terranova in Philadelphia. He owes me big-time. Wasn't for me he wouldn't be head of his own family down there now."

"What do you want from him?"

"Tell him I want four, five of his best guys; guys the cops up here don't know their faces. And I'm not talkin' about muscle. I want guys can think."

Molino thought for a moment, then: "I'm gonna do whatever you say, Vinnie, you know that, but it ain't gonna be easy to snatch her up, even for guys the cops don't know. They'll have the place they're keepin' her locked up tighter than a bank vault."

"Fuck snatchin' her up. I want that fuckin' cunt gone. Dead. When the rest of the business is taken care of, she's all they got. Without her, I walk."

"Yeah, but the money, Vinnie. She's the only one knows where it is."

"Fuck the money. We worry about that later. I end up in the joint for twenty-five years, how the fuck I'm gonna get the money then, huh? We get this straightened out, I'll set things right with the other Families."

"If you just want her dead, maybe we should think about bringin' in the Cuban."

"Yeah? We used him before, right? What's his name?"

"Antonio Zamora."

"So what do you got in mind?"

"Forget about the guys from Philly, let the Cuban handle it."

"You know where this guy is?"

"Miami. Reason I thought of him, he took care of a touchy piece of business for Richie Oliva down there. Last year. That federal judge Richie paid off? Took the money, then fucked him? The Cuban did a real quick, clean job. I could get him up here, maybe tonight yet."

"Yeah? You think he's that good."

"I met him a couple years ago. Spooky motherfucker. Looked into his eyes. Scared the shit out of me without even tryin'. Like he's got no soul."

"What makes you think he's better for this than our own people?"

"For one thing, he's outside the Family, so he can't be traced back to us. And he works alone, a real specialist."

"Specialist at what?"

"He was some kind of assassin for Castro. Russians trained him. He could sneak up on you and slit your throat, or take you out with a sniper rifle from two thousand yards. Came to the States about ten years ago. He did some work for the Colombians and built a rep. Charges half a million a job, half up front, half when he's done. Don't care who the target is. Satisfaction guaranteed. Word is he's never had to give no money back."

Genero stared at the floor for a moment. "Okay. Yeah. Do that. Bring him in. And you keep workin' your source inside the Intelligence Division. Find out where the fuck they're keepin' that whore and tell the Cuban he makes sure she don't walk into no grand jury room, or the last thing I do, he don't walk around no more, period."

Genero heard a car pull up in front of the house. "Sounds like they're here." He turned and posed in front of the mirror. "How do I look?"

"You look great, Vinnie. Like always."

"If it's like the last times, after the whore picks me out of the lineup, the cops'll take me down to Central Booking, then they'll stick me in the Tombs until the arraignment tomorrow morning, then over to Rikers until the grand jury." He gestured toward the living room, where Kasanoff was sitting with his drink, out of earshot. "The shyster in there will make sure you get in to visit me. You make sure you show, every fuckin' day."

"Hey, Vinnie. Didn't I always?"

Genero embraced his underboss, kissing him on both cheeks. "Nothin' personal, Carmine. I'm a little edgy. You know how I fuckin' hate bein' locked up."

"I'll get things done real fast. You'll be outta there in no time."

Genero opened the front door and stepped outside to see Detective Joe Early and his partner Tommy O'Brien get out of their unmarked car. Two blue-and-whites pulled in behind them. The uniformed officers got out and joined the two detectives. Kasanoff came out and stood beside Genero as Early and O'Brien approached, not in the least surprised that the Mafia boss knew they were coming.

"Vincent Genero, you're under arrest for the murder of Michael Onorati," Early announced. "You have the right to remain silent. Anything you say can and will—"

"My client is well aware of his rights, detective."

"Well, if you don't mind, counselor, I'm going to give them to him anyway."

Early continued as O'Brien snapped the handcuffs in place and guided Genero into the back seat of their car. O'Brien climbed in beside him.

"You're going directly to the Seventeenth Precinct station house for a lineup, I presume?" Kasanoff said.

"You presume right, counselor," Early said, and got behind the wheel.

"Don't start until I get there."

"Wouldn't dream of it."

With that, Early drove away, followed by the two blue-and-whites. Big Paulie pulled the black Mercedes out of the garage and Kasanoff climbed in the back.

"Stay with them," Kasanoff ordered.

Jack Kirby stood at a second-floor window looking down on the media circus at the entrance to the 17th Precinct station house. Genero was swarmed by reporters and cameramen the moment he stepped out of the unmarked car. He smiled and joked, shouting witty quips to the eager reporters as Early and O'Brien, each taking an elbow, steered the Mafia don into the station through a forest of microphones and camera lenses.

Nicole Bass was in a small room off the detective squad room, to prevent her from seeing Genero being brought in for the lineup. She had just finished giving O'Brien her statement when the door opened and Early entered.

"You ready, Ms. Bass?"

Bass nodded and stood up, following Early and O'Brien across the squad room to another room where Kirby waited with Genero's lawyer and Kendal Taylor.

Bass stood before the one-way glass and looked into a larger room as eight men entered from a side door and stood beneath numbers tacked to the wall above their heads.

Rizzo had personally selected the men for the lineup himself. All of them were dressed in suits, Italian-looking, and approximately the same physical size and age as Genero. Six were detectives from the Intelligence Division, and two were reluctant volunteers from an Italian restaurant down the block from the station house frequented by the de-

tectives of the 17th squad. It was as fair and balanced a lineup as any de-
fense attorney could hope for.

Bass's eyes moved slowly down the line, stopping abruptly at the
man standing beneath the number 6. He was smirking and looking directly at her as though he could see her behind the one-way glass. She
felt a sudden chill and a small knot forming in her stomach. She averted
her gaze, then looked back.

"Take your time," Taylor said anxiously.

"I don't have to take my time. Number six is the man I saw kill
Michael Onorati."

"There's no doubt in your mind?"

"Absolutely none. It's number six."

Taylor smiled broadly at David Kasanoff. "Looks like you've got
your work cut out for you, Dave."

Kasanoff smiled back. "See you in court, Kendal."

"I'm looking forward to it."

Kirby led Bass out into the squad room, where he pulled a chair out
for her alongside Early's desk.

"Can we go now?"

"Detectives Early and O'Brien are leaving in a few minutes to take
Genero down to Central Booking. The press will follow them, then we'll
get out of here."

Kirby got them both a cup of coffee and sat at Early's desk across
from Bass. He had seen the change in her after she picked Genero out of
the lineup. There was no turning back now, and she knew it. And she
was afraid. With good reason, he thought.

31

JOHNNIE SOCKS AND Big Paulie sat slouched in the front seat of a black Lincoln Continental parked alongside a deserted warehouse in a seldom used section of the Brooklyn docks. They had done as Totani instructed; the car was parked out of sight, hidden from view by massive shipping containers, empty and left to rust, from some long-departed freighter. The front windows of the Lincoln were down and cigarette smoke drifted out into the night air as the two men sat staring at the lights of Manhattan reflecting off the dark waters of the East River.

Big Paulie lit another cigarette off the one he was smoking. "Nino say what we was gonna do tonight?"

"He just said meet him here eight o'clock. Stay outta sight."

"Maybe he found the broad and we're gonna go whack her."

"Yeah. Maybe." Johnnie Socks looked at his watch; it was a few minutes after eight. "Should be here anytime now."

He had no sooner finished his sentence than Nino Totani pulled in behind them, leaving the lights on high beam and the engine running as he stepped out of the car.

The two men in the Lincoln looked back and squinted against the glare of the headlights as Totani came up to the driver's side window. Without a word, he shot Big Paulie in the head, then leaned in to do the same to Johnnie Socks as the huge man, stunned by what had just happened, stared dumbfounded and in utter confusion at the sound-suppressed pistol pointed at his head. Totani finished the job with two more shots into the head of each man, then walked back to his car and drove away.

• • •

Thirty-five minutes later Totani drove through the open gate in the chain-link fence enclosing Carmine Molino's construction company in Queens. He crossed the gravel parking lot and pulled in at the prefabricated one-story office building to see Molino come out and walk around to the rear of the car.

"Hey, Nino. Pop the trunk. I got somethin' to put in there."

Totani got out of the car and came around to unlock the trunk.

"You take care of that piece of business?"

"It's done."

Totani had his back to Molino, and as the trunk lid swung up, Molino shot him twice in the back of the head. As Totani toppled forward, Molino grabbed his legs, tossed him into the trunk and locked it, then calmly walked around and got behind the wheel and drove out of the parking lot.

Antonio Zamora's American Airlines flight from Miami arrived at New York's La Guardia Airport at eleven-thirty that night. He took a cab into the city and, never one to deny himself any of life's luxuries, checked into the Plaza Hotel forty minutes later.

The tall, handsome Cuban was well dressed and well spoken and had no trouble passing for what he purported to be, someone in the import-export business. The night-vision telescopic sight, the disassembled custom-built sniper rifle, and the semiautomatic 9-millimeter pistol, both weapons fitted for sound suppressors, concealed in his two suitcases, gave the lie to the role he was playing.

Zamora called Carmine Molino's pager at twenty minutes past midnight, entering the number for the Plaza and the room he was in after the beep. Molino called back within five minutes.

"You got the picture of the broad and the cash okay?" Molino had used the fax machine in the office of his construction company to transmit the eight-by-ten photograph of Bass that Nino Totani had taken from the escort service office, and within one hour of his telephone call to Richie Oliva in Miami, two large nylon duffel bags containing $250,000 in cash were delivered to the location Zamora specified.

"Yes. I received both. The fax of the photograph is virtually worthless. Have a messenger service drop the original off with the concierge at the hotel in an envelope with my name on it. Do not bring it your-self."

"Yeah. Sure."

"Since we last spoke, have you managed to get the address where the police are keeping the target?"

"Yeah," Molino said. He had talked with his Intelligence Division source two hours earlier. "She's at 150 East 69th Street, between Lex-ington and Third. A high-rise. Apartment 20-B. Faces the street and got a balcony."

"How many people are guarding her?"

"One stays inside the apartment with her all the time. Couple more inside the building. My source ain't sure where. Probably the lobby. And an unmarked car at each end of the block in front of the building. Two detectives in each of them."

"And when is she scheduled to testify before the grand jury?"

"We ain't sure yet. But my boss's lawyer says they got to get the indict-ment within six days of when they busted him, or they got to cut him loose."

"I'll need to know when and where the grand jury hearing will be held. You will let me know as soon as you have that information."

Molino's eyes hardened. Fuckin' spic givin' me orders. "Anything else you want?"

"Not at the moment."

"So I call the hotel and leave a message when I wanna get in touch with you, or what?"

"No. You will call the number I gave you for my cellular telephone. And do not call unless it is information regarding the movement of the target. I will call your pager when and if I need any further information from you. Is that understood?"

"Yeah. Sure." Molino took the phone away from his ear and made a face at it. Who the fuck this guy think he is? But he said nothing, recall-ing their one and only face-to-face meeting and the man's cold, dead eyes. He was about to ask when Zamora was going to make the hit when he heard the click on the other end of the line.

"Fucker hangs up on me," Molino muttered.

. . .

Antonio Zamora left the Plaza Hotel shortly after twelve-thirty. He walked north on Fifth Avenue, along the edge of Central Park, until he reached Sixty-ninth Street. He then crossed the avenue and headed east, across Madison and Park to Lexington, where he stood on the corner, across the street from Bass's apartment building.

He quickly spotted the two unmarked police cars at opposite ends of the block. The four detectives in the cars appeared bored to distraction. He began walking slowly along the sidewalk on the opposite side of the street from the apartment building, and just as quickly determined the blind spot between the two cars. He stood there, beneath the overlapping branches of two maple trees, and studied the front of Bass's building, counting the floors until his eyes stopped at the twentieth, then scanned back and forth at that level.

He turned to look at the buildings behind him, those with a direct line of sight toward Bass's building, and assessed their suitability as sniper posts. None would do. They were mostly brownstones, and those with the best line of sight were at least ten stories too short. Any shot from their rooftops would be at a severe upward angle. At best he would have a partial head shot at someone standing on the balcony. Far from optimum conditions.

Zamora walked east to Third Avenue, then one block north, and turned west on East Seventieth Street. The block paralleled the street where Bass's apartment was located. He was looking for a building that was high enough to give him a straight-on shot at her balcony or through the sliding glass doors. He judged the distance would be no more than two hundred yards, an easy shot, if he could find the right building. But again, he found nothing suitable.

He decided to concentrate on the one time he was certain his target would be out in the open: when she was transported to the grand jury hearing. He would have two windows of opportunity: when she left the apartment building, and when she entered the building where the hearing would be held. Unless something happened that provided him with an earlier opportunity, he would kill her then.

He continued along East Seventieth Street, walking west until he reached Central Park. He was enjoying the crisp night air filled with the scent of autumn, a welcome change from what had been an unusually hot and humid week in Miami. He wanted to walk some more before turning in for the night, and he entered the park and followed one of the meandering paths leading back toward the hotel.

As he walked deeper into the near-deserted park, he saw a flicker of movement off to his left at a juncture with another path. Two men stood in the shadows of a tree. The light in a nearby lamppost was out, and in the bright moonlight, Zamora saw the broken glass at its base and immediately understood the circumstances. As he drew closer, he judged the two men to be mere teenagers. They remained standing at the point where the paths intersected, leaning against the trunk of the tree, their feral eyes locked on him, following his every step.

At sixteen years of age, both were accomplished muggers with three years of experience under their belts. They usually selected their victims closer to their home territory of Morningside Heights, and the easy pickings around Columbia University, seldom venturing much below West 106th Street. Tonight they had decided to expand their territory and their horizons. Had they seen the small smile that creased the corners of their intended victim's mouth, the instincts and street smarts that had allowed them to survive this long would have told them they were about to make the worst mistake of their young lives.

Zamora's eyes were fixed on the taller of the two teenagers. The shorter one stood slightly behind him to the left, designating his companion as the leader. The taller kid's hands were deep in the pockets of an oversized New York Knicks jacket, which hung heavily to one side; the pocket containing the gun, Zamora knew. Always welcoming any opportunity to hone his skills in real-life situations, enjoying the pure sport of it, Zamora gave the two kids added incentive to carry through with their plan. He pulled back his coat sleeve in an obvious display of checking the time; the eighteen-karat Rolex President, its bezel inset with diamonds, glowed in the moonlight.

The taller kid made his move as Zamora reached the point where the paths intersected. Grinning, cocky, certain of an easy score, with visions of the flashy watch on his skinny wrist, he stepped out of the shadows and began to draw the gun from his jacket pocket.

Zamora's gun appeared from nowhere, and in an instant his target was in his sights. The first shot struck the taller kid squarely between the eyes. The second struck his companion just an inch more to the left. The shots came less than one second apart. Both of Zamora's targets were dead before they crumpled to the grass at the side of the path, the specially loaded 9-millimeter bullets blowing out the backs of their heads.

Zamora lowered the hammer on his gun, slipped it back into his shoulder holster, and continued through the park toward the hotel. He had never stopped walking. Never even paused or adjusted his stride or pace. Had someone been there to check his blood pressure and pulse rate, they would have found no more of an elevation or increase than if he had simply swatted two flies.

32

IT WAS JUST past noon of the third day after Bass picked Genero out of the lineup at the 17th Precinct station house. She and Kirby had not been out of her apartment except for a once-daily ride in the elevator to the lobby to get her mail—a small concession Kirby had granted when Bass made a case for allowing her at least some semblance of a normal existence.

Their meals were delivered from nearby restaurants and delicatessens and eaten in Bass's kitchen/dining room. What Bass missed most was her five-mile run each morning. She was unable to convince Kirby to run with her, despite her argument about the difficulty of hitting a moving target, to which Kirby countered that bad guys with fully automatic weapons had been known to drive by and take out everyone on a sidewalk, moving or not.

Kirby sat on the sofa in the living room, trying to concentrate on the magazine article he was reading. He looked up to see Bass, still dressed in shorts and a sweatshirt from her workout, pacing back and forth. He put the magazine down in frustration. If he had been honest with himself, he would have admitted that part of that frustration was due to living in close quarters with someone so desirable and alluring, and so completely unattainable. But instead, he simply attributed it to her getting on his nerves.

"Would you mind sitting the hell down? You're driving me nuts here. If you're not tapping away on that damn computer like a crazed woodpecker, or clanking weights around, or wearing out the StairMaster, you're pacing back and forth like a caged lion."

"That's exactly how I feel. Like a caged lion."

"Well, knock it off. How the hell do you expect me to read?"

"Try moving your lips."

"Very funny."

"You're no treat either, Kirby. You sit there playing solitaire for hours on end, snapping the cards like some automaton. You grunt like a warthog when you do your push-ups and stomach crunches. You've got your bedroom looking like someone tossed in a hand grenade, not to mention the guest bath; it looks like Slappy the Seal's been living in there."

"Hey! This arrangement was your idea, not mine. Want me out of here? I'll get you a replacement *real* fast."

Bass ignored the remark and continued on her rant as she paced. "Your choice in television shows leaves a lot to be desired, too. If I have to watch another football game, or one more rerun of *Cheers* or *M*A*S*H,* I'm going to throw up. Which reminds me, you've got the palate of a crow. You'll eat anything. And no more pasta."

"What do you have against pasta? Besides, you're the one who orders it."

"Yes, but I don't slurp my damn noodles."

Bass stopped pacing, stared at Kirby, then burst out laughing. Kirby couldn't help but join in. She flopped down on the sofa beside him, tossing a leg over his lap.

Almost as a reflex response, without any conscious thought, Kirby began to massage her calf, then caught himself and quickly removed his hand. "I'm sorry, I shouldn't have done that."

"Why not? It felt great."

"Considering the situation, it's way off base; about as unprofessional as a cop can get."

Bass smiled and removed her leg. "You're an anachronism, Kirby. Just one of your many charms."

"Right. I'm a real charmer. A prince among men."

"You can be, when you want to." Bass held his eyes for a moment, then changed the subject. "If we don't get out of this apartment, you're not going to have to worry about Genero killing me; we'll end up killing each other."

"Only three more days until you go before the grand jury. Then we'll go upstate, somewhere out in the country where you can get outside,

maybe even ride a horse. You'll feel like you're back in the hills of Tennessee."

"What would a city boy know about the hills of Tennessee?"

"I know that people down there consider roadkill a delicacy, marry
their first cousins, and the men get emotionally involved with their live-
stock."

Bass laughed, playfully punching him on the arm. "We're going out
tonight. Dinner and dancing. My treat. I know just the place."

"No way."

"There wasn't a question in there. We're going out. I'm not under arrest—I can go anywhere I please."

She was right, and Kirby knew that if she wanted to walk out the
door at that moment, there was nothing he could legally do to stop her.

"I can't guarantee your safety by myself."

Bass flashed a knowing smile. "Behave. You think I haven't noticed
the two plainclothes cops in the lobby when we go down for the mail?
And how many more do you have out on the street?"

"You made the guys in the lobby?"

"They're black, Kirby. There isn't a black tenant in this entire building. They stand out like a couple of raisins in a bowl of rice. How many
do you have outside?"

Kirby saw no point in denying what she already suspected. "Two
cars, at opposite ends of the block. Each with two detectives."

"Which means they'd know if Genero's men were watching the
building. Which I assume they aren't, with all the cops around. So your
men can escort us to dinner."

"It's too dangerous, and it would take too long to set up the proper security."

"You and I can go in the car with the two detectives in the lobby, the
two cars outside can position themselves in front and behind us. We can
drive a route, take surveillance detection measures, make sure no one is
following us. I could do that myself if I had to. And besides, no one's
going to expect us to go to the place I have in mind."

"You've got this all worked out, don't you?"

"What else have I had to think about?"

"Why don't we just take a long walk after dark. That way we can put
some body armor on you and surround you with cops."

"Body armor?"

"A bulletproof vest."

"Oh, great. I just bet I'd look terrific in that."

"It's meant to stop a bullet, not to look good. Besides, you'd look terrific in anything."

"Why, Detective Kirby, I do believe you just paid me a compliment."

"I lie a lot. What do you say? A long walk after dark?"

"No deal. I'm going out tonight, with or without you. I need to do something that makes me feel like a normal person. A bullet in the head is beginning to have more appeal than staying cooped up here any longer. Now, are you coming with me or not?"

"Like I have a choice. Where do you want to go?"

"A nightclub down in SoHo. The Golden Cockatoo. They have terrific food, Brazilian. And a great salsa band that starts about nine o'clock. If we get there at seven, we can have a nice leisurely dinner and then dance for a while."

"I don't dance."

"I'll teach you."

"Others have tried. It's a lost cause, believe me." Kirby stared at her for a moment. "I thought salsa was something you dipped taco chips in."

"You've led a sheltered life, Kirby."

"And by the way, I don't slurp my noodles."

Bass winked and smiled. "Yes you do."

"Anyway, a crowded place like that, it'll be a nightmare trying to protect you."

"As you well know, detective, it's a lot easier to go unnoticed in a crowd. And if no one follows us, no one will know we're there. I can assure you, it's not a Mafia hangout. It's pretty much a Latin crowd."

"You've been there before?"

"Only once. A client took me there last year. Not a place I'd go on a regular basis, but it was great fun, terrific atmosphere. Loud, lively, guaranteed to make you forget your problems, mainly because you can't even hear yourself think once the music starts."

"That's a hell of an endorsement."

"Right now it's what I desperately need."

"What's the location?"

"Just off Spring, on Mercer Street."

"I'll have to clear this with the lieutenant. And we'll have to get some security in place before you get there."

Kirby got up and took the cordless phone with him outside onto the balcony, closing the sliding glass door behind him.

"I was just about to call you," Tony Rizzo said.

"What's up?"

"Genero's systematically eliminating anyone who can tie him to Onorati's murder."

"Big Paulie and Johnnie Socks?"

"They were found this morning on the Brooklyn docks, their brains all over the inside of a Lincoln Continental. And Nino Totani took two in the back of the head; his body turned up in a Dumpster in Yonkers."

Tommy Falconetti's face flashed before Kirby. "Did you bring Falconetti in?"

Rizzo hesitated. "We can't find him, Jack."

"What do you mean, you can't find him?"

"I have people lookin' everywhere. He hasn't been back to his apartment in three days and nobody's seen him around."

"Ah, shit, Lou."

"Yeah, I know. But let's not think the worst yet. We're talking to every snitch we've got that's wired into Genero's crews. And there could be a number of reasons why Falconetti might have dropped out of sight and hasn't called in yet."

But Kirby knew the most likely was that Falconetti's luck had run out. He forced the disturbing thought from his mind. "Any signs of them trying to find out where we are?"

"That's something else that's bothering me. We've got surveillance on all of Genero's crews. Every last one of his soldiers are accounted for. They're hanging around the social clubs or out doing their usual crap. And the detail outside Bass's apartment hasn't seen any of them anywhere near the place. It's like they've given up on her."

"You can bet your ass Genero hasn't. She's the only one left now who can tie him to Onorati's murder."

"It's possible his lawyer told him to back off; maybe he knows something about her we don't, and thinks he can discredit her as a witness."

"Or Genero's brought in some outside talent from Chicago or Philadelphia, people we don't know."

"I thought of that, too. I'm checking with the organized-crime units there and a couple other cities where Genero has strong ties to see if any of their known shooters left town in a hurry."

"I've got another headache for you. You're gonna love this. Bass insists on going out tonight."

"Out where?"

"A club called the Golden Cockatoo, down in SoHo. I'm going to need some help other than the guys I've got here."

"You can't talk her out of it?"

"I tried, but I think it's more than just wanting to get out. I got the feeling that being under protective custody again is dredging up a lot of things from the past she doesn't want to think about. At times she looks like she's on the verge of going postal."

"What time does she want to go out?"

"Dinner at seven, then hang around for the band later."

"I don't like it, but the risk should be minimal as long as you make damn sure nobody follows you. I'll send some of our people over to cover the outside. You can post the people with you inside the club. What precinct is that in?"

Kirby thought for a moment. "Fifth, I think."

"I'll check it out and ask the patrol sergeant to have his radio cars and his anticrime people in that sector make some sweeps of the area, make sure no one's hanging around they aren't used to seeing. Call me right before you leave the apartment and I'll fill you in on the setup."

"How about putting some of the people from the squad on the street in front of the club starting a few hours before it even opens?"

"Good idea."

"And Lou? Let me know the minute you come up with anything on Tommy."

"I will. First thing."

Kirby went back inside to find Bass sorting through one of her bedroom closets. "Do I have to get dressed up for this place we're going?"

"Sport coat and jeans are fine." Her mood had changed. She was cheerful and more animated than he had ever seen her.

She stopped what she was doing and came over to him. "Every once in a while I get snakes in my head, and I have to get completely away from what I've become; try to find some thread of what I used to be." Bass surprised him by giving him a quick hug and a kiss on the cheek. "You don't know how much this means to me."

Kirby stood transfixed for a moment. Bass's scent, the warmth of her skin, and the feel of her body against his lingering. "I think I do."

Bass gave him a curious look, then returned to the closet and held up two dresses: one black and the other a deep red. "Red or black? What do you think?"

"I think you're nuts." He considered telling her about the murders of Johnnie Socks, Big Paulie, and Nino Totani, and of the possibility of outsiders being brought in, perhaps changing her mind about going out. But he decided against it, doubting that after what she had just told him she would change her plans regardless of the arguments for her doing so, and there was also the possibility that the knowledge of the killings might push her over the edge and cause her to have second thoughts about testifying.

"Choose one," Bass said, holding both dresses in front of her.

"Black."

"Black it is. Smile, Kirby. I promise you, you're going to have fun in spite of yourself."

"I'm aglow with anticipation."

Janet Morris left the Intelligence Division headquarters building shortly after noon on her way to a delicatessen, with a list of sandwich orders for herself and five OCMU detectives. Before completing her lunch run, she stopped at a public telephone in the same block as the delicatessen and dialed a number she knew by heart. She hated herself for what she had been doing for the past six months, but she had accepted that she had no choice. The consequences for refusing to do what they demanded were too great.

Almost one year ago to the day, her husband had realized his life's dream and opened a restaurant in the TriBeCa section of lower Manhattan. Within three months his optimistic expectations were tempered by the harsh realities of the restaurant business, and an additional fifty thousand dollars was needed just to remain open. The bank where he had borrowed the money to remodel and cover operating costs for the first month was not eager to throw good money after bad, and with no more collateral, and nowhere else to turn, David Morris, desperate to hang on to his dream, made the terrible mistake of borrowing the needed funds from a Gambino Family loan shark at 5 percent interest per month.

Carmine Molino had personally approved the transaction, based on the discovery that Janet Morris worked for the NYPD Intelligence Division. The loan provided the operating capital Morris needed, and he was soon on solid footing, with his customers increasing steadily. That was until Molino set his well-thought-out plan in motion and went about making certain the restaurant never had a chance at success.

Deliveries were not made on time. The chef quit without explanation. His replacement lasted no more than two weeks before suffering a broken leg during a "mugging." Twice on busy Saturday nights, with the restaurant packed with steady customers, tough-looking men, standing at the bar, started fistfights that turned into all-out brawls, requiring the police to come and break them up. Word of the restaurant's problems soon spread, sounding the death knell for David Morris's dream.

After Morris missed three consecutive interest payments, Molino began applying direct physical pressure. Johnnie Socks broke Morris's right thumb first, then two months later, and two more missed payments, he broke his left arm. Morris had told his wife that the broken thumb was the result of an accident at the restaurant, but his weak explanation for the broken arm, when viewed in the context of the accompanying bruises on his face and ribs, led to Janet Morris learning the full extent of her husband's troubles.

Carmine Molino offered a solution to all of their problems. As long as Janet Morris provided him with occasional information on the activities of the Organized Crime Monitoring Unit, no further interest payments would be required, and Molino would personally see to it that the restaurant's problems vanished overnight. Janet Morris at first adamantly refused, and tried, without success, to find the money to pay them off. Then one evening upon returning home from work, she found an envelope in their apartment mailbox. Inside the envelope was a photograph of their six-year-old son, being pushed on a swing in the playground of his school. The man pushing the swing was Johnnie Socks. The message was clear: we can get him anytime we choose. From that day on, Janet Morris gave Carmine Molino whatever information he wanted, without question or hesitation.

The call she was about to make was the fourth this week, and she was more frightened than she had ever been in her life. She knew that the OCMU would eventually realize the source of the information she was passing on had to be inside the unit.

"You don't worry about that," Molino told her when she voiced that concern. "You ain't the only one workin' there. Could be anybody. Keep your mouth shut, they'll never know."

"But if they already suspect that someone is doing it, they may be watching all of us."

"We already had this discussion a couple months ago, Janet. You just keep the information comin' and I got a nice bonus for you once we got our little problem solved."

"What bonus?"

"No interest. No principal. The slate's wiped clean. Your husband don't owe nothin' no more."

"Do I have your word on that?"

"Absolutely. The boss will be very appreciative. I already talked to him about it," Molino lied. "So you're sure about this Golden Cockatoo? Seven o'clock tonight?"

"Yes. Lieutenant Rizzo pulled six detectives off other assignments and reassigned them to a security detail there."

"Good. Look at the bright side, Janet. Maybe tonight it'll all be over and you can forget about us for good."

The fact that someone had to be killed before it was all over made Janet Morris physically ill. She had gotten precious little sleep since seeing the beautiful young woman Kirby had brought in and realizing that she would be indirectly responsible for her death. And then there was Kirby himself. She liked and respected him. Would they kill him, too, if he got in the way? But she already knew the answer to that.

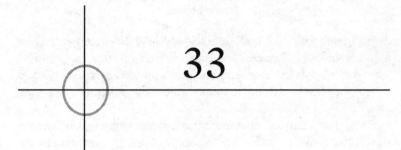

33

ONCE A NO-MAN'S-neighborhood of run-down nineteenth-century buildings and decaying warehouses on quaint cobblestone streets that only a fool or a felon would walk after dark, SoHo, following its startling transformation during the seventies, became a mecca for the city's artists. The high ceilings and large windows of the deserted industrial lofts made perfect studios, with ideal locations for galleries on the first floors.

Living in a SoHo loft soon became fashionable, and the smart set moved in as the old buildings were converted into pricey apartments with rents equal to those of Greenwich Village and the Upper East Side. Chic restaurants, high-tech art galleries, and glossy boutiques now lined the streets of the trendy neighborhood; the type of place where you could find a living statue posed in the window of one store, and a hyacinth macaw sitting on a perch in front of another. Usually packed with uptown and out-of-town tourists, its shops offered everything from Bangkok suits to Bolivian sandals, and the diversity of its nightlife rivaled that of any other neighborhood in the city.

Directly across the street from the Golden Cockatoo, Antonio Zamora sat at a table in the window of a café that offered fifty different brands of coffee. He watched the steadily growing crowd of hopefuls as they queued outside the renovated old warehouse that housed the popular club, pleading their cases with two no-nonsense bouncers who decided who would be allowed to enter.

The criteria for admittance seemed to be that those with the fewest rings through their ears, eyelids, noses, and lips, and those wearing the least amount of black leather and chains, got the nod of approval. Most who were allowed in were dressed in bright, colorful, expensive clothes, and appeared to be dancing to music heard only in their heads as they swaggered and strutted inside.

Earlier that afternoon, after receiving Carmine Molino's call, Zamora scouted the area around the club for escape routes, and took note of the two side exits and the rear exit of the club. He considered, then dismissed, the idea of using his sniper's rifle from a rooftop position on the opposite side of the street; getting off the roof would have posed a problem if the police quickly determined where the shot had come from. His decision was reinforced when the crowd began gathering at the entrance. With so many people milling about, he would have had difficulty getting a clear shot at his target.

Before Zamora entered the café, he had spotted the two cops posing as homeless men, slouched in doorways on opposite sides of the street, and another, a woman, who had walked the block a few too many times before entering a small restaurant on the corner and taking a window seat that gave her a view of the club's entrance and one of the exits on a side street.

Zamora sat sipping a special blend of Ecuadorian coffee as he watched four men dressed in sport coats and slacks get out of a dark blue four-door sedan. Two of them joined the selection committee at the entrance to the club, flashing their shields and then standing off to the side to watch the crowd. The other two went inside, to check out the interior of the club, Zamora reasoned, then reappeared on the sidewalk fifteen minutes later to join those at the entrance. Zamora also noticed the slow drive-bys of the police radio car and the unmarked car carrying two young cops dressed in street clothes he guessed were from the precinct's anticrime unit. The heavy police presence did not bother him in the slightest; it was simply something else to factor into his plan.

Five minutes after he saw one of the detectives at the entrance speak into a small portable radio, a car pulled into the curb at the front door of the club. Jack Kirby and Nicole Bass got out of the back seat and were immediately surrounded by four men who climbed out of two more cars that pulled in behind them. Zamora noted that the driver and the man in the front passenger seat of the car from which Kirby and Bass had emerged remained in the vehicle, in the event a hasty departure was required.

Zamora's eyes fixed on Bass. She was wearing a sleek black dress that ended at mid-thigh and complemented her stunning figure. He would have no trouble spotting her inside, regardless of the size of the crowd. Kirby's well-worn charcoal-gray tweed sport coat and maroon turtleneck, worn over jeans and running shoes, drew looks of disapproval from the doorkeepers. One of them placed his hand on Kirby's shoulder to deny him entrance, only to have it brushed aside and a detective's shield shoved in his face. The bouncer backed off, made an apologetic gesture, and held the door open for Kirby and Bass and the four detectives accompanying them.

Inside, the former warehouse that now housed the Golden Cockatoo was spacious and open and high-tech industrial in design. A large grid of multicolored neon lights, in varying hues of red and green and blue, hung suspended from the steel I beams just below the roof, casting an eerie glow over the dimly lit interior. Huge concrete columns, adorned with neon lights matching those of the suspended grid and spread evenly around the massive room, supported a semicircular balcony that overhung half of the lower floor space on three sides. The railing along the balcony was lined with dining tables, and behind the tables patrons stood six-deep at the upper-level bar. Open, spiral staircases led to the lower level where a huge dance floor in front of the bandstand was ringed with rows of tables jammed into every available space. Behind the tables, the back wall was lined with tufted black-leather banquettes.

Kirby chose a banquette in the far corner against the rear wall where he had a commanding view of most of the lower level. No one could approach from behind or from the left side, leaving only the areas directly in front and to the right to be observed. He positioned a man at each of the side exits and the rear exit, and another just inside the front door. All four of the detectives inside the club, as well as those posted outside, had experience in providing security for visiting high-profile dignitaries and politicians—another of the Intelligence Division's areas of responsibility.

Kirby's eyes moved constantly over the crowded tables. He estimated there were at least four hundred people in the club, with more arriving each minute. And Bass had been right: it was a mostly Latin crowd, twenty-something couples and singles, with a scattering of gays and lesbians and funky older couples thrown into the esoteric New-York-at-night mix. The dining area sparkled with lively chatter and the clink of glasses. Greetings, apologies, and passes filled the air as single men made their approaches to clutches of attractive women who were there for just that reason.

Kirby occasionally picked at the dinner he had allowed Bass to select and order for him, which she did in flawless Spanish, to his surprise; her protracted, animated conversation with the waiter left no doubt in his mind that she was fluent in the language. He found the heavily marinated steak too spicy for his taste, but she appeared to relish her entrée: a fish dish swimming in a red sauce that he suspected might rival the corrosive properties of battery acid after giving in to her requests to taste it. After a comment to that effect, he continued to watch the crowd in silence, having said little since they sat down.

"Well, what do you think, Kirby? Do you like the place?"

"It's alright. I haven't been down to this area in a long time, but I can remember before the artsy-fartsy crowd took over you pretty much had to shoot your way in and out of most of the joints around here."

"It's changed a lot since then."

Bass sat watching him as his eyes again moved over the crowd. She knew much about the secret motivations of men, and understood the double-edged nature of their emotions, and the multifarious little stresses that mysteriously determined the way they reacted in various situations, but she knew little about the man to whom she had entrusted her life, other than the superficial observations that he was complex, with a quiet self-possession, and sometimes a quizzical, humorous expression that was pleasantly reassuring. She had seen flashes of his anger, but his composure never deserted him, and he had a deceptively easy smile and charm. She wanted to know more about him, and she leaned forward, making direct eye contact.

"What happened to your marriage?"

Kirby held her gaze for a long moment, taken aback by the personal question. "I screwed it up. Enough said."

"No significant other in your life at the moment?"

Kirby smiled at the term. "My last 'significant other' told me I was incapable of sustaining a meaningful relationship or conversation with anyone who wasn't carrying a gun or pointing one at me."

"Was she right?"

"Probably."

"What are your plans . . . when this is all over?"

"I don't have any plans."

"Everyone has plans, or dreams of where they want to be, or a goal they want to reach. Things they're working for."

"I don't. I used to. I worked hard to get my gold shield. A good home and a good life for my wife and my . . . and the rest of it. Then it all turned to shit, and let's change the subject."

Kirby lapsed into another long silence. He avoided looking directly at Bass. It was not just his sense of professional responsibility that kept his eyes on the crowd, but also the fact that Bass, in the simple, figure-flattering black dress, with little makeup and no jewelry other than a watch, still managed to look absolutely stunning. He had never been so physically attracted to a woman, and he was afraid if he allowed himself to look at her he would be too distracted to do his job.

Bass again broke the silence. "What's wrong, Kirby?"

"Nothing."

"That look on your face says it's something."

"I'm a little preoccupied here, Bass. I don't have time for idle chatter. I'm trying to keep you alive."

She reached across and refilled his water glass, then poured herself some more wine. And then, completely misreading Kirby's lack of attention to her, she said, "You don't approve of me, do you?"

Kirby did not answer immediately, then: "I'm the last guy in the world to pass judgment on you or anyone else. My father, on the rare occasions when he was sober, used to say that we're all put on earth for a reason, even if we have to make it up as we go along. And we've all got baggage; in my case it's a couple of steamer trunks."

"But you don't approve of what I do for a living?"

"I don't understand why you do it. I mean, look at you. You're beautiful, intelligent, and you've got a personality that could charm a starving man out of his last piece of bread. You could probably be successful at anything you tried."

"And your question is, why am I a prostitute?"

"I didn't ask a question, it's none of my business. You brought it up. I just don't understand why, when you obviously had other choices."

Bass's face clouded over. "I can assure you I'm not proud of myself,

Kirby. I plan to get out of this business in a few years, but not until I have enough money invested that I'll never have to even talk to anyone I don't like, let alone be in a position where they can tell me what to do."

"I hope you get what you want. I really do. And if you get it, I hope there's enough left of the person you were when you started out that you can enjoy it. Now if you're finished with your dinner, let's get out of here."

"I told you, I want to dance."

"And I told you, I don't dance. And I'm not going out on that floor to make a fool of myself for you or anyone else."

"Fine. Have it your way. I'm sure I won't have any problem finding someone to dance with me."

Kirby didn't rise to the bait. "Okay, Bass, since you've been asking all the questions, let me ask you one."

"Go ahead."

"Someone told me you charge a thousand dollars an hour with a two-hour minimum. Not for nothin', but I never lied for it, fought for it, or paid for it in my life, and I'm curious—just what the hell is it you do that guys are willing to pay a minimum of two grand for?"

Bass couldn't resist the opening. "If you've got the two thousand dollars, Kirby, I've got the time." She finished the remark with a salacious smile and a wink.

"Sorry I asked." Although the thought did cross his mind that if he had the money to burn he would be sorely tempted to take her up on it.

Bass smiled. "I was only joking. What do I do for a thousand dollars an hour? I give comfort and pleasure to lonely, unhappy men. And it isn't all about sex. It's about listening and caring and making a man believe he's the center of your attention, hanging on his every word, being nonjudgmental and convincing him that he's needed and appreciated, and all the other little things that make someone feel good about themselves."

"Yeah?" Kirby feigned deep thought for a moment, then: "What if I skip the caring and understanding and listening and center-of-attention stuff and just take the sex? Think a couple of hundred would cover it?" He finished with his own mischievous smile and wink.

Bass laughed and reached across to touch Kirby's hand. "Something tells me you need the caring, understanding, and listening stuff more than you need the sex."

"Maybe, but it sure as hell wouldn't feel as good."

Kirby's attention quickly turned to a nearby table where a waiter was clearing away the dinner dishes. He had seen the man staring at Bass earlier and dismissed him, along with a number of others he had classified as slack-jawed mouth-breathers who had gaped at her in open admiration. But the waiter was at it again, and this time his hand was inside his white jacket. Kirby's eyes were fixed on him, until he saw that what the waiter was reaching for was the check for the couple seated at the table he had just cleared.

Kirby removed his hand from the grip of the pistol in the shoulder holster inside his sport coat and looked across to see the band members setting up on the stage. He turned back to Bass.

"I can't let you go out on that floor with a complete stranger. So what about a compromise?"

"What do you have in mind?"

"We don't dance, we just listen to the music for a while."

Bass smiled. "If you agree to dance just one slow dance with me, I'll sit out the rest."

"That I can handle, as long as your toes can take the punishment."

Antonio Zamora stood at the railing on the far end of the balcony, at an angle where he could see beneath the semicircular overhang, down across the breadth of the lower level and into the banquette on the back wall in the opposite corner. He leaned against one of the support posts, hidden by deep shadows as he watched Bass and Kirby.

Earlier, he walked the entire lower level, spotting the cops posted inside at the exits and the entrance. He thought about making his move while Bass and Kirby were eating, kill them both and take the cop out at the rear exit. But Kirby gave him pause. He judged him to be someone who was aware and capable and not to be taken lightly. He decided to wait until they got up to leave, as they made their way through the crowd now packed shoulder-to-shoulder on the dance floor waiting for the music to begin.

But then he saw Kirby and Bass settle in after paying the dinner check. Bass ordered something from the waiter, who shortly brought her another split of red wine. They sat watching the band remove their instruments from cases, plug in their amplifiers, and set up music stands, giving every indication they were waiting for them to begin playing.

Zamora knew that as soon as the music started the dance floor would be jammed with even more people, hundreds of them, moving rhythmically, erratically, a perfect cover and diversion for him to make his approach.

34

THE ATMOSPHERE INSIDE the Golden Cockatoo changed dramatically when the music began. The lights in the neon grid suspended from the ceiling dimmed to a soft glow as multicolored spotlights came on and swept back and forth across the impossibly crowded dance floor. Onstage, six lively singers, the men in black pants and white-silk blouson shirts open to the navel, the women in brightly colored skirts and scooped-neck blouses with puffed sleeves, danced and gyrated at their microphones, shouting out the lyrics to the up-tempo songs in rapid-fire Spanish as the twelve-piece salsa band rocked and swayed.

The brass section reared back, their horns blaring as the rhythm section launched into a precision, arm-flailing, head-bobbing onslaught on drums, gourds, hollowed sticks, and cowbells. Down on the dance floor, hundreds of bodies, with little space between them, moved ecstatically with the driving rhythms. The lead singer stepped forward, the brass section wailed again, and the dancers responded, rocking into high gear. People danced alone or with partners, on the dance floor, on the spiral staircases, among the tables, at the upper- and lower-level bars, anywhere they could find an open space, caught up in the music and the energy of the huge crowd.

Normal conversation was impossible with the amplifiers cranked up to hearing-damage level, the music filling every corner of the sprawling interior space. For Kirby, the scene was a protection nightmare. Any semblance of order or predictable ebb and flow of the place had deteriorated to pure bedlam. His head was on a swivel, his eyes flicking from dancer to dancer, assessing, dismissing, reassessing. Bass sat opposite him in the banquette, smiling, moving with the music, dancing with her head and shoulders as she watched the frenetic crowd out on the floor.

Kirby watched the same people, but with a different point of view. He scanned back and forth, studying faces and hands and body posture. Was there a frowning face among the smiling crowd? Any nervous head movements or darting eyes in their direction? A holstered gun peeking out from under a suit coat? Was anyone moving against the rhythm of the crowd, possibly searching for the best angle of fire? Was anyone carrying anything that could conceal a weapon? Any sudden arm movements out of sync with the dancing? Anyone approaching with hands where he could not see them? His eyes never stopped moving.

He leaned across the table, shouting to be heard. "So this is salsa music?"

Bass shouted back. "The first two songs were. The last two were soca."

"Never heard of it."

"It's Caribbean. Part calypso, part American soul music. Great to dance to. Like it?"

Kirby rolled his eyes. "It's a real toe-tapper."

The band finished a five-song set, and after a short pause, during which no one left the dance floor, the spotlights switched to a soft blue and the music changed to a romantic ballad. A dreamy-eyed, would-be Julio Iglesias stepped up to the microphone, his hand inside his shirt, rubbing his chest as he sang.

Bass slid out of the banquette the moment the ballad began. She took Kirby by the hand and led him through the near-solid mass of couples standing along the edge of the dance floor, who were doing little more than holding each other's asses and slowly turning in place to the music. Bass angled and inched her way out to the middle of the floor, dragging Kirby with her.

Kirby tensed at the improbability of his situation, finally relaxing with the thought that if he had to find his own mother among the mob surrounding them he would be hard-pressed to do so. Bass turned to face him and flashed a wicked smile.

"Time to perform, Kirby."

She came easily into his arms. She was graceful and light on her feet, and Kirby had no trouble moving smoothly with the music in the small space he staked out for them. Bass was wearing two-inch heels, and it occurred to Kirby that she was the only woman he had ever held in his arms who was on eye level with him. He held her at a decorous distance, but Bass was having none of it. She moved in. Their bodies touched. Her cheek lightly against his. Her breath warm on his neck.

She moved her hand up and ran her fingers through his hair where it curled over the collar of his coat. Kirby felt a pleasant tingle run down the center of his spine.

"What's a cop doing with Hollywood hair?" The words were spoken only inches from his ear, her voice low and soft.

"It's undercover hair. We've got to blend in with the general public. Can't go around looking like a cop."

"You lied to me."

"About what?"

"You're a good dancer."

"You've got more to do with that than me."

"No, you move well when you let yourself relax."

She kept her hand at the back of his neck, and every so often, without thinking about it, she gently, tenderly massaged it with the tips of her fingers as they danced.

Despite himself, almost on a subconscious level, Kirby surrendered to the moment. It had been eight months since his one brief affair after his divorce, and Bass's touch elicited feelings he had since denied and kept at bay with alcohol and long hours at work. He responded by moving his hand across her lower back, holding her close as his other hand cupped hers and held it to his chest.

The band segued into a second ballad, and Bass received no protest when she kept him dancing. She felt comfortable in his arms. He had an inadvertent seductiveness that she found provocative and enticing and made her think of other times, of lovers of her own choosing, and of sincere and heartfelt passions she believed she would never experience again. She had kept her real self bottled up for so long that she had almost forgotten how it felt to simply let go, to lose herself in honest emotions. She snuggled her head into the crook of his neck and pressed her body firmly against him until they moved as one, locked in a sensual embrace.

Kirby breathed deeply of Bass's scent, captivated by her intense physical presence, enjoying the feel of her body moving against his.

Then something snapped him out of the pleasant reverie. A flicker of movement seen in his peripheral vision, out of sync with the slow, rhythmic motion of those around him. His eyes moved slowly over the nearby dancers, then past them, deeper into the crowd. He steered Bass in a tight circle, searching for whatever it was that had caught his attention.

He saw it again. Only a fleeting glimpse. Cast in the bluish glow of one of the spotlights sweeping back and forth across the floor. Someone tall, dark hair, dancing with a shapely blonde off to his right. Eyes fixed on him and Bass too long to be a casual glance. And then he was gone, lost in the shifting mass of bodies and the deep shadows left behind as the spotlight moved on.

Bass felt Kirby's body tense; his dancing no longer had the smooth, gentle rocking motion of a moment ago.

"Is something wrong?"

"I think we have a problem."

Bass raised her head from his shoulder. She saw his eyes go cold and hard. They were fixed on the dancers off to their right.

"What is it?"

Then Kirby saw him again. Thirty feet away across a sea of swaying bodies. Their eyes met for only an instant, but long enough to tell him that the tall Latin-looking man knew who they were and was working his way across the floor toward them.

He gripped Bass even tighter. His primary concern was to get her safely away from the area and to avoid a confrontation that would put her in danger.

"We're going to continue dancing, but I'm going to move us slowly off the floor." His voice was low, his tone compelling. "When we're clear of the floor, we're going to make a run for the exit. Do not let go of my hand for any reason. Do you understand?"

"Yes." Her voice was tight and strained now. "What is it, Kirby?"

"Someone just made us. I don't know who he is, but he knows who we are."

Bass turned her head to look in the direction Kirby was staring. She saw nothing out of the ordinary. "One of Genero's men?"

"If he is, he's one I haven't seen before."

"Maybe it's nothing."

"It's something."

Bass was still dancing close to him, and when his right hand left the small of her back, she felt it move across her abdomen and inside his sport coat. She looked down to see him unsnap the retaining strap on his shoulder holster, remove his gun, and slip it inside his waistband at the front of his jeans.

"You're scaring me, Kirby."

"That makes two of us." He took the small portable radio from his pocket and whispered into it, alerting the men posted inside and out to the situation as he continued dancing, turning in a slow circle, scanning the crowd.

"This is Kirby. I've got a possible out on the dance floor. Subject is tall, dark hair combed straight back, maybe Latino. Dark blue or black sport coat. White shirt open at the neck. I'm heading for the side exit at the north end of the building. Outside detail, move to that location and be prepared to cover us when we come out. Everyone else hold their positions."

Kirby held the radio to his ear and heard a series of acknowledgments from the protection detail. Bass continued to look around the floor as Kirby began to dance them toward the exit. He shouldered and edged his way through the couples in their path, sometimes lightly prodding, sometimes bulling his way past those who resisted.

Zamora saw Kirby talking into the radio and now knew that he was fully aware of the threat to Bass. He danced his blond partner in the same direction Bass was moving and had no trouble keeping her in sight; she was almost a head taller than any woman on the floor. Without so much as a parting word, he released the blonde from his embrace and abruptly left her when he realized that Bass was being led toward the exit directly ahead of him.

He moved along the perimeter of the dance floor, shoving people out of his way as he kept pace with his intended target on a parallel course. A beefy Puerto Rican, bleary-eyed from too much champagne, resented being shoved and reached out to grab Zamora by the shoulder as he went by.

Zamora's response was quick and decisive; he delivered a precise, lightning-fast blow to the Puerto Rican's throat with the knife edge of his hand. The stunned man dropped to his knees gasping for breath. Zamora moved on, never even bothering to look back at his handiwork, his attention riveted on Bass.

Kirby estimated the exit was eighty feet away, with at least sixty feet of it jam-packed dance floor. Their progress was painfully slow. His eyes searched the crowd ahead and to his left for the tall man with the blonde. An overhead spotlight swept past, shining directly into his eyes, destroying his night vision in the darkened club. He held his eyes closed for a few moments to get it back, then opened them to see the blonde, standing alone, an indignant look on her face as she stared after some-one. Kirby followed the direction of her gaze and saw Zamora pacing them along the edge of the dance floor.

Zamora made eye contact with Kirby again, then looked toward the exit and saw the cop posted there craning his neck, trying to find Kirby and Bass. Zamora decided to make his play before they reached the rel-atively open area between the dance floor and the exit, where he would have to contend with the other cop as well.

He moved out onto the floor, roughly shoving people out of his way. His eyes searched the brief open spaces between the couples as they danced in small circles. He caught a quick glimpse of Kirby's hand go-ing to his waistband for his gun. Zamora drew his own weapon from the holster at the small of his back—a compact 9-millimeter semiautomatic with a stubby sound suppressor affixed to the barrel. He held the gun in-side his jacket and took a direct line toward Bass.

Kirby saw him make his move. He released Bass from his embrace and grasped her left hand firmly. Bass had finally seen the man Kirby was now staring directly at. He was in the middle distance, between them and the edge of the dance floor, his eyes locked on her.

With her right hand Bass undid the clasp on the small evening purse that hung from a thin strap over her shoulder and was tucked under her arm close to her side. Unnoticed by Kirby, she slipped the semiauto-matic pistol out of the purse, flicked off the safety, and held it down and out of sight, along the outside of her thigh.

Kirby checked on Zamora's position—he was closing fast. "We're going to make a run for the exit. Hang on."

With all pretense gone, Kirby pulled Bass along, pushing his way through the mass of couples locked in embrace, eliciting snarls and curses and receiving a few elbows in the ribs from those who responded more aggressively.

Zamora was within ten feet of them, almost in position for a clear shot at the back of Bass's head, when a man reacted to being shoved by grabbing him as he passed by. He caught hold of Zamora's jacket, pulling it open and revealing the gun in his hand. Zamora swung around and brought the barrel down hard on the man's head, clubbing him to the floor. The woman dancing with the man screamed, "He's got a gun! He's got a gun! He's killing him!"

The reaction was instantaneous and volatile. People quickly backed away from Zamora, clearing the immediate area around him as they scattered in all directions. The panic spread like ripples on a pond, out across the dance floor and beyond. Afraid of being caught in the cross fire if a gunfight erupted, men and women, in an effort to get out of the club, tripped and fell over each other or were shoved to the floor to be trampled by those who were stronger and more agile. A mad chorus of shouts and piercing screams filled the huge room, resounding off the walls and ceiling, drowning out the music. The band stopped playing, shocked and confused by the chaos before them.

The panic reached those on the upper level, who had not heard the woman cry out about the gun. Believing that the building had caught fire, they added to the mass hysteria, jamming the spiral staircases to the lower level. Those who tried to restore order were quickly overcome by the frenzied mob.

Kirby and Bass were within twenty feet of the exit at the north side of the club when they were caught behind a dense mass of bodies trying to get out of the building the same way. Kirby looked for a way around them, or the path of least resistance to an alternate exit. But the situation was impossible. He scanned the crowd behind them for Zamora and saw him at the precise moment he leveled the gun at Bass.

Bass saw him, too. Not fifteen feet behind her with an almost clear field of fire as people scrambled to get away from him. She was about to raise her gun and fire at him when Kirby reacted first. A split second before Zamora fired.

Zamora's shot was well aimed. He squeezed the trigger, certain that he would strike his target in the side of the head, just above the ear. It was only Kirby's quick response to the threat that saved Bass from certain death. He pulled her off her feet, catching her as she fell, then holding her low, bent over, as he moved her out of Zamora's line of sight and forced his way deep inside the near-solid mass of people fighting to reach the exit ahead of them.

Zamora's shot struck the man who had been standing directly in front of Bass, impacting in the back of his neck and killing him. The sound-suppressed shot went unheard, the fallen man ignored.

A woman beside the man who was shot put her hand to her cheek and brought it away to see the smear of warm blood that had spurted from his carotid artery and splattered across her face. She screamed, again and again, believing she had been shot or stabbed. The mob responded with a renewed effort to reach the exit, moving as one now, people carried along by the momentum of the mass. The double doors at the exit flew open and the outside street light spilled in, revealing the anguished, terrified faces of those who rushed through the narrow opening and out onto the sidewalk like a torrent through a floodgate.

The crowd inside surged, moving steadily forward now, sweeping the cop posted at the exit out into the street with them. Zamora ran toward the exit, searching for Bass. He saw her, now in front of Kirby, his hands on her shoulders, his body shielding hers from behind as he shoved her toward the open doors.

Zamora saw no possibility for a clear shot at her. Continuing the pursuit would only bring him in contact with the cops outside, who, judging from the piercing sound of sirens, had called for backup. He had lost his chance, and quickly decided on a strategic retreat to regroup for a later attempt. He looked to his left and saw that the rear exit doors were open and the crowd rushing through them was thinning out. He glanced over his shoulder to see Kirby and Bass go through the side exit, and then ran toward the rear of the building.

The two detectives who had driven Kirby and Bass to the club had moved the car and parked it directly across the street from the exit, with the motor running. They stood on the opposite sidewalk with the rest of the outside detail, clear of the crowd spilling out of the building. Their guns were drawn when they rushed to surround Bass as Kirby led her to the car and into the front passenger seat. Bass slipped her gun back inside her purse as Kirby told the two men who had driven them that he would take her back to the apartment, instructing them to meet him there.

The people running from the club quickly dispersed in all directions, and Kirby pulled the car onto Mercer Street and sped uptown with another of the unmarked cars close behind. Bass was visibly shaken, as much from the terror of being caught in the frenzied crowd as by the man intent on killing her.

"How did they know we were at the club?"

"I don't know. He's an unknown face, and if he was alone, we could have missed him tailing us, or . . ."

"Or what?"

"The local precinct was told we were going to be here and asked to provide extra security around the building."

"And one of the cops could have told them?"

"Maybe."

Bass looked down to see blood speckling her right leg. "I'm bleeding."

"It's not you. It's from the guy who got shot next to you."

"Someone was shot?"

"It was meant for you."

"That was when you pulled me off my feet and into the crowd?"

"Yeah. Just before he fired."

"I saw the gun in his hand, but I never heard the shot."

"Neither did anyone else. He had a silencer."

"Oh, God, Kirby. I'm so sorry. This was all my fault." Bass stared out the window, watching the street scene speed by as Kirby put the swirling red light on the dashboard and used the siren to run the traffic lights.

"This isn't going to work, you know. Unless I spend the rest of my life locked in my apartment with cops outside the door, you can't protect me any better than I can protect myself. At least I wouldn't give anyone advance notice of where I'm going to be."

"I'll make sure that doesn't happen again. And if you do precisely what I tell you to do for the next few days, you'll come out of this just fine."

"Just fine? Hiding for the rest of my life under an assumed name? Wondering when they're going to find me? Getting up every morning and thinking, this could be the day? That's what you call just fine?"

"You've got to understand how these wise guys think. Once Genero is convicted and sent to prison for the rest of his life, he's out of the picture. In a couple of months, when his appeals aren't going anywhere, he won't have a power base anymore. A handful of wannabes will jockey for position, allegiances will change, and when it's over, someone else will head the Family. And when whoever that is assumes power, he won't be interested in going after the person who put Genero away. In some respects you'll have done him a big favor."

"Can you guarantee that?"

"I can't guarantee anything, but it's not like the old days. These scumbags have no honor; they laugh at the old traditions. They don't give a shit about anything but money and power. If you're no longer a threat to them, you've got nothing to worry about."

Bass didn't respond. Kirby's argument was valid if revenge for testifying against Genero was the only reason they would come after her, but its flaw was in his not knowing about the computer disk in her possession. The disk was the only bargaining chip she had left, and she was not about to give it up until she was certain it would insure her safety.

They sat in silence for the remainder of the ride uptown, until Kirby turned off Third Avenue onto East Sixty-ninth Street and into the driveway to Bass's apartment building, where he parked at the front entrance. Before getting out of the car, he turned to her, giving her a roguish smile.

"Anyway, thanks for the dance. You were right. I enjoyed that part in spite of myself."

Bass returned the smile as she slowly shook her head. "You're a real piece of work, Kirby."

35

AFTER SHOWERING AND bundling herself in her terry cloth robe, Bass took a glass of wine into the living room and sat on the sofa, tucking her legs under her as she turned on the television to watch the eleven o'clock news.

Kirby was outside on the balcony, reporting to Tony Rizzo, who had the same newscast on in his basement recreation room with the volume down low.

"How is she?"

"She'll be okay. Rattled enough that she won't make any noise about going out again."

"So you have no idea who the shooter was at the club?"

"Never saw him before. He definitely isn't one of Genero's soldiers, or any of the other Families, unless they've added some new talent we don't know about. And he looked more Latin than Italian."

"You think he tailed you from the apartment?"

"It's possible, but I don't think so. It's more likely he knew where we were going before we got there."

"I sure as hell hope not."

"Yeah, well, we'll just have to keep her under wraps until the grand jury."

"What we've got to do is move her out of that apartment. They could go after her again, when we transport her for the hearing."

"I'm on shaky ground here, Lou. She's not going to go for it."

"Then first thing in the morning I'm putting some people in the stairwell on her floor, and a couple more in the lobby."

Rizzo fell silent and Kirby could hear the volume on the television in his recreation room being raised. "Hold on, Jack."

Rizzo watched as a live shot of the exterior of the Golden Cockatoo filled the screen. He listened to the reporter to get the gist of the story, then flicked on the mute.

"Two people trampled to death, eighteen hospitalized, and the guy you saw shot is dead. The D.A.'s gonna love this."

"What's the press attributing it to?"

"Right now they think it's gang- or drug-related."

"With a little luck that's all they'll get."

"I wouldn't count on it. The fact that we had a protection operation going on will probably get out sooner or later. I'll call you first thing tomorrow about the additional security at the apartment."

Kirby went back inside to find Bass sitting on the sofa in tears. He looked at the television and saw the Channel 4 News reporter outside the Golden Cockatoo and immediately understood what had upset her.

Bass stared at him, looking forlorn and helpless, tears streaming down her face.

"Three people dead, Kirby, and all because I insisted on going out tonight."

"It's not your fault."

"Yes it is."

Her lower lip quivered and her hands shook so badly the wineglass tumbled to the floor. Kirby sat beside her and took her in his arms to comfort her, stroking her hair, her head resting on his chest.

"It's going to be alright. I promise you."

"There's no way to make this mess right."

"If what happened tonight is anyone's fault, it's mine. I knew better, and I should have done whatever it took to keep you from going out."

"There's nothing you could have done. It was my stupid decision."

He turned off the television and sat holding her until she stopped shaking and the tears subsided. "Why don't you try to get some sleep."

Bass got up and Kirby followed her to the hallway leading to the bedroom. She stopped and turned to him, then held his face in her hands and kissed him softly on the lips, a fleeting contact filled with tenderness.

"Thank you for saving my life."

He looked deep into her eyes, his eyebrows knit together in a frown, his face lightly flushed with pleasure from a kiss that carried with it an alluring hint of her taste and sent a surge of sensation coursing through him. "It's what I do," he finally said, the awkward attempt at humor falling flat.

"You put yourself between me and that man. He could have killed you. No one's ever done anything like that for me before."

"It was my job to protect you."

"What you did tonight had nothing to do with being a cop. It had to do with character and integrity and selflessness. It was what you are inside that made you do it."

Bass kissed him again, this time passionately, her tongue flicking in and out of his mouth. He was at first reluctant, tentative, then he responded, taking her in his arms. She pressed her body to him and felt his rising hardness against her.

Kirby's thumb traced the outline of her lips, his eyes focused on their sensual fullness. He kissed her firmly, a gentle pressure that shaped her mouth to his. His tongue slipped inside and she lightly sucked on it. A small tremor shook his body and Bass heard him groan a faint, deep sound of pleasure.

She untied her bathrobe and let it fall open, guiding Kirby's hands to her breasts. He cupped them gently, and his mouth moved slowly down her neck toward them. Her hands went to his waist, to unfasten his belt, when he abruptly stopped and took a step back, pulling her bathrobe closed.

"We can't do this."

"I want you, Kirby."

"For the wrong reasons. You're frightened and vulnerable, and you feel obligated to me after what happened tonight."

She embraced him again and laid her head on his shoulder. "No. I want you for all the right reasons." Her voice was just above a whisper.

Kirby stepped back and held her at arm's length. "We just can't do this. Not now. Not in this situation. And believe me, that's one of the most difficult things I've ever had to say. And I can't believe I just said it."

"Okay, Kirby. I'll respect that." Bass tied her bathrobe around her waist and smiled. "But I think you should know, you have the sole distinction of being the only man to ever turn me down."

Kirby's lips formed a humorless smile. "And along with that comes the moron-of-the-month award."

Bass laughed and kissed him lightly on the cheek before she turned and walked down the hall to her bedroom. Kirby continued to watch as the door closed, a thin sliver of light shining beneath it. He thought of how her entire demeanor had changed that evening. For a few short hours during dinner she had been playful and charming, almost happy, the ever-present sadness and cynicism visible just behind her eyes gone, however briefly. Whoever she was, before the DEA exploited her and ruined her life, had not been destroyed, but hidden deep inside, denied to those who would hurt her again, though still very much there, encased and protected and kept alive by an indomitable spirit.

A strong, tactile memory of kissing her and holding her in his arms came back to him; her scent still with him, the warmth of her skin, the firmness and fullness of her breasts, the feel of her body against his, all still evoking responses deep within. It took all of his self-control to keep from following her into the bedroom, taking her in his arms, and knowing the consummate pleasures that awaited him.

He told himself to get a grip and went into the kitchen, where he opened the refrigerator, reached for a bottle of beer, changed his mind, and opted for a soft drink instead. He then went into the living room and sat on the sofa to watch the rest of the news before checking the locks on the door and turning in for the night.

Bass, still wearing her terry cloth robe, sat propped up in bed listening to an oldies-but-goodies station on the clock radio, the volume down low, the green glow from the digital readout the only light in the room. It had been an emotional roller coaster of an evening, having run the entire gamut, from terror and confusion to anger, remorse, passion, and disappointment, completely upsetting her equilibrium in a way she had never experienced. She was still not fully recovered from it.

Her thoughts went back to when she and Kirby sat on the sofa, how he took her in his arms without a word, comforted her, and held her until she was calm and back in control. He had a kindness, compassion, and gentleness she had not expected, and she had wanted to make love to him more than she had ever wanted any man.

Bass forced the troublesome image of him from her mind. She believed she knew what made her do what she did that night: twisted fragments of painful memories of what the DEA had forced her to do, lying buried in her mind, concealed and sometimes forgotten, had taken hold and caused the irrational and self-destructive behavior. It had happened before, but this time it had cost the lives of three people and nearly the life of a good and decent man who was prepared to sacrifice himself for her.

She made her decision and looked at the clock radio. It was three-fifteen in the morning. With no time to waste she got up and began to pack her carry-on bag, taking only a few essentials, planning on buying what she needed when she reached her destination.

She double-checked to make certain she had included all of the important things she would need: the small leather passport folder she had kept hidden in her closet for the past eighteen months, the neatly banded packets of cash totaling fifty thousand dollars from Michael Onorati's briefcase, the original and the copy of the computer disk with the information on the bank accounts, and a spare magazine of ammunition for her pistol.

She had heard Kirby going to bed hours ago, but just to reassure herself, she cracked the door and listened for a few minutes. Hearing nothing, she then quickly pulled on the clothes she had laid out: a pair of gray lightweight gabardine slacks and an off-white silk blouse to wear with her black blazer. She next went into the bathroom, turned on the light, and stood before the mirror to put on her blond wig. Returning to the bedroom, she secured her pistol in an inside-the-belt holster on her right hip, slipped into her raincoat, and picked up her bag.

She paused to listen again, then went out to the living room, where she put her laptop computer into its case and slung the carrying strap over her shoulder. She tiptoed toward the door and undid the locks. Once out of the apartment, she let the door close slowly until it quietly clicked shut, then she hurried to the end of the hallway and took the stairs down twenty flights to where a door opened onto the lobby. She opened the door a few inches until she could see the reception desk just inside the entrance to the building. One of the night doormen sat behind the desk reading a magazine. Across from him she saw one of the detectives sitting in a lounge chair with his back to her. She looked for the second detective, but he was nowhere in sight.

To the left and around the corner from where the stairwell door opened to the lobby was another door that led to a basement storage area and the utility rooms. The door from the basement led to a passageway outside and was locked from the inside. Anyone who managed to break in that way still had to come up to the lobby to take the elevators or the stairs to get to any of the apartments. Bass had noticed on her trips down to get the mail that the cops, obviously aware that an intruder coming in through the basement would have to enter the lobby to get to her, had not bothered to position anyone where they could see the door to the basement.

The lobby was still and quiet, and, holding her breath, Bass opened the stairwell door just enough to get through, then gently closed it behind her. She then quickly moved around the corner and through the door to the steps leading to the basement, where she paused at the bottom to listen for anyone who might have seen her and followed. She heard only the night sounds of the building, and hurriedly unlocked the outside door and skipped up the steps to a walkway that led down the side of the driveway behind a row of trees and high shrubs to the street. She ran down to the sidewalk, then slowed to a walk as she turned right toward Third Avenue.

She spotted the car with the two detectives in it parked near the east end of the block on the opposite side of the street, facing in her direction. The man in the front passenger seat appeared to be nodding off, but the one at the wheel saw her, his eyes following as she approached and came abreast of where they were parked.

Bass soon realized he was not suspicious of her, rather simply bored and she was the only person on the street at that hour of the night. As she had correctly assumed, his antennae would be up for anyone approaching the apartment building, not someone walking away from it.

She headed north on Third Avenue, walking six blocks before she heard a manhole cover clang and turned to see a taxi speeding up the avenue behind her. She hailed it to the curb and climbed in, beginning the roundabout route and three changes of cabs she would use to get to her interim destination.

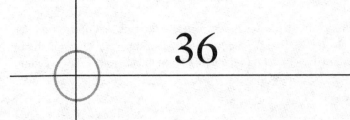

36

KIRBY WAS UP and exercising in the living room by six-thirty. After finishing his stomach crunches and push-ups, he started some coffee, expecting Bass to come out of the bedroom in her workout clothes at any moment to do her stretching exercises, followed by an hour on the StairMaster and a light workout with the dumbbells. He ate a bowl of cereal and a banana as he watched *Good Morning America,* going over in his mind the reassuring speech he had planned for her.

When she was not up and about by eight o'clock, Kirby walked down the hall to knock on her bedroom door. Getting no response, he opened it a few inches and called out. When no one answered, he looked in and immediately noticed that the bed had not been slept in. He entered and checked the empty bathroom, and then, with a dreadful certainty, he knew what had happened.

He went into the kitchen and used the building intercom telephone to call the doorman, who brought one of the two detectives on duty in the lobby to the phone. The detective informed Kirby that Bass was not there, nor had the night doormen, or the detectives who had worked the graveyard tour and just left, said anything about seeing her. A call to Intelligence Division operations, who patched him through in turn to the detectives who had been parked outside that night, yielded results on the second call. One of the men in the car parked at the east end of the block recalled seeing a tall blonde walking toward Third Avenue around three forty-five that morning.

After kicking in a cabinet door beneath the sink, and throwing a left hook into the wall that caused two of his knuckles to swell, Kirby calmed down and went into the living room to call Tony Rizzo, catching him just as he walked into his office.

Bass paid cash for a first-class ticket on the American Airlines flight leaving New York's JFK Airport at nine o'clock that morning and arriving on the Caribbean island of St. Martin at two o'clock that afternoon. Peter Bechtal's invitation to join him on his yacht had reminded her of the place she decided on as a final destination, a place she had fond memories of and was only a short distance from St. Martin.

Before entering the airport, Bass put her pistol in her carry-on bag, inside her makeup kit, and then checked it through to her destination, keeping her computer with her. She felt vulnerable and unprotected without the gun, but she was not about to rely on dumb luck or an inattentive X-ray machine operator to get it past the security checkpoint. Getting caught trying to smuggle it aboard the plane would have resulted in her immediate arrest, and then she would have been right back where she started, with even more trouble than she already had. Going through customs at her destination with the gun in her bag was another problem, but one she had dealt with successfully on other occasions and felt confident she could handle when the time came.

With forty minutes remaining until her flight's scheduled departure, she walked about the airport, carefully watching for faces she had seen before, ducking into shops, and making erratic changes of direction in the concourses. She stopped at a newsstand to purchase last night's final edition of the *New York Daily News* when she saw the bold headline and the photograph of bodies being carried from the Golden Cockatoo.

When she was certain she was not being followed, Bass went directly to the ladies' room near her boarding gate. She locked herself in a stall and sat reading the newspaper. On the second page of the paper a follow-up story on Vincent Genero's arrest caught her attention: MYSTERY WITNESS IN GENERO MURDER CASE. The story had no accompanying photograph of her, and if they had her name, they did not reveal it, simply identifying her as a high-class call girl who had witnessed the murder and was now under police protection. Bass stayed in the bathroom stall until her flight was announced over the intercom, then hurried to the boarding area and onto the plane.

The huge jet rumbled and roared down the runway, lifting off and climbing rapidly away on a southerly heading. Bass asked the flight attendant not to disturb her, then reclined her seat and closed her eyes. She thought of Kirby—by now he would know she was gone. She had considered leaving him a note, but there was nothing to be said. Her leaving had closed that chapter of her life, for better or worse.

Rikers Island, known to those incarcerated there as the Rock, is a 415-acre island in New York City's East River, a few hundred yards off the shore of Astoria, and one hundred feet from the end of Runway 22 at La Guardia Airport. Accessible only by a two-lane bridge, it is not one large jail, rather a compound of ten separate jails, and is the largest urban corrections center in the world. The inmate population, in excess of sixteen thousand, is housed in an amalgam of overcrowded, old-style penitentiaries, modern prefabricated jails, an eight-hundred-bed prison barge, two converted Staten Island ferries docked at the northern tip of the island, and six aluminum and fabric structures that resemble tennis bubbles. The two categories of prisoners are housed separately and live under different rules: detainees, who have not yet been to trial and could not make or were denied bail, and convicts sentenced to one year or less. Prisoners with sentences exceeding one year are sent to state prisons.

Vincent Genero was housed on the third tier of the North Infirmary Command, the jail used for high-security and high-profile prisoners, and in a separate section, prisoners with AIDS. His single-occupant, six-by-nine-foot cell contained a bed, a toilet, and a sink. The noise in the cell block was constant throughout the day and into the night—the corridors echoing with senseless chatter, off-key singing, the sound of television sets with the volume raised, and the intermittent roar of jets leaving La Guardia Airport.

At nine-fifteen on the morning of Bass's disappearance, the door to Genero's cell clanged open and a guard arrived to escort him to the visiting room. As a detainee, as opposed to a sentenced prisoner, he was allowed to wear his civilian clothes while in the jail, but before entering the visiting room, he had to strip and put on a gray one-piece prison jumpsuit, a measure taken to assure that the guards had no problem telling the visitors from the detainees at a glance.

Genero entered the visiting room, a large open area filled with tables and molded plastic chairs, to see Carmine Molino stand as he approached. The two men embraced, then sat opposite each other across a table in the middle of the room, out of earshot of the guards.

Molino noticed the changes in Genero in just the three days since his incarceration. He was edgy, his eyes darting back and forth, settling nowhere for more than a few seconds. His face was taut and the circles under his eyes were deep and dark. Molino remembered the other occasions when Genero had spent a few days to a week in jail, until his lawyers got him out on bail. He hated being confined under any circumstances, dreaded it, and regardless of how short the stay, had always done hard time.

"What are you doin' here this early in the morning?"

"We got a problem, Vinnie. But maybe not as much a problem as it might sound like. Could end up bein' in our favor if things go a certain way instead of the other way. Could actually be a blessing in—"

"What the fuck are you babblin' about, Carmine? Get to the fuckin' point!"

"The Cuban tried to take care of that piece of business last night."

"Tried?"

"Things got outta hand. He missed his target, guy got shot by mistake, people panicked, a few of them were trampled to death."

"You talkin' about that thing I heard on the news this morning? That nightclub down in SoHo?"

"Yeah. Same thing."

"So let me get this straight. This spic you hired for half a million to take care of things, supposed to be a top pro, goes after the hooker, shoots some guy by mistake, and starts a stampede in a crowded nightclub? That about it?"

"It's okay, Vinnie. He'll make it right. Guy never quits till he does."

"Guy's walkin' around with a quarter million of my money up front, he better fuckin' make it right!"

Molino sat looking at his hands for a moment, trying to think of some way to put a positive spin on what he had to say next.

Genero's eyes narrowed. "There somethin' else?"

Molino braced himself for the reaction he knew was about to come, comforted only by the reasonable certainty that Genero probably would not explode and come across the table after him with the prison guards standing around.

"The broad skipped."

Genero clenched his fists and leaned across the table, his face turning bright red until he managed to get control of himself. "Skipped? What do you mean skipped? The cops moved her and you can't find her, or what?"

"She's gone. The cops don't know where she is neither; they're lookin' for her. But that's the good part, Vinnie. They find her, we find her. No problem. My source inside is solid. But if the cops don't find her, that's even better. She ain't here to testify before the grand jury two days from now, they got to cut you loose, right? That happens, you got some breathin' room till we find her again."

Genero nodded, gaining control over his anger and frustration. All he wanted was out, he didn't care how. He tugged at the ill-fitting prison jumpsuit that bunched at his waist and made him look as though he had a paunch.

"This fuckin' place is full of moron, degenerate animals. I got some fuckin' eggplant on the tier below me singin' rap songs all fuckin' day. Drivin' me crazy. I shout down, nice-like, ask him to knock it off. Fuckin' spade calls me a wop bastard. Believe that shit?"

"I'll see about gettin' somebody to have a talk with him."

"You tell whoever does it, kick the fuck until he's dead."

"You get that stuff I sent in for you: the salami, the cheese, and the bread?"

"Yeah. One of the guards slipped it to me last night. Guy says if you send in some real food, like a dinner, he'll heat it up for me. So take good care of him, and get me some veal and peppers from Roselli's. Send it over tonight. And some more Italian bread."

Genero's eyes darted about the room, his temper rising again. "You know they got scumbags with AIDS in here? That shit could get in the ventilation system or somethin', you never know."

"Couple more days, Vinnie. That's all."

"The longer that hooker's out there walkin' around, Carmine, the longer I'm in here. I'm countin' on you to make sure she don't show for no grand jury. She does, you whack the fuckin' Cuban, first thing. Then get somebody knows what they're doin'."

Shortly after 10 A.M., Kirby entered Tony Rizzo's office at Intelligence Division headquarters. Rizzo was on the telephone, nodding his head and occasionally answering with a curt "Yes, sir" before whoever was on the other end of the line abruptly hung up.

"That was our dear friend, A.D.A. Kendal Taylor. You can imagine what he had to say about last night's fiasco and losing Bass. You come up with anything?"

"Nothing. I got Janet Morris checking all the airlines for anyone making reservations under the name of Nicole Bass, Martha Johnson, or Catherine Adams, the name she used at the Carlyle. We've got people watching the bus and train stations, checking the hotels again, car rentals, but with the head start she got, something tells me this time she's already left the city, maybe even the country."

"She have a current passport?"

"Yeah. I checked."

"What about the DEA?"

"What about them?"

"Did she have any phony ID they gave her when she was working out of the country for them?"

"I don't know. I can ask Charlie Castanza."

"Check it out."

Kirby went back to his desk to make the call. Castanza said he would check with his group supervisor, Cliff Mahanes, the man who had been involved with the operation involving Bass, and get back to him as soon as possible. The return call came fifteen minutes later.

"Mahanes says CIA gave her a passport under another name in case her cover got blown and she had to make a run for it out of Bolivia."

"Is it still valid?"

"Let's see. She got it what? Three and a half years ago? So, yeah. It's still good for another six and a half years."

"Do you know what name was on the passport?"

"Nancy Maguire."

"Thanks, Charlie. Next beer's on me."

"Next beer my ass; next two dinners."

"You got it."

"Answer me something. Rumor is that mess at that club in SoHo last night was a protection operation. Didn't happen to be your people and Bass did it?"

"Yeah. But you didn't hear it from me."

"I didn't hear it at all."

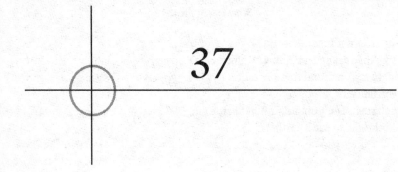

37

KIRBY TOOK THE steps to Janet Morris's office two at a time, startling her when he suddenly appeared at her desk.

"I need the printouts you did on the passenger manifests for all the flights leaving JFK, La Guardia, and Newark since six this morning."

Morris gathered up the thick stack of papers from her desk and handed them to him. "Is there anything I can help you with, Detective Kirby?"

"No thanks. We just may have gotten a break. I think I know what name Bass might be using."

"Oh, great. I can check the lists for you, if you like."

"That's okay. I'll take it from here."

Morris watched Kirby leave the room, wondering if his reluctance to confide in her was any indication he was suspicious. She decided it was not; Kirby was more circumspect than most of the detectives in the unit, and someone who preferred doing his own work.

Kirby took the passenger manifests to his desk in the OCMU squad room and quickly scanned the lists of names and destinations. Six pages into the stack, he found that a Nancy Maguire had left JFK Airport at nine o'clock that morning on an American Airlines flight to the Caribbean island of St. Martin.

Acting on the hunch that anyone who saw Bass was not likely to forget her, he made a call to the American Airlines ticket counter at the airport, identifying himself as a police officer. After talking to three of the six agents working that morning, he found the one who had issued Bass's ticket. When asked to describe Nancy Maguire, the agent did so in glowing terms, leaving no doubt in Kirby's mind that it was Bass the man had waited on.

Kirby rushed into Tony Rizzo's office, told him of the passport under the name of Nancy Maguire, and showed him the American Airlines passenger list. "I want to go after her, Lou. I think I can convince her to come back with me and testify."

"I'll have to talk to the captain and he'll have to get approval from the chief, but I don't think there'll be a problem. Hell, the ADA will probably pay your expenses himself. Without Bass, he's got no case, and I guarantee you he's not looking forward to a press conference where he has to explain why he cut Genero loose on a murder rap."

"I'm going to check on flights to St. Martin, see how soon I can get down there."

"Keep in mind, Jack, your shield doesn't carry any weight there, and you can't take your gun with you."

"If I can get to her before any of Genero's shooters do, I won't need it."

Kirby found a Continental Airlines flight leaving Newark airport at two-fifteen and arriving in St. Martin at seven that evening after a stop in San Juan, Puerto Rico. The San Juan leg of the flight was booked full, and the reservation agent told him the best she could do was to place him on standby. Kirby declined the offer, hoping that once again, he could put Janet Morris's computer hacking skills to good use.

"I need you to access Continental Airlines's reservation computer and bump someone from their two-fifteen flight from Newark to St. Martin. Is that possible?"

"Anyone in particular?"

"Definitely not a first-class passenger; the cheapest seat you can find me."

Morris again accessed the airline's computer with ease, scrolling the manifest for the flight until she found an economy-class passenger without a predesignated seat assignment. She deleted the man's name from the list and inserted Kirby's.

"Your reservations are confirmed, detective," she said with a smile.

"That's it? It's done?"

"Done. Just get there early to pick up your ticket and check in at the boarding area, that way if the man I deleted was preticketed and starts ranting and raving, you're not the one who'll get bumped."

"You're a genius, Janet."

"If you like, I can check on hotel reservations on St. Martin for you; find out where Bass is staying on the island. I'll need the name she's using, though."

"No. I'll have to play it by ear. I don't even know that St. Martin is her final destination. She may catch a flight out of there to somewhere else."

"I can check and see if she has a connecting flight."

"I already checked. She doesn't. But that doesn't mean she won't book one when she arrives. I can find that out when I get there." Kirby looked at his watch. "Her flight gets to St. Martin about the same time I leave Newark, which gives her a five-hour head start by the time I arrive. With a little luck, she'll still be on the island."

Morris did not risk pushing any harder to learn the name Bass was using. "Anything more I can do, just let me know."

Kirby returned to Rizzo's office, informing him of his flight to St. Martin. "I'm going to head out now, Lou. Go to my apartment, pack a bag, and get over to Newark to pick up my ticket. I don't want to sit around here waiting for the A.D.A.'s approval and take the chance of missing the plane. I'll check in with you before the flight leaves to make sure it's okay."

The call for permission would be perfunctory; Kirby had already decided he was going after Bass, official sanction or not. Wanting to put Genero in prison for the rest of his life was only part of the reason. He had given Bass his word. With Genero's men still hunting her, he had no intention of deserting her when she might need him, even though it had been her decision to run.

Rizzo got up and walked out of the building with him, shaking his hand as they reached the sidewalk. "Just remember, even if you can't find her and get her back here within the next two days, and Genero is cut loose, we can always rearrest him when you do find her, and the D.A. can start the process over again. So don't take any unnecessary risks. We've got options."

"Bass doesn't. Not if Genero finds her first."

After again accessing the airline's computers, to determine what flight from the New York area arrived in St. Martin at two o'clock that afternoon, Janet Morris volunteered to make the lunchtime sandwich run to the nearby deli, stopping on the way at the pay phone on the corner to call Carmine Molino.

"You got the name she's using?"

"I couldn't get it."

"If you know the flight she's on, how come you can't figure out which one of the broads on it is her; process of elimination or somethin'."

"I checked the passenger list after Detective Kirby left. There are thirty-two women on board that flight. I have no way of knowing which of them is Bass."

Molino's voice took on a cold, hard edge. "You go the fuck back to work and get the goddamn name she's usin'."

"I can't, Mr. Molino. I've asked too many questions already. They'll know."

"I need that name, Janet. You want me to give your husband a reminder of what happens when you don't do like I say? Or maybe your kid?"

"No. Please."

"Then get the name."

"Maybe you won't need it."

"Yeah? Why's that?"

"Bass arrives in St. Martin at two o'clock this afternoon. If you can have someone there when her flight lands who knows her on sight, the name won't be necessary."

Molino looked at his watch. It was twelve-ten. "By the time we line up a private jet, it'll be at least one, one-thirty. No way it's gonna make it there in a half hour, not unless it's the Space Shuttle or somethin'."

Molino decided not to push Morris to the point where she fell apart on him, reasoning that he might need her later. He had another idea. "Okay. We'll try it this way. You said this Detective Kirby gets there at seven tonight?"

"Yes."

"Since he knows the name Bass is using, we'll have someone waitin' for him when he lands, let him do the legwork and lead us to her. In the meantime, if you can get the name without bein' too obvious about it, you call me right away."

"And when you find her, it's over? And my husband owes you nothing?"

"What I said before."

• • •

Kirby had just left his apartment on the Upper West Side when his cellular phone rang. It was Tony Rizzo.

"The A.D.A. gave the go-ahead. The D.A.'s office will pick up your expenses."

"I'm on my way to Newark now."

Rizzo's voice took on a somber tone. "Jack, I'm afraid I have some bad news."

"What is it?"

"The Harbor Unit pulled a floater out of the East River under the Williamsburg Bridge this morning. It was Tommy Falconetti."

With Bass's disappearance, and the rush to find her, Kirby had all but forgotten about Falconetti. He now saw his face before him; the bright, tough, twenty-two-year-old kid he first met six years ago. Eager to fight the good fight, confident of his own immortality.

Rizzo sat listening to a prolonged silence, then: "Jack? You there?"

Kirby blinked away the image of Falconetti's youthful face, swallowed hard, and cleared his throat. "Where's the body?"

"At the morgue."

"I'm going over there to make sure it's him."

"The fingerprints are a match, Jack. I'm sorry."

"I knew I should have brought him in." Kirby's voice broke as he spoke. "I goddamn knew it, and I let him stay under."

"Don't beat yourself up, Jack. He wanted to keep at it until we found Bass. It was his decision."

"But I knew better. I saw the signs. I shouldn't have let him do it. That fuckin' Genero. I'll kill that motherfucker myself."

"We'll get him, Jack. The right way. For him, spending the rest of his life in a cell is far worse than dying."

After another long silence, Kirby said, "I'll call you as soon as I have anything on Bass, Lou." And then he hung up.

In a refrigerated room in the basement of the chief medical examiner's office in lower Manhattan, a poker-faced morgue attendant pulled out a stainless steel drawer and stepped aside.

It was not that Kirby doubted the body the Harbor Unit pulled from the East River was Tommy Falconetti; fingerprints did not lie. He simply needed to see him. If for no other reason than to say goodbye. "Part of closure is the process of accepting what has happened and going on with your life," he remembered the Department shrink telling him after his daughter's death.

He stared at Falconetti's bloated body, its skin a mottled bluish-green. The ligature marks on the neck were still clearly visible, and Kirby had no doubt how Falconetti had suffered and died, and who had done it. Strangulation was Johnnie Socks's preferred way of killing. Kirby found no solace in the irony that the man who had killed his friend was now dead himself, by order of the same man who had ordered him to kill Falconetti.

Kirby reached out and touched one of Falconetti's hands; it was cold and spongy. "I'm sorry, Tommy. Sorry I let you down. But you rest in peace, partner. I'll get the son of a bitch for this. I promise you that."

Kirby slid Falconetti's body back into the locker himself, then quickly left the room. Out on the sidewalk he paused before getting back in his car, drawing in huge breaths of fresh air in an attempt to purge his senses of the faint, sickening-sweet smell of death that permeated the building.

The deep sorrow he felt about Falconetti's death brought with it memories of that fateful morning fourteen months ago. His daughter, Kathleen, lying dead on the bedroom floor, a bullet wound in her chest, put there by his own gun. By his carelessness, his stupidity. He relived the wake and the funeral, and was almost overcome by the terrible emptiness that had been with him ever since.

He was driving slower than he realized, lost in a fog of painful memories, when he glanced at his watch as he came out of the Holland Tunnel. With only forty minutes until his flight took off, he placed the flashing red light on the dashboard and used the siren for the rest of the drive.

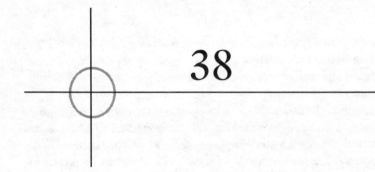

38

TWELVE MINUTES AFTER Antonio Zamora boarded the chartered Learjet at La Guardia's Marine Air Terminal, the sleek aircraft reached altitude and streamed southward, the dark blue waters of the Atlantic stretching east to the horizon thirty thousand feet below.

Zamora looked at his watch. It was one thirty-five. The pilot estimated the flight time at three and one-half hours, which would put him in St. Martin two hours before Kirby's plane was due to arrive. The seventeen thousand dollars the chartered flight had cost him for a round trip, with an additional fifteen hundred dollars for the plane and crew to lay over in St. Martin for the three days he had allotted to find Bass, did not come under normal operating expenses, and he had informed Carmine Molino that he expected to be reimbursed when the job was completed.

Zamora left his suitcases containing his sniper rifle along with the rest of his things with the concierge at the Plaza Hotel until his return, taking with him only the sound-suppressed semiautomatic pistol and the clothes he would need. He opened the carry-on bag he packed for the trip and removed what appeared to be a video camera. He then released a hidden catch and opened the camera casing to reveal a hollow interior specifically designed to hold his semiautomatic pistol and two spare magazines of ammunition. He removed the pistol from his briefcase and placed it inside the camera case, securing the hidden catch in place and returning it to the bag. The innocuous-looking device, ostensibly an ordinary video camera, was a familiar sight to customs officials the world over, and had served Zamora well since he had it made, never once arousing the slightest suspicion.

Zamora was at first angered that Molino was unable to provide him with the name Bass was using, not wanting to depend on following Kirby in order to find her. But upon reflection, he realized the method had its merits. He would not have to spend hours, or possibly days, showing Bass's photograph to innumerable people, exposing himself to any number of them who would remember him and be able to provide a description to the police after Bass's body was found.

He pulled the small curtains across the plane's windows, casting the cabin into a subdued light, then reclined his seat and closed his eyes and went back over what had happened at the SoHo club the previous night. He detested failure, and it was the first time he was forced to make a second attempt on a target. He blamed Kirby for that, and decided to kill him for his interference even if it was not necessary to do so to fulfill his contract to eliminate Bass.

Nicole Bass was greeted by a gentle trade-wind breeze as she got off the plane and crossed the tarmac to the terminal at Juliana International Airport on the island of St. Martin. She removed her blazer and held it across her arm as she moved slowly along in the line waiting to go through customs. In preparation for what she had planned, she had taken off her bra in the lavatory just before the plane landed, and as she approached the long counter where officious men in crisp white uniforms were examining the arriving passengers' luggage, she unbuttoned the first and second buttons on her silk blouse.

Upon reaching the counter, she smiled at the sullen-faced customs official and slipped the laptop computer case from her shoulder, placing it before him. She then leaned forward to unzip her carry-on bag, feigned fumbling with it as she handed it to him, and sent it tumbling on its side. The panties and bras purposely placed on top spilled out onto the counter.

"Oh, how clumsy of me. I'm so sorry." She began to hurriedly stuff her underwear back into the bag, using her best embarrassed look.

The man offered a small smile, his eyes lingering on Bass's breasts, clearly visible through the deep V of the unbuttoned blouse as she bent over the counter. He ignored the computer case and patiently waited until she had the bag in order. Bass held her breath, hoping he would not find the gun hidden inside her makeup kit, or the forty-five thousand dollars in cash zipped inside two inner compartments.

Bringing the money through customs on an island with any number of casinos would not arouse suspicion in and of itself, though it could compound a more serious problem if the gun was discovered along with it. But her diversion worked; the customs official's attention never wandered far from Bass's open blouse as he conducted a perfunctory examination of the bag, doing no more than running his hand around the interior before passing her through.

Bass stepped out of the terminal into the bright Caribbean sun and was immediately approached by a smiling island native who took her bag, almost wrestling it from her hand. He was a porter, who had an arrangement with his cousin, a taxi driver, to steer the more prosperous-looking tourists to his cab. One look at Bass's clothes, the soft leather carry-on, the computer case, and the Rolex sport watch on her wrist told him she would probably tip well.

"I'll carry this for you, miss. And where is it you will want to go? The French side of the island or somewhere here on the Dutch side?"

"The French side. Marigot Harbor."

Bass kept a watchful eye on her bag as the porter carried it to a waiting taxi, then handed it to her as he opened the rear door for her.

The porter gestured toward the cabdriver, who was leaning on the fender of the car, his arms folded across his chest, smiling pleasantly. "This man is the best and safest driver on the island, miss."

"And your brother, right?"

"Oh, no, miss. Certainly not. He's my cousin."

Bass returned his cheerful smile and gave him a five-dollar tip. He did a graceful little bow, and told his cousin where she wanted to go.

"Where in Marigot do you wish me to take you, miss?" the driver asked as he pulled away from the curb.

"Just drop me anywhere near the marketplace."

The spectacular island scenery unfolded before her as the driver expertly negotiated the narrow, winding road through the countryside. Villas and condominiums dotted the low mountains that rippled through the center of the island and trailed off to hilly spurs that ran down to the ocean, creating picturesque seaside valleys. The scenic drive to the French side of the island began to put Bass in the easy, relaxed Caribbean mood. The salt air, brilliant sun, and broad vistas of a sparkling turquoise sea were already weaving their magic spell as she forced all thoughts of the past week from her mind and felt the tension slowly drain from her body.

She left the cab in the heart of Marigot, pausing on the sidewalk for a few moments to take in the quaint beauty and Gallic charm of the old harbor town, reminiscent of the French Riviera with its bustling sidewalk cafés and bistros and exclusive European boutiques. October was the off-season, and the town was nowhere near as crowded as she remembered it from when she had been there in January.

She was standing in front of a sidewalk café, and became aware of a handsome young waiter staring at her. Their eyes met and he smiled, then approached and offered her a prime people-watching table. She politely refused his offer and moved across the street to the quay, noticing that he was watching her every move with open admiration.

A steel-drum band played somewhere off in the distance, and along the waterfront the colorful open-air market was in full swing. Local fishermen arrived in small, brightly painted boats bringing fresh snapper, lobster, conch, and shrimp, while stalls crowding the quay brimmed with tropical fruits, vegetables, and exotic spices, and the handmade jewelry and woven hats and baskets of the natives.

Out in the harbor luxury yachts and sailboats rested at anchor with hand-built island skiffs and the occasional freighter as counterpoints. Bass breathed deeply of the salt air mixed with the sweet, pungent scent of the open-air market as she stood looking out across the harbor toward her final destination.

Barely visible in the distance, across six miles of open water, no more than a twenty-minute trip by powerboat, she could just make out Anguilla, a low-lying coral island only sixteen miles long and a few miles wide, but with some of the most beautiful beaches in the Caribbean.

Bass had visited it only once, the previous winter, but it left a lasting impression. Far less developed than St. Martin, Anguilla still maintained much of the look and feel of the simple, unspoiled island wilderness that most of the islands had lost through overdevelopment. With no golf courses, jet skis, parasailing, casinos, or shopping arcades, it was a beachcomber's island at heart, a step through time to the Caribbean as it was years ago.

Her companion on her visit had been an English diplomat from the United Nations. Since he was another no-sex client, she had her own bedroom in a beachfront suite, and they spent the entire week sailing to outlying islands and secluded bays for picnics and lying in the sun. In the evenings they took long walks on the beach, and she listened as he talked about the love he still felt for a wife who had died the previous year, how wonderful their life together had been, and of his deep regret that it had been a childless marriage.

An inter-island airline flew small prop planes to Anguilla from the Juliana airport, but Bass did not want to arrive on the island in a way that would make it easy for anyone who might trace her to St. Martin to learn her final destination. The ferry that took day-trippers from Marigot to Anguilla was just leaving the pier when she got out of the taxi, and the next one was not scheduled for another half hour.

Bass noticed two small charter boat services at one of the finger piers near where the ferry docked, and she approached a tall, slender man with flawless mahogany skin who was filling the gas tank of a twenty-foot, rigid-hulled inflatable boat equipped with twin outboard motors. A sign nailed to a post on the pier read NOBLE SAMUELS: FISHING. SIGHT-SEEING. WATER SKIING. SCUBA DIVING AND SNORKELING.

Noble Samuels finished topping off his gas tank and looked up to see Bass standing on the pier. He smiled broadly, both for the prospect of a needed charter and in appreciation of the beauty of the woman before him.

"Noble Samuels at your service." He had the lilt of the Caribbean in his voice and the twinkle of the rascal in his eyes.

"Can you take me over to Anguilla?"

"Of course. Anywhere you like."

"I'd like you to drop me on the beach in front of Cap Juluca."

"I can do that."

"What do you charge?"

"For such a lovely woman as yourself? Fifty dollars."

"And for everyone else?"

"Fifty dollars." Samuels flashed another sparkling smile.

Bass laughed and handed him her bag and computer case. "Sounds like a bargain."

Samuels helped her down into the boat and took his place at the center steering console. He backed slowly away from the pier, and they were soon skimming across the gentle swells in Marigot Bay, heading northward to Anguilla.

As they drew close to the island, an incongruous vision, straight out of an Arabian Nights fantasy, rose on the horizon like a mirage. Nestled along a near-perfect semicircle of bone-white beach more than a mile long and anchored at either end by rocky promontories was the romantic, glamorous resort of Cap Juluca. The Moorish-style luxury villas with their whitewashed arches, domes, turrets, and parapets, partially visible through a lush screen of palm trees and tropical plants, glistened in the midday sun. Surrounded by crystal-clear, iridescent turquoise water as far as the outer reef, and then the cobalt blue of the sea separating Anguilla from St. Martin, it was a place far removed from the mainland of one's ordinary cares.

Noble Samuels cut back on the power, using the switch on the center console to raise the propellers out of the water as the boat rode the gentle surf up onto the edge of the near-deserted beach. Bass rolled up her slacks and took off her shoes before stepping out of the boat, enjoying the feel of the sand between her toes and the warm water lapping at her ankles. Samuels handed her carry-on bag and computer to her, along with one of his business cards.

"I know the best places to snorkel and dive. Very close by. You call me from the hotel and I soon come. Thirty minutes, no more."

Bass thanked him and helped him shove the small boat back into the surf, where he lowered the props, spun around in a tight circle, and waved before roaring away.

Bass walked across the beach to the main lobby of the resort and requested and got the same accommodations she had on her previous trip: an oceanfront villa at the eastern end of the crescent beach with its own private swimming pool inside a walled-in courtyard. A graceful keyhole archway covered with purple bougainvillea led from the courtyard of the ultraprivate quarters to the beach not fifty feet away down a narrow footpath landscaped with more spectacular flowers and surrounded by sand dunes.

Bass tossed her bag on the bed, immediately undressed, and slipped into a bathing suit. She took a beach towel with her and left for an ocean swim she had been anticipating since getting on the plane in New York City.

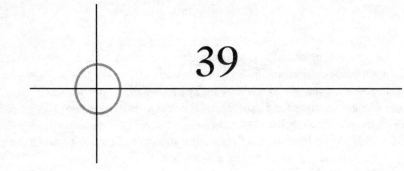

39

FOLLOWING THE ADVICE of a helpful flight attendant, a cop buff who struck up a conversation with him midway through the flight from Newark to Puerto Rico, Jack Kirby managed to arrive on St. Martin earlier than scheduled, avoiding the one-hour-plus layover in San Juan by changing to another airline that had a plane leaving fifteen minutes after his flight arrived.

He was first in line through customs, and walked out of the Juliana airport terminal shortly after six o'clock in the evening, still feeling stiff and cramped from spending most of the day immobilized in too-narrow seats with precious little leg room. He held his hands high above his head in an exaggerated stretch and stood looking about the area just outside the terminal, taking in the porters and the taxis lined up at the curb along with a few vans from nearby resorts awaiting passengers still working their way through customs.

The warm evening breeze coming in off the ocean felt good against his skin, and he took off his leather jacket, stuffed it through the handles of his carry-on bag, then rolled up his shirtsleeves. He decided to start with the porters. He showed the picture of Bass taken on the beach at Fire Island to three of them before the fourth man's face clearly registered that he had seen her, though he said nothing to that effect as he handed the photograph back and eyed Kirby with suspicion; he had spent three years in New York City before returning to the islands, and recognized Kirby's cop attitude.

"You've seen her, haven't you?"

"Many people have arrived here today. I can't remember all of them."

"But you remember her."

"Maybe. Maybe not."

Kirby took out his shield and showed it to the porter. "I'm a cop. I'm here to help her, not arrest her, and I'd appreciate anything you can tell me."

The porter smiled at the shield. "You're a policeman in New York City. Not here."

Kirby pulled a bill from a wad of twenties. "Does this help your memory?"

The porter palmed the twenty-dollar bill and slipped it into his pocket. "This afternoon. She came in on the two o'clock flight."

"Did she take a taxi or a van to one of the resorts?"

"I'm not sure. I was very busy. With the other passengers, you know."

Kirby handed him another twenty, which also quickly disappeared into his pocket. The porter motioned for Kirby to follow him, and led him to his cousin, who was leaning against the fender of his taxi parked at the curb.

"Johnathan, that lovely woman I brought to you this afternoon. Do you happen to remember where you took her?"

The taxi driver shrugged. "I can't be sure. It was a busy day."

Kirby let out a short, gruff laugh. "You guys practice this routine, or what?" He peeled off another twenty from the roll in his pocket and handed it to the cabdriver.

"Oh, yes. She wanted to go to the French side of the island."

"You wouldn't happen to remember exactly where you dropped her off, would you?"

"Let me think about that."

Kirby gave him another twenty. "That's all you're going to get. So let's have it."

"I could take you there, you know."

"How much?"

"Forty-five dollars is the fare to Marigot; that is where I took her." He had added twenty dollars to the usual fare, to be split later with his cousin.

Kirby tossed his bag through the open window of the cab. "Let's go."

By sheer luck Antonio Zamora had seen Kirby as he passed through customs. Not expecting him for another hour, he was sitting in the small café just inside the terminal nursing a cup of coffee and reading a magazine when he happened to look up at the same moment Kirby came out of the customs area and left the terminal.

Zamora stayed inside, watching through the glass doors until he saw Kirby get in the taxi and drive away. He then hurried outside and climbed into the first cab in line, holding up a one-hundred-dollar bill for the driver to see.

"It's yours, and another one just like it, if you follow the taxi that just left without letting them see us."

"No problem," the driver said, and pulled out immediately. With the recent arrival of a flight, another cab behind Kirby's on the road to Marigot would arouse no suspicion as long as it did not get close enough that Zamora could be identified if Kirby turned to look behind him. The driver had no trouble keeping Kirby's cab in sight, maintaining a respectful distance and speeding up only when it disappeared around a sharp curve.

As Zamora's driver crested a steep hill leading down to the outskirts of Marigot, Kirby's taxi could be seen at the bottom of the hill, slowing for the increased traffic as it entered the harbor area. Zamora's driver slowed to stay well behind, but still close enough to notice any turnoffs from the main road.

Near the bottom of the hill, with Kirby's driver still in sight as he continued along the waterfront, a tourist couple on a motorcycle pulled out from a side road, cutting in front of Zamora's cab. After going only a few hundred yards, the motorcycle skidded to a panic stop to avoid two goats crossing the road. Zamora's driver slammed on the brakes just in time to avoid rear-ending the motorcycle. Zamora leaned forward from the back seat and looked through the windshield to see Kirby's taxi disappear around a curve.

"Go around them!" he ordered the driver, who sat impatiently waiting as the man on the motorcycle, stopped sideways on the narrow road, tried to restart his stalled engine.

The cabdriver maneuvered his way to the shoulder, but could not pass without going into a ditch. Finally the motorcycle sputtered to life and drove off. Zamora's driver honked his horn and swung around them, driving as fast as the road would allow until he again slowed when he entered the congested harbor area. Kirby had been out of sight for a full two minutes, and Zamora's eyes frantically searched the road ahead.

"There!" he shouted, pointing at the distinctive pale blue cab just as it turned off the main street through Marigot.

"I see him," the driver said, and continued to follow, turning onto another narrow coastal road that led to the other side of the island.

They were too far behind to tell that the man in the cab they had been following was no longer Kirby. Another man, a tourist looking for a ride back to his resort hotel seven miles further up the coast, had grabbed the cab when Kirby got out in the middle of Marigot. With his attention on the road ahead, Zamora did not notice Kirby standing on the sidewalk as they drove past.

Kirby's driver dropped him precisely where Bass got out of the cab that afternoon, directly in front of the sidewalk café across the quay from the ferry dock. The outdoor market was closed for the day, the stalls and stands disassembled and taken away, and the cafés lining the sidewalk were filled with giddy, rummed-up day-trippers back from excursions to nearby islands, and fishermen telling tall tales of the ones that got away. The lights on the sailboats and yachts anchored just offshore sparkled like jewels on the surface of the dark water as a deep purple dusk slowly settled over the harbor. Along the quay charter boat crews exchanged the latest news and gossip, and young off-season honeymooners, beet-red from the tropical sun, strolled arm in arm, oblivious to anyone but themselves.

Kirby followed his cop instincts and began his canvass of the area by starting with the café directly behind him. He first showed Bass's picture to the bartender, who had only been on duty for the past hour. He shook his head, but Kirby's luck held. The young waiter who had admired Bass earlier that day leaned over to look at the photograph as he picked up a drink order for one of his tables. Without hesitation, he told Kirby he had indeed seen her, and pointed him in the direction Bass had gone, indicating the ferry dock.

"Where does the ferry go?"

"To Anguilla, and to St. Barts," the waiter said with a thick French accent.

"Did you see her get on the ferry?"

"No. It left just before I saw her. Another was not due for perhaps thirty minutes. She walked over to the dock, but when I looked again a few minutes later, poof, she was no longer there."

Kirby thanked him for his help, then crossed to the waterfront and stood at the dock where the ferry was tied up for the night, having just returned from its last run of the day. He showed Bass's picture, with no success, to the woman who sold tickets for the ferry as she was closing up the stand, and to three of the ferry's crew who were getting off the boat. None of them could recall seeing Bass aboard for any of the runs that day.

He interrupted the lively, animated conversation of a group of locals gathered on the quay, none of whom recognized Bass, then he continued along the dock to a finger pier where two small charter boat operators had their boats tied up. He stopped before Noble Samuels's sign and looked down to see the tall, slender island native cleaning his boat after a disappointing day of little business.

"Can I talk to you for a minute?"

Thinking he might have a potential charter for the next day, probably a scuba diver, he guessed, judging from the look of Kirby, he swung gracefully up onto the dock and extended his hand. Kirby shook it and introduced himself.

"Noble Samuels, Mr. Kirby. How can I help you?"

Kirby decided to try using his shield again, hoping to save some money. He flipped open the small leather case and held it up for Samuels to see.

"NYPD Blue!" Samuels exclaimed in recognition of the shield. "Lieutenant Fancy. Detectives Sipowicz, Simone, and Martinez. And that beautiful blond woman. What is her name? Abandando."

It took a few moments for Kirby to realize what Samuels was talking about. "The television show?"

"My favorite."

"You get that down here?"

"Of course. On the satellite."

"World's getting smaller every day."

"What can I do for you, detective?"

"I'm looking for someone." He took the photograph from his shirt pocket and gave it to Samuels, who held it up to the light on the post above his sign.

"Another beautiful woman."

"Have you seen her around here? About two-thirty or so this afternoon?"

"Surely a woman this beautiful is not a wanted criminal?"

"Nothing like that. Does she look familiar?"

Samuels held Kirby's gaze for a moment, then looked away. "That's hard to say."

"What's hard about it? Either you saw her or you didn't."

Samuels hesitated. "You're not here to arrest her?"

"Absolutely not."

"Ah, an affair of the heart then, as my French friends would say."

"She's in danger and I'm trying to save her life."

Samuels nodded. "I might have seen her, but I can't be certain."

Kirby chuckled softly and shook his head. "What is this? Everybody down here take the same course on how to extract money for information? I've got snitches back in New York who cost me less."

"Information is a valuable commodity, yes?"

Kirby gave him twenty dollars. "Do you know where she went?"

"I do" was all Samuels said with a smile.

Kirby gave him another twenty dollars. "Okay, by the numbers. Where did she go?"

"To Anguilla."

"And where's that?"

Samuels pointed out across the harbor to the open water. "It is a small island. Six miles that way. Only twenty minutes in my boat."

"Did she go to a resort there?"

Samuels nodded, grinning. "Since I enjoy your television show so much, I will take you there for my normal fee."

"Which is what?"

Samuels made a thoughtful face. "This time of night? After I've already cleaned my boat?"

"How much, Noble?"

"One hundred dollars."

"What about the forty I just gave you?"

"That was for information. Now we're talking about transportation."

Kirby tossed his bag down into the boat. "Cast off, you goddamn pirate."

Samuels laughed and dropped down into the boat with Kirby. Once clear of the harbor, he opened up the twin fifties, sending the light, agile craft speeding across the gentle swells at forty knots, leaving an impressive goose tail in its wake. Kirby sat in the front of the boat as Samuels had instructed, helping to keep the bow down and the sea spray to a minimum.

A crescent string of lights twinkled on the horizon as Kirby stared ahead at the distant island, looming larger by the minute. He thought about what he was going to say to Bass when he found her, wondering if she would be willing to listen to anything he had to say. And he again thought about what she had been through. He could not blame her if she refused to have anything more to do with the police or the courts. But even if she refused to return with him and testify, Genero would not quit until he eliminated her as a threat, and Kirby knew it was only a matter of time until someone found her and killed her. And he had resolved to do whatever it took to prevent that from happening.

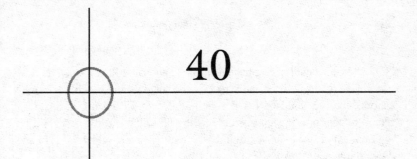

40

NICOLE BASS SAT on the beach in front of her villa watching the day give way to what the French called *l'heure bleue*—the blue hour—when the last rays of sun disappear beyond the horizon. The sunset had been magnificent; the sky glowing with pinks and scarlets and ever-deepening reds as the sea changed from luminescent turquoise to deep blue to onyx and dusk darkened into night, leaving behind a gentle offshore breeze and a cloudless blue-black tropical sky twinkling with the pin lights of countless stars.

The ocean rose in gentle swells, breaking listlessly onshore with a soothing sound enhanced by the soft rustle of palms and the echo of the surf on the distant reef. Bass got up and walked down to the edge of the white, powdery sand, letting the warm water curl gently over her feet in tiny wavelets. The events of the past week were fading fast as the primal island rhythms invaded her very soul, bringing a sense of calm and well-being that coursed its way through her body, diminishing the last of the tension and stress to insignificance.

She felt hungry, and realized that, other than a small bag of roasted almonds on the flight, she had eaten nothing since the dinner at the Golden Cockatoo the previous night. She recalled the excellent food at the resort's main restaurant, and visions of a sinful meal filled her thoughts. She decided on another swim, then a shower, followed by a leisurely dinner under the stars.

• • •

Noble Samuels cut the engines back to idle and raised the propellers out of the water, letting the small boat ride the surf into the beach. He came ashore near the same spot where he had dropped Bass off, almost directly in front of a stretch of sand leading up to the resort's main building on a small rise overlooking the ocean, only one hundred yards or so down the beach from Bass's private villa.

Samuels pointed in the direction of the main building. "The lady walked in that direction."

Kirby took his carry-on bag, slinging it over his shoulder as he stepped out of the boat onto the sand. He thanked Samuels for his help, then watched him shove off and pull away in the light of a rising moon. He walked slowly up the beach, pausing for a moment to look around, admiring the spectacular setting and the fairy-tale feeling of the place. He stared off to his left, to where a rock promontory jutted out into the water and the resort's private beach ended. The light of the full moon shimmered across the surface of the ocean, and in the distance, fifty yards from shore, he could just make out someone swimming slowly, expertly, toward the beach with smooth, graceful strokes. He continued watching the lone swimmer as he walked up to where palm trees lined the sand and the stone pathway to the main building began.

The sounds of reggae music and cocktail-hour chatter drifted down to the deserted beach from a small pavilion off to his right as he started up the path. Something made him stop and again look back toward the ocean. The swimmer had drawn closer to the beach and stood waist-deep in the gentle surf. He could now see it was a woman. She ran her hands through her hair, sweeping it back, before walking slowly through the water toward shore.

It was when she came out of the ocean, clad in a brief, high-cut bikini, her skin glistening with beads of seawater, her magnificent figure silhouetted in the moonlight, that Kirby realized it was Bass he had been watching. She stood motionless at the edge of the water for a moment, looking in his direction, but he knew she could not see him where he stood in the shadows beneath the palm trees.

He began to move along the edge of the beach, staying inside the tree line, hidden from view. He stopped when he came abreast of where Bass walked up the beach to pick up her towel and continue on toward a low, stark white villa shining in the moonlight.

Bass had poor night vision, but as she swam in from the reef, she had heard the boat come into shore farther up the beach. And she had seen the indistinct form of a man get out and pause to look in her direction, then disappear beneath the palm trees in front of the main building. She thought the boat was the same one, or of the same type, that brought her to the island, but she wasn't sure; she saw it only as a dark, blurry image in the failing light.

Her heart raced as she imagined the worst, then she calmed herself, rationalizing that it could be someone arriving on the island just as she had. And even if it was the same man who had brought her here, that was what he did for a living. It did not necessarily mean he had led someone to her.

But she had learned hard lessons about denying her instincts. She remained calm, acting as if she had seen nothing out of the ordinary. She picked up her towel and walked up the beach to disappear behind the lush tropical foliage along the path leading to the walled-in courtyard off her villa.

Kirby moved quickly through the trees along the perimeter of the beach until he reached the path Bass had taken. He slowed his pace, staying in the shadows until he came to the keyhole-shaped archway opening into the courtyard. He went through the archway, keeping to the wall as he skirted the small private swimming pool, then paused on the terrace off a softly lit, glass-walled living room.

The sliding glass doors were open to the night breeze and the distant sound of the ocean, and he peered inside. He saw no one and heard no one moving about a second room he assumed to be the bedroom, partially visible down a short hallway. As he took a step toward the open doors, he was startled by a voice from a darkened corner behind him. He instinctively reached for a gun that wasn't there before he realized who it was.

"How did you find me?"

Kirby dropped his carry-on bag to the terrace and turned to see Bass, barely visible in the deep shadows, lower the gun she had pointed at his head.

"What? No 'Hi, Jack. Good to see you'?"

"How did you find me?" Her words spoke more of disappointment than anger.

"It's what I do."

"Please, Kirby, don't be cute. If you found me, so can Genero. Where did I mess up?"

She stepped from the darkness into the soft light spilling out onto the terrace from the living room, and Kirby's attention was diverted for a moment by her bikini, which left little to the imagination.

"A friend at DEA told me about the Nancy Maguire passport."

"My file was supposed to be sealed."

"It is. I just lucked onto someone who was involved with Operation Armani."

She gave him a questioning look, then: "That's what they called it?"

"Yeah."

"I never knew that. How clever of them." The bitterness was evident in her tone.

Bass expelled a long, slow breath and seemed to slump in defeat, all of her energy and whatever fight she had left deserting her at that very moment.

"You're like a bad penny, Kirby."

"Yeah. My father used to say that about me."

"I'm not going back with you."

"Bad choice. Like you said, if I found you, so can Genero."

"You can't protect me any better than I can protect myself. Last night proved that."

"I give you my word that won't happen again."

Bass didn't reply. She felt trapped, as she did almost four years ago that evening in Milan, when all her troubles began. And as she stood there on the terrace, she was overcome with the feeling that it had never really ended and never would. The fear, the helplessness, her friends deserting her, the intolerable time spent with a man she truly hated and the self-loathing it had engendered, it all descended on her like an unbearable weight, crushing what remained of her spirit.

After a prolonged silence she looked directly at Kirby, her eyes pleading. "I'm not as strong as I thought I was. I can't take any more of this. Please, if you care about me at all, just leave. Go back to New York. Tell them you couldn't find me."

Kirby saw her pain, the hopelessness in her eyes. "This isn't just about getting Genero anymore, Niki, not for me. It's also about getting you out of this alive. And there's only one way out. And that's through it. You've got to trust me on this. You can try running around it, over it, under it, pretend it isn't happening, but the only way through it is through it."

"And what is that supposed to mean?"

"It means get it over with, once and for all. Come back with me. Help me put Genero away. Then it'll end. I promise you."

Bass held Kirby's gaze, her face a mask of sorrow and regret. Without a word, she walked from the terrace into the living room. Kirby followed her to a wet bar in the corner of the large open room where she put down the gun and removed a bottle of champagne from an ice bucket and poured herself a glass. She finished most of it with one long drink.

She turned to face him, her voice soft and plaintive. "I'm tired, Kirby. Tired of running. Tired of being afraid. Tired of not having any control over my life. I didn't ask for any of this. I don't want it. I just want to disappear and forget it ever happened."

"I know." He hesitated, looking into her saddened eyes. "And I know about Bolivia and Calderon, and what the DEA made you do."

Bass looked away, to some distant place only she knew of. "No, you don't. You only know the words."

"I'm sorry. I know that's a meaningless, stupid thing to say, but I am sorry for what happened to you. No one deserves to be used that way."

The abhorrent image of Calderon when Kirby spoke his name, the rush of emotions long suppressed, the stark terror and near-constant pressure of the past few days, were finally all too much for her. She turned her back to Kirby. He saw her shoulders tremble, and then he heard the soft, almost inaudible sobs. Without hesitation, he embraced her from behind, one arm around her shoulders, the other around her waist, feeling the warmth of her bare skin, her body quiver with each short, troubled breath.

He stood there holding her, squeezing her tightly until she stopped trembling and the sobs diminished. He kept her in his embrace as he turned her around to face him. Her eyes were red from crying, her face stained with tears. He tried to think of something to say that would comfort her.

"It's going to be okay," he whispered softly. "We'll get through this. I won't let them hurt you. I won't let you down."

It had been years since Bass allowed her emotions to rule, and she

was afraid she was about to lose complete control. She believed that
Kirby truly cared for her. It was not so much in what he had said, but the
compassion in his voice, the tenderness of his touch, and how he had
been willing to sacrifice himself for her the previous night. She put her
arms around him, clinging desperately.

"Hold me, Kirby. Please, hold me."

She raised her face to his, their eyes met, and then their lips. He was
surprised by the forcefulness and depth of her kiss, her tongue alive in
his mouth, darting in and out. He took her head in his hands and responded with equal, eager passion, breathing her breath. He lowered his
hands to cup her breasts as she clung to him, moving her hips in a slow,
sensual circle, pressing herself against him with all the strength of her
emotions.

Bass abandoned any semblance of self-control, letting herself go
completely. Nothing rehearsed or practiced or mechanical, none of the
cold, calculated detachment, or feigning of passion and erotic sensations
in response to an unwanted touch she had taught herself to evoke to
make the time with Ernesto Calderon bearable, the same emotionless responses that later made it possible for her to work for Carolyn Chambers. Giving only her body, nothing of her soul.

She responded to Kirby's gentle, reassuring touch with an almost forgotten freedom, an unbridled, impatient passion that overwhelmed her
with its intensity. She slipped out of her bikini, then unbuttoned Kirby's
shirt, stripping it from him as they continued to kiss and caress while
she finished undressing him. They dropped to their knees on the soft,
woven rug in the middle of the floor, kissing and touching each other
until she placed her hands on his shoulders and leaned forward, lower-
ing him onto his back and straddling him, her hands on his chest, her
forehead against his, her tongue flicking in and out of his mouth as she
reached back to guide him inside her, the silky warmth eliciting an involuntary sigh of pleasure from him as she moved slowly, rhythmically,
taking him in all the way, then rocking back and forth, withdrawing to
the very tip of his erection to drive the full length of him back inside at
the precise moment he arched toward her, reaching her very depths.

They climaxed together, suddenly, her chest rising and falling with
short, murmuring breaths as she tightened herself to keep him deep inside, then one final glide up and down and she shivered in exquisite
pleasure and tossed back her head. She leaned forward, ever so slowly,

until he was no longer inside her, then slipped off him to lay at his side, her mouth open, breathing sighs of contentment next to his ear.

They remained silent, said not a word, their bodies wet with perspiration, their muscles tingling from exertion. Bass rolled toward him, placed a leg across his thighs, and traced small circles on his chest with her fingers. Kirby turned his head to look into her eyes. She smiled back, a warm, wonderful smile he had not seen before.

He lay there feeling completely drained, a sense of satisfaction and fulfillment he could not remember having experienced before her. He knew what had happened between them was for reasons more than physical, something they both needed on an even deeper level. She had given herself to him completely, without reservation, without restraint, and he had responded in kind, in a way he never had with anyone else.

Bass rose on one elbow and leaned over to kiss him, gently biting his lip, then got up, naked and unashamed, and crossed the room to the bar, bringing back a glass of champagne for both of them. Kirby sat up and propped his back against the sofa. Bass sat leaning against him, her head resting on his chest as they sipped the ice-cold sparkling wine.

Kirby kissed her forehead as he ran his fingers through her hair. "Thanks."

"Compliments of the management."

"What?"

"The champagne."

"No. I mean, thanks. I didn't want it to end."

Bass smiled and snuggled her head into the crook of his neck. After a moment or two she began nibbling his ear, her warm breath tickling him. He ran his hand lightly over her face, tracing its contours, admiring her beauty. She took one of his fingers into her mouth and sucked it. Kirby felt himself growing hard again, and Bass moved her mouth down over his body, her lips brushing his chest and stomach until she reached his erection. She looked up with a playful smile and took a drink of champagne, holding the cold, fizzing liquid in her mouth for only a second before letting it trickle down the length of him, then immediately took him into her mouth to the back of her throat, then out again until just her lips held him, again and again, sucking in long forceful strokes.

The sudden chill and then the warmth and pressure of her mouth sent a jolt through Kirby's body. It was the most erotic sensation he had ever felt, and he climaxed almost immediately, exploding in powerful spurts.

He went momentarily limp with immobility and sat staring at her, a languid smile and a look of enormous pleasure on his face.

She continued to stroke him, taking him back into her mouth, tickling the tip with her tongue, and he was surprised to find himself hard once again. He bent down and kissed her passionately, then rose to kneel before her. Without further encouragement, she rolled onto her stomach and got to her knees. He entered her from behind, the angle and position making everything feel tight and new again. Later, they swam naked in the small, private pool in the courtyard, then lay, sated and exhausted, entwined in each other's arms, drifting on a cushioned float.

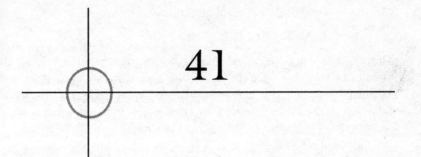

41

ANTONIO ZAMORA WASTED more than an hour at a resort on the French side of the island of St. Martin before he discovered that the man dropped off there by the cabdriver he had followed was not Kirby. He backtracked to the airport to find the same pale blue taxi and, after a short discussion during which fifty dollars changed hands, he learned where the driver had dropped Kirby off in Marigot.

Zamora's first thought was that Kirby had taken the ferry, but upon being told that the last run of the day was completed before Kirby got there, he did the same thing Kirby had done before him and asked others on the quay if they had seen him or Bass, using the photo of her taken from Carolyn Chambers's office.

Noble Samuels had left for the evening, but his competitor and friend, Johnno Thomas, who operated his own small charter service from an adjacent finger pier, was still there. He had gotten back late from a snorkeling charter and was just finishing hosing the salt spray off his twenty-foot Boston Whaler when Zamora approached him and paid him fifty dollars to learn that shortly after Thomas returned from his charter, Noble Samuels arrived back at Marigot Harbor from dropping Kirby off at Cap Juluca. When Zamora gave him another fifty dollars and showed him Bass's photograph, Thomas told him that it might be the woman his friend Samuels had taken to the same place earlier that day.

Zamora at first tried unsuccessfully to get Thomas to take him to Anguilla, Thomas arguing that he was finished working for the day. The five hundred dollars Zamora offered him changed his mind immediately.

. . .

Thirty minutes later, after a high-speed run back from Anguilla, Johnno Thomas tied up his boat at the dock in Marigot Harbor, whistling and snapping his fingers as he crossed the street to a bar frequented by locals. He found his friend Noble Samuels at a table in the back eating a steaming bowl of goat stew. Thomas sat down across from him, grinning as he took out his wallet.

"Your tourist friends are very popular, thank God." He showed Samuels the total of six hundred dollars Zamora had given him.

"And where did you get that?"

Thomas told him about Zamora and his interest in both Bass and Kirby. Samuels stopped eating and stared thoughtfully at his friend.

"The detective I took there said the woman was in danger; that he was trying to save her life. Was your tourist another American policeman?"

Thomas shrugged. "Could be. But I don't think so. He asked me to take him in to the beach where no one at Cap Juluca would see him come ashore."

"And you did that?"

"At first I suggested we go into a fishing pier further down the bay, but the look he gave me was not one I care to see again. So I did as he asked."

"And just what did you think he was up to, Johnno? Certainly no good."

"I don't ask. I don't know. No problems."

Samuels shoved the bowl of goat stew away. "Where did you drop him?"

"Why? If there's trouble, it's not our concern."

"Perhaps not your concern. But the detective asked me not to tell anyone of his interest. And what is the first thing I do with my big mouth? I tell you. And you tell someone who is looking for him and the woman and wants to sneak ashore and not be seen."

Samuels finished his beer in one long gulp and got up from the table. "I don't know why I let myself get involved in these things. I should have known there would be trouble. Easy money, Johnno. There's always the devil to pay."

Thomas shrugged, not sharing his friend's concern.

"Now tell me, where exactly did you drop this man?"

"In Shoal Bay West, just on the other side of the rock outcropping from Cap Juluca beach."

Samuels went to the pay phone at the back of the bar and called the registration desk at Cap Juluca. He asked to speak to Jack Kirby, and was informed there was no one registered at the resort by that name. He did not know Bass's name, and when he asked about a beautiful young woman who had arrived there at approximately three o'clock that afternoon, describing the clothes she had been wearing, the man on the desk grew suspicious and hung up after informing Samuels that they did not give out information about their guests.

"A lightning rod for trouble, Noble Samuels, that is what you are," he muttered to himself as he left the bar. "Your mother said it is so and it is."

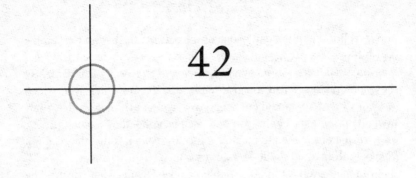

42

THE MAIN DINING room at Cap Juluca, an open pavilion on a coral outcrop only six feet from the water's edge, provided a romantic view of the ocean and the lighted domes, turrets, and parapets of the villas along the length of the crescent beach. The off-season guests, their faces browned or lightly burned from a day in the sun, were a mix of honeymooners, families with children, and happy older couples whose greatest pleasure in life seemed to be each other's company. The reggae beat of a local band lured the younger couples onto the small dance floor by the bar, but most of the guests in the less-than-half-full dining room simply relaxed and enjoyed their meal and the spectacular setting.

Bass and Kirby had talked all through dinner, and then Kirby's mood suddenly changed and he sat staring silently out across the water.

"A penny for your thoughts."

"I was thinking about Kathleen, my daughter."

"How old is she?"

"She would have been eight five days ago."

Bass saw the pain in his face and reached across the table to squeeze his hand. "I'm sorry. What happened to her?"

Kirby hesitated, then, for the first time since the terrible tragedy, talked openly about his daughter's death and how he would never forgive himself for what had happened.

"She was like one of those ocean birds you see down here, riding the wind, all natural grace. She was the most beautiful, wonderful thing in my life. I loved her so damn much it hurt, and I destroyed her. I failed at the most important job any father has—to keep her safe."

"Is that why your marriage broke up?"

"Kathleen's death was just the final straw. We were well on our way to splitting long before that. It's an occupational hazard with cops. You work all night then sleep all day. You forget about your family, lose track of days, weeks, months, women you've slept with, lies you've told, bars you can't get back into. Pretty soon all you have or think about is the Job." He shrugged and looked away. "I guess, in the end, we all get what we deserve."

A sad smile crossed Bass's face. "No. We get what we settle for."

They sat quietly for a few minutes, each with their own private thoughts, then Bass lightened the mood by changing the subject and ordering a bottle of champagne. She laughed when she saw Kirby's expression as the waiter filled his glass, the recent erotic experience clearly in his thoughts.

"Get that silly look off your face, Kirby. You're grinning like a mule with a mouthful of briars."

"That's one I haven't heard before."

Bass affected a quick-cadence, twangy, mountain voice. "You forget, I'm a Tennessee hillbilly. We've got a lot of sayings like that."

"I've never met a real hillbilly before."

Bass clinked champagne glasses with him and winked. "See what you've missed?" Her eyes softened, her voice just above a whisper. "Are you going to stay with me tonight?"

"Is that an invitation?"

Bass leaned over and kissed him lightly on the cheek. "Yes. We can go back tomorrow."

"We?"

"Yes. We. I've thought about what you said, and you're right. I've got to see it through or I'll never find any peace."

Antonio Zamora had found his way off the beach to the main road around the island, following it the short distance to the entrance to the grounds of Cap Juluca. He noticed that none of the villas had numbers on their doors, and were obviously left unlocked; he had seen people entering and leaving without locking or unlocking their doors. He spent a half hour or so getting oriented, walking the lighted, lushly landscaped footpaths through the resort until he came to the path leading to the main dining room. He stepped out into the open briefly, then moved back beneath the palm trees when he spotted Kirby and Bass at a table on the edge of the terrace. He retreated deeper into the shadows and watched them until they left the restaurant and followed a path down to the beach where they walked arm in arm along the water's edge, only fifty feet from where he stood beneath the palms.

He could have easily shot them both at that moment, the sound of the surf and the night breeze rustling the trees hiding the hiss and finger-snap sounds as he fired the sound-suppressed pistol. But he noticed two couples walking ahead of them, and then others coming down from the restaurant for a walk on the beach before retiring for the night. He decided to wait until Kirby and Bass got back to wherever they were staying and kill them there. No one would find them until the next day, giving him ample time to get off the island before their bodies were discovered.

Zamora stayed in the shadows beneath the trees, following a parallel course with Bass and Kirby as they walked slowly along the beach. He saw them stop and embrace and kiss, and he smiled to himself. They would make love that night, he was certain of it. He would kill them as they lay together. Perhaps watch them make love first, putting an end to their lives as they were about to climax—a nice, personal touch, he thought.

Bass and Kirby entered the private courtyard of her villa to see that after turning down the bed, the maid, in keeping with the romantic theme of the resort, had turned out the lights in the living room and the bedroom and lighted small oil lamps, their flickering flames casting playful shadows about the rooms.

Bass crossed the courtyard terrace and walked through the open doors to the living room and began to unbutton her blouse. "It's only ten o'clock. I'm in the mood for a moonlight swim. How about you?"

Kirby raised an eyebrow. "In the ocean?"

"Of course. It's beautiful at night."

"It's also when everything that's in there does most of their feeding. Like sharks."

"That's not true."

"It's what I heard."

"If you want to be a wimp about it, we can swim in the pool."

"Pool's fine."

Antonio Zamora, thinking that the archway entrance to Bass's private terrace was a common area, mistakenly stepped into the courtyard before realizing it was part of her villa. He was out in the open where they would easily see him through the glass doors if they looked in his direction. He reacted instinctively, and in his haste compounded the mistake by forgetting what he had learned during his training years ago: never move quickly against a stationary background—back away, or lower your profile slowly until you are under concealment—since rapid movement draws attention where slow movement will not. Without thinking, he moved quickly to his right, into the shadows against the interior wall of the courtyard.

Kirby was taking off his shirt when, out of the corner of his eye, he saw the sudden movement in the shadows just inside the archway. For an instant he thought it was just the night breeze swaying the broad leaves on one of the potted palms placed around the terrace in large urns. But it had been an unnatural movement, and he immediately grabbed Bass and pulled her to the floor behind the sofa.

Bass laughed, thinking he was clowning, playing the part of the overanxious lover. "Seduction and foreplay aren't your strong points, are they, Kirby." She raised her head to kiss him and saw the intense look on his face. "What is it?"

"Someone's outside on the terrace."

He peered over the top of the sofa, his eyes moving quickly across the courtyard, searching the area to the left of the archway. He saw nothing, and ducked back down beside Bass. "Stay down!" His voice was an urgent whisper.

"My gun!"

"Where is it?"

"In the purse I took to dinner." She pointed to the table against the wall opposite the sofa. He would have to cross five or six feet of open space to get to it.

Kirby crawled on his elbows to the end of the curved sectional sofa, then darted across the open space, grabbing the purse from the table and diving to the floor as a bullet missed his head by mere inches and impacted in the wall above him.

He had heard the sharp click made by the gun as the receiver went back to inject another round into the chamber, and he caught a brief glimpse of the muzzle flash that escaped from the tip of the suppressor, telling him precisely where Zamora was: to the left of the pool, along the courtyard wall. He rolled back behind the sofa beside Bass, and took the gun from the purse.

"How many rounds in the magazine?"

Bass thought for a moment. "Six. And one in the chamber. The safety's on."

Kirby flipped the safety off. "Stay here. I'm going to try and draw him out into the open."

With the element of surprise gone, Zamora had no choice but to act immediately. He muttered an oath in Spanish, then kept to the shadows along the courtyard wall as he moved toward the open door to the living room, looking for an angle that would allow him a clear shot behind the sofa.

The living room was lit only by the dim glow from the oil lamp, and the dancing shadows from the flickering flame made him spin to his left and almost fire before he realized what he was seeing. A moment later he saw a much larger shadow dart from behind the sofa. He fired twice, his shots shattering a vase behind a silhouetted figure he identified as Kirby as the figure disappeared into the hallway leading to the bedroom.

Zamora realized what Kirby was doing. Moving to outflank him. What he did not know was whether both of them had a weapon. He doubted that Kirby, as a cop, would risk smuggling a gun into another country. But had Bass? And if she did, who had it now? He guessed Kirby, and that the purse he had grabbed off the table when he fired at him had contained Bass's gun. He reminded himself that although Bass was his primary target, he first had to deal with the person he believed had the weapon.

Kirby was counting on Zamora going after Bass first, and had moved into position to get a clear shot at him when he approached the living-room door. At the end of the short hallway to the bedroom, he peered around the edge of the glass door open to the terrace, then immediately pulled his head back inside. He had hoped the quick look would reveal Zamora's position, but he saw nothing moving in the shadows where he had seen the muzzle blast earlier.

The moment Kirby disappeared into the hallway, Zamora moved

around the far side of the pool to the opposite end of the terrace. Zamora was behind Kirby when he peered around the edge of the door, hidden in the darkened corner where the villa and the courtyard walls joined. He was just about to fire when Kirby pulled his head back inside. He stood motionless in the corner, waiting for Kirby to come outside, his gun held firmly in a two-handed grip, aimed at the precise spot where he had appeared moments ago.

The oil lamp in the bedroom was on a table next to where Kirby crouched at the door. He reached over and snuffed out the flame, casting the room into darkness. He came through the door onto the terrace in a low crouch, and flattened himself against the solid part of the villa wall between the glass doors of the living room and the bedroom. He was partially hidden by a large urn filled with an overflowing flowering shrub, and he looked in the direction he had last seen Zamora, watching the deep shadows against the courtyard wall and the urns containing the broad-leafed palms.

Zamora took careful aim at the back of Kirby's head and slowly squeezed the trigger. As he was about to shoot, he saw Bass step out onto the terrace from the living-room door, not ten feet from where Kirby was crouched. Kirby also saw her, the oil lamp from the living room in her hand, her attention focused behind him. She had peered out from behind the sofa when Kirby ran into the bedroom and had seen Zamora moving around the far side of the pool. With no other weapon available, she had picked up the oil lamp and moved across the room to where she had a view down the short hallway to the glass doors of the bedroom and saw Zamora step out of the shadows behind Kirby. The moment she came through the living-room door onto the terrace and saw Zamora ready to fire, she threw the oil lamp at him.

Kirby spun around to see Zamora use his gun hand to deflect the lamp, shattering the glass chimney. Hot oil splattered across his face, searing his skin and blurring his vision in one eye. He cried out in pain, then fired three shots in rapid succession. The shots were high and wide of their mark, and ricocheted off the wall above Kirby's head just as he returned two well-aimed shots that struck Zamora in the chest.

The .380-caliber bullets were not powerful enough to kill him quickly, and Zamora staggered backward and dropped to his knees. He brought his gun up to fire again, but Kirby fired first, this time killing him instantly with two shots that tore into the side of his head above the ear. Zamora dropped onto his side, his body from the waist up hanging over the edge of the swimming pool, his head in the water.

Kirby got to his feet and immediately went over to Bass to make certain she had not been hit by any of Zamora's shots. She stood staring at Zamora, the blood from his head wounds swirling about in the circulating pool water.

"You okay?"

Bass nodded, still staring at Zamora. "Was he the one at the club last night?"

"I think so."

"How did he find me?"

"He didn't find you. He found me. He must have followed me from New York."

Bass looked at Kirby and her eyes widened in alarm. In the glow from the pool lights she could see blood on the side of his face and on his chest where his shirt hung open. "Were you hit?"

"No. It's his. Blood splatter from the head wounds. By the way. Thanks. You saved *my* life this time."

Bass shrugged and pulled a face. "It's what I do."

Kirby couldn't help but laugh. "Look, we've got to get out of here. Fast. I guarantee you the four shots I fired were heard all over this resort. We can't wait around for the local cops to arrive, they probably take a dim view of the tourists killing each other."

"The resort is less than half full, and there's no one in the villas on this end of the beach. Maybe no one heard the shots."

"Trust me on this one. They were heard. Someone's going to check it out."

"How are we going to get off the island at this time of night?"

"I haven't figured that out yet. But if we're here when the cops arrive, they're going to lock us up until they sort this out, which could take a few days. And if our friend dangling into the pool over there brought anyone else with him, you'll be a sitting duck in a local jail cell. So grab your things, we'll work out a plan later."

Bass ran back into the villa, stuffing the few clothes she brought with her into her carry-on bag. She grabbed her laptop computer off the table in the living room and waited at the door to the terrace as Kirby washed the blood from his face and chest and put on a clean shirt.

"Did you check into this place as Nancy Maguire?"

"Yes. They kept my passport for a few hours and then gave it back."

"Good. There's no record of my being on the island, so we're clear. When they start asking questions about Nancy Maguire, they'll hit a dead end when the State Department tells them it was a phony passport. They'll probably find a long record on our friend over there, chalk the whole thing up to a drug-related killing, and that'll be the end of it."

"Where are we going now?"

"As far away from here as we can get. We'll take the beach until we're clear of the immediate area—we don't want to run into the local cops on the road."

They hurried out of the courtyard and down the path to the beach, staying just inside the tree line at the edge of the sand until they reached the far end of the resort's property. They saw no one, and Kirby reasoned that either hotel security, if they had any, had not determined the direction from which the shots had come, or they had simply called the police and were waiting for them to arrive and investigate.

Kirby was about to lead Bass over a low point on the rock promontory where the resort's private beach ended when he heard the roar of outboard engines just offshore. He turned to see a twenty-foot, rigid-hulled inflatable boat heading into the beach under full power. He stopped and watched as it drew closer. In the light of the full moon he could make out that the man behind the controls was Noble Samuels. He continued racing toward shore, then cut back on the power, raised the props, and brought the boat up on the beach not ten feet from where they stood.

Kirby and Bass ran over to him and tossed their bags inside. "We got a little problem here, Noble," Kirby said. "We could use your help."

"I thought that might be the case."

Bass took the helping hand Samuels offered and got in the boat as Kirby shoved them off the beach, leaping in as a retreating wave pulled them out into the surf.

Samuels lowered the props and gave the twin outboards full throttle, almost sending Kirby over the side until he dropped to his knees.

"I thought I heard gunshots," Samuels shouted above the roar of the engines as the boat pulled quickly away from shore. The sharp reports when Kirby had fired had carried a considerable distance out across the water. Samuels heard them as muted popping sounds over the noise of his engines.

"You thought right." Kirby got to his feet and held on to the control console as he stood beside Samuels. Bass sat in the very front of the boat, helping to keep the bow down.

"I'm sorry if I put you in any danger, Detective Kirby. I made the mistake of telling a friend about you. When he told me he brought the other man to the island, I thought I should make sure you were okay." Samuels backed off on the throttle slightly to help drop the bow some more. "Was anyone hurt?"

"You could say that."

"Is the other man chasing you?"

"Not anymore."

Samuels stared at Kirby, then nodded his understanding.

"I hope I'm not putting you in a situation you can't talk your way out of, but I've got to get her back to New York, alive."

Samuels grinned and laid on the island accent thicker than usual. "No problem, mon. Not my island. I wasn't even here."

The ocean swells were broader, the troughs deeper, than when Kirby had crossed the open water earlier. The small boat pounded in and out of the troughs in a bouncy, exhilarating ride interspersed with bone-jarring jolts that had Bass smiling and Kirby close to losing his dinner by the time they pulled into the dock at Marigot Harbor. Kirby was the first one out of the boat, thankful for a surface that didn't move under his feet. A few deep breaths and his queasy stomach settled.

Kirby looked around at the near-deserted quay, hoping to see a taxi, but there weren't any. "We'd like to get to the airport, Noble."

"No more planes tonight. First one out is tomorrow morning at eight o'clock. It goes to San Juan, then on to New York City."

"Know a nice quiet place near the airport we can spend the night?"

"I do. A small guesthouse in the hills on the Dutch side. A friend of mine owns it. Very private. Just the place for you. And only a few minutes from the airport."

"Sounds perfect. How do we get there?"

"I will take you there. My car is just across the quay."

"I don't want to put you out. If you can call us a cab, that'll be fine."

"No, I insist. I still feel guilty about your problems."

They arrived at Samuels's friend's guesthouse forty minutes later. Before getting out of the car, Bass leaned forward from the back seat and handed Samuels ten banded packets of money totaling ten thousand dollars she had taken from her carry-on bag.

"This is for you, Noble. For helping us."

Samuels stared at the packets of money in disbelief. "This is a whole lot of money."

"You were a whole lot of help."

Samuels, grinning from ear to ear with his good fortune, accompanied them into the small hillside guesthouse where he had a private conversation with his friend as Kirby and Bass waited in the sitting room/lobby.

After a few minutes he came over and sat across from them. "There are no other guests tonight, and there will be no need to register. My friend Nelson will take you to the airport tomorrow morning, first thing."

Kirby and Bass thanked him again for his help and watched him drive away down the narrow mountain road. They had every intention of making love that night, but exhausted from a long, full day that ran the gamut of emotions, they instead fell asleep in each other's arms, the louvered doors of the small bedroom open to the soft mountain breeze.

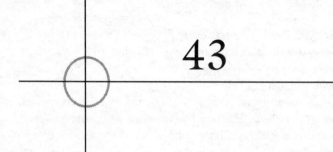

43

KIRBY AND BASS arrived at New York's JFK Airport on a connecting flight from San Juan, Puerto Rico, at two o'clock the following afternoon. Waiting for them the moment they stepped off the plane were Tony Rizzo and four OCMU detectives, who immediately surrounded them and escorted them down a stairway outside onto the tarmac where two unmarked police cars and a police van with heavily tinted windows were parked. The carry-on bags they had checked were immediately separated from the flight's other luggage and put into the van with them and they were driven swiftly away, led by an airport security vehicle.

When the van and the two unmarked cars left the airport by a side exit, the security vehicle stayed behind and two blue-and-whites joined the procession into the city, one in front and one bringing up the rear. The lead blue-and-white used its light bar and siren to keep those behind moving at a fast clip.

Twenty-five minutes later they arrived at Bass's apartment building on East Sixty-ninth Street. An unmarked car with two detectives in it was parked at the end of the driveway, with two more at opposite ends of the block. Bass and Kirby got out of the van at the entrance to the building and were again surrounded and escorted past four detectives in the lobby and taken directly up to Bass's twentieth-floor apartment where a detective was posted outside the door and another in the stairwell landing at the end of the hall. The four detectives with Rizzo left to relieve those in the lobby when he and Bass and Kirby entered the apartment.

Bass and Kirby spent the next half hour briefing Rizzo on all that had happened in St. Martin and Anguilla. Rizzo noticed a subtle difference in Kirby's behavior and attitude toward Bass, deferring to her at times in a way he knew was not Kirby's usual manner. He guessed what had happened between them, but said nothing.

"You'll testify before the grand jury tomorrow morning at eleven o'clock," he said to Bass. "We'll transport you there under heavy security around nine, so the A.D.A. can go over your testimony with you beforehand. Immediately after you testify you'll be moved to a permanent location outside the city until the trial starts. For your own safety I don't want you leaving this apartment for any reason until we come for you tomorrow. You want anything, you tell Detective Kirby and he'll make sure you get it."

"Have they decided on where I'll be staying until the trial?"

"Not yet. You'll have some input on that." Rizzo smiled. "The A.D.A. isn't too eager to incur your wrath again."

Rizzo stood and addressed Kirby. "I want to talk with you privately for a minute."

Kirby led him out onto the balcony off the living room and slid the door closed behind them. "What's up, Lou?"

Rizzo's eyes bored into him. "Are you sure no one on that island where you shot the guy can connect you to the Department?"

"One person. The guy who got us out of there. But he's in no position to talk about it to anyone without causing himself some problems. Besides, he's from St. Martin, not Anguilla, different country, and nobody was around to see him pick us up."

"I sure as hell hope you're right. I don't know the laws down there, but I guarantee you, you broke more than a few by not calling in the local cops and leaving the scene."

"It was a judgment call, Lou. If nothing else, they would have busted her for bringing a gun onto the island. We'd have been in limbo down there for what? A couple weeks? Plus my being busted along with her would have put you and the chief in the jackpot back here. All things considered, it was the only choice; this way nothing's going to come back on us. They've got no way to tie me or the Department to it. And they don't even know Bass's real name."

"You're involved with her, aren't you?"

Kirby was caught off guard by the question. "In a word? Yes. But it's not a problem."

"Don't let it become one. I know you well enough to know what this is about. You feel sorry for her because the DEA raked her over the coals."

"There's more to it than that."

"Whatever. Just remember that lady in there isn't any Girl Scout. She had to be tough and resourceful to go through what she did and come out the other side. And the odds are she got bent in the process."

"So what are you saying?"

"I'm saying, keep your perspective; don't let the little head do the thinking for the big head. And don't forget what she did for a living for the past eighteen months."

"Don't worry about it. It's not going anywhere."

"Because you don't want it to, or because she doesn't?"

"Same difference. I'm a cop, Lou, looking forward to a cop's pension. I've got nothing to offer her and nothing she wants."

"You know, Jack, for a smart guy, sometimes you say some pretty dumb things. A couple days ago you told me your gut feeling was she wasn't leveling with us. Well, my gut tells me the same thing. I think she has an agenda of her own we haven't figured out yet. Keep that in mind."

Carmine Molino drove out of the Rikers Island prison compound badly shaken. Ten minutes earlier, when he told Vincent Genero that Bass was back in protective custody and he had not heard from the Cuban, Genero exploded in a violent outburst, grabbing him by the lapels of his suit coat and dragging him halfway across the table before the guards in the visiting room intervened. It took a total of four guards to remove him from the room, screaming at the top of his lungs as they pulled him through the door.

"Get it done, Carmine! Get it fuckin' done you wanna keep breathin', you cocksucker!"

It was not the first time Genero had cursed and threatened him, and Molino attributed the outburst to the toll being locked up was taking on him. But he knew Genero better than anyone; if he got it into his head that someone had betrayed him, he would have them killed without giving it a second thought, regardless of the depth of any past relationship or their status within the Family.

Molino thought back on the order to kill Totani, a man whom Genero had respected and trusted, and who had served him well. Others over the past six years had suffered the same fate when Genero turned on them for disobeying him, causing him the slightest inconvenience, or in response to an insult or threat to his power, real or imagined. Molino did not kid himself that he was exempt from his boss's retribution, and if he did not soon eliminate Bass, Genero would find someone else to do it and eliminate him in the process.

With no word from the Cuban, Molino had to accept the fact that Bass would testify before the grand jury. There was no way to stop her; security would be too heavy and they would be expecting an attempt on her life. His only hope was to make new arrangements as soon as he learned where they were going to keep her until the trial. He would have to move fast. Genero would remain in jail for at least another six months after the grand jury indicted him, until his trial began, and each day he stayed locked up would make him crazier than the last. Molino comforted himself with the thought that he still had Janet Morris inside the Intelligence Division, and she had not failed him yet.

He pulled through the gate to his construction company in Queens and parked in front of his office. He had his back to the parking area, unlocking the office door, when he heard someone pull in behind him. He turned to see a panel truck with no rear windows and bearing the logo of a dry-cleaning company stop beside his car. The driver kept the engine running as the man in the front passenger seat got out. Molino recognized him as Artie Salerno, a Genovese Family soldier, and immediately slipped his hand inside his coat to grip the butt of the pistol tucked into the waistband at the front of his slacks.

Salerno grinned and held his hands up in mock surrender. "Yo, Carmine. Easy. This is a friendly visit. Somebody wants to talk to you."

Molino walked toward the panel truck, keeping his hand on his gun and his eyes on Salerno as Salerno pulled open the side door and gestured for him to get in. Molino stopped halfway there, cocking his head to peer inside. The back of the truck was fitted with two leather armchairs facing forward and two facing the rear. He could see the legs of a man who was sitting in the front-facing chair closest to the open door. He took another step forward to a spot where he could see who it was, and at the same moment, Salvatore Conte, the head of the Genovese crime Family, leaned forward into full view.

The most reclusive and least visible of the New York Mafia dons, Conte ran his complex criminal enterprises and his Family with the strictest secrecy, and consequently they were the only Family not to be decimated by high-level defectors turned government witnesses during the trials that put the upper echelons of the other Families in prison six years ago. An even-tempered, intelligent, and thoughtful man, he held the most influence with the heads of the other Families, with the exception of Vincent Genero, who despised him and considered him a weak leader. Molino had not seen Conte in person in five years, nor to his knowledge had anyone outside of the Genovese Family.

"We need to talk, Carmine. You have nothing to fear from me. This is a business meeting."

"I don't know. You should be talkin' to Vinnie if it's Family business. Not me."

"That's not possible right now, is it?"

"I can't agree to nothin' without Vinnie's say-so."

"Just get in, Carmine. We'll drive around and you'll hear me out. If you don't agree with what I have to say, this meeting never happened."

Molino, intrigued by what Conte might have to say, looked about the construction company yard to make certain no one was watching him. The yard was empty, the employees gone home for the day, and Molino got in the back of the truck and sat facing Conte. Salerno closed the door, climbed in the front passenger seat, and they drove off.

Conte held eye contact with Molino as he lit a cigarette and reclined his leather armchair. "I'm aware of the problem Vinnie has with the woman who saw him hit Onorati."

"We're gonna have that taken care of real soon."

"That's what I want to talk to you about; that and the cop who got inside one of your crews that Vinnie ordered hit."

Molino remained silent, acknowledging nothing.

"Vinnie's causing a lot of problems, Carmine. The cops are putting the pressure on all of us about the death of one of their undercovers, and about the attempts on the witness's life. It's bad for business and it's got to stop."

"I'll tell Vinnie what you said."

Conte sat smoking his cigarette for a few moments, then leaned closer to Molino. "Vinnie's the problem, Carmine. Not the solution."

"What do you want me to do about it? He's the boss."

"What I want you to do is listen to what I'm going to say. I met with the heads of the Bonanno, Lucchese, and Colombo Families this morning. Along with the problems I already mentioned, they share my concern about Vinnie rolling over for the cops if he ends up with a life sentence. He knows too much about all of our operations for us to let that happen. So we came to an agreement and we have a proposition for you."

"I don't think I wanna hear this."

Conte's voice took on an edge. "Just listen to what I'm telling you."

"I'll listen, but I ain't makin' no decisions without talkin' to Vinnie."

"The decision's already been made, Carmine. Vinnie's got to go. We're taking care of that. What we need to know is if we can depend on you to help keep your people from starting an all-out war, which isn't going to do anybody any good. If you can do that, we can guarantee that you'll take over your Family."

Molino saw Conte's offer not only as a means of attaining power, but as a way out of his current dilemma with Genero. But as a veteran of numerous internecine Mafia wars, he knew the pitfalls inherent in any power play.

"How are you gonna do that? A lot of the guys ain't gonna like Vinnie gettin' whacked."

"Vinnie has no friends, Carmine. Only people who fear him. When he's gone, so's their loyalty. The only reason we let him head the commission was to stop the war he started six years ago. Without going into details right now, I can tell you that we know for a fact most of the capos in your Family will back you as the new don. The few who don't will be dealt with before they cause any trouble."

Molino shook his head. "That broad don't testify? And Vinnie gets out? He's gonna start a war you wouldn't believe. And guess who he's gonna whack first?"

"You're not listening, Carmine. Vinnie is a liability we can't afford any longer. It's not a question of what's going to happen to him; the question is, are we going to make an arrangement with you right now to keep the peace."

Molino's answer was cautious and indirect. "I got no beef with you or the other Families."

Conte reached over and patted Molino's knee. "Good. Because that's how things should be. We all got our own interests to look out for, and nobody is moving in on anybody else's territory. Nobody wants any more problems than we already have."

Molino sat quietly for a few minutes. Conte watched him like a cat with a cornered mouse, knowing that he would have to kill him if he refused their offer. When Molino finally spoke, Conte knew the commitment was made.

"There's another problem you don't know about."

Conte smiled. "The money? We know about that. Somewhere between fifteen and eighteen million is the figure we got."

"How'd you find out?"

Conte shrugged. "That's another reason we don't want the witness dead. We want our share of the money back, Carmine, and we expect you to get it for us."

"Gettin' to the broad ain't gonna be no walk in the park."

"With Vinnie gone, there's no trial. She's not a witness anymore. Nobody's protecting her. So after things calm down you deal with her then."

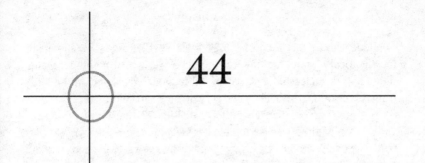

44

CARMINE MOLINO DROVE out of his construction company yard in Queens and headed for his home on Staten Island knowing that he would get little sleep until the transition of power within the Family was complete. The days that followed would be a dangerous and volatile period, and he would need to move swiftly and surely once Genero was dead, to consolidate his position with the other ranking members of the Family, making certain they kept their soldiers in line. He felt no sense of loyalty to the man he had served for the past six years as underboss and confidant, and no sense of remorse over his death sentence. It was the way things were in the life they had chosen, he told himself. Vinnie had made too many mistakes and too many enemies, and backing him now would only mean going down with him.

As Molino came off the Verrazano Narrows Bridge onto the Staten Island Expressway, his thoughts were interrupted by the chirp of his car phone. He picked up the receiver to hear Janet Morris's voice.

One mile behind Molino, in an OCMU surveillance van, a sophisticated ultrahigh-speed scanner, programmed to automatically scan cellular channels in the New York City area, intercepted the call. After the death of Tommy Falconetti, the OCMU had asked for and got a court order to put a Title III wire on Molino's home and business phones and to intercept his cellular calls, and on that same day, the Intelligence Division's technical unit, while Molino was visiting Genero at Rikers Island, had also installed a state-of-the-art tracking device on his car.

Hidden under the hood of the Cadillac Seville, disguised as part of the electrical system, the tiny transmitter, a black cube no bigger than a thumbnail, broadcasted a signal to a directional indicator on the electronics console in the back of the surveillance van. With a range of over thirty square miles, the transmitter, capable of being remotely deactivated when Molino was having his car swept for bugs, enabled the surveillance team to locate their target and follow at a safe distance without fear of being spotted or losing track of him.

A second, equally sophisticated transmitter was expertly concealed inside the roof liner of Molino's car, to capture the conversations of any passengers. It was this bug that picked up the chirping noise of the car phone and transmitted it to the OCMU surveillance van, alerting the detectives in the rear of the van to the incoming call and prompting them to turn on the scanner and the reel-to-reel tape recorder linked to it.

Within seconds after Molino answered his car phone, a mountain range of blue peaks danced on the screen as the scanner found and locked onto the call and the reels of the recorder began to turn, capturing the conversation on tape.

"They're picking Bass up at her apartment at nine o'clock tomorrow morning," Janet Morris told Molino. "They'll take her to the Criminal Court Building and use the side entrance to the district attorney's office."

"Okay, Janet. That's good. But listen. Don't call me no more about this thing. I'll get in touch with you when I need you."

"Does this mean my husband's debt is satisfied?"

"No, it don't. Not yet."

"But you promised, Mr. Molino."

"Hey, Janet. It ain't over till I say it's over. I'll be in touch."

The detective at the electronics console in the back of the surveillance van did not want to believe what he had just heard. He removed his headset and looked over at the other OCMU detective sitting beside him. "Shit."

"Yeah. I recognized the voice, too. Janet Morris, one of our PAAs."

"That explains how they've known about every move we've made."

"The lieutenant's not going to be a happy camper."

With that the detective picked up the telephone on the console and dialed the number for Lieutenant Tony Rizzo's office at OCMU.

· · ·

That evening, when Janet Morris was about to start dinner for her husband and son, she answered the door to see Tony Rizzo and two detectives from the OCMU standing outside on the landing. The look on Rizzo's face, a mix of disappointment and anger, was enough to cause her to start sobbing hysterically.

"Oh, my God, Lieutenant Rizzo. I'm sorry. I'm so sorry. They threatened to hurt my son."

Rizzo's expression softened. "You should have come to me, Janet. We could have done something. Now it's too late."

One of the detectives moved to put handcuffs on her, but Rizzo waved him away. He took her by the arm and led her outside to his car as her husband and son looked on.

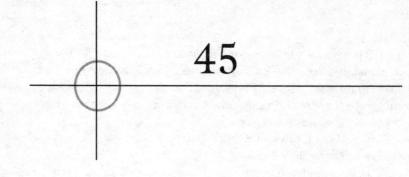

45

THE SECURITY AROUND the Criminal Court Building in lower Manhattan, where Bass was due to arrive momentarily, rivaled that provided for a presidential visit. Vehicular traffic was denied access to Hogan Place, the one-block-long side street where the entrance to the district attorney's office was located, and anyone attempting to enter the street on foot was instructed by uniformed officers manning police lines at both ends of the block to use other avenues of approach to their destinations.

The windows and rooftops of every building with an unobstructed view of where Bass would arrive and depart, out to a distance of two thousand yards, had been checked by countersniper advance teams from the Emergency Services Unit. They had gone through each of the buildings with the building supervisors, checking the rooftops for any place a sniper could hide, then, floor by floor, determined which windows opened and which did not, which way they opened, and if there were any vacant rooms or offices.

Seven three-man countersniper teams were then assigned to observe the designated buildings from rooftop vantage points. One hour before Bass was due to arrive, using binoculars and tripod-mounted spotting scopes, they began the continuous scanning process, looking for windows that were not supposed to be open, suspicious persons or objects that appeared in those that were closed, or any objects on the rooftops that were not there during their initial survey. Down on the street, parked in unmarked cars near the designated buildings, was an ESU response team for each countersniper team, ready to respond to any situation spotted from the rooftop observation posts.

The van transporting Bass and Kirby, led and followed by an unmarked police car carrying four detectives, turned onto Hogan Place at precisely eight fifty-five. The van stopped directly in front of the entrance to the district attorney's office, and as one of the four detectives inside got out to open the sliding side door, the detectives from the other cars lined the sidewalk to the entrance.

Kirby got out of the van first, then helped Bass out. She had a blanket over her head, concealing all but the lower half of her legs, and she wore a flak jacket as well as a Kevlar helmet. Kirby led her to the entrance, surrounded by a swarm of detectives. Her exposure from the time she left the van until she entered the building was no more than five seconds.

Assistant District Attorney Kendal Taylor was waiting when Bass and Kirby got off the elevator on the ninth floor. After Bass removed the flak jacket and the helmet and gave them to the detective holding the blanket shed upon entering the building, Taylor led her to a small anteroom adjacent to the grand jury room to prepare her for her testimony.

Taylor, dressed in an impeccably tailored three-piece, chalk-striped, charcoal-gray suit, stood holding the door open for her. Bass paused in the doorway to give him an appraising look up and down.

"Where did you get that suit, Taylor?"

The A.D.A. beamed. "Bergdorf's Men store." Known to be overly proud of his wardrobe, and vain about his personal appearance, he anticipated a compliment for his excellent taste. "It's English. Turnbull and Asher."

"Is it new?"

"No. I got it last year."

"So then it's too late to return it."

Taylor's smile turned to a frown.

"Lighten up, yuppie. I was only teasing." She turned and winked at Kirby, who stood leaning against the wall nearby, slowly shaking his head.

Kirby recognized the sarcastic humor for what it was: Bass's way of dealing with the stress she was feeling about testifying. She had been nervous and on edge since arriving back in New York, and despite Kirby's reassurance that she would be well protected, while he lay awake for other reasons after they made love, he had heard her up most of the night moving about the apartment.

"You're going to be here when this is over, aren't you?" she called to him from the doorway.

"Absolutely."

"I'm counting on it."

As she walked past Taylor into the room, Kirby heard her say, "Did you pick out that tie all by yourself?" and then the door closed.

The guard on the third tier of the North Infirmary Command Jail on Rikers Island opened the door to Vincent Genero's cell at nine-fifteen to escort him to the visiting room. It was the same guard who smuggled food to him from the outside each evening, and Genero nodded a silent good morning as he stepped out of the cell.

The guard usually engaged Genero in conversation, but this morning, after telling him that his lawyer was there to see him, said nothing more as he walked ahead of him on the narrow walkway along the front of the cells lining the tier. Genero, frustrated and angry with the thought of facing another six to nine months in jail until his trial, or until they finally got to Bass, hoped his lawyer was there to tell him that she, for some reason, had changed her mind about testifying before the grand jury. He looked at his watch and realized that, according to the information Molino had given him, Bass was scheduled to take the stand any minute.

The guard paused to look back at Genero following a few steps behind, then opened the gate leading out of the cell block. He hurried through, then quickly closed and locked it behind him. Genero stood at the gate, puzzled by the guard's behavior as he watched him disappear inside the control room outside the tier.

"Hey! We goin' to the visiting room or what?"

There was no answer, and at that moment the survival instincts of the street that had kept Vincent Genero alive and enabled him to rise to the head of the Gambino crime Family told him what was happening. The Mafia don who had gained and held his power by brutality and fear, for the first time in his life felt the same cold fear he had instilled in others.

He heard a cell door open behind him, and he spun around to face a short, heavily muscled man who stepped out into the narrow walkway. The man's name was Jorge Gonzales, and he was a "bull" in the prison vernacular, an enforcer within the inmate hierarchy. He was bare-chested and wore a beaded necklace displaying the colors of the Netas, a Hispanic gang.

Gonzales had his right hand behind his back, and smiled as he brought it out into plain view, his fingers wrapped around the taped handle of a homemade knife fashioned from a piece of a metal chair leg and patiently sharpened into a four-inch blade on the cement floor of his cell.

"You gonna kill me, punk?" Genero shouted. "Huh? You think your spic ass is gonna build a reputation by killin' *me?* Vinnie Genero? I'll leave you in pieces, then have your whole fuckin' family whacked."

Gonzales continued to smile as he moved slowly forward. Genero lowered himself into a half-crouch fighting stance, waiting for Gonzales to make his move. As a young man, Genero had been a street brawler and enforcer in his own right, and he knew how to handle himself in a fight. At six feet tall and 220 pounds, his edge had always been his ability to outmuscle his opponents and pound them into unconsciousness, not in his agility or speed. Gonzales, a veteran and accomplished knife fighter, was twenty-two years old, his speed and reflexes and strength at their peak.

Genero reached out to grab Gonzales's forearm when he made his first lunge and sweep with the knife, but Gonzales was too quick, slashing and retreating out of Genero's reach. Gonzales stepped back and stood grinning at him.

"What the fuck you smilin' about, punk? Come on! Come on, tough guy!"

"You don't even know you already dead, asshole." He stared at Genero's stomach, his smile widening.

Genero followed Gonzales's gaze and looked down. Such was the power of the adrenaline surging through his body in anticipation of the fight that it was not until that precise moment that he felt the searing pain in his stomach and saw the blood gushing from a deep wound across the breadth of his abdomen.

Gonzales lunged again. Genero sidestepped him and the blade sunk into his rib cage on his left side, wide of its intended mark in the center of his chest. The knife stayed there, buried to the hilt, as Gonzales lost his grip on the handle when his momentum carried him past Genero, off to his side. He was momentarily off-balance and Genero grabbed him from behind and slammed his head into the cell door, stunning him. The knife had punctured and collapsed one of Genero's lungs, and he nearly passed out from the excruciating pain in his chest and stomach. He looked down again to see his intestines spilling out from his stomach wall. He felt his strength deserting him, his legs becoming rubbery, his head spinning. He summoned the strength to slam Gonzales's head into the metal bars of the cell door again, then locked a powerful forearm around his attacker's neck and slid to the floor still holding on to him.

Gonzales was barely conscious and offered little resistance as Genero tightened the choke hold on his neck, cutting off his air. With Gonzales sitting on top of him, Genero sat slumped against the cell door, on the verge of losing consciousness, the life slowly ebbing out of him as blood continued to gush from the massive stomach wound and a sharp pain in his chest jolted him with each breath. But through strength of will and a white-hot hate, he held Gonzales, gagging and gasping, in the death grip, jerking and twisting his neck until he died, only moments before Genero took his last painful breath and collapsed on the floor, his arms still locked around his assailant's neck.

Bass came out of the grand jury room smiling and relaxed now that it was over. She looked around for Kirby and saw him further down the hall involved in an intense, animated conversation with Tony Rizzo, who had just arrived and pulled him away from the group of detectives he had been talking with.

Bass walked over and Rizzo stopped talking. Kirby looked at her and smiled, then looked at Rizzo, who nodded his consent to the unspoken question.

Bass noticed the interplay between the two men. "What's wrong?"

"Nothing's wrong. It's a wonderful day in the neighborhood."

Bass smiled at the Mister Rogers imitation. "What are you talking about?"

"Vincent Genero is dead."

Bass stared at him, stunned. "When? How?"

"Someone stabbed him to death in prison this morning. About twenty minutes ago, while you were testifying."

Bass did not react the way Kirby had anticipated she would. She simply looked away, deep in thought for a few moments, then turned back to him.

"Who killed him?"

"Another inmate, but it had to be a setup. I guess Vinnie's goombahs thought he was becoming too much of a liability and decided to cut their losses. No pun intended."

Kendal Taylor came out of the grand jury room and was immediately approached by one of his assistants, who told him of Genero's death. The look on Taylor's face told anyone who knew him what he was thinking: gone were the daily press conferences on the courthouse steps, the film clips on the nightly news, the chance of advancement following the successful conclusion of a high-profile case. He took a moment to compose himself, then walked over to where Bass stood with Kirby.

"Well, Ms. Bass, it appears you're off the hook."

"I'm still holding you to your word. I want to go into the Witness Security Program. Just because Genero's dead doesn't mean his friends still won't come after me for whatever twisted reasons."

"Although I don't believe it's necessary, I will keep my word. If the police will continue to protect you for one more day, I'll make arrangements for the U.S. marshals to pick you up at your apartment tomorrow morning. You were already approved for admittance to the program when the trial ended, so I don't anticipate any problems."

"Thank you."

Taylor nodded curtly. "It's been a pleasure, Ms. Bass," he said, his tone thick with sarcasm.

Bass's eyes narrowed. She called after him as he walked away. "By the way, Taylor. A word of advice. The next time you go shopping for clothes? Take someone with you."

Taylor paused, made a half turn, then changed his mind and continued down the hallway without a word.

Kirby pulled Bass aside as Rizzo left to return to his office. "You don't have to go into the program, Niki. It's over. You're home free."

"You can't guarantee that."

"I'm ninety percent sure of it. Let us continue with your protection detail for a few more days, until we see how this is going to shake out with the Gambino Family and the others. We've got confidential informants who'll tell us what's going on. Genero's death wasn't any random prison killing. He was set up, and that means someone ordered the hit, probably with the sanction of the other Families."

"I'm not willing to take the ten percent chance that you're wrong. I don't have to tell you that we're not dealing with rational people here. Maybe they'll do nothing right now, but that doesn't mean they won't come after me later."

"They've got nothing to gain by killing you. You're no threat to any of them now. As stupid and vicious as they are, they don't do things that could put them behind bars for the rest of their lives without a reason. And the bottom line is, they've got no reason to kill you."

"I'm not going to make it easy for them if they decide otherwise."

Kirby stared at her, trying to understand. This was someone with as much personal courage and intuitive intelligence as anyone he had ever met, and her decision wasn't in keeping with what he knew of her. "What's going on here?"

"What do you mean?"

"Don't insult me, Niki. What aren't you telling me?"

"About what?"

"About why the hell you want to go back into the program when there's no good reason for you to do it."

"I think there is a good reason, and it's my decision to make, and I just made it. I want to get as far away as I can from what I've been for the past eighteen months and begin a new life I can be proud of, and I don't want to be constantly wondering when one of Genero's sick friends is going to kill me."

Kirby searched her eyes. What she had said rang true, but it wasn't all of it. He had little doubt that she was lying about her real reasons for what she was doing. He also knew why he was having difficulty accepting her decision. And it had nothing to do with what was best for her. It was about him. He was taking her decision personally. He simply did not want her to leave. To go somewhere he could not find her, out of his life forever.

He knew that if this was any other witness under the same set of circumstances, he would not hesitate to accept and respect their choice, regardless of any ulterior motives they had for making it. And as much as he did not want to admit it, he also knew that whatever there was between him and Bass at that moment was all there ever would be. It wasn't meant to be, and could never be, anything more than what it was: a brief, meaningless affair between two people thrown together by circumstances, and when the circumstances no longer existed, neither did the relationship. He had no right and no business interrogating her about something she obviously did not want to admit to or discuss. Finally accepting all that, he reached down and took her hand.

"Okay, if that's your decision, I'll leave it at that. But if there's something or someone else you're afraid of, another element of this you haven't told me about, don't shut me out. I'll help you, regardless of what it is. Do you understand?"

Bass squeezed his hand. "Yes, I do."

Part of her wanted to confide in him, to let him know what she was doing and why she was doing it, but something inside her, something forged and hardened by what had gone before him, would no longer allow her to trust him or anyone else. And he was a cop; his advice about what she planned to do would only have been not to do it. For her, that was no longer an option. She saw a golden opportunity to get the security that could give her peace of mind and protection from those who would use her, and she was not about to relinquish that for anyone.

"I'm sorry, Kirby," was all she said, then looked away.

"Yeah. Me, too."

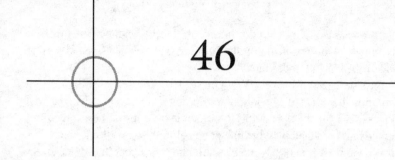

46

THE U.S. MARSHALS assigned to Bass's protective detail agreed to her request to let Kirby drive her to La Guardia Airport's Marine Air Terminal. She took four suitcases full of clothes and personal items with her; the rest of her belongings, including the furniture from her apartment, would be packed and shipped by a moving company under contract to the Marshals Service, to be stored in a warehouse until her relocation.

Kirby and Bass said little to each other during the thirty-minute drive to the airport other than brief comments about the weather and the traffic and the general decline of the city's highways, the long silences in between broken only by intermittent transmissions coming over Kirby's portable radio tuned to the Intelligence Division's frequency.

The previous evening had been just as difficult. When Bass had finished packing, they sat on the sofa watching television, Kirby keeping to himself until Bass slid over, curled up beside him, raised his arm and put it around her, and laid her head on his chest. She attributed his aloofness to his putting up a wall to protect himself from emotions that would only make things more difficult when the morning came, and later, when she embraced him to kiss him goodnight, he gave her only a brief hug, then kissed her on the cheek.

She had held on to him, the inner turmoil tearing her apart as she again fought back the urge to tell him what she was doing and why she was doing it, but in the end the hard lessons of the past prevailed and all she said was, "I'm sorry, Jack. I really am."

Kirby had simply run his hand through her hair and looked deep into her eyes, then said goodnight. It was a troubled moment for Bass, the conflict of emotions bringing her to tears when she went into the bedroom and saw him standing there at the other end of the hallway, watching her like a lost soul as she closed the door. She heard the television on in the living room as she lay awake most of the night.

In the morning she faced a stranger who spoke to her in the precise, clipped, detached voice of a cop as they sat drinking coffee, waiting for the marshals to arrive. The drive to the airport was even more strained and awkward as the time for Bass to leave drew near.

They drove through the security gate at a side entrance to the airport and followed the marshals' car out onto the tarmac, stopping alongside the glistening white Gulfstream II jet that would take Bass to the Marshals Service's new Safesite and Orientation Center in Washington, D.C., where she would remain under their protection until final arrangements for her relocation were made.

Kirby and Bass got out of the car and stood together in silence as the marshals put her luggage on board the plane. Then one of them motioned to her from the door of the aircraft, indicating they were ready when she was. It was then that Kirby could no longer deny the sense of loss he was feeling, knowing he was never going to see her again. He turned to her and took both her hands in his, but the words he wanted to say would not come.

"You take care of yourself, huh?"

"I will."

"Good, you make sure you do that."

"I won't forget you. You not only saved my life, you saved me from myself."

"It's what I do."

Bass forced a weak smile. "Goodbye, Kirby."

"Yeah. Goodbye."

She started toward the plane, then turned and came back to embrace him and kiss him passionately. Kirby held her tight, breathing deeply of her scent, wanting to remember it, lost in the feel of her body pressed against his. She raised her head to look into his eyes.

"I meant all the things I said when we made love, Jack."

"I know."

"But you don't know what you meant to me in those moments. What you did for me. I felt real emotions I didn't think I was capable of feeling any longer, and you showed me that I still could. And I'll always love you for that."

Kirby had to look away. Then despite himself, he told her how he truly felt. "I'm in love with you, you know that."

"I know." Her eyes brimmed with tears and she forced a smile. "You know what they say: 'If you love something, set it free.'"

A small smile creased the corners of Kirby's mouth. "You forgot the rest of that saying."

"And what's that?"

"If it doesn't come back in about four or five months, hunt it down and kill it."

Bass laughed and brushed away a tear. "I'll miss you."

"And I'll miss you. Now get the hell out of here before I make a complete ass of myself."

Bass hesitated for a moment, the tears now flowing freely. She started to speak, then shook her head in frustration and turned and ran up the steps and into the aircraft.

Kirby stood where he had last held her as the plane taxied out onto the runway. He continued to watch as it took off and climbed away to become a small dot in the distant sky. Only then did he get back in his car and drive slowly away.

That evening Tony Rizzo found Kirby where he knew he would be, in a back booth in Eddie Boyle's Tavern on Manhattan's Upper West Side. He stopped at the bar to say hello to Boyle and get a beer, then slipped into the booth and stared across at Kirby and the eight empty beer bottles lined up in front of him.

Kirby looked up through slightly out-of-focus eyes and saw Rizzo eyeing the empties. "I don't wanna hear it, Lou. I'm off-duty."

"Hey. Easy. That's not why I'm here. I just stopped by to see how you're doing. So how are you doing?"

"Breathin' in, breathin' out."

"You really went off the deep end for her, didn't you?"

Kirby nodded and took a long pull on his beer. "I'll get over it. I don't know who the hell I thought I was kidding. Women like Bass don't go for guys like me. For a while there I forgot who I was."

"Stop beating yourself up, Jack. You're human, just like the rest of us. She was a beautiful woman."

"She was a lot more than that."

"Speaking of which, what do you think it was she wasn't telling us?"

"I don't know."

"You going to look into it?"

"What for? She kept her part of the bargain, and even though it didn't go exactly the way we planned, the end result was the same, it ended right. That piece of shit Genero's dead."

"Yeah, but that lady had her own agenda, and I'll be damned if I can figure out what it was. Aren't you at least curious?"

"No. I have no interest in digging up something that might hurt her. With a little luck, maybe she's found some of the happiness they stole from her four years ago." He made a dismissive gesture with his hand and took another drink. "Anyway, enough of this shit. Tell me something I don't know. Like what's happening with the greaseballs?"

"The word is Conte ordered the hit on Genero, not Molino."

"I didn't think Carmine had the balls to make a move on his own. So how'd the other capos react to it?"

"Two of them, Vicarro and Fauzio, turned up dead this morning. Double taps to the back of the heads. Everybody else seems to have fallen into line. Looks like Molino's going to be the new don."

"Fat slob's gonna have to go on a diet and get a whole new wardrobe. The Gambinos like their dons to look sharp."

Rizzo laughed and got up to leave. "Tommy Falconetti's funeral is tomorrow. Up in New Haven. We're giving him a real send-off. Full honors."

"I know. I'll be there."

"See you there, then, huh?"

"Yeah. See you there."

Rizzo nodded to Boyle on his way out, then looked back at Kirby. "By the way, Jack, I got some ideas about bringing Molino down. We'll talk about it later."

Kirby raised his beer bottle in response as Rizzo went through the door.

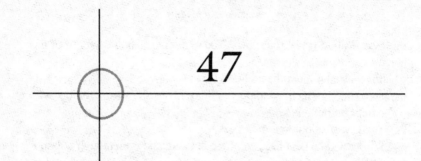

47

NICOLE BASS SPENT less than three weeks at the Safesite and Orientation Center in Washington before being relocated to Chester County, Pennsylvania, where she had been living for the past six months as Ann Hayes. The home the U.S. Marshals Service found for her to rent was an old stone farmhouse on ten acres of woods and pastureland near the town of Chadds Ford, not far from where she had also found a job working in a small art gallery that featured local artists.

Bass appreciated the beauty of the gently rolling countryside with its lush green meadows and stately trees, where upper-income residents commuted from mini-estates and horse farms to offices in Philadelphia less than an hour away. Parts of it reminded her of where she had grown up in Tennessee. But it was not where she wanted to be, it was where they had allowed her to go, one of five choices, the other four being less desirable. She wanted to be in the city, but they insisted that Philadelphia, where the Gambino crime Family had ties to the local mob, would not be a sensible choice if she wanted to avoid the possibility of being seen and recognized by the very people she was hiding from. They had also recommended that she cut her hair short, change its color, and wear nonprescription glasses when out in public. She had compromised, wearing the glasses, but keeping her hair the same color and wearing it in a ponytail or a twist.

It was just past eight o'clock on Friday night, a night Bass usually worked at the gallery, but she had gotten a coworker to fill in for her so she could attend a lecture at the Winterthur Museum outside of Wilmington, Delaware, only a short drive across the state line. She was on her way home from the lecture when she slowed for the traffic light in Chadds Ford and saw the swirling red and blue lights as she stopped at the intersection of Route 1 and Route 100.

At first she thought someone had been pulled over for speeding, but then she saw three more state police cars and an ambulance in the small parking lot behind the cluster of quaint shops and boutiques on the corner across the intersection.

The art gallery where she worked was among the shops on the corner, and when the light changed, she pulled across the intersection and swung into the parking lot and walked down the steps into the small cobblestone courtyard surrounded by the shops. She immediately saw that the center of activity was the art gallery, and she rushed over to join the group of onlookers gathered at the yellow crime scene tape set up by the state police to cordon off the area. She angled her way through the crowd until she reached the front, then watched as two emergency medical technicians carried a stretcher with a body bag on it from the gallery.

"Oh, my God!" she gasped, knowing who was zipped inside the body bag, the only person it could be. Joyce Hill. Her friend and coworker who had taken her place at work that night.

Bass ducked under the crime scene tape and ran toward the gallery, hoping against hope that she was wrong. One of the state troopers at the scene grabbed her by the arm as she reached the entrance.

"You have to stay on the other side of the tape."

"What happened to Joyce?"

"Did you know the victim?"

"We worked together."

"Looks like a robbery, but we aren't sure yet."

"We only kept about two hundred dollars in the office. Joyce was so meek she would have given it to anyone who even yelled at her. Why would someone kill her?"

"They don't need a reason these days, lady."

The trooper escorted her to the yellow tape and held it up as she crossed back to the other side.

Bass spotted the man who ran the candy shop standing nearby and asked him if he knew what had happened. He knew no more than what the state trooper had told her. She looked around at the people gathered outside in the courtyard and saw one of the women who worked in the leather crafts shop adjacent to the art gallery. She had seen some of what happened and told Bass what she had told the police.

About twenty minutes earlier she heard two gunshots and saw four men run from the gallery across the courtyard to the parking lot, then speed away in a dark-colored car. She then ran to the gallery and saw Joyce Hill lying dead on the floor just inside the door, the front of her blouse drenched in blood.

Bass stood watching until the ambulance carrying Hill's body pulled away. She was angry and incredulous that someone could be killed for no more than the small amount of money they kept in the shop. But then she reminded herself that the trooper was right, and if it had happened in New York City, or Philadelphia, or Washington, where people were killed for much less on a daily basis, it would have made no impression on her at all. But here, in a quiet, upscale community, such senseless violence still had an alarming effect on people who did not yet accept it as a part of their daily lives and in many cases had moved away from the city to escape it.

But even a relatively rural area like Chadds Ford was not immune to big-city crime problems. In the past five months Bass could recall six armed robberies in the immediate area—four convenience stores where two of the clerks had been shot, and two shops not far from the gallery where the owners were beaten and brutalized.

The fact that it could have been her in the body bag, had it not been for a spur-of-the-moment decision to go to the lecture that evening, was not lost on Bass as she drove home, the windows of the Jeep Cherokee open to the sweet scent of spring meadows on the cool late April evening. The six months in the country had been more enjoyable than she had anticipated, and the time away and distance from the life she left behind had allowed her to gain some perspective on the events of the past four years. She had even found a place nearby to lease a horse on a monthly basis, allowing her to spend her weekends riding through the picturesque countryside.

But she was only biding her time until she felt the moment was right for her to leave the Witness Security Program and get on with what she had planned for the rest of her life. The murder of Joyce Hill left her shaken, bringing back memories of things she desperately wanted to forget, and made her decide to move up her timetable. She would call the marshal assigned to her case in the morning and tell him that she had decided to leave the program, as she had done two years ago. They were never wholly convinced that it was necessary in the first place, doubting that she was in any real danger with Vincent Genero dead and the dynamics of the Gambino Family changed. They would readily accept the fact that the past six months had given her sufficient time to think things over and come to the same conclusion.

The state troopers had secured the art gallery until the Crime Scene Unit and the detectives who caught the case arrived and began their investigation. One of the detectives going through the small office off the exhibit room picked up a bank deposit bag lying on top of the desk and unzipped it to find $230 in cash inside. He turned to look at his partner beside him, raising an eyebrow.

"Four guys rob an art gallery, and the owner says none of the paintings are missing, some of them worth a couple grand, price tags on them. The victim's purse had eighty-six dollars in it, plus a bunch of credit cards. And she had a pretty expensive gold necklace, an engagement ring worth a couple thousand, and a watch worth five or six hundred. None of it was touched, plus they miss over two hundred in cash in a deposit bag laying right on top of the desk. Unless they're the dumbest bad guys in the world, this wasn't any robbery."

His partner nodded in agreement. "One of the witnesses, a customer who was coming out of a shop across the courtyard, said he heard the victim scream and caught a glimpse of her struggling with two of them in the doorway. He said it looked like they were trying to drag her outside when one of the guys starts shouting something at the guys who had ahold of her, then the guy who was shouting pulls out a gun and fires two shots into her at point-blank range."

"What the hell was she fighting with them for if they didn't steal anything?"

"Maybe before they got a chance she started screaming, they panicked, tried to shut her up, shot her, and then just ran."

"Maybe, but I'll bet you a six-pack and a pizza that isn't what we're going to come up with when we start digging into this."

Joey Arcaro turned off the headlights as he pulled the black Pontiac Grand Prix into a narrow, wooded farm track off a secondary road a few miles from Chadds Ford. He had driven in silence, seething with anger, from the time he left the art gallery, none of the three men in the car with him daring to utter a word. He cut the engine and turned sideways to glare at Tony Buzzaro, seated beside him in the front passenger seat. Then, without warning, he slapped him hard across the back of the head. The two men in the rear of the car remained silent, not wanting Arcaro's anger directed at them.

"You goddamn moron!" he screamed at Buzzaro. "What the fuck is wrong with you, huh? That wasn't her, asshole. You take us in to grab the wrong broad and we end up killin' her? Fuck!"

Buzzaro ran his hands through his hair, smoothing it back in place. "Hey, Joey. How was I supposed to know?"

"You're supposed to know, you fuck. You're the one they gave the information to."

"I thought it was her." Buzzaro held up his hand, ticking off each reason on his fingers. "She was tall. Dark hair. Good-lookin'. And the information they give me was she worked there alone on Friday nights. I wrote it all down." He took a folded sheet of paper from his jacket pocket and shoved it toward Arcaro. "It says right here, see." He reached up and switched on the interior dome light.

Arcaro immediately turned the light off, then grabbed the paper from Buzzaro, crumpled it into a ball, and threw it at him.

"Why are you showin' me that? Huh? You wrote it down, you fuckin' moron. You're showin' me somethin' you wrote down wrong, like it's proof."

"It ain't my fault, Joey. And you gotta admit that picture they gave me I showed you looks somethin' like the broad was there."

"Just shut the fuck up! 'Looks somethin' like her.' " Arcaro lit a cigarette and sat staring out through the trees to a moonlit pasture off to his left. "We gotta finish this tonight. Before the broad and the cops figure out what the fuck's goin' on."

Buzzaro carefully unfolded the crumpled sheet of paper and held it up again. "Yeah. We could do that easy. I got directions right to where she lives. Even a little map I drew. It's a stone farmhouse couple miles from the art shop."

"Gallery," Arcaro corrected him. "It's a fuckin' art gallery, not art shop."

"Yeah. Anyways, we go to her house, we grab her, take her to New York like they want. Then everything's okay. Right?"

"You drew a map, huh? We'll probably end up in fuckin' Arizona we follow your map."

"Gimme a break, Joey. Guy gave me good directions, right to the house."

"Yeah? You sure you wrote that down right? 'Cause I could just see it now. We go to some farmhouse, end up whackin' John Boy and the whole fuckin' Walton family 'cause you screwed up again."

"Come on, Joey. I made a mistake, okay? We'll make it right. And don't hit me no more."

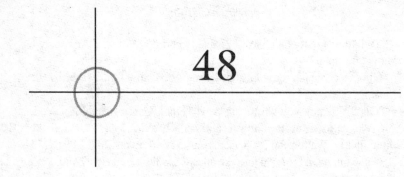

48

AFTER TAKING A shower and changing into jeans and a sweatshirt, Nicole Bass sat curled up on the sofa in the small den off her kitchen, eating a cup of yogurt and watching television, staring at anything that would take her mind off the murder of Joyce Hill. She channel-surfed until she found an old movie, lost interest in it, and picked up the packet of brochures she had received that morning from an international realtor specializing in properties in the south of France.

A scratching noise at the kitchen door made her look up and smile. Mojo was paying his nightly visit. The black Labrador retriever belonged to her nearest neighbors, a retired elderly couple living just across the road at the top of her driveway. Mojo was a moocher of the first order, showing up each morning to run with her, and for the dog biscuits Bass gave him when they got back, and then returning each evening for another snack. A sucker for a dog with soulful eyes, Bass looked forward to his daily visits.

She got up from the sofa and went into the kitchen, taking a handful of dog biscuits from the box she kept for him on the counter. She opened the door to see Mojo standing on the mat, his tail swishing back and forth.

"Mojo the moocher. What a surprise. And how are you tonight?"

At the sound of her voice Mojo sat obediently, his eyes on the biscuits in her hand. Bass knelt down to rub his head, feeding him his treats one at a time until they were gone. Mojo cocked his head, his eyes pleading for more. Bass laughed and gave him a hug.

"Go home, Mojo. See you in the morning."

Mojo sauntered down the walkway leading from the house to the parking area in front of the small bank barn at the bottom of the driveway. Bass walked back through the kitchen, pausing as she reached the doorway to the den. She heard Mojo bark twice, then stop, then twice again. She was about to ignore it when the barks became louder, one after the other.

Bass went over to the kitchen window, turned off the light, and looked out. In the light of the moon, she could see Mojo standing stiff-legged in front of the barn, his barks now interspersed with low, mean growls. Mojo was known to be at war with any and all raccoons, ever since four of them tried to drown him when he made the near-fatal mistake of chasing them into the pond at his home when he was eight months old. Bass suspected he had cornered one near the barn.

She put on her running shoes to go outside and send him on his way before he ended up at the veterinarian's again, his muzzle covered with scratches. She took a light jacket from the hook just inside the door, and again looked out the window as she pulled the jacket on over her sweatshirt.

Mojo was slowly stalking toward a corner of the barn deep in shadows. Bass lost sight of him and heard a sharp yelp. The silhouette of a man stepped out of the shadows, looked toward the house, then quickly disappeared back around the corner of the barn.

Bass moved away from the window and pressed herself flat against the wall. She waited a moment, then peered around the edge of the glass to look out toward the barn again. She saw a man run from the shadows and disappear into the stand of pine trees just off the driveway at the front of the house. Then another darted out from the same spot and stopped behind the Jeep Cherokee parked at the foot of the walkway to the kitchen.

Bass ran into the den and grabbed the pump shotgun she kept propped behind the door. She took the cordless telephone from the table next to the sofa, turned off the light, casting the first floor of the house into darkness, then sat tucked into a corner of the room, the shotgun in her lap as she dialed 911.

The call was answered by the 911 center in the nearby town of West Chester. Bass remained calm, telling the dispatcher who she was and where her home was located and that there were prowlers outside her house.

"Stay on the line, please. I'm calling the state police barracks in Avondale now."

Bass stayed scrunched into the corner of the den where anyone looking in the window could not see her and she had a clear shot if someone came through the doorway. She had the phone to her ear, held in place by her shoulder as she used both hands to pump a shell into the chamber of the 12-gauge shotgun. In the background she could hear the dispatcher relaying the information to the state police.

Bass heard a loud thump at the far end of the hallway off the den. Then another, and the front door flew open, slamming against the inside wall.

"They're in the house!" she whispered into the phone.

"Stay on the line with me," the dispatcher said. "The police are on their way now."

Bass heard someone moving down the hall toward the den. She put down the phone and crawled to the doorway, where she raised herself into a low crouch. She took a deep breath to calm herself, then came out of the den firing a blast from the shotgun down the length of the hallway toward the front door to cover her as she ran into the kitchen.

In the split-second flash of light from the muzzle blast, Bass saw a large man ten feet away. He cried out in pain and fell heavily to the floor. She stayed in a low crouch as she ran to the kitchen door, then stood up, flattening herself against the wall. She pumped another shell into the chamber of the shotgun and took a quick look out the window and found herself face-to-face with Tony Buzzaro on the other side.

Buzzaro, startled by the sudden appearance of Bass, raised his pistol, but did not fire, the dire warning that she was not to be killed fresh in his mind. There was no hesitation on the part of Bass. She fired before Buzzaro could recover and get away. The powerful blast blew out the entire center section of small panes in the window, sending a storm of glass shards and shotgun pellets into Buzzaro's face and neck. He died instantly, the force of the blast knocking him back into a bed of shrubs.

Bass heard the wail of a police siren in the distance, then another joined in, followed by a shout from a man near the front of the house.

"Joey! We gotta get out of here! Now!"

Bass saw two men run across the driveway and disappear behind the barn. She heard a car start and an engine roar, followed by the crunch of gravel as the car took the back way off the property to a secondary road a short distance away through the woods.

The sirens grew louder, and Bass stepped outside to see a police car, its light bar swirling and flashing, slam on its brakes and swerve into the driveway and speed toward her. The state police cruiser skidded to a stop in front of the house just as a second one turned into the driveway behind it. The troopers were only two miles away at the art gallery crime scene and had responded immediately when they heard the call coming over their radios.

The first trooper to arrive heard the second shotgun blast only moments before. He got out of his cruiser, his gun drawn, using the hood of the car for cover. The second trooper stopped directly behind him and jumped out of the car to take up the same defensive position.

"They're gone!" Bass shouted to them from where she stood just outside the kitchen. She put the shotgun down as they cautiously approached, their eyes continuously moving over the area around them.

Both of them stopped when they saw Tony Buzzaro, half of his face missing, lying in the shrubs only a few feet from where Bass stood.

"There's another one inside the house. In the hallway by the front door."

One of the troopers entered the house; the other one stayed with Bass. "Are you okay?"

"I'm fine. But I've got to find Mojo."

"Who's Mojo?"

"He's a dog." Bass started walking toward the barn. The trooper followed, his gun still drawn, his eyes watching the shadows.

Bass found the Labrador around the corner of the barn. He was lying motionless on his side. The trooper shined his flashlight on him as Bass placed her hand on the dog's chest and felt him breathing. She stroked his head and he whimpered at her touch.

"He's alive. Thank God."

The trooper bent down to shine the light into Mojo's eyes, then felt the bump on the top of his head. "He'll be okay. Looks like he just took a knock on the head."

Mojo struggled to his feet, sitting listlessly at Bass's side, leaning against her as the second trooper came out of the house and walked over to the barn.

"The house is clear. One dead from a shotgun blast to the chest. He had a 9-millimeter lying beside him. The dead guy off the kitchen had a .45."

His partner looked at Bass. "You mind telling us what happened here?"

"Four men tried to break into my house. I shot two of them, the others ran away."

"You were here alone?"

Bass nodded that she was. The trooper studied her face. She did not seem anywhere near as frightened or unnerved as he thought she should be. His expression was a mix of thinly veiled admiration and disbelief.

"Where'd they go?"

"They drove out the back road through the woods."

"What kind of car?"

"I don't know. I didn't see it. They parked behind the barn. I guess they came in the back way, too."

The trooper who had gone through the house was shining his flashlight on the driver's licenses he had taken from the wallets of the two dead men. "Two guys from Philadelphia," he said to his partner. He next unfolded the sheet of paper he had found in Tony Buzzaro's pocket. His brow knit as he read it. When he finished, he looked at Bass.

"Is your name Ann Hayes, or Nicole Bass?"

Bass stiffened. "Ann Hayes."

"Who's Nicole Bass?"

"I don't know anyone by that name."

"According to what's on this sheet of paper, these guys were looking for someone named Nicole Bass, and your name, Ann Hayes, is written underneath hers. They had directions to this house, and your work schedule at the—"

The trooper stopped in mid-sentence, realizing the significance of what he had just read. He showed the paper to his partner, pulling him aside for a private conversation.

Bass looked on in silence. It had not been necessary for the trooper to complete his sentence. She had made the connection as soon as she saw the men approaching her house. They had first gone to the art gallery looking for her, and killed Joyce Hill when they realized their mistake.

One of the troopers went back to his cruiser and radioed the detectives at the gallery, informing them they would need the Crime Scene Unit at Bass's house. The other trooper came back to Bass.

"You know what this is about, don't you?"

"No. I don't."

"I think you do. I think these same men were looking for you earlier tonight at the art gallery and killed another woman by mistake."

"I know. I mean I know Joyce Hill was killed tonight. But that's all I know."

"If you don't level with us, Ms. Hayes, we can't help you."

"I've told you what I know."

"And you have no idea why these men were trying to kill you?"

"None."

"When the detectives from the art gallery get here, they'll want to talk to you. I suggest you be a little more forthcoming with them."

"I can't tell them anything more than I've already told you."

Despite their patient interrogation, the state police detectives learned no more from Bass than she had already told the troopers. With the bodies of the two men removed, and the Crime Scene Unit finished, the detectives left shortly after midnight, failing to convince Bass that for her own safety she should get out of the house and stay with a friend until they could determine if there was still a threat to her life.

The moment the detectives pulled out of the driveway, Bass picked up the phone and dialed the twenty-four-hour emergency number for Paul Faust, the U.S. marshal assigned to her case. The call was forwarded to his home in Gladwyne, a suburb of Philadelphia.

"How did they find me, Paul?"

"How did who find you?" His voice was full of sleep.

Bass told him all that had happened that night, her words angry and bitter.

"Did you tell the state police you were in the program?"

"No, I did not."

"Good. I'm going to send someone over there to pick you up right now. We'll bring you in and take you back to the Safesite and Orientation Center until we can find out what happened and get you relocated somewhere else."

"No. I'm leaving right now."

"That's a bad idea. You're not thinking straight. Just sit down and relax until I get some of our people over there."

"I'm leaving the program, Paul. Tonight. So I'm no longer your responsibility. But I think you damn well better look into how those people found out who I was and where I was before you get someone else killed who thinks you've got them safely tucked away."

"We'll find out how it happened. I promise you. But whether you know it or not, the last thing you want is to be out there on your own."

"And how could that be any worse? I guarantee you, they're not going to find out where I am from me."

Bass hung up before Faust could respond, leaving the phone off the hook. She ran upstairs to the master bedroom and pulled two suitcases from the closet, packing them full of only her favorite clothes and a few personal items and photographs along with the twelve thousand dollars in cash left from what she had taken from Michael Onorati's apartment. After checking to see that the magazine for her pistol was fully loaded, she slipped the gun inside the waistband of her jeans, then took the suitcases and her laptop computer and put them in the cargo area of the Cherokee.

Mojo was lying on the kitchen floor, mostly recovered, but still a little dazed. Bass put him in the car with her and took him home. Forty minutes later she was driving north on the New Jersey Turnpike.

49

JACK KIRBY HUNG up the telephone in the OCMU squad room and sat drumming his fingers on his desk as he drank the last of his morning coffee. He looked across the room to see Tony Rizzo in his office and went over and knocked on the door, entering after Rizzo waved him in.

"What's on your mind, Jack?"

"I just got off the phone with our Marshals Service liaison. He got a call from the regional inspector in Philadelphia this morning. Someone tried to kill Nicole Bass last night."

For a moment the name escaped him. "The witness from the Genero case? I thought they relocated her under a new name."

"They did."

"They know who it was?"

"The two guys she killed were a couple of buttons from the Philadelphia mob."

"She took out two wise guys?"

"Yeah. With a shotgun."

"My kind of woman. Is she okay?"

"She skipped. Told the marshal in charge of her case she was leaving the program. He alerted the office up here in the event she shows up."

"It can't be connected to Genero. He's dead and gone, and Molino's got no reason to send anybody after her."

"I know. It doesn't make any sense. And if it was them, how did they find her?"

"The feds aren't immune to what happened to us. The wise guys spread enough money around, or muscle the right person, they'll find someone just like Janet Morris who'll get them what they want."

"It just doesn't make any sense," Kirby repeated, more to himself than to Rizzo.

"Maybe she's back at her old line of work and got involved with the Philadelphia mob under her new name. Did something to piss them off. It doesn't take much."

"Something's wrong about this, Lou."

"It's not our problem anymore."

"If you don't mind, I'd like to ask around. See if anybody knows anything about it."

"Like I said, Jack, she's not our problem anymore. If you don't have enough work to do, I'll find some for you."

"Look, I admit, part of this is personal. I didn't have to say anything to you—I could have checked it out on my own. But I'd like your support."

"Alright. You're going to do it anyway no matter what I say, so I'll give you one day to look into it. Then that's it."

"Thanks, Lou."

"And Jack. I haven't forgotten how you felt about her. So just remember, you're a cop. We both knew she wasn't leveling with us six months ago, so whatever it is she's got herself jammed up over, you can bet your pension she's not an innocent party. Keep yourself and the Department out of it."

Within one hour of leaving Rizzo's office Kirby had tapped three of his confidential informants and learned nothing. All three were low-level thieves on the fringes of the mob, and as such seldom if ever had inside information unless they happened to overhear a loose conversation. Kirby knew Rizzo would go ballistic over what he was going to do next, but he needed to know what was happening to Bass, for reasons that had nothing to do with the OCMU.

He drove through the Ozone Park neighborhood until he spotted Louie Toma standing on the sidewalk in front of a bodega with three of his mob friends. Toma was known as "Louie the Mouth" because he was constantly mouthing off and getting into fights. At forty years of age he had been a member of a Gambino Family crew since his early twenties, but was still not a "made man" and never would be, partly because of his habit of picking fights with the wrong people, and partly because he was a borderline moron.

He was tolerated because of his innate ability as a burglar, specializing in jewelry stores, and for his never failing to share his take with the capo in charge of his crew. He was a reluctant informant, but over the years, Kirby had managed to get information out of him by playing on his limited intelligence and threatening to put the word out that he was a snitch for OCMU.

Kirby went into his act the moment he pulled into the curb in front of the bodega. He jumped from the car and ran toward Toma, shouting at the top of his lungs.

"You think you can beat up a cop and get away with it, scumbag?"

The three men with Toma backed away when Kirby grabbed him by the lapels and threw him against the wall. The startled Toma stared at Kirby in complete confusion.

"What the fuck you talkin' about. I didn't beat up no cop."

"Just because he was off-duty and in civilian clothes doesn't get you off the hook, asshole. You're goin' down for this one."

"It never happened."

"Get in the car!"

"This ain't right."

"I said get in the goddamn car! Now!" Kirby dragged him off the sidewalk by the scruff of his neck and shoved him into the back seat, face first.

Before closing the door, he shouted at him again, for the benefit of his friends, "If he can make a positive ID on you, you're goin' away for assaulting a police officer."

With that Kirby jumped in the car and sped off with Toma in the back seat, wondering if he might have punched a cop and forgotten about it. When they were well away from the neighborhood, Kirby pulled in and parked behind a supermarket, then turned in his seat to face Toma, who sat staring at him, still confused.

"Hey, Kirby. I'm tellin' you again, I didn't hit no cop."

"I know you didn't. But I needed to talk to you so I thought I'd make it look good."

"Talk about what?"

"Why is Carmine Molino trying to kill the woman who was going to testify against Genero before he got whacked?"

Toma said nothing. He avoided Kirby's gaze and looked out the window.

"Come on, Louie. Don't jerk me around."

"What's in it for me?"

"A hundred."

"Two hundred."

"Fifty, and I drop the assault charges."

"You just said you knew I didn't hit no cop."

"That was before. Now I think it might have been you." Kirby sat watching him chew his lip, his mind working at its usual snail's pace.

"Okay. Fifty and you drop the charges."

"Deal. Let's hear it."

"No big mystery. You steal money from all four Families, you're in deep shit."

The fifty thousand dollars in cash Kirby had seen in Bass's carry-on bag at the Carlyle Hotel flashed before him. "Molino put out a contract on her because she took fifty grand? It had to cost him more than that to find out where she was."

"Fifty grand? That ain't what I heard. More like fifteen million. And it ain't no contract. He wants her snatched and brung to him."

Kirby stared at him in disbelief. "Fifteen million? In cash?"

"No. Some kinda secret bank accounts. Where you're only a number to them, ya know? This guy Genero whacked, his accountant? He was like in charge of investing money for all the Families. He stole fifteen million from them, put it in them number accounts. Anyway, the broad got her hands on the secret numbers and they can't get to the money without them."

Suddenly it all fell into place for Kirby. Why Bass had thought she could make a deal with Genero. Why she had insisted on going back into the Witness Security Program. Why they were still looking for her. And as he put it all together, he also believed he knew where she was going and what she was going to do.

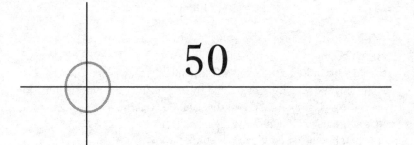

50

AT 9:35 A.M., Nicole Bass finished her breakfast and went to a pay phone at the rear of a coffee shop located across the street from New York's Madison Square Garden. During the weeks following Vincent Genero's death, she had read with interest the series of stories about the brief power struggle within the Gambino crime Family that had appeared in the *New York Times*. She recalled one of the stories mentioning that Carmine Molino was now the head of the Family, and that he lived on Staten Island.

She found twenty-two listings for Molino in the Staten Island telephone directory, but none with the first name Carmine. Eight of the numbers were listed for women, four had only initials after them, none of them a *C*. Thinking that Molino's telephone might be under his wife's name, she began calling the women listed and got Angela Molino on the fifth try.

"Wait" was all the woman said when Bass asked to speak to Carmine Molino. She heard a door opening and closing, muffled voices, then a man picked up the phone.

"Yeah. Who is it?"

"Nicole Bass, Mr. Molino." She waited for him to reply, hoping it was the right Carmine Molino.

After a brief hesitation Molino responded as though he was talking to an old friend. "Oh, yeah. I wanna talk to you but not on this phone."

"I'm not giving you the number I'm calling from."

"I'm gonna give you a number where you can call me back in twenty minutes. Is that okay with you?"

"Yes. That'll be fine."

Upon becoming head of the Gambino crime Family, Molino had also become a far more cautious man. Three months ago, suspecting that his car was bugged, in a fit of anger and frustration after the man he hired to sweep it found nothing, he took his Cadillac Seville to a salvage yard and had it crushed into a four-foot cube.

Molino now used only pay telephones to discuss business. He had a list of fifteen scattered about the city, choosing the one he would use each day at random, secure in the knowledge that no one could possibly get court orders to tap any of them without being able to show that their primary use was for criminal purposes. By making and receiving no more than three calls from each phone in any given week, and constantly adding new locations to replace old ones, he assured that none of them were tapped.

Molino gave Bass the number of a public telephone in a bar a few miles from his house. The OCMU detective monitoring the call from the operations center at Intelligence Division headquarters wrote down the number.

One block from Carmine Molino's house Jack Kirby sat slouched behind the steering wheel of his car. Parked at the curb on the same side of the street and facing away from the house, he still had an unobstructed line of sight to the driveway through his right side-view mirror.

Within thirty seconds of Bass's call, the OCMU detective monitoring Molino's home telephone radioed Kirby to report the contact. The telephone company had given him the name of the bar and its location, but rather than go directly there and wait for Molino, Kirby decided to follow him when he left the house to see if he made any stops en route.

Five minutes after the call from Bass, Molino and his driver came out of the house and walked toward the black, twelve-cylinder BMW sedan parked in the driveway. Kirby had to smile as he watched Molino get into the car; part of his earlier prediction had come true. Although Molino had not lost any weight, he was dressing better, that morning wearing a double-breasted Armani suit that almost, but not quite, made him look stylish—the suit fit him as though it was one he had stolen off a truck without first checking the size.

Kirby did not bother to start his car, knowing well the habits of

Molino's driver. He would pull out of the driveway and floor the BMW, race up the one-way street in the wrong direction, watching his rearview mirror to see if anyone was following. At the end of the second block, he would pull a screeching U-turn and come speeding back past the house.

Parked facing in the right direction on the one-way street, Kirby simply waited until the BMW roared past him and turned the corner, then he pulled out to tail it.

Molino waited in the hallway at the back of the bar opposite the rest rooms, alternately looking at his watch and the telephone mounted on the wall beside him. Bass's call was twelve minutes overdue.

For the past half hour he had been thinking about how he would handle her. All he and the other Families wanted was the money. They could care less about Bass after that. If he didn't scare her off, and he got the money back, he knew his position as head of the Family was secure, but if he did not, he was just as certain that the other Families would find some way to get rid of him. He had heard rumors that they were already approaching capos within his own Family, an indication that their patience was wearing thin. And after his failure the previous night he could imagine them at that very moment calling a meeting that would seal his fate.

Molino grabbed the receiver off the hook the moment the telephone rang. He waited to speak until he was certain the caller was Bass.

"Mr. Molino?"

"Yeah. So what do you wanna talk about?"

Bass hesitated, once again going over in her mind the things she had rehearsed on the drive into the city and all that morning. "I want to make a deal with you."

"How do I know you're not settin' me up; got the cops listenin' in?"

"You don't believe that, or you wouldn't have had me call you back. Besides, we both know that no matter what the police or the government promise me, they can't deliver. I learned that last night."

"Yeah, I heard about that. Okay. What kinda deal you got in mind?"

"Your money for my life."

"That I can do."

"Your predecessor made the same promise to me."

"My what?"

"Vincent Genero. Then he sent people to kidnap me."

"Vinnie had another reason for goin' after you. That reason don't exist no more. You got my word that ain't gonna happen again."

"I'd like to believe that, Mr. Molino."

"If I said it, you could believe it. So how you wanna handle this?"

"I'm going to send you a computer disk that will give you access to the accounts with your money in them."

"You don't send me nothin' through the mail. Somethin' goes wrong, then I got a federal rap to worry about."

"I'll send it to you UPS—they're not the government."

"No, that's not the way it's gonna be. I ain't takin' no chances of that disk fallin' into the wrong hands. We meet face-to-face and you give it to me then."

Bass had anticipated his reluctance to having the disk sent to him. "Alright, Mr. Molino. But I want you to understand, if you don't come alone, if I even suspect you brought people with you, I promise you, I'm gone and so is your money."

"I won't bring nobody else. Just the guy who drives me and he'll stay in the car."

"No! Come alone, Mr. Molino, or I'll shoot you and your driver on sight. I'm not bluffing, and I'm not afraid of you. I've got nothing to lose."

"Alright. Alright. I believe you."

"Then come alone."

"You got it. I'll drive myself. Where do you wanna meet?"

"Are you familiar with Battery Park?"

"Yeah, I know where it is."

"What kind of car will you be driving?"

"A black BMW."

"I'll meet you at the dock where the ferry leaves for the Statue of Liberty and Ellis Island. In one hour."

"I'll be there."

"*Alone*, Mr. Molino."

"Hey, I said I'd be there alone, I'll be there alone. I ain't Vinnie. With me a deal's a deal. Ask anybody, even the cops. You keep your part of the deal, we got no further problems."

51

KIRBY PULLED HIS unmarked car into the curb on State Street as soon as he saw Molino's BMW make the turn into the lot at the north end of Battery Park. He got out of the car and ran across the street, following a path through the park to a grassy area behind Castle Clinton, where he again picked up Molino as he walked along the Promenade overlooking Upper New York Bay. He was surprised that he had come alone, and felt less concern for Bass's safety, certain that Molino was not about to kill her himself in a crowded public area.

Kirby mingled with the weekend crowd as he paced Molino on a parallel course, his eyes searching ahead for Bass. And then he saw her, to the right of a group of tourists queued for a ferry arriving at the dock on its return trip from the Statue of Liberty and Ellis Island. She was standing at the seawall staring at Molino as he approached, a breeze off the bay tossing her hair, looking even more beautiful than he remembered.

He saw her slip her hand inside the center section of her shoulder bag, and for a moment it crossed his mind that she might have called Molino there to kill him, but he immediately dismissed the notion. He moved closer to the Promenade and stopped at the war memorial, where he stood at the corner of one of the huge stone monuments, no more than fifty feet from where Bass and Molino met at the seawall.

Thirty minutes earlier Sammy Casella got off the Staten Island Ferry where it docked at the south end of Battery Park. He had followed in-

structions and arrived well before Molino. After leaving the ferry terminal, he walked along State Street looking for any surveillance vans in
the area, then continued through the park to make certain there were no
undercover cops waiting to set up his boss. He finally stopped at the
flagpole in the center of the park and, from a distance, watched Molino
leave the parking lot and walk along the Promenade and stop to talk
with Bass. When Casella was certain Bass's attention was on Molino, he
began to move in closer, staying out of her line of sight.

Kirby spotted Casella as he moved away from the flagpole. He approached him from the rear, watching him carefully as he moved closer
to the seawall. He saw him stop behind a statue and put his right hand
inside his jacket. Kirby moved quickly, closing the distance. He grabbed
Casella by his hair and spun him around.

Casella almost threw a punch before he saw it was Kirby who had
grabbed him. "Goddamn, Kirby, that hurt."

"Take your hand out of your jacket; real slow."

Casella did as he was told, bringing out a pack of Marlboros. "Just
gettin' a smoke, for Christ sake."

"You're coming up in the world, Sammy. Working for the don now,
huh? Last time I looked, you were stealing cars and hijacking trucks for
Nino Totani."

"Yeah, well, Nino ain't around no more, is he?"

"What are you doing here?"

"That's none of your business. I ain't breakin' no laws."

Kirby reached inside Casella's jacket, relieved him of the 9-millimeter
pistol secured in a shoulder holster under his left arm, and tucked it inside his own waistband.

"You got a permit for this?"

"Come on, Kirby. That's a bullshit beef."

"Unlawful possession of a firearm, Sammy. It's a felony."

"I won't do no time for that. I'll be back on the street before you finish the paperwork."

"You got a short memory, sport. You're on parole. You can't afford
even a bullshit bust. If I remember right, you still owe the state seven
years on that hijacking rap. I'll violate you right here—by tomorrow
you'll be back in Attica with all your old buddies."

"What do you want?"

"Why are you here?"

"This ain't what it looks like."

"Yeah? And what does it look like?"

"I ain't here to do nothin' to the broad. Just to watch the boss's back and follow her if she doesn't come through with her end. Tell him where she goes."

"You sure about that? Nobody else with you?"

"Nobody. The boss says if he leaves the same way he came into the park, that means he got what he came for and I don't follow her, she walks away clean. No harm, no foul."

Kirby took out his handcuffs, snapped one end on Casella's left wrist, and secured the other end to a metal ring attached to an old hitching post, drawing the attention of a group of tourists as they walked by.

"Hey, what's this? I told you what you wanted."

"Relax, Sammy. I just want to know exactly where you are until this is over. So shut up and stay right here until I get back."

Casella rattled the cuffs. "Like where am I gonna go."

Molino extended his hand and Bass shook it, tentatively. "You wanna sit on a bench in the park where it's more private, or you wanna talk right here?"

"Here." Bass put her hand back inside the center section of her shoulder bag to again grip the gun. She studied the people around her, then those walking about the park, her eyes stopping only once before continuing on as she looked for anyone Molino had brought with him. She had watched him pull into the parking lot and get out of the car alone, but was not wholly convinced he had kept his word.

Molino saw what she was doing. "Hey. I'm alone, okay? Let's get down to business. I don't like this kinda open exposure no more than you."

Bass took the computer disk from the pocket of her coat and handed it to him. "This is what you want."

Bass held her breath as she watched Molino's mind working. She had remembered Vincent Genero's words to Michael Onorati the night he killed him: "The accountant says fifteen to eighteen million." She was counting on Molino still not knowing the exact amount.

Molino looked at the disk, then slipped it into the inside pocket of his suit coat. "So how much money are we talkin' about?"

Bass breathed a silent sigh of relief. She had guessed right. "You don't know?"

"Course I know. I just wanna make sure you didn't skim none off for yourself."

"I'm not smart enough for that, Mr. Molino. It's all there. All fifteen million dollars of it. At least that's what was in the accounts when I found the disk in Michael Onorati's briefcase six months ago."

"You're the only one had it since then, so that's gotta be what's in there now. Right? Or is there somethin' you ain't tellin' me?"

"What I meant was, there's probably more. Whatever interest the money has earned in six months."

Bass had added an additional $225,000 to account for the 3 percent interest $15 million would have earned in that period of time, knowing from her own offshore accounts that that was what two of the banks paid to investors who deposited large amounts of suspect cash.

"Okay. If the fifteen million plus interest is in there, then our business is finished."

"And you won't send anyone else to kill me?"

Molino's eyes narrowed and his voice took on a rough edge. "Hey! I gave you my word. You insult me again, I'll have you whacked just for pissin' me off."

"I'm sorry. I just wanted to be sure."

"Like I said. I get the money, we got no more problems."

Molino started to walk away, then stopped and turned back to Bass. "By the way, I gotta hand it to you. The only thing I respect is balls, and for a broad, you got some set of balls on you."

Bass suppressed a smile. "You're the second person who's said that to me, Mr. Molino, and I'll take it the way it was intended."

"You do that."

With that, Molino abruptly left, walking directly back to the parking lot. Bass watched him until he was out of sight, then continued to stand at the seawall and stare out across the bay. She turned slightly to one side and, out of the corner of her eye, saw Kirby walking toward her from the veterans' memorial where she had spotted him earlier. She waited until he was only a few feet away, then turned to face him and smiled.

"Hi, Kirby. Miss me?"

Kirby smiled back. "Oh, yeah."

"Couldn't sleep? Couldn't eat?"

"Don't get carried away with it."

Bass laughed. "I thought about you, a lot."

"Me, too. So, did you give it all back?"

"You found out about that, huh?"

"It's what I do."

"Are you asking me that question as a cop?"

"Nope. As a friend. Besides, if you've done what I think you've done, it has nothing to do with me—that's the feds' jurisdiction."

"Are you going to tell them?"

"Not a chance."

"Then I'll answer your question. Molino thinks he got it all back. So who am I to argue with him?"

"How much did you keep?"

"A little over three million."

Kirby smiled and shook his head. "How did you pull it off?"

"I was pretty sure they didn't know precisely how much was missing, or where the money was, so I just opened new numbered accounts, transferred the funds into them, and kept a little something for my trouble."

"And if they figure out what you did?"

"They won't. Without the original account numbers, they have no way of finding out what was in them, and those accounts no longer exist."

"I can't believe you tried to walk away with all of it."

Bass shrugged. "Nothing ventured, nothing gained."

"That venture damn near got you killed last night."

"That's why I decided to make a deal. You think Molino will keep his part of it and forget about me?"

"Yeah. All they wanted was their money."

"What about the guy you handcuffed to that post over there?"

Kirby grinned. "You don't miss much, do you?"

"I try not to."

"He was just here to cover Molino, and to follow you if you didn't come through with your end of the deal."

"I know you think what I did was wrong, Kirby, but somehow I don't consider it stealing, not from people like that. And I wasn't about to turn it over to the police. There's this little voice in the back of my head that keeps telling me I earned it, starting in Italy about four years ago."

"Can't argue with that. What are you going to do now?"

"Visit a few places until I decide where I want to live."

"You finished with your former profession?"

"That was only the means to an end. And I just reached the end."

"I hope you're right, and I hope it works out for you."

"Are you going to come and see me when I get settled?"

"I don't know. To be honest with you, you scare the hell out of me, for any number of reasons."

Bass smiled and winked. "That's not all bad. It'll keep you in line."

She took his face in her hands and kissed him. "I did miss you terribly." She looked out across the bay and saw another ferry approach the dock. "Ever been to Ellis Island?"

"Never got around to it."

"My father told me my great-grandparents came through there, when they left Ireland during the potato famine."

"Mine, too. From the same place and for the same reason."

"There you have it. Our meeting was fated by things that began over a hundred years ago. We're talking predestination here, Kirby. Maybe our great-grandparents arrived there on the same day. Maybe they even knew each other, or spoke to each other in passing, or just sat across from each other and exchanged a smile, and set off a chain of events that ended with us standing here right now."

"And maybe you should cut back on those calls to the psychic hot line."

Bass laughed and gestured across the bay toward Ellis Island. "You know, their archives have a record of everyone who ever came through there; we could look up our families and take a walk down memory lane."

"I don't have that many pleasant memories."

"Me neither. But maybe we can start some of our own."

Bass looked off to her right and began to laugh. Sammy Casella was gesturing toward Kirby and pointing at the handcuffs. Bass drew Kirby's attention to him.

"What are you going to do about him?"

"Fuck him. I'll cut him loose when we get back. If I think about it."

Bass slipped her arm through Kirby's and led him toward the ferry just then arriving at the dock. "I'll treat you to dinner tonight at Nello's. It's my favorite restaurant. You'll love it, great pasta."

"Then you think maybe later we could have some more champagne at my place?" Kirby wiggled his eyebrows and grinned. "What do you think, huh?"

"Only if you're a very good boy and don't slurp your noodles at dinner."

"Kiss my ass."

"Maybe that, too."

Acknowledgments

I owe a special debt of gratitude to the following members of the New York City Police Department:

Deputy Chief William P. Conroy of the Intelligence Division, for opening the doors to the Byzantine corridors of his fascinating and arcane operations.

Detective Salvatore Rizzo of the Organized Crime Monitoring Unit, for patiently and unerringly guiding me through those corridors.

Detective Patrick J. Early of the Tenth Precinct Detective Squad, who never failed to have the answers I needed.

And a note of thanks to Detective Sergeant Robert D. Fiston, Commanding Officer of the Tenth Squad; Captain Michael B. Herer; and Detective Richard O'Brien. All were more than generous with their time and highly specialized, hard-earned knowledge.